ABOVE, BELOW, AND BEYOND THE SEA

A Collection of Historical Fiction Short Stories

W. M. Ashley   Michelle Dennis Christensen   Kyro Dean

D. Ogden Huff   Stephanie Kilpatrick   Rachel Kirkaldie

L.P. Masters   Erin Mindes   Holly D. Morgan   Leah Moyes

H. Linn Murphy   L.M. Ontiveros   Jaclyn Rose   Skye Rosey

C R Simper   Amy Trent

American Night Writers Association

Compiling Editor: Shauntel Simper

Cover Design: Broken Candle Book Designs

Formatting: Shauntel Simper

Edited by Shauntel Simper, Jaylee Kennedy, and Carrie Snider

ISBN: 979-8-3303-5693-5

TABLE OF CONTENTS

The Salt of the Sea 1

Swaying the Scientist 8

Together at Trafalgar 35

Harmony's Melody 58

Drinking Water From the Sea 79

Stoneheart's Soul 95

Pearl Island 124

Love, Lies, and Pirate Allies 138

Keep Your Blade Sharp 164

The Ghost of the Pirate Queen 188

Seaflower 215

The Mesmerizing S.S. Mesmer 240

Secrets of the Celtic Sea 267

The Sirens of Whitby 282

Tail of Rope and Stone 292

Beware the Sea 310

About the Authors 330

About ANWA 335

The Salt of the Sea

Kyro Dean

Captain Arla looked out over the ocean, sticky sweat hot on the back of her neck. The calm of the waves was deceptive. The deep ceruleans and azures a mockery of their fate. So oft' was the case on open waters. But theirs was a burden she couldn't carry on her own. She'd have to put it to a vote.

She turned back to the deck and blinked away the bright spots of white that always came from staring at sunlit water too long. Her crew stared back, beleaguered. It didn't take a genius to know that things had gone terribly wrong in the storm. They just didn't know how much.

"During Neptune's wrath, we lost half our water stores," she said, looking each in the eye with the respect and gravitas the situation required. "We're drier than a desert summer."

Silence stretched with the *shushoosh* of waves lapping against the side of the boat.

"Three days' supply of threadbare rations. Three days to die of thirst after that. We won't make it the week without some rain, and the gods have already shed their tears. There's not a dark spot in the sky."

Hushed whispers broke out amongst the crewmembers, worry carving deep ravines on their sun-leathered faces.

First mate Hicks spoke first, his dark beard scruffy and unkempt. "So we change course. We're not but five days northwest of Terceira. We restock there and head back out."

"But what of the Queen's charge?" Arla asked, keen eyes on their faces and a tilt to her head. "Her Majesty herself was sick when we left our plague-ravaged homeland. Every day we delay returning with the cure, a thousand die. Terceira will add ten days to our trip. Ten thousand additional souls lost because of our lack of water. Is sparing our lives worth darkening our souls? Are we so traitorous?"

"But home is nearly two weeks away," Hicks countered, cracking his knuckles and rolling back his shoulders. "We won't make it otherwise. And late medicine is better than none at all, which is what they'll get if we all perish."

A cacophony of cries ensued, a line forming between officers, between crew. There was the travel to Terceira group, the honor-bound, and those who wanted to talk things through. Shouts turned to fists, and Hicks grabbed Cook and shook him.

"Enough." Arla snapped, yanking her gun from its holster. When no one minded her call to order, she aimed at the blue sky and pulled the trigger. A deafening crack broke the ocean's calm and separated the brawlers. Three sides parted, spitting at each other's feet.

It was Calenthia who spoke next, her dark braids and green eyes glistening. The sharpest lookout in the seven seas, she often saw more than the rest of the crew. "There is another way."

"Witchcraft no doubt," Hicks sneered. "We all know you dabble."

Arla leaned her gun against her shoulder, chin raised. A silent threat. Hicks shut his mouth and narrowed his eyes.

"The great Molpe has been known to help sailors reach their destination," Calenthia said in a whisper that carried more than a scream.

Arla shivered, the sweat on her neck chilling despite the sun. "A sea witch?"

"A siren."

Shouts rose up again, but Calenthia silenced them all with a hiss. "She can help us reach the shore, increasing our speed so that for every one day, we travel the speed of two."

Hicks spat again, his saliva coating Calenthia's toes so she growled. "If your precious siren is so helpful, why have we never used her before? Hm? Perhaps it is because sirens eat men and drag them beneath the waves to a horrible death!"

Calenthia kicked her foot free of spit, her green eyes daggers. "Molpe does not work for free any more than you or I do. Her services require a price that is not always worth the service."

"The price of a man's life." Hicks gnashed his teeth.

"One for every day of speed." Calenthia grinned.

Hicks raised his fist and charged, but Arla stepped between, shoving her gun into his belly.

"Stand down, Hicks. You were willing to sacrifice the lives of ten thousand, including our queen, why so up in arms about the life of one man? Or is it because it could be your own?"

He sneered, uneven teeth set so they were yellow and mean. He met her eyes with malice. "And what of you, Captain? Are you willing to give your life to the sea?"

She studied his face. Calenthia's. Garon's, the navigator. The boatswain, Chalene's. Cook's. The clean's. On down the line until she gazed once more upon Hicks.

"How does it work, Calenthia? This sacrifice to the siren?"

"You call her name and throw salt into the sea." Calenthia pulled a small pouch of salt from her waistband and held it up for all to behold. "Then she comes for the trade in the black of night. Legend sings that she takes but one, sight unseen, whose heart of shame shines bright and keen. Each day, one more, the dirtiest soul, and drags them down, down, down, to place their bones in the shoal."

A cold wind whipped across the deck, riffling the sails overhead and pulling them taut.

Eyes widened.

Faces drew gaunt. Tight.

Shushoosh, gugoosh.

Arla swallowed, feeling the thirst of the days ahead.

Hicks grabbed for the salt, but she snatched it first, the weight of the leather heavy in her hands. She licked her lips. Felt the rhythm of her pulse. And tucked the white grains into her front pocket.

"We vote." She tucked her gun back in its holster and stepped to the nearest rope, an arm's width thick, and pulled strands of manila free. With a swift hack of her boot knife, she'd severed them all into equal pieces, then turned and faced the group. "Leave it straight to return and collect supplies before making our way home. Tie a knot to proceed. Whether we go forward on our own or with the help of the siren, our people die. If we turn back, so could our families back home and possibly our queen. Choose wisely. You get one cast."

Each crew member took a strand until her hand was empty. Arla took her coin pouch out and emptied it on the deck. The silver clattered and rolled in the stifling quiet, bouncing against boot and barrel alike. She held the soft leather open and each man and woman dropped their thread in from a closed palm. Anonymous. So they could speak freely, though the siren would see.

She cinched the satchel closed and retired to her quarters with her morning rations.

A finger length of the sun's journey later, she returned, face grim. "All but three voted to be loyal to their queen. All but three voted to call upon the sea. Those who shamefully betrayed their country and families be warned. Poseidon's daughter sees. Calenthia, raise the siren."

The shrewd green eyes of the lookout widened, the tease from earlier gone. "Captain?"

"I said raise it." She stared her subordinate down with equal ferocity.

No one moved.

Arla's lips pinched tight. "What do you want?" She raised her arms to the crew, shaking the pouch that decided their fate. "We will lose all of us rationing and thirsting. Six if we cut down a few of our own now to save their water and spare the rest. It is the same loss if we give to the sea gods, only we arrive faster and save many, and then only the shameful will die. Are your consciences so unclean?"

Calenthia's wide mouth clenched shut. She nodded and stepped to the railing.

"Oh, no, you don't!" Hicks yanked her from the sea.

Calenthia toppled backward with glaring eyes, rubbing the elbow that caught her fall.

He glared at Arla, insurrection as clear on his face as the sun on the sea. "Three years we have followed you at the Queen's command, but out at sea, you are only captain because we say so. And after you drove us straight into that storm and threatened us with thirst, I say no. You don't deserve to lead."

Arla smirked. "One of the three."

He snarled, fists balled tightly, and turned to the crew. "Who's with me? Hm? We shouldn't have to die to save others. We are merchants, not soldiers, only assigned this job because we're the fastest on the sea. Should our prowess be our punishment? If we could not make it back in time, no one else could have been faster. We will arrive with the medicine when we can do so with all of us intact. This, I promise you, if you vote for me."

Shaken Cook now nodded. So did Garon and Chalene. They cast the vote quickly for all to see. All in favor of his cowardice. Not just three. They tied Arla up to the main stay in thick cords, low enough to twist her back in pain and high enough she couldn't rest on her knees.

The ship changed course, heading to Terceira. To water. To safety.

Night fell and an ethereal sound carried across the waves. Music, strange and sad, as wistful as the sea.

In the morning, the sun rose quickly, blinding Arla before she'd fully awakened.

A cry rang out of misery.

The boatswain was gone. Chalene. And their ship traveled too quickly, pushed by breath from a being unseen, headed back the way they had come and away from home, to the southwest.

"What is this?" Hicks thundered up the steps from his new chambers, dagger in hand and pointed at Calenthia, who stared at the sea. "Why did you call the beast?"

"'T'wasn't me," she hardened, eyes wide and fists clenched. "I gave instructions on how to call Molpe for the whole crew to hear. It could have been Cook or Chalene as easily as me."

Hick's face crumpled and reddened. "But Chalene is dead."

"So it would seem."

"Make it stop! Undo what has been done!"

Calenthia turned back to the horizon, voice soft and listless, unlike the sea. "The siren will not give up her salt any more than the ocean will give up its dead."

He spluttered and started twice, then thrice, before turning on his heel. "You did this," he snarled, stomping over to Arla with murder in his eye. "You called the siren, and now we head nowhere helpful. Two days wasted, not one on this blasted journey. What of your cause? What of your queen?"

Arla looked up at him, back sore and temples throbbing.

"Speak!" He snapped.

She closed her eyes. He seethed.

The crew worked tirelessly to slow the boat. To change its direction without tipping into the ocean at such high speeds. The sails snapped all day. The water cut at their coming, sprinkling those on the edges of the deck with sprays of salt and seaweed. But it wasn't until nightfall that the ship came to a rest.

Hicks posted a guard with Arla to quell the restless ranks and ensure their safety. Tibby, the curly, copper-haired cooper who watched the stocks and supplies at night anyway. She mercifully gave Arla a small share of water and chided her for her deal with the sea.

"But I'm not worried. No, not me." Tibby rambled, her feet kicked up and her hands behind her head as she leaned against the backside of the mainstay. "I've got nothin' to be ashamed about. Live my life honest and good. I'm not one of the three."

The song came again that night, closer and stifling and just as far away and free. The cries of woe followed in the morning. The Gunner, Mr. McPhewen, had been swallowed up by the sea. Their ship headed true south this time, as directionless as the crew with just as much speed, waves crashing and splashing as the sun rose high.

Hicks was back again, swearing and spitting at Arla. "You'll be the death of all us, you sea wench!"

She gazed up at him, steady and calm. "Us? Or you, Hicks? Us or you?"

He foamed and frothed and ranted, kicking barrel and hoist, rail and anchor. "I'll kill you and feed you to the siren. Solve our disappearing problem and turn us toward Terceira." His knife gleamed.

But a hand caught his shoulder.

Calenthia's mouth turned sour. "You promised if we voted you in, we'd all make it back to port. We're down two already. Do you really want to make it the proffered three?"

He spat at her again and retired to the captain's quarters, in charge of the ship as he had wanted to be. The crew's effort to slow the ship came in at half as much as the day before. The wind whipped and stung at eyes and ears, drying skin and splitting lips. The choppy waves turned stomachs. A few of the crew hurled over the edges, their vomit whisking away in the breeze.

"I'll watch her meself," Hicks declared that night, anger in his eyes and sputtering speech. The boat had slowed, but the ship lurched and groaned as if she still felt the wake. "I'll watch her meself."

They sat in silence. *Shushoosh. Gugoosh.* Waiting. *Gugoosh. Huroosh.* Until the song carried across the sea.

Hicks stabbed a knife in the dried wood above Arla's head. "Make it stop," he half-snarled, half-pleaded. "Stop feeding the siren."

The boat shuddered, the call of the sea echoing louder and louder, like a seagull's screech swirled up in a conch. His eyes widened and spit dribbled from his chin.

"Stop feeding the siren! Stop feeding the sea!"

A blue washed over the edge with a gulp of salt water, but instead of washing back into the ocean, it stood and walked toward Hicks. He turned frantic toward Arla.

She looked up through her salt-stained lashes. "Two plus Hicks makes three."

The light flashed over them, dragging Hicks to the sea with hands like ice and fire and fish and green. The fingers of blue reached for Arla, too, touching her face and pulling at her coat, her hair, her fingers.

"Take us home," she whispered.

The light flickered. The blue grew wide and thin, wide and thin. It brushed her cheek, tasting the salt of her skin. Not yet. Not yet. Not yet for the sea. The light gave her water as fresh as a spring which she gulped down thirstily, enough to live one day, no more. She remained tied and shackled, and she slept.

The next morning the cries came again. Heart-wrenching and fearful. Panic seized the crew without a leader, but no one looked to Arla. The ship sped northeast. Toward home at last. No one tried to slow it down. No one fought the will of the sea. They would honor their queen. They would sacrifice as necessary. Four days more off course plus the eleven that could have been six. They would do what was right now. Now that they had lost the three.

But the siren could see.

Night after night, a body disappeared and Arla drank. Garon was five. Calenthia thirteen. But not a night death. The crew had taken to fury and folly, fighting and throwing each other overboard in hopes of sparing their own lives next. Unnecessary deaths in their attempts to be free. It was only her and Tibby in the end. But they were still a day off from shore. A night. And the song came as it always did, the sea as predictable as a stray cat come for feed. Tibby chattered through the whole thing, though her words were nonsense as the blue poured over the side and dragged her down to the sea.

A ghost ship pulled into Queen's Cove the next morning. It was a full hour before dockhands found the courage to venture onto the ragged ship. They found Arla there, lips bloodied from the wind and sun, hair wild in dark tangles, eyes shut until they snapped open. She flashed them at each of the dockhands, not seeing.

One stepped forward and offered her a canteen. She slurped the water and spat it back out. "Impure. Imperfect. Shameful."

He frowned and pulled back, anxiously eyeing the others. "What happened to you? To your ship and crew?"

Arla laughed, a dry, broken, haunted thing. "They all voted black. To betray the queen. So in my chambers, I called to the siren with the salt of the sea. And I could do it. I could send them all to the ocean's black because . . . because there were never three. Not even two, not even me. When I took the vote, we all voted black, and that's when I could see . . . we all deserve the depths of the sea."

Swaying the Scientist

D. Ogden Huff

Early May, 1829

Athena sucked in a deep breath of salty air and pulled her thick coat tighter around her. The air had grown chillier in the evenings as *The Albion* sailed south toward the tip of Africa and neared the Cape of Good Hope.

Mother wouldn't like that Athena lingered above deck without her. Athena had escaped their tiny cabin after begging for a breath of fresh air, but that wasn't the only reason she had chosen this time to go above deck. This was the magic time when the sailors gathered.

Athena was waiting for their stories. The legends of adventure called to her in a primal way—much more exciting than her proper English life in India where her parents kept her safe and protected. She adjusted her skirts to cover her feet as she sat on a large coil of hemp rope.

Soon, a sailor called, "Saul, give the lads a tale!" A rousing cry for a story echoed over the splashing waves.

Saul stood, his back bowed. His gnarled hands gripped the ship's rigging beside him. He pulled his stocking cap farther over his ears. His serious expression was softened only by the twinkle in his eyes.

"Every sailor worth 'is salt knows the sea 'olds its secrets. Only the bravest scallywags would venture forth on tubs o' wood," Saul slapped the worn railing, "to face the squalls, the sea monsters, an'...the legends."

Every evening, Saul began his tale the same way, except for the order of the last few words. On nights that he told of mysterious beasts, he ended the list with sea monsters. On nights he told of storms, he emphasized squalls. Tonight, the sailors would hear a tale of a legend.

"Bravest?" the quartermaster called out. "A bit o' rum gives anyone courage."

The sailors hooted and booed the ribbing.

"Ah...." Saul called the attention back to himself. "But this 'ere tale needs more than grog. It needs true nerve to face superstition. The legend o' *The Flyin' Dutchman* is no' for the faint o' heart."

A shiver ran down Athena's spine—her vertebrae—she automatically translated into the academic term her father taught her. She grinned from the thrill of the story. This was why she'd returned above deck, rather than hide below like that silly scientist in a cabin near hers. He'd hardly left his cabin, always making excuses of "specimens to catalogue" to avoid leaving.

Every head nodded, including Athena's, and murmurs of agreement rippled over the group. Apparently, they knew the story well. That didn't stop one sailor from saying, "Git on with it then."

"Almost two 'undred years ago, in the year of our Lord 1641, the ship, *The Flyin' Dutchman*, neared the Cape on a dark, moonless night."

Athena looked up at the nearly full moon, grateful that it shone brightly. She remembered vividly the trepidation of being at sea without the light of the moon. They'd been on the boat for a little more than a month, and she'd already seen one moon cycle since they'd waved goodbye to Father and sailed from Madras, India in early April.

"Cap'n Vanderdeck'n finished successful tradin' to the East an' was returnin' to Amsterdam with 'is lucrative cargo." Saul waggled his eyebrows and rubbed his hands together like a miserly old man.

"As the ship rounded the point, a fearsome storm overtook 'em. The sailors begged 'im to turn aft an' seek shelter in port, but 'e 'ad profits on 'is mind."

The crowd hissed their disapproval. Athena wrapped her arms tightly around her ribs—her thoracic cage—she translated again. She dreaded their first storm at sea and prayed it wouldn't be at night. Thus far, the weather had obliged and stayed calm.

"The cap'n swore on all things 'oly that 'e would finish the journey even if it took 'im 'til Judgment Day."

At the blasphemous words, several sailors rubbed religious tattoos. Many of the sailors had star tattoos between their index finger and thumb or crucifix tattoos elsewhere. Athena crossed her fingers. She wasn't superstitious, like most sailors, but when in Rome....

"The devil 'eard 'is boastin,'" Saul continued in a rousing voice of warning. "'Try,' the devil challenged the cap'n, 'or else sail the seas forever.' The ragin' storm swallowed the ship, and the cap'n and 'is crew were condemned to sail the oceans for eternity."

"On days no' unlike this day," Saul punctuated his words with a flourish of his arm, *The Flyin' Dutchman* ghost ship can still be seen racin' under full sail through an angry storm."

As a girl, Athena's father had read the tale to her in a story called "Vanderdecken's Message Home." But reading it in the safety of a warm study and hearing it told on the chilly ocean where the ship wrecked was quite different. She shuddered at the thought. Her eyes refused to rise to the dark horizon, despite the fact that she knew the story was only a tall tale.

"But beware," Saul finished by wagging a warning finger, "the ghostly sailors still be tryin' t' hand off their letters to the vessels of the livin'."

"No thank ye," a deep sailor voice boomed. "They can deliver their own cursed mail."

Athena shuddered once more and retreated to the warmer safety of the tiny cabin she shared with her mother.

It was mid-morning the next day before Athena received permission to go above deck again. Her mother had scolded her the night before for dawdling on deck too long, and thus insisted on accompanying Athena.

But Athena couldn't stay in her cabin when the ship was due to round the Cape within the hour. It was a sight to be witnessed once in a lifetime, and she wouldn't miss it.

The chances were almost non-existent that she would ever pass this way again. Mother was accompanying her back to England for her first London season. Father remained in India to care for his successful business ventures. Their expectation was that Athena would marry and stay in London.

"Bundle up, my dear," Mother said as she donned her cloak. Mother wrapped not one, but two scarves around her own neck, until she looked like a painting that Athena had seen in the British Museum years ago of Queen Elizabeth I wearing a high lace collar. Athena obeyed, although she limited her scarves to one.

Summer in the southern continent had ended a month previous, but even autumn this far south felt like winter in London, compared to the hot, balmy days she'd left in India.

Mother opened the cabin door and promenaded down the dark corridor toward the steep stairway leading above deck. She paused halfway down and turned toward a neighboring doorway.

Athena groaned inwardly. Mother wasn't going to attempt to converse with that man, was she?

"Good morning, Mr. Downes." Mother nodded toward the open doorway. "Would you care to join us above deck to watch the ship round the Cape?"

Athena peeked inside. The cabin was identical to theirs but contained a single bed and a makeshift desk made of crates and a wide board. Hunched over the tiny desk, Mr. Ezra T. Downes, *Esquire* looked up from the pile of papers in front of him, blinking in surprise.

"Oh," he said and looked back down at his pages. "Mrs. and Miss Foggity. You're going up, are you?"

"Yes," Mother repeated patiently, "to see the ship round the Cape."

"Oh. Is that today? I'd like to see that. But...." He glanced back down at his papers. "Maybe I'll join you in a while." He bowed over his pages and resumed scribbling.

Mother nodded gracefully and turned toward the stairs.

Athena shook her head. Why did Mother even bother? The man, despite being absurdly handsome, was insufferable. Work, work, work, with no patience for conversation or respect for the enviable freedom he could have any time he desired. That had left only Mother, the busy captain, and the quartermaster for Athena to converse with for a full month—whenever she was *allowed* on deck.

According to the captain, Mr. Downes was a scientist who had spent the last year in India studying ants, of all things. Ants! Whoever heard of such a pursuit? But did he want to discuss ants with Athena? No! He only wanted to rewrite his notes before they reached England. *Poppycock*!

Athena took a steady breath to calm herself. She would enjoy this day—with or without Mr. Downes—*Esquire* or not.

The sun shone high and had burned off all the morning mist by the time the ladies completed a turn about the deck. A strip of land was visible off the starboard side. Maybe if it had ants, Mr. Downes would actually come up on deck.

"The Cape o' Good 'ope!" The quartermaster, a large, burly man, pointed as the ladies neared.

Athena offered him a smile. "So we see, Mr. Brown. Any storms in sight?" She looked to the ocean horizon past the port side of the ship.

"Nary a one." The man beamed like he was personally responsible for the clear skies.

Mother walked on, her eyes on the captain pacing the quarterdeck ahead. She believed a lowly ship's master should be beneath her daughter's notice. But Athena needed the company of someone other than her mother. Anyone was more interesting than the absent Mr. Ants, *Esquire.*

Athena leaned over the railing and studied the horizon again. She thought she'd seen something far out to sea.

Yes.

There it was again. A ship. Or not. Maybe it was too high off the water to be a ship.

"Is there … something … out there?" Athena squinted as she asked Mr. Brown.

Mr. Brown pulled a spyglass from his pouch. "Shouldn't be." He held the eyepiece to his eye. "The water's much choppier out there. All cap'ns steer clear o' that area."

The man's Adam's apple bobbed in his neck as he swallowed hard. "That's…." He paused too long, and Athena studied his nervous reaction. "…nothin'…to worry 'bout, Miss Foggity." He swallowed again.

He was hiding the truth. Athena was sure of it. "May I see?" Athena reached for the telescope before he could argue. She almost had to pull it from his grip. He reluctantly handed over the device.

Athena raised the glass to peer through the eyepiece. Although she could clearly see waves in the distance, the ship farther out appeared blurry, almost transparent. And something was odd about how it sat on the water. It didn't really sit *on* the water but *above* it. A faint red light, as of a phantom ship aglow, emanated from the vision.

She swallowed hard as she remembered the legend of the night before. "That almost looks like a...ghost ship? Perhaps it's *The Flying Dutchman?*"

Mr. Brown grabbed the telescope out of her gloved hands. "Shhh. Do no' speak so loud. The crew, they be a suspicious lot. They believe a sightin' of the ghost ship warns of a near disaster. They be petrified of seein' it."

Mr. Brown seemed a reasonable man, yet *he* believed this was the ship of legend? Could the story be true? Athena stared at the image on the horizon, the mystery making her stomach clench. Yet, she was witnessing it with her own eyes. Undeniable evidence.

Mr. Brown bit his lip. "Best not to dwell on it, Miss Foggity. Many a man," he nodded at her, "or woman 'ave been driven to the brink by visions at sea. I'd best warn the cap'n."

The quartermaster hurried away toward the quarterdeck and the captain, who was in conversation with Athena's mother. Athena followed after.

Mother's keen ears overheard Mr. Brown reporting on the ship sighting. "What's this, Captain Ralph? Another ship? Will we be troubled by pirates?"

"No, no, ladies. There's nothing to concern yourselves about." He threw a stern look to Mr. Brown. "The ocean plays tricks on the eyes. See here—there's not a thing out there." Captain Ralph passed his own spyglass to Athena's mother.

She looked for a moment and shrugged. "Nothing to see." She passed it to Athena, who searched the horizon, over and over, for any sign of the ship or the red glow.

Athena knew what she'd seen. Mr. Brown had witnessed it too. She would not be dissuaded. The fact that the ship wasn't visible now only confirmed that it could be the ghost ship that they'd sighted.

After the drama of spying a ghost ship, the rounding of the Cape of Good Hope was anticlimactic. More water. A short view of land, which they quickly left behind. The peninsula had faded from view when Mr. Downes came rushing up from below deck.

He looked around and spied the Foggity women. He smiled brightly at them, one side of his full lips rising higher than the other. His eyes warmed with recognition. Athena's heart jumped in her chest, but her body's reaction made her frown. Why was her heart racing? And her stomach aflutter? She didn't even like the man.

It's natural to have a physical reaction to a handsome man, she told herself as she tempered her expression. It was simple biology. Athena's father was interested in medicine and anatomy, and he'd allowed her the use of his extensive medical library, which Athena had found *very* informative.

Not that Mr. Downes would ever know. They'd have to converse first.

He eventually wandered over, concentrating on the ocean on the starboard side of the ship while he walked. His gaze finally landed on her, but his brows pulled together. "Didn't you say today was the day we rounded the Cape?"

She tilted her head, not attempting to hide her exasperation. "Yes. It was. You missed it."

He stepped back and scratched his cheek. "Oh. Already? You came above deck at...." He checked his pocket watch. His expression deflated. "That long ago? I really missed it, didn't I?"

"You really missed it." She didn't tell him she'd been unimpressed.

"There was quite a bit of excitement, Mr. Downes!" Mother said. "We're sorry you weren't here."

Mr. Downes' brows rose. "Excitement?"

Athena tried to deter her mother with a look, but her mother ignored her.

"Athena saw a ship." Mother leaned closer to whisper to Mr. Downes. "There was talk of it being the ghost ship, *The Flying Dutchman.*"

"A ghost ship?" Mr. Downes laughed, drawing the attention of several sailors nearby. "Your daughter saw *The Flying Dutchman?*"

His dismissive reaction needled Athena, and she spoke before she thought. "I certainly did!" Maybe it was the trepidation of seeing a cursed ship. Maybe it was the comparative doldrums of rounding the Cape. Whatever it was, Athena had no patience for Mr. Downes.

Athena heard whispering behind her. When she turned to look, the young cabin boy and his equally young shipmate scurried away. They went right to a group of sailors and resumed whispering.

When Athena turned around again, Mr. Downes offered her an amused grin. "You know this ghost ship was most likely a figment of your imagination?"

Athena's temper ignited, setting her tongue ablaze. "It was not. If you knew anything about me at all, you'd know I have a keen mind, not a childish one."

Mr. Downes' amused grin widened. "Keen enough to see a ghost ship?"

Athena wanted to stomp her foot, but that would negate her argument. "Yes, and I wasn't the only person to see the ship. Mr. Brown witnessed it as well."

"Well." Mr. Downes' brows lifted, and he actually looked impressed. "There's corroborating evidence, is there?"

Athena lifted her chin. "So, you believe me now?"

Mr. Downes thought for a moment and then shook his head. "I'm afraid not. Something so fanciful, I'd have to see for myself before I'd believe."

Athena's eyes narrowed as she studied the handsome man, his chestnut curls ruffled by the wind. He hadn't seen the ship round the Cape. He hadn't scanned the horizon with a spyglass and scrutinized the image of a ship on the horizon. He only ever saw his papers. If it was within her power, she vowed, she'd find a way to make him see *The Flying Dutchman.*

The Albion had laid anchor in Cape Town Bay for the night to take on supplies, but Captain Ralph had demanded that the ladies stay aboard.

"A port is no place for a lady," he'd insisted.

Athena had spent some time on deck watching the lowering of the whaleboats filled with lucky crew members with a few hours of shore leave. Mr. Downes had hurried aboard the whaleboat, with only a glance at her. Sometime later, as the ladies sat in their room with the door open, he'd returned with a packet of paper and a new inkwell.

They set sail the next morning, but with the bustle of the crew storing supplies and setting sail, it was after dinner before Athena and her mother took a walk above deck. Surprisingly, the main subject of conversation above deck wasn't Cape Town, but rather the news of Athena's sighting of *The Flying Dutchman.* Rumors had spread like cholera through the crew. Every few feet of their walk, sailors asked Athena to describe the ghost ship. The questions didn't stop.

"Did ye spy the black spotted crew?"

"Were they flying thar colors?"

"Will they be back wit' thar mail?"

Athena didn't know the answers to any of their questions. For the first time, Mr. Brown looked grim when she approached him.

"Why the frown, Mr....Quartermaster?" Athena stopped right before she made an embarrassing rhyme. *Heavens.* She'd have to watch herself.

"It's the blasted crew.... Excuse me language ma'am. They're sceered of the Dutchman sighting. They be a superstitious lot." He rubbed the cross tattooed on the back of his hand. Seemed to Athena that he was a bit spooked himself.

Mr. Brown's frown deepened. "A few 'ave asked the cap'n if we be turnin' back."

"Turning back? Heavens, no!" Turning back would mean they'd arrive in London just as the season was beginning, without time to order a wardrobe. But Athena's London season wasn't the only thing at stake. The ship was loaded with a shipment of father's spices. Turning back would cost father more to hire a new ship and increase the risk with a significantly longer trip.

"I warned ye." Mr. Brown sighed with defeat. "I asked ye no' to tell the crew. They fear a calamity, but they be spendin' so much time watchin' the horizon that they no' bein' careful. They be the cause o' their own ruination."

"I apologize for my part," Athena said. "But I didn't inform the crew. A few sailors overheard my mother tell Mr. Downes, and then he teased me for claiming to see the ship."

Mr. Brown's eyes widened. "But we both saw the ghost ship."

"As I told him."

"Did 'e believe ye then?"

"Not until he sees it with his own eyes."

"Fool scientist." His eyes flashed. "If it appears again, I'll inform ye." With a bow, Mr. Brown hurried on.

Fool scientist indeed. If Mr. Downes saw the ship himself, would he believe her then? If so, maybe the ship appearing a second time would be a good thing.

But, there would be a greater chance of Mr. Downes seeing the ghost ship if he actually spent some time above deck. How could she convince him to lounge about up here? Thankfully, Mr. Downes wasn't the only one with a scientific mind. She prided herself on her own academic knowledge.

Aristotle's Modes of Persuasion might help. Athena tried to recall them from her lessons with her father. *Ethos*, establish credibility. *Logos*, appeal to logic. *Pathos*, use emotion. And what was the last one? That's right. *Kairos*, choose the right moment. Now, how could she apply them to her challenge of convincing Mr. Downes to loiter above deck for a while?

Athena leaned over the railing to watch the waves splash against the side of the ship, but her brain was calculating a plan. A brilliant plan. He'd rue the day he ever questioned her judgment.

The next day, Mother cried off their walk with a headache, so Athena decided it was the perfect opportunity to put her plan into action.

Ethos, Athena reminded herself as she approached Mr. Downes' door, *relies on credibility to convince others.*

She intended to convince Mr. Downes by bribing him with an intellectual discussion...which should begin with confidence. So, Athena rapped determinedly on Mr. Downes' door.

Something clattered behind the closed door. Perhaps she'd rapped a little too decidedly and surprised him.

The door opened quickly. Mr. Downes stood there, without a jacket or boots, wearing only his trousers and shirtsleeves. "Oh. Miss Foggity. Is something wrong?" He ran his fingers through his dark hair, but he only succeeded in mussing it more. *Drat the man. He looked even better mussed.*

Athena realized he was watching her, awaiting an answer. "I'm sorry to startle you, Mr. Downes. No, nothing is amiss. Well...except for Mother's headache, but that's nothing to cause alarm."

Mr. Downes stared at her for a moment longer, then he seemed to recollect himself. "Can I help you with something?"

Credibility, Athena reminded herself. "I was hoping to help you."

"You? Help me?" Mr. Downes looked taken aback, and Athena would have liked to kick him in the shins.

Instead, she smiled sweetly, in accordance with her plan. "I find, when I'm entrenched in scholarly work, that it's helpful to take some physical activity to clear the mind."

Mr. Downes stared at her as if she'd sprouted horns. Athena fought against her desire to bite her lip. Perhaps Father had been right. He'd warned Athena that some men might not appreciate her intellect and think her a bluestocking. Was Mr. Downes one of them?

But Athena liked her keen mind. She liked her hard-earned knowledge. She lifted her chin and attempted a confident smile.

He rubbed his cheek. "You're right. I could use a recess. I've been staring at my pages so long I feel like I'm going cross-eyed."

"Would you care to join me for a turn about the ship?"

He looked down at his disheveled appearance and grimaced. "Perhaps I might join you in a few minutes?"

Athena nodded, and Mr. Downes smiled gratefully and closed his door.

Most likely, he'd get distracted by his work and forget all about her offer. *Oh, well*, she thought. *It was a worthy attempt.*

Athena made her way up the stairs and wandered over to the railing. Just in case, she studied the horizon. Ocean, ocean, and more ocean, with nary a ghost ship in sight. Still, the contrast of a brisk breeze and the warm sun invigorated her, and she didn't regret the moment, despite her lack of success.

"It really is quite a beautiful day, isn't it?"

Mr. Downes' rich, baritone voice behind her made her jump. "I'm sorry to startle you, Miss Foggity."

When Athena turned, the blasted man wore that amused grin again. Maybe he'd surprised her as retribution for Athena catching him off guard earlier.

Well, she wouldn't give him the satisfaction of reacting more. "It *is* indeed, Mr. Downes. Shall we take a turn around the deck?"

He nodded and offered her his arm. The muscles beneath his newly donned jacket tightened at her touch, and she forced down the thrill coursing through her. She could almost picture the page in Father's book, *The Anatomy and Physiology of the Human Body* by the Bell brothers, with its drawings of the muscular system of the human forearm. For some reason, learning how the muscles worked and feeling them work were quite different.

He led her toward the port side of the ship, and they strolled forward. Mr. Downes coughed nervously into his fist. "Am I correct in assuming that you share some qualities of your namesake?"

"Excuse me?"

"The goddess Athena. She was known for her..."

"...wisdom and warfare." Athena smiled. "Yes, I suppose I share some of her qualities. I only hope I'm not driven by her cold logic. I like to think I have some of the goddess Hestia's warmth."

Mr. Downes laughed. "Let's hope so. I wouldn't want to start a feud with you."

Too late, Athena thought.

"So...what scholarly pursuits do you find of interest?" he asked.

Athena considered her answer in light of her goals, all the while watching the horizon for a ship. "My father tutored me in languages and the classics, of course. But I have a particular interest in Human Anatomy."

Mr. Downes stopped walking right before the steps up to the

quarterdeck and turned to her. "Anatomy?"

Athena nodded and climbed the stairs. "As a child, I showed an interest in Greek statuary. Father was of the belief that science would de-sensationalize the sight and...make it normal. He gave me access to his medical books, which I studied on my own."

Athena dared a glance behind her at Mr. Downes. He blinked at her several times as if altering his view. "Your father is a man of medicine?" He joined her on the quarterdeck.

Athena had hoped he was seeing *her* in a different light, but apparently his thoughts were on her father. A drizzle of disappointment threatened to drown her optimism. "No, a spice merchant. But he specializes in plants with medicinal value for the medical trade, so he educates himself about medicine."

"Wonderful!" Mr. Downes sounded practically giddy. "I would very much like to meet him someday and discuss the medicinal properties of ants. Are you joining him in England?"

Athena barely stopped herself from huffing. Her father had sparked his scientific interest, not her. She wasn't doing a very good job of establishing credibility.

"No. He stayed behind in India."

"Do you share his interest in medicine? Or is Anatomy all that fascinates you?" His eyes gleamed with teasing.

Athena blushed. "Sir, are you mocking my academic pursuits?" She turned and climbed the steps up to the poop deck. She scanned the horizon while Mr. Downes scrambled after her.

"Heavens, no! I only find it fascinating that a woman would indulge in a study of the human body."

Athena turned to face him, her hands on her hips. "*Fascinating* is a bit of a neutral word. Do you intend for it to mean laudable or improper?"

Mr. Downes laughed. "You really don't believe in idle chit-chat, do you?"

Athena lifted an eyebrow. "Is that what you prefer?"

Mr. Downes crossed his arms and shook his head. "Wisdom and warfare. I see the resemblance now."

Athena looked away, toward the horizon over the bow of the ship. This wasn't going at all like she'd hoped. No ghost ship and no credibility. She'd never get a chance to prove she saw the specter.

"Actually," he said, his tone softer. He took her gloved hand and slipped it into the crook of his arm again. Athena fought back her inclination to trace his biceps brachii muscle and forced her fingers still. *Purely scientific motivation,* she told herself.

"I have no experience with intelligent conversation with a woman," he continued. "I'm finding this walk quite invigorating...both mentally and physically. I wouldn't mind repeating this experiment."

Maybe there *was* hope of more opportunities to spend time with him above deck. The thought sent a colony of ants scurrying inside her stomach.

Maybe she was nervous that *The Flying Dutchman* might not make an appearance again. Athena crossed her fingers and smiled sweetly at Mr. Downes. His answering grin turned the scurrying ants into swarming bees.

Drat the man's effect on her own anatomy. Why did he have to be well-formed *and* agreeable?

What method should I attempt today? Athena wondered as she stood in front of Mr. Downes' door the next morning. She hypothesized that, for him, logic would be more persuasive than emotion.

Logos it is.

She'd enjoyed the conversation with Mr. Downes the day before—more than she'd expected. But for some reason, it left her feeling slightly discomposed. She'd spent part of the night attempting to scatter the metaphorical scurrying ants but had been unsuccessful. So, her knock sounded braver than she felt.

Mr. Downes opened the door, and this time he wore his boots. His overcoat lay over the end of his bed, as if he'd prepared to go out ahead of time. *That might be a good omen,* Athena thought.

He smiled at her. "Miss Foggity." He leaned out the door and looked down the hall towards her room. "Is your mother still not feeling well?"

Athena shrugged. "Her headache is better, but she's still not up to walking in the sun."

"Is there anything I can do?"

"Thank you, but no. I gave her something for a headache that my father sent with us. She should be fine shortly."

They stared at one another for a moment. Mr. Downes finally grinned. "Are you taking another turn around the ship?"

His smile brought on another case of the buzzing bees. She studiously ignored them. "I...am. Did I interrupt your work?"

He reached for his coat. "No. I am at an impasse in my analysis." He frowned at the stack of pages on his small desk. "As you suggested yesterday, perhaps some exercise might help." With a wave of his hand, he encouraged Athena to go into the narrow passage before him, which she did. He followed her, closing the door.

Athena didn't need to use Aristotle's *Logos* persuasion method to get Mr. Downes above deck this time, but it seemed a waste not to use such a perfect opening for a logical argument. Once she'd climbed the steps to the upper deck, she turned and suggested, "When I've reached an impasse, I've found it beneficial to discuss my findings with someone else. I often see things in a new light."

Mr. Downes chuckled as he climbed the last few steps. "Are you hiding knowledge of *Hymenoptera* too?"

Athena was taken aback at the unfamiliar word. She used the moment to search her memory as she scanned the horizon for the ghost ship. When both came up blank, she finally asked, "*Hymenoptera*? Is that an opera about the Greek god, *Hymenaios*?"

Mr. Downes barked out a laugh. "An opera...about the Greek god of...marriage?" he finally choked out as he offered her his arm.

Athena took his arm but fought back a frown. Showing irritation at his teasing wouldn't help her accomplish her goals. Instead, she smiled sweetly. "It was all I could recall. What is *Hymenoptera*?"

They started their walk as he started his lecture. "*Hymenoptera* is an order of insects that includes bees, wasps, hornets, sawflies, and..."

"Let me guess...ants." No wonder ants and bees had been tormenting her. Metaphorically, anyway.

Mr. Downes beamed proudly at her, and the bees in her stomach droned. "The word *Hymenoptera* comes from *hymen*, the ancient Greek word meaning membrane, and *pteron*, meaning wing."

Athena recognized one of those words from her studies of female anatomy, but that would hardly be a subject for discussion in polite society, let alone with a man. She stayed silent and didn't contribute her knowledge.

Mr. Downes was happy to continue without her prompting. "Are you familiar with Carl Linnaeus' classification system that involved grouping organisms into a series of hierarchical categories: kingdom, phylum, class, order, family, genus, and species?"

He rattled them off so fast that Athena was glad to have read about the subject and found it interesting. "If I remember correctly, he named our species *Homo Sapiens*. We are classed as Mammals in the grouping with orangutans and chimpanzees. My father agreed, but Mother was incensed when she heard we were included with orangutans."

Mr. Downes chuckled. "You are correct. Our order is Primate. An ant's order is *Hymenoptera*."

"Ahh." Athena nodded. "So what is it that keeps you occupied in your room all day?"

"While in India, I traveled all over the country collecting specimens of ants and other *Hymenoptera*. I'd lay food traps wherever I'd go and come back a few hours later to collect samples. Now, I'm studying each specimen and categorizing them according to Linnaeus' system. I hope to take my specimens and notes to Frederick Smith, an entomologist who also draws illustrations, in hopes he will publish my findings."

Athena stopped at the place where she'd seen *The Flying Dutchman* and leaned on the railing. Her eyes scanned the horizon. The longer she could keep him talking, the better the chance of seeing the mysterious ship. Besides, she had to admit she was curious about his work and enjoyed his conversation much more than she expected.

Handsome, agreeable, and interesting. Drat.

She needed to keep him conversing. "And what has perplexed you today?"

Mr. Downes sighed and followed her example by leaning on the railing. "I'm having a difficult time categorizing a certain ant I collected. It has characteristics of the *Crematogaster* but also a few differences."

"*Crematogaster*?" Athena grimaced. "Cremated...stomach?"

Mr. Downes nodded. "Very good. Literally, it means 'burning stomach,' but probably means 'suspended stomach' instead. They're also known as acrobat ants because the ant, when defending itself, arches its 'stomach' over its head with its stinger facing forward."

"Fascinating." Athena scanned the horizon once more.

When she glanced at Mr. Downes, he scratched his cheek. "Oh, you don't have to feign interest. I know ants don't stir curiosity in most people."

Athena smiled. "But I am curious. If there are similarities and differences with the *Crematogaster*, is there a chance that you might have discovered a new species?"

Mr. Downes' eyes gleamed and he leaned toward her, almost giddy with excitement. "That is exactly what I hope."

His enthusiasm infected Athena, and she clapped. "Oh! That would be so exciting. Would you get to name it?"

"Possibly." His grin tilted, and his eyes widened. She hadn't really noticed his eyes before. His irises were blue, like shallow water near a beach, but rimmed with navy, like the deep ocean. She stared at them for a moment, caught in a whirlpool, before pulling her gaze away.

Blinking, Athena made a show of placing a finger to her temple, as if contemplating. "May I suggest that you name it *Crematogaster Athenia*?"

One side of Mr. Downes' lips edged up at her reaction, but he laughed good-naturedly. "It sounds very distinguished. But would you want an ant named after you?"

"I would," Athena smiled mischievously, "if it displayed both wisdom and warfare."

His brows pulled together as he seriously considered her requirements. "Well, warfare describes most ants when defending themselves. I'm not sure about wisdom, but they do work in a cooperative society."

Athena smiled. She couldn't help but appreciate his enthusiasm for his work, even if his scientific brain meant he didn't believe her about seeing *The Flying Dutchman*. "Sounds wise to me."

"*Crematogaster Athenia*, it is then."

Athena couldn't help smiling for the rest of their stroll. And Mr. Downes smiled back.

"Are you well enough to take some fresh air today?" Athena asked her mother.

Mother looked up from her embroidery and raised an eyebrow. "Do you wish me to be?"

"Of course, I wish you to be healthy." Athena tugged a little too hard on her thread and it made a knot she'd have to pick out.

Mother tipped her head down and sent her a look, as if she saw right through Athena. "But do you wish me along for your stroll? It seems to me you've returned the last two days with an extra sparkle in your eyes." Mother's brows rose suggestively.

Athena gave up on the knot in her thread. "Whatever do you mean, Mother?" It came out too sharp.

"I think you enjoy Mr. Downes' company more than you are admitting."

Mother was right. Athena *might* even *like* the man now. But she also wouldn't admit her real motive for seeking his company. Enjoyable conversation or not—*Esquire* or not—she still hadn't forgiven him for dismissing her claim after she saw the ghost ship. If she could prove it to him, she would.

She'd yet to decide on a strategy to persuade Mr. Downes to take another walk with her. Of Aristotle's methods, *Pathos* was left.

Emotion.

One could gather more ants with honey than vinegar, so the emotion should be positive. But her own emotions were in a bit of a flutter. Since their walk the day before, Athena had relived their conversation multiple times. She couldn't stop thinking about him. And it was driving her to distraction. She needed to focus on spotting *The Flying Dutchman*.

A knock on their door made them both jump. Athena scrambled to her feet, eager for a change from Mother's line of questioning.

When she opened the door, Mr. Downes stood, fully dressed, coat and all, also wearing a hopeful look. Athena's heartbeat sped up. Annoyed at her body's reaction, she attempted a calm smile.

He touched his hat and nodded. "Good morning, Miss Foggity, Mrs. Foggity."

"Good morning, Mr. Downes." Mother spoke first. "What brings you by this fine morning?" She nodded toward their small round window.

"I was hoping you ladies might want to join me for a stroll up top."

Mother beamed at him. "I'm still recovering, but I'm sure my daughter could use a change of conversation." She smiled knowingly at Athena.

Athena fought back the irritated look she would have liked to give her mother and, instead, smiled sweetly at Mr. Downes. "Yes, I could use a diversion."

Mr. Downes waited while Athena donned her bonnet and cloak. She was grateful she hadn't slipped off her shoes, as was often her habit. Mother grinned the whole time.

As quickly as possible, Athena closed the door behind them. She led Mr. Downes into the narrow hallway without even a glance at him.

When they reached the upper deck, Mr. Downes offered her his arm. When she touched his coat, a shiver rolled through her, her body betraying her once again.

"Are you cold?" he asked, his brow furrowed. "Do you need to return below?"

"No. Not too cold." The day was warm, by southern Africa standards. The sun shone overhead. Far ahead to the north, thin, dark clouds lined the horizon, but on the ship, the day was perfect.

Athena searched the port horizon, hoping for a glimpse of *The Flying Dutchman*.

"What surprises of conversation do you have for me today?" Mr. Downes asked.

Athena glanced at him. His ocean-colored eyes gleamed with teasing. She lifted her chin. "Whatever do you mean?"

"Ghost ships, Anatomy, wisdom and warfare, opera about Greek gods. Each conversation has surprised me."

Athena sniffed. "Perhaps it's your turn to surprise me."

"Hmmm." He glanced to the bow of the ship where Captain Ralph and Mr. Brown conversed on the quarterdeck and, with a slight frown, he led her south, toward the stern. "Let me think."

If she didn't think the idea ridiculous, she might have imagined that Mr. Downes was jealous. But he'd have to be interested in something other than ants to be jealous.

They approached a group of sailors looking the other way at the line of clouds far to the north. As she passed the sailor nearest her, she heard him whisper, "'Tis but a calm 'fore yon storm."

Mr. Downes, though farther away, apparently overheard. "Here's something that might surprise you: my great-grandfather was knighted because of a storm."

Athena smiled, despite the sailors' warning.

"I love a good story."

He led her around a coil of ropes narrowing the walkway. "My great-great-grandfather was the quartermaster on the *HMS Stirling Castle*, a warship in the Royal Navy. Have you heard of the Great Storm of 1703?"

Athena nodded gravely. "Of course. I read Daniel Defoe's account. It was horrific."

Mr. Downes nodded. "Hundreds of ships sank and thousands died. Grandfather's ship was lost on the Goodwin Sands near Dover. Violent seas swamped the ship. She filled with water and sank onto the sands, with only the stern exposed for a few survivors to cling to."

They stopped at the *Albion's* stern and leaned over the railing.

"How did that lead to him being knighted?" Athena asked.

Mr. Downes stared at the dark water churning below. "His ship was transporting a British ambassador home to England—a man who was a particular friend of Queen Anne. During the storm the ship tilted, a crate came untied from the deck and knocked the ambassador unconscious into the churning water."

Athena gasped and covered her mouth with her fingertips.

"My grandfather risked his own life, saved the ambassador, and pulled him onto the exposed stern. Once the ambassador returned home, he sung my grandfather's praises to the queen."

Athena clapped. "Who showed her gratitude by knighting him."

Mr. Downes beamed at her.

Athena looked over at the horizon again. Lost in the excitement of the story, she'd forgotten to search for the ghost ship.

But, wait. What was that in the distance? She squinted to see clearer, but it didn't help enough. She looked around frantically.

"What's wrong?" Mr. Downes asked.

"A spyglass! Don't the sailors keep a spyglass at the stern?" Athena spotted the case, hanging on the railing. She ran to it and pulled the glass from the leather pouch. She lifted it to her eye.

When it focused, she almost cheered. There, in the distance, *The Flying Dutchman*, sailed above the horizon.

She thrust the spyglass into Mr. Downes' hands. "Look!" she demanded.

He lifted it to his eye. "By jove! That ship looks like it's floating above the water."

"It's *The Flying Dutchman!*"

He spun to her, his eyes wide. "What?" he almost shouted.

"Shhhh!" she hissed, covering his lips with her gloved fingertips.

He smiled beneath her fingers. His eyes gleamed with a fire that unnerved her. "Why a secret?" he mumbled. "I thought you might want to crow over being right."

She quickly withdrew her tingling fingers. "The crew is afraid of the ghost ship!"

As one, they turned to the bow of the ship where much of the crew had gathered to watch the approaching storm. The clouds to the north had grown darker, billowing gray in the distance. None of them were looking behind them where the ghost ship lurked.

"We can't tell them we saw *The Flying Dutchman* again. They think it's a bad omen. They'll want to turn around."

"Turn around?" Mr. Downes blanched. "Toward the specter?"

"Ah, so you believe me now?"

Mr. Downes shrugged. "I did witness it with my own eyes. As a man of science, I respect evidence."

Athena studied the approaching storm. The clouds were moving faster than she'd thought at first. "Even if we turned around, I doubt we could outrun the storm fast enough to return to Cape Town."

Mr. Downes frowned. "Maybe that blasted ghost ship *is* a bad omen." He held the spyglass to his eye again. "By jove! The ghost ship is gone."

Mr. Downes had stayed up top to help "batten down the hatches," but the Captain had ordered Athena to her cabin to "ride out" the storm with her mother. Mr. Downes glared at Mr. Brown while the quartermaster stopped her and suggested a few techniques to help, including handing her a lidded bucket. Athena hadn't had time to wonder about Mr. Downes' annoyed reaction because of the wall of clouds flying toward the ship.

"Do not worry." Mr. Downes took her hands in his larger ones and held her gaze for a long moment.

Was he worried? Jealous? She studied his eyes, trying to read the unspoken message, but her inexperience made it indecipherable.

He squeezed her hands, sending a shiver up her arms and down to her toes. She wasn't sure her reaction was from fear or the bees suddenly swarming in her stomach.

"Do you think the ghost ship...." Athena stopped herself and shook her head. It wouldn't help to dwell on the bad omen. "Be safe."

As she'd hurried away, her hands tingling and her insides buzzing, the captain and quartermaster took turns hollering at the sailors.

"Fit the deadlights!"

"Bowse up the cannon!"

"Rig up the lifelines 'n case she ships a sea."

Sailors scurried around, covering hatches with oilcloth, shortening the sails, and rubbing their religious tattoos.

Despite clear orders to go right to her room, Athena paused in front of Mr. Downes' door. If the storm was severe enough there might be damage to the ship. Were his papers stowed? Was everything prepared to be tossed around?

Athena opened his door and peeked inside. Pages covered the desk and a few personal items lay about. She slipped into the room and carefully placed the items in the large, still open chest next to his bed, which was filled on one side with waxed paper envelopes. Ant specimens, most likely. She wrapped the papers into an oilcloth pouch, locked the chest with the key in the lock, and pushed his mattress on top. It was all she could do before she headed back to her own room.

The storm hit with a ferocity that shocked both Athena and her mother. "Ride out" the storm was an appropriate term, for Athena felt as if they were clinging to a bucking horse. They lay in a U-shaped depression in their mattress created by shoving items under the two sides, as Mr. Brown had suggested. The valley protected them from some of the buffeting but shoved them together tightly.

The room was dark as a cave, the round galley window having been covered from the outside by a round metal plate. Everything smelled of seasickness vomit from the covered bucket and the slippery floor when they'd missed the bucket. Mother alternated between whispered prayers and whimpering. Athena silently prayed for the men above while she clung to her mother.

The storm raged for hours, screaming like a swarm of angry bees. In the muffled voices barely audible over the roar of the tempest, Athena could recognize the deep bass of Mr. Brown barking orders. But she hadn't heard Mr. Downes lately. Was he safely in his room? Was he still helping above deck? Surely there would be a commotion if someone went overboard.

A loud clunk sounded at the bow of the ship and, then, a scraping on the outside of the wall nearest Athena.

"Oh, heavens," Mother whispered. "What was that?"

The grating moved from the bow to the stern, as if something rubbed against the outside of the ship.

"I think we hit something."

The voices above grew louder. Footsteps pounded the deck, hurried down the stairs, and ran past their room to the cargo area where her father's spices were stored.

More shouting. More pounding footsteps.

Then the ship rocked toward the port side. Athena sat up to avoid Mother rolling on top of her.

The ship didn't right itself but remained listing to port. Athena struggled to her feet. The floor tilted, even as the ship continued to shudder on the bucking waves. The tilting grew steeper as Athena waited, holding her breath, straining to hear.

A loud knocking sounded on the door, but it was thrown open before Athena could move to answer it. Mr. Downes stood in the doorframe, water dripping from his entire person, his face a grim mask.

"The ship is taking on water." He wiped his hand across his drenched face. "We hit a rock."

Mother gasped, reaching for Athena, who helped her stand. They clung to each other as the ship continued to toss. Mr. Downes gripped the doorframe to steady himself and reached a hand to them.

Athena pushed her mother forward first, and Mr. Downes pulled her up into the hallway. Mother gripped the doorframe and edged out into the hall.

Mr. Downes leaned forward once more to reach for Athena.

She took his hand as the ship groaned and listed more. Athena tripped backward, but Mr. Downes caught her and pulled her, now more uphill, into the hallway. She wasn't expecting the force of his pull, so she stumbled forward and landed in his arms.

Mr. Downes didn't let go of her. He stared down into her eyes, his expression a mix of hope and fear, his eyes suddenly a stormy ocean. She couldn't look away. Her brain cataloged a variety of sensations: his strong arms clutching her waist, her fingers gripping his broad shoulders, his breath catching and holding, the sound of her heart beating in her ears even over the howling storm, the scent of rain still dripping off a curly lock of hair hanging in his eyes. His eyes darted to her lips, and he leaned forward slightly.

The ship groaned and moved. Mother cried out.

They both turned toward Athena's mother. She'd fallen against the hallway wall, leaning precariously.

Athena nodded toward her mother. "Assist her, please!"

With a determined nod, Mr. Downes let go of Athena. She immediately felt the loss. He moved quickly down the tilted hall, toward her mother.

Mr. Downes looked back and waved her forward. "Hurry! We must get to the lifeboats."

"Lifeboats?" Athena stumbled forward, her hand on a wall to steady her. "Are we leaving the ship?"

His furrowed brow conveyed the gravity of the situation. "The ship is sinking, Athena," he yelled over the storm.

Athena's heart leapt at hearing her name on Mr. Downes' lips, but she pushed forward. He didn't seem to notice his slip.

Mother clung to Mr. Downes. He threw a mournful look at the

closed door to his room, but Athena knew the chest with his bug specimens was too large for the lifeboat. Specimens that represented a year of work. His life's work. The thing that mattered most to him. Her heart broke for his loss.

Mr. Downes pushed past his door, valiantly keeping Mother upright, his expression even grimmer. Athena only hesitated a second as she reached the door. She reached up and tried to push it open, but the makeshift desk had tumbled toward the door and blocked her entrance.

"Athena! Leave it!" Mr. Downes yelled over the roar of the storm. He'd reached the stairs and was helping Mother climb.

"But your work!" she called back.

"It's replaceable. You're not!"

She didn't have enough time to argue or analyze his meaning as the ship listed more. With a frustrated growl, she hurried after them.

The sight up top was harrowing. Waves crashed over the port side, almost reaching the stairs where Athena emerged. On the starboard side, sailors had lashed themselves to the railing as they worked on the tilted deck to lower the lifeboats.

Mr. Downes climbed to the starboard railing and reached back to help Athena and her mother do the same. They crept along, clinging to the slippery wood, until they reached the sailors.

Three lifeboats tossed in the waves, tethered by ropes and drenched sailors. Athena pulled her coat tighter around her and watched as Mr. Downes helped her mother climb over the railing. Sailors handed her down, over the now exposed side of the ship, to the nearest lifeboat. Sailors filled the other two lifeboats in a similar manner.

Athena gripped the slippery wood and climbed over the railing. She looked back at the ship, now listing at almost forty-five degrees. The masts were bare, sails having been stripped down to storm sails to reduce friction. The drift anchor, a long rope with barrels attached, was pulled tight as the ship strained against its tether.

She climbed down into the lifeboat and huddled under a large oilcloth on the far side of her mother. Mr. Downes climbed into the other outside seat. Other sailors soon joined them, and last, the captain.

"Stay afloat, my girl. Stay afloat." Saluting his ship, he shouted, "Cast off!" He turned to face East, toward what Athena hoped was land, although the storm reduced visibility to twenty feet.

"Oars in. Stroke. Stroke. Stroke."

Athena's last thought as she watched the lifeboat pull away from the ship was that maybe Aristotle would think it appropriate. His last method of persuasion was *Kairos*–the right moment. Mr. Downes had certainly appeared at exactly the right moment to save them.

The storm tossed the lifeboats around, but also pushed them toward land.

"What happened?" Athena yelled.

The captain bellowed an answer. "The storm blew the ship too near Possession Island. She hit an underwater rock outcropping. The only good news is we're near land."

Despite the oilcloth over her head, Athena was drenched from head to toe after only a few minutes. Water splashed over the sides of the boat, soaking her skirts and filling her boots. Rain pelted the oilcloth and drenched her sleeves. Everyone was shivering by the time a rocky shore peeked through the mist.

Athena squinted through the water dripping into her eyes. Some kind of animal huddled in groups on the flat rocks ahead.

"Penguins!" the captain shouted over the crashing of the waves.

Mr. Downes' head popped up. "Penguins? Capital! Any chance we could bring home a specimen?"

Despite leaving their ship, despite losing a year of his work, despite no guarantee that they'd be rescued, Mr. Downes hadn't lost his enthusiasm. Despite the frigid cold, warmth filled Athena from head to toe, and she laughed. She laughed until tears streamed down her cheeks and every person on the rowboat, including Mr. Downes, roared along with her.

Six months later, November 1829
London, England

Athena joined in the polite applause echoing in the lecture hall of The Royal Society of London. She clapped like a lady, but she wanted to cheer like a sailor safe on land after a stormy shipwreck.

No.

She wanted to cheer like boatloads of sailors who, as the sun had risen in a clearing sky, discovered their ship hadn't sunk but had been run aground instead.

That was a moment she would never forget. She'd cheered just as loudly as the rest.

But this moment was almost as good.

At the podium in front of her, Ezra T. Downes, *Esq.*, her betrothed, glanced down and smiled widely at her, a smile that still warmed her from head to toe. He adopted a more serious expression and bowed, once again, to the audience. His subject, *Hymenoptera of India*, didn't stimulate the audience like Michael Faraday's upcoming Royal Institution Christmas lecture on electricity, but it excited Athena nevertheless.

She waited patiently while a few people approached him to ask questions. Finally, he descended the podium steps and beelined straight for her, his expression jubilant.

"You'll never guess who introduced himself!" he gushed. "Frederick Smith, the artist and entomologist! He *asked* to draw my specimens and publish my notes and his drawings."

"Ezra! That's wonderful. That's exactly what we'd hoped for after all your hard work."

He tipped his head to her. "And I owe it all to you."

Athena laughed. "Hardly. Thirty seconds of effort pales in comparison to your years of hard work." She slipped her hand around his now familiar arm and fell into step beside him.

He smiled gratefully at her acknowledgement as they walked toward the north exit of Somerset House, the home of The Royal Society. "But if you hadn't stored my notes that day and closed and locked my chest, it would have all been lost. Can you imagine trying to collect *ant* specimens from the water that filled my cabin?"

Athena shook her head. It had been hard enough to help Ezra dry out the wax paper envelopes containing his thousands of specimens before mold formed. Athena and her mother had both helped for hours once they'd been allowed back onto the ship.

"I'm still amazed you stopped to help Mother and me escape, rather than kicking down the door and saving your life's work."

Ezra looked around and pulled her into a shadowed area outside the large doors. He placed his hands on her shoulders and leaned forward to whisper, "I have you to thank for that too."

His breath brushed her neck, sending shivers down her spine. He leaned back to look at her and smiled knowingly, as if he knew the effect he had on her.

Athena raised an eyebrow. Two could play at this game. She dropped her voice to a purr. "Do tell." She held his gaze.

He gulped, but then he grinned and didn't answer right away. He guided her out of the shadows and through the lofty arches of the North Strand entrance.

As they crossed the plaza overlooking the River Thames, he finally explained. "Since we've met, you've taught me to care more for people than pursuits. If I'd lost my research on that ship, I'd probably always regret it, but if I'd lost you in pursuit of insects, I wouldn't be able to live with myself."

Athena appreciated the changes she'd seen in him. Although he was still enthusiastic about his work, he didn't obsess over it. Much.

The pair headed toward a favorite spot overlooking the river and leaned on the railing. She stared at the river before them, alive with illumination. Boats floated past, each one adding glimmers of light that reflected in the rippling water.

Water still reminded Athena of that fateful storm and the miracles that had followed. She counted them off with every footstep. No lives lost. Miracle one. Ship run aground with damage accessible. Miracle two. A passing ship saw them that happened to be loaded with supplies to repair the damage and extra manpower to help. Miracles three, four, and five. And Father's shipment of spices saved too. Miracle six.

Take that supposed bad luck from seeing the ghost ship.

That thought reminded Athena. "Oh! I forgot to tell you. I learned something new."

Ezra laughed and patted her hand at his elbow. "Always my curious scientist, aren't you?"

"You'll enjoy this one. I found a scientific explanation for our sightings of *The Flying Dutchman*."

"Really?" His brows rose. "But you won. You already convinced my scientific brain of the ghost ship curse."

Athena smiled sweetly. "But *was* it a curse if it gave us two extra weeks on the ship to spend together?"

Ezra laughed. "I'll concede your point on the supposed curse. And this scientific explanation? What of it?"

"*La fata Morgana*," Athena announced with a wave of her hand, as if performing a magic trick.

Ezra grimaced. "The fairy Morgana? I thought this was a scientific explanation."

Athena raised a hand to ward off his questions. "*La fata morgana* are ocean mirages caused by the right atmospheric conditions."

"Ahh. A mirage?"

Athena nodded. "When the sun heats up the air above the ocean, it creates layers of temperatures. Near the cold water, the air layer is cooler, but sitting above that is a layer of air that is warmed by the sun."

Ezra's eyes widened with understanding. "And light must refract between layers of air, like it bends between layers of air and water."

"Yes." Athena smiled widely. She loved their intellectual discussions. "In fact, some *fata morgana* images can actually be refracted cities and ships from beyond the horizon."

Ezra's eyes narrowed in thought, and he tapped his chin. "So we might have seen an image of the ship that rescued us."

"Exactly." Athena pulled back to stare at him. "Wait...*might* have seen?

Ezra smiled mischievously. "I'm not dismissing a ghost ship as an explanation, either."

Athena giggled, and soon they were both laughing.

"Well, Ezra," she said. "I believe we've traded places. I'm looking for scientific explanations, and you're seeing ghosts."

His eyes softened, and he leaned toward her. "Now that you mention it, something *has* been haunting my dreams lately."

Athena recognized that look. Eagerly, she tipped up her chin and met him halfway.

"You," he whispered against her lips.

She answered with a kiss that promised a lifetime of exploration.

Together at Trafalgar

Stephanie Kilpatrick

James Evans thought there was nothing quite like the feel of a rough halyard pulling taut in his hands as a sail billowed into place, adding its snap to the din of busy sailors on the deck below. It was serene and exciting at the same time. At least, it was when he wasn't seasick.

James breathed in the salty sea air and placed a hand on his queasy belly. Twenty-one years old with the stomach of a child. He'd been a sailor for four years now, but he still lost his sea legs whenever he left the ship for more than a few days. Of all the midshipmen aboard the *Belleisele*, only he had this problem. At least he'd earned enough respect that no one bothered him about it. Still, it irked him that his body betrayed him when he had duties to perform.

"Oi! You clumsy lubber!" Lieutenant Smith's high-pitched voice grated in James's ears. "How am I supposed to make my reading like this?"

James turned to see the Lieutenant berating a lad tangled in Smith's long-line. They often picked up a few new boys or seamen when they put into port. Especially a port like Plymouth—one of the largest maritime towns in England. And this new crew mate seemed exceptionally inexperienced.

James tried not to laugh at the boy's flustered expression. It was like the look his younger brother, George, got whenever Mother caught him trying to sneak a "pet" into the apartment. James would bet the boy was around fourteen too, just like George.

"Stop moving! You're making it worse!" Smith's face grew red.

Despite the joy it brought James to see Smith frustrated, he left the side of the gunnel to lend a hand.

"Sir." The boy touched his forehead in salute as James approached.

"Can you believe this?" Smith threw up his hands. "You deal with this mess." He commanded and stomped off.

"Yes, sir." James bent to untangle the scrawny legs. Lieutenant Smith was impatient, arrogant and, as far as James was concerned, incompetent. He only had the position because of his family's rank. James had recently passed his examinations for promotion to lieutenant, so he recognized all the errors the officer made. James knew *he* could do a better job. But, there was military discipline to maintain, so he kept his thoughts to himself.

"What's your name, sailor?" James deftly untangled the boy's legs.

"Timothy." He stepped free of the line and rubbed his left ankle. "Thank you, sir."

"It's your first day?"

Timothy nodded.

"You'll get the hang of things quick enough. But you may want to keep away from Lieutenant Smith until you do."

"Aye, sir. Thank you, sir." Timothy saluted and scuttled away.

James chuckled and bent to coil the log-line, his stomach flipping with the movement. A cool breeze blew his hair over his eyes and James shoved it out of the way, pulling out a couple brown strands by accident. He wished this queasiness would pass. He'd hoped to ask Captain Hargood for a promotion recommendation today. That recommendation was the last thing James needed to put in for lieutenant, and he was anxious to have it done. Hargood was a fair and quiet man that expected the best from his men. And while James had never had any negative interactions with him, he didn't want to appear weak. If the captain denied his request, it would be months before he'd be able to try again. Months of holding his tongue at Smith's arrogant inefficiency. Months more of supporting his family on the lower wages. Months in which others could fill the open positions… Breathing deep, he focused on the horizon.

White clouds were smeary whisps across the light blue sky. Plymouth port was just a smudge in the distance now, like a weevil resting along the rim of a plate. After seeing him off at the ship that morning, his family would be going about their day. Mother would be tending to her seamstress duties, and George better be at school.

A pang of guilt hit him as he thought back to the argument he'd had with his stubborn brother just before shipping off. Ever since their father's death in battle two years ago, taking care of their family had become James's responsibility. But George wouldn't accept James's charge to take care of their mother and go to school. George *wanted* to join the navy. James understood. The boy wanted to follow in their father's footsteps, as James had. George wanted to sail and do his duty to defend England. But James couldn't risk Mother losing her youngest son. And James couldn't lose another member of his family. He knew he was doing what a responsible big brother should do. Still, he felt bad about the way they'd left things. George hadn't come to see him off as he'd boarded the ship that morning. And that didn't sit well.

He shook his head trying to clear his thoughts. He'd deal with that later. For now, he needed to focus on doing his part to keep England safe from the threat of Napoleon. And to do that, he first needed to win the battle against the waves of nausea.

"James! There ya are." Charles Thomas appeared, stepping around the coiled line at James's feet. His Scottish friend seemed relieved. "I've been lookin' high and low for ya." The blue tails of Charlie's midshipmen jacket fluttered in the wind as he clapped James on the back. "Sick again?"

James nodded, swallowing hard and setting his jaw. "Just a bit." Charlie had been his best friend since they'd transferred to the *Belleisele* about two years before. As the only two new midshipmen at the time, they'd bonded and been close ever since. Charlie often joked about James's green gills, but James didn't want him to think he couldn't do his job. He could. "I'm fine." No matter what, James would do his duty.

"Right. Well, come on. Cap'n's called all the officers to his cabin for a meetin'."

James followed his friend below the quarter deck. Why was the captain inviting *all* the officers to a meeting? It wasn't typical. Something of note must have happened. Then it hit him: if he could keep from heaving, after the meeting would be the perfect opportunity to ask about the recommendation he needed. They'd have the privacy of the captain's cabin, no one bothering them, and the business of the day momentarily off to the side. Plus, the captain was always in a good mood after giving one of his inspiring speeches. He may not get a better chance.

James straightened his coat and stepped inside.

The captain's cabin was stuffy and warm, crowded with men who were already sweating. James gulped, missing the fresh sea air, and wedged in next to Charlie as the captain started speaking.

"Gentlemen, the crown is lucky to have such fine officers." Captain Hargood leaned back against his table and studied the silent group.

Through the crowd, James could see Smith straighten like a proud peacock at the proclamation, as if it was meant specifically for him. James rolled his eyes at the idiot, just as the captain's gaze hit James.

Captain Hargood paused for a moment, tilting his head with a raised eyebrow.

Stupid! James couldn't believe his luck. This was *not* a good way to preface his request for a recommendation. He shook his head, trying to communicate that he wasn't rolling eyes at the captain, but Hargood had moved on.

"Another chance to demonstrate your courage and skill has come," Captain Hargood said. "The crown has received intelligence that Napoleon has sent his fleet to invade England. And we are being sent to stop him."

James leaned forward. Was this it? Was it finally happening? They'd been expecting Napoleon to make such a move for almost a year now. The British Royal Navy had dominated the seas, so some thought Napoleon wouldn't dare. But the French Emperor was set on ruling the world. James knew it was only a matter of time before he tried to invade England.

The grumbling about Napoleon quieted the moment the captain resumed.

"Our orders are to rendezvous with Lord Nelson's fleet at Trafalgar and stop the allied French and Spanish fleet from reaching the shores of England." Captain Hargood paced, making eye contact with the men as he spoke. "Officers, I expect you to ready the crew and see to the preparations necessary. This is our occasion to defend our families, our homes, and the crown from French tyranny." He lifted his hat into the air and cried, "Huzzah for King and Country!"

"Huzzah for King and Country!" Every officer shouted back in chorus, including James.

"It's about time we show old Boney the true might 'a the British Navy," Charlie said as the crowd dispersed.

The excitement of the announcement had chased James's sickness away. "He doesn't stand a chance against Lord Nelson." Lord Nelson was the greatest naval commander in British history! "I can't believe we get to fight with him."

"Do ya think we'll get to meet 'im?" Charlie wondered.

James shrugged, imagining it. "Who knows." What would he say to such a legend?

Charlie started to lead him out, but James pushed him ahead. "Go on. I'll be just a moment."

Charlie glanced from James to the captain. "Ah. Good luck." He tilted his head and ducked out the door. While Charlie was supportive, James knew he wasn't thrilled with the prospect of James getting a new commission and leaving him behind. James would likely be reassigned to a different ship, and they may never see each other again. Friendships were more of a brotherhood in the service. You trusted each other with your lives. But this was war. Positions changed, transfers happened, and lives often ended. Still, it was a hard thing to lose people you saw as family, even when you knew to expect it.

When the last of the officers cleared the room, James approached the captain who was hunched over the table, scrutinizing a map.

"I, uh, wasn't rolling my eyes at you, sir..." James babbled like a nervous child, trailing off as the captain glanced up with an expression as if wondering why James was still there.

James's stomach flopped and he couldn't tell if it was from sea sickness or anxiety. Last he'd checked, there were only a handful of lieutenant openings within the Royal Navy. It was competitive. He needed a *really* good recommendation, and he was blowing it.

"May I help you, James?"

"Uh, well..." James wiped sweat from his brow, trying to settle his stomach. "As you probably know, I've passed all my examinations for lieutenant. To apply for promotion, I only need your recommendation."

"You sick?"

Was it that obvious? "A bit. Probably something I ate before shipping off." So much for not appearing weak.

Captain Hargood raised both eyebrows, as if he doubted the story. "You *are* an excellent midshipman. I heard you scored top marks on your exams. Your father taught you well."

James unconsciously placed a hand on the knife sheathed at his belt—the knife his father had given him as a going away gift when James joined the *Belleisele*. He'd spent his first couple years in the navy serving under his father, who, as a commander, had requested James be assigned to his ship. He'd hated it. Father had been harsh and critical with him. It was the reason James had secretly put in for a transfer to a different ship.

But a month after James left, his father was gone. Killed in action against a French frigate. And James hadn't been there to help. He'd abandoned his father, and he had died. He didn't know which was worse, the guilt at not being there, or the fact that their last interaction had been an argument about tying a cleat hitch.

"I'm sorry for your loss." Captain Hargood's voice pulled him out of his distracted thoughts. The captain spoke in a gentle, careful tone. He must have sensed James's shift in mood. The tall, gray-haired man placed a hand on James's shoulder. "He was a good man, your father. Excellent seaman. A true patriot." With a pat to the shoulder he said, "Fight well in the battle ahead and survive, and you shall have your letter of recommendation."

James let out a relieved breath. "Thank you, sir! I—"

There was a knock at the door.

"Enter," Captain Hargood boomed.

James didn't care about the door or being cut off. He barely paid attention as a ship's boy stepped in. They were going to beat Napoleon, and he'd get his glowing recommendation!

The boy saluted and passed a paper to the captain. "Message from the watch officer, sir."

The familiarity of the voice tore away all James's thoughts of Napoleon, his recommendation, his father, and even the awareness of seasickness. It couldn't be. James stepped out of the shadows, scrutinizing the boy, and froze in disbelief. *How?*

"George?!"

George stepped back, obviously startled. Had he secretly joined on at Plymouth thinking he could avoid James indefinitely? What a dimwit! Sure, it was a large crew, but George *had* to know James would find out eventually.

Captain Hargood looked from James to George. "You know each other?"

James spun toward the captain. "Sir, this is my little brother. He shouldn't be here. He's supposed to be home, in Plymouth. With our *mother.*" He glared at George as he said that last word.

George stared at the floor with slumped shoulders, his face growing as red as his hair.

"Ah, I see." The captain let out a breath and gave James a sympathetic look.

"Sir, we have to take him back," James pleaded. Not only was

George likely to ruin his chance at promotion, but they were headed into war! All that Mother had left was on this ship—she'd be devastated if they didn't come home.

But the captain was shaking his head. "I'm sorry, James. We cannot alter our course. I understand your situation, but we must all do our duty now." He tapped a finger on his lips. "Tell you what, he's your charge. See to his training. You can keep your eye on him, but he's your responsibility until we get back to Plymouth. Understood?" It wasn't a question.

"Yes, sir." James mumbled. Great, now he was in charge of the selfish bugger.

"Understood?" The captain directed this to George, who looked up and nodded.

"Sir. Yes, sir." George bit his lip, avoiding eye contact with James, whose glare hadn't softened.

"Very well. Dismissed."

James grabbed George by the arm and hauled him out to the sunlit deck. "What were you thinking? Mother's probably worried sick. Here we are headed for the biggest battle we've ever seen, and you don't know how to load a gun, or tie rigging, or follow orders, apparently. You can't even swim!" And now it was *his* job to fix all that and try to keep him alive. This was just like his brother. Always doing what he wanted, regardless of how it affected anyone else.

"Hey!" George pulled his arm free. "I'm not an idiot. I left Mother a note. Besides, she's not helpless, you know. You don't give us enough credit. And you know most sailors can't swim. Also," —he straightened his back—"I've been studying knots."

James stared at him like he was joking. "Knots? Oh, well then. You're all set. What do you need me for?"

"I *don't* need you." George flung the words like a slap, then softened his voice to lessen the sting. "Look, I just want to be like you and Father. Can't you support that? My friend Timothy joined, and he had his family's blessing. They were proud—I wish I knew what *that* felt like. Besides, I'm not a child. There are younger boys than me on this ship." As if that would justify him being there.

James held in his thoughts that *yes*, George *was* a child, and this selfish behavior was proof. Nothing he said would change their situation. All he could do now was train George so he'd have a chance at survival.

James took a deep breath, pinching the bridge of his nose. "So you tagged along with Timothy? I met him. He'll be lucky to survive."

George opened his mouth to retort, but James waved his arm to cut him off.

"I'm not saying that to fight." James gazed at the sails, taut and full of autumn wind. Resting a hand on the knife at his waist, he sent up a silent prayer for help. "I'll train him too. I'll get approval from the captain while you retrieve him. Your training starts now. You're going to need all you can get before we reach Trafalgar."

"Fine." George started to leave, then turned back. "I know ships are often in battle, but why do you keep talking about this like it's something *different*?"

"This is no ordinary ship-to-ship engagement. Napoleon is sending a fleet to invade England. We've been ordered to meet up with Lord Nelson's fleet and stop him. This is *the* battle, George. For King and Country."

"Oh." The fight and pride dimmed a bit in George's eyes as the weight of that sunk in. Then he turned and headed off to find Timothy—who hopefully wasn't tangled in a line somewhere.

"No, no! Like this." James flung the rope around, tying a swift and perfect bowline knot. "You *have* to be faster."

"It's fine," George complained. "It looks just like yours, why—"

"Again!" James threw the line down at his brother's feet, dredging up memories of his father yelling *"Again!"* at him . . . Serving under his father, James had been pushed harder than his fellows. Father had forced him to learn skills that weren't required and do tasks again and again. While his crewmates played cards or told stories, James got drilled and criticized on work that was already better than most others'. Despite his arguments, his father hadn't relented. And it wasn't until these past two weeks, drilling and training Timothy and George, that James had finally understood why. His father had requested James be stationed with him, had spent his free time teaching him, even forcing him to learn to swim, all because he wanted James to have the skills and instincts that would provide the best chance at success and life.

James traced a finger along the handle of the knife linking him to his father. He'd done everything in his power to help his son, because he loved him. And James had repaid him by transferring to a different ship and leaving him to die.

James squeezed his eyes, trying to banish the guilt. What was done was done. Training George well was the least he could do —for his father, *and* for himself. He couldn't lose another person he loved. But two weeks . . . It wasn't enough time.

Next to George, Timothy picked up his rope and got to work, while George glared at his brother.

James sighed, peering over their heads at the silhouette of Lord Nelson's fleet, hull up against the sunset. Tonight, they'd join the formation and prepare for battle. This was it. He'd done all he could. And despite the captain commending him for his hard work with the lads, James knew it wasn't enough. They weren't ready.

James placed a hand on his brother's shoulder. "I'm sorry for being hard on you. I just want you to be alright."

George's scowl softened. "I know."

James bit his lip, knowing that what he was about to ask wasn't going to go well. "You've learned a lot these past two weeks, but it's not enough. I want you to stay below deck during the battle."

"James! I'm not going to cower—"

"You're my charge, so it's my call. You're not ready."

"I'm not going to leave you up here. I want to fight by your side."

The words struck James in the heart, which was probably what his little brother intended. As children, they pretended to be sailors together, like their father. They'd fight invisible enemies with their makeshift swords. *"I'll always fight beside you."* That's what George would say at the end of each victorious imaginary skirmish. Now here he was, saying it again.

James's eyes started to water as he looked at the tall young man George had grown into. He wasn't much younger than James had been when he'd joined. His once wild red hair was now combed under a real navy cap, and here he stood, ready to fight together. Like they had when they were kids. But George didn't know what he was getting into. This wasn't pretend. It was too real. And dangerous. James couldn't risk it.

He stepped in close, taking George by the shoulders. "You are the bravest brother a man could have, George. Someone I'd be proud to fight alongside. But you and Mother are all I have. If anything happened to you . . . Please." James wasn't sure if it was his pleading tone or something in his eyes, but George backed down.

"Fine. I'll stay below." He gave James a disappointed shake of the head then left with Timothy to enjoy the rest of their free time, not giving James a chance to say anything else.

James stared after him, relieved.

"Ya can't protect 'im forever, ya know." Charlie patted James on the back then bent to retrieve the practice rope.

James sighed. "I know. But—"

"Nah, I understand." Charlie tossed the rope aside. "Come on. How's about another round 'a dice while we still got time?"

Stars reflected off the dark glassy ocean. Things were calm. Too calm. No snapping of the sails, no slapping of water, and no talking.

The lookouts had spotted a line of mast tips along the horizon before sunset, and Lord Nelson had formed their fleet into two columns, intent on cutting the Spanish and French line in half.

The *HMS Belleisle* had taken its place in the lee column, behind the *HMS Royal Sovereign*—captained by second-in-command, Admiral Collingwood. And then the wind had died to a wheeze, causing the fleet to spend the night creeping forward like logs on a stagnant river.

They were in no position to fire upon the enemy, facing them head-on as they were. The goal had been to swoop in, cut through like a knife, and engage them in ship-to-ship combat. But without the wind, speed and maneuverability were gone. As soon as they were within range, they'd be sitting ducks.

Standing near the port side of the ship, James could barely make out the neighboring line of British ships. The weather column was led by Nelson himself. This was the closest James had ever been to the naval legend. Thinking about it boosted his courage. Despite their circumstances, with Nelson leading the battle, they couldn't lose. Right?

His right hand began to ache and James realized he'd been squeezing the handle of his knife. Releasing his grip, he flexed his fingers. "I wish you were here, Father." James shifted his gaze from the knife to the stars. "Put in a good word for us with God, 'eh? I never killed an albatross… that ought to count for something."

A clunking splash sounded through the darkness from the water up ahead, pulling him away from thoughts of his father.

The enemy had fired occasional lobs all night, waiting for them to get in range. Lined up as the British were, the lead ships—*Sovereign* and *Victory*—were bound to take raking fire as they approached. Still, as second in line, the *Belleisle* wasn't likely to reach the enemy unscathed.

At least for now they had darkness on their side. It would make it difficult for the enemy to target them accurately. But that would only last until the sun came up. Which would be soon.

George appeared at his side, hunched down and whispering. "Anything new?"

James shook his head. "No. Now get back below with Timothy." He'd made sure George was tucked safely away in the middle of one of the lower decks. Well, as safe as one could get on a ship in a battle—there was never any guarantee. But George kept coming up for updates, since it was taking much longer than anticipated.

The long, drawn-out approach was bad for other reasons. It was giving James too much time to worry about what was coming. About how England was at stake. About his father. About George.

Another splash, only this time, a drop of water hit James in the face. His eyes widened as he wiped the salty splotch from his cheek. They were in range.

There was nothing they could do but move forward, hoping the incoming shots didn't do any critical damage. Once they were closer, Nelson and Collingwood's ships could shoot their forward guns at the enemy, but it wouldn't do much against such a broad line. What they needed was wind.

They endured another hour of splashes and occasional whistles as shots passed too close.

James steeled himself for the inevitable.

"Down!" The yell was distant, coming from the ship ahead. Then, a loud crack and a splash.

The *Sovereign* erupted in commotion, and James knew they'd been hit. But there was nothing to do but keep going. They'd figure it out and fix what they could. None of their masts seemed to be damaged. He hoped everyone was alright.

The sky had begun turning purple on the horizon—the sun was coming. Any other day, James would have enjoyed the sight. The swelling pinks and oranges mirroring off the flat water were surreal. But right then, he'd have preferred the dark. The faint light lit up their ships like a beacon.

A whizzing sound grew from up ahead on his side of the ship. "Down!" he yelled as he threw himself to the deck. He heard a crack from behind and turned to see a three-foot section of the stern rail missing—the edges broken and splintered.

Nothing major. He stood, wiping the sweat from his brow.

Something snapped above him.

He crouched, ready for the worst, as he glanced up.

The sails were moving!

A cheer went up from the men as the ship speed increased and the breeze cooled their thoughts.

"We have the weather gauge," someone called. That was the best news he'd heard since this whole thing had started. Not only did they finally have wind, but it was in their favor, blowing right at the enemy line. Victory and promotion were within reach.

Signal flags flapped to life above the *HMS Victory*. A message from Lord Nelson to the fleet!

"What's it mean?" George was at his heels again. The stupid boy.

"Get out of here!"

"First tell me what it says."

With only two weeks to train him, James hadn't bothered with signal flags. He'd focused on tying rigging, loading and firing guns, and knowing the commands he'd need to understand in a high intensity situation.

Before James could answer, Captain Hargood's voice boomed out, relaying the message to the crew. "Lord Nelson says, 'England expects that every man will do his duty.'"

The crew cheered.

Captain Hargood graced George and James with an approving nod before continuing his own speech. "This is it, men! Stand firm. Remember your training. Think of your families and defend them well. Let's show them the might of the Royal Navy. For King and Country!"

"For King and Country!" was the chorus of replies.

"There. Now get down below." James shoved George's shoulders, but he didn't budge.

George scrunched up his eyebrows, probably about to argue that he needed to stay up here to do his duty, but before he could, another shot whirred overhead.

James threw him down as it passed, thankfully missing the ship and its crew, and splashed overboard.

"Go! That's an order!"

George picked up his cap, glaring back before disappearing below deck once more.

The quiet was gone. Noises filled the morning as the two columns of ships sped to close the distance between them and the enemy fleet. Splashes, cannon fire, orders being yelled, and beneath it all, the beating drums of battle.

Both columns shifted apart as they came upon the enemy, cutting the French and Spanish line in half. Vessels turned, readying for close quarters fighting. The *Sovereign* moved north, revealing a French flag off to starboard, and the *HMS Belleisle* moved to engage it.

Another crack as an incoming shot damaged a minor spar, splintering a span of timber.

This was it.

Pipes blew, calling him to the starboard side. James took up position behind his gun crew, ready to coordinate their efforts.

"See ya on the other side." Charlie clapped James on the back as he passed, heading to manage the gun crew on James's left.

"Indeed. You owe me a rematch of dice when this is over," James quipped, trying to lighten the mood. Charlie usually beat him when they played ship, captain, and crew. He doubted a rematch would go in his favor, but James would be happy to play him. That would mean they both made it through this alive.

Charlie winked and started barking orders to his gun crew.

James did the same, and as the *HMS Belleisle* maneuvered to pass alongside their opponent, their gun was ready and waiting for the order to fire.

Lieutenant Smith paced behind their line of guns. What was he waiting for? They were close enough. James's gun had a clear shot at the deck of the French warship.

A blast rocked the *Belleisle* as an enemy round hit the bow, wrecking their careful aim.

"Fire as they bare!" Smith finally yelled.

"Fire!" James commanded his gun crew. The cannon flew backward as a shot exploded toward the enemy ship. It missed the mast by a yard, skipping off the French deck and landing in the water. James ground his teeth in frustration at Smith. They'd missed their one shot!

Light flashed from the hull of the enemy ship across from them.

With a boom, the deck to his right exploded in wood shrapnel, throwing his team down like dice from a cup.

James's ears rang as he struggled to his feet. Brushing slivers of wood from his uniform, he checked on his gun crew. Aside from being a bit dirty and dizzy, they were alright.

Another team down the line cheered as the enemy mainmast

splintered and cracked, falling onto the deck of the French ship.

James let out a relieved breath. They'd gotten it.

Smoke swirled in the air as they passed the ship, firing off guns as they went. The enemy vessel was dead in the water and would be easy pickings for the superior British Navy.

The *Belleisle* sailed down the line towards the next enemy ship.

"Prime!" James ordered, and his crew got to work loading gunpowder.

"Load!" A ball and charge were loaded.

"Pull!" The sailors tasked with hauling the cannon back into place yanked their lines.

"Aim!"

James's crew glanced from him to the enemy ship ahead.

"Hold!" His gun was ready for Smith's order the moment they were in range.

This time, Smith got it right.

"Fire as they bare," the lieutenant called.

"Fire!" James yelled, and a shot blasted from their gun in a cloud of soot.

The ball sailed true, hitting the enemy mainmast with a loud crack.

His gun crew whooped in a brief moment of triumph, then got back to work.

The battle continued. Debris was everywhere, and the air was clouded with smoke. The smell of blood mixed with the acrid sulfur scent of spent powder, making it hard to breathe. Booming cannons weren't enough to drown out the shrieks of the wounded and the moans of the dying. All James could do was focus on his small group—on fulfilling their duty. He hoped Charlie was alright, and that George was safer below decks, but he couldn't think about that now.

Joe, one of his men in charge of running out the gun, stumbled back. A fist-sized shard of wood lodged in his chest.

"Don't worry, mate. I'll get you to the surgeon." James grabbed Joe under the arms and hauled him over to the seaman taking the injured below to the sickbay.

Joe disappeared out of sight, and James said a quick, silent prayer for the man.

He rushed back to his gun crew, taking up Joe's place.

They fired again and again—doing massive damage to the French and Spanish line.

If Napoleon thought he could overcome the British—the dominant naval power in the world—he had another thing coming. The British

Navy was better trained and better motivated. After all, they were fighting for the freedom of their country.

"Fire!" His voice came out hoarse from overuse. The cannon flew back as their gun blasted another mainmast. It cracked and tilted over.

Just then, an enemy shot hit the gunnel in front of them. Before he knew what was happening, James was tackled to the side as their heavy gun came flying toward where he'd just been standing.

He blinked, trying to bring things back into focus. George was on top of him. George had pushed him out of the way. George!

"What are you doing up here?" James growled as he wiped a warm trickle off his forehead. This was the worst time for his brother to be here. Everything was chaos and blood.

"Saving your life!" George retorted, pulling James to his feet.

"You disobeyed a direct order!" James's left knee buckled, and he grabbed George's shoulder to steady himself. His head was pounding. His body ached. But he was too worried about George to dwell on the fact that he'd almost died. "Why can't you stop being selfish!"

"Selfish? You'd have been smashed by that gun if it weren't for me. You keeping me below is selfish. I can help!"

"Sir!" Kip, the sailor in charge of loading the charges approached. "Jack's down. We need another hand."

James looked from his diminished gun team, trying to put their cannon back into place, to his brother. George was right. Maybe James was the one being selfish. They had a duty to England and needed everyone willing to do their part. George was brave and willing. Stupidly so. But he was old enough to help, and like Charlie had said, James couldn't protect him forever. He didn't want to lose George, but it wasn't up to him anymore. It was up to fate.

George bent, retrieving something from the debris cluttered deck. "Here." He held out James's knife. Their father's knife.

Resigned, James let out a frustrated sigh and snapped his knife back into its sheath. "Fine."

Beaming, George placed a hand on James's arm. "Let's fight together."

"Keep firing!" Smith yelled as he assessed the ragged gun crews—their uniforms singed and torn and spotted in blood.

James set his jaw and nodded once to George. "Run out the gun."

George jumped into position.

Once Kip had loaded the shot, George and James hauled the cannon into place and fired.

The blast from their cannon was a pin-drop in the cacophony. But it was a solid shot to the gun line along the port side of the enemy's top deck.

"Nice shot," George called, obviously thrilled that his first contribution to the battle had been a success.

"Again!" James yelled.

After two more rounds, James's spirits lifted. The enemy ship was tilting, beaten and taking on water with a hull pocked full of holes. Things were looking good. They'd bested every ship they'd engaged and, while they'd endured casualties, their ship was still in fighting shape. The battle was almost won, and George was still standing uninjured! After this, James was sure he'd get a good letter of recommendation. Soon, he'd be a lieutenant.

A loud crack overwhelmed the other sounds, and James jerked around to see the top of their mainmast falling. Right towards his brother.

"George! Move!"

George dove towards the port side of the ship just as the tangled mass of rigging, timber and sails hit.

A loud thud reverberated through the deck as orders were yelled and men dodged to avoid being tangled in the lines. But James moved closer.

"George? George?!"

"Evans!" Smith yelled to him. "Remain at your post!"

James hesitated, looking from Smith to the broken segment of mast that was now tipping over the port side of the ship. George was under there somewhere. He needed help! But before James could voice his protest, a corner of the canvas rippled and flipped as someone climbed out from under the piece of sail. George! He was alright.

George stood, swaying for a moment, then brushed off his pants and grinned at James.

James released his breath. Shaking his head, he smiled back at his brave, idiot brother. "Come on, you."

George took a couple steps then froze, glancing down at his right ankle.

James gaped in horror as a loop of rigging pulled taut around George's leg, hauling him back.

The mast was going overboard, and George was caught like a rabbit in a snare.

George stumbled backward, trying in vain to free himself from the line, but it was too tight and too quick. His body slammed against the gunnel, pulled by the weight of the mast as it dropped into the sea.

"No!" James rushed forward but was caught in the chest by Smith's outstretched hand.

"To your post, sailor," the lieutenant ordered. "We need that gun. Now!"

"Sir, my brother!" James pointed. Everyone else was either too far away to help George or too busy trying to keep themselves alive. A few sailors had jumped up what was left of the mast, cutting the rigging to disengage the broken portion and keep it from pulling the ship over.

While the entire nightmare had taken only seconds, time seemed to slow, as if to mock him. Then everything went silent as he witnessed his worst fear. All the yelling, cracking, and booming were gone—swallowed up by the heartbeat thudding in his ears and George's cry for help as he was jerked overboard. "No! GEORGE!"

"This is battle, sailor. Now, do your duty." Smith shoved him back.

James didn't move. "He can't swim!" Most of the sailors up here couldn't either. No one else was going to jump overboard after George. His world was spinning. His only sibling, his little brother that looked up to him like some kind of hero, needed his help.

Smith's face was red, from fury at being ignored or from the rush of battle, James couldn't tell.

James knew death was the price of war, but this was different. It was family. Yes, he had a duty to his country and his shipmates. And he couldn't disobey a direct order without serious consequences. Certainly his desire for promotion would be forfeited, and the brig was likely. But what did that matter if George was dead? He could never live with himself if he didn't try to save his brother. James hadn't been there for their father, but he could be there for George. First and foremost, his duty was to his family.

James pushed past a sputtering Smith and ran for the port gunnel where George had gone overboard. Tying a line around his waist, he jumped over the rail and splashed into the chilly water below. The salt stung his cuts, but fear for his brother shoved the discomfort out of mind.

"George? Where are you?!" James swam towards the flotsam, silently thanking his father for making him learn to swim.

A gurgling moan broke through his splashing. "George?" James sped towards the sound. He reached a jumbled mess of canvas and wood and rope and heard the sound again. James pulled the knife from his belt, thanking his father once more, and pushed through the dangerous debris. He wove through the wreckage, careful to avoid getting caught like a fish in a net. The gurgling moan was close. James flipped over a flap of sail, and there was George.

His brother was wrapped around the thick mast, a tangle of rigging holding him prisoner against the splintered wood. Blood trickled down George's forehead, rinsing off with each wave that covered his face and left him spluttering.

"I'm here, George. I'll get you out." James began hacking the ropes with his knife.

George grunted in recognition, but his eyes were half closed, as if struggling to remain conscious. He must have been hit in the head. There was no way he could get out of this mess alone.

"Stay with me, George." James continued working on the rigging, but cutting wet ropes proved to be much harder than cutting dry ones.

A cannonball hit the water to their right, sending a salty spray into James's eyes and narrowly missing the tip of the piece of mast. It created a wave that bobbed the wreckage and covered George's face in seawater.

James stopped his work on the ropes to hold up his brother. He managed to get George's head high enough for him to breathe until the rippling waves subsided.

James glanced around, really taking in their situation. Not only were they exposed out here, at risk of getting shot, but the wreckage was slowly floating away from the *Belleisle*. If he didn't hurry, his safety line would run out and they'd be unable to get back to their ship. He felt like a drowned rat surrounded by feral cats. Or—James's eyes went wide as he spotted a gray fin cutting through the water off to his left—sharks. "Lord preserve us." He shouldn't be surprised. Sharks were common in these waters and often followed ships, attracted by all the garbage they threw overboard. Not to mention the blood and bodies that the battle had put into the sea. Still, right then, it seemed like everything was conspiring against them.

Drowning, drifting away, getting shot, or eaten by sharks . . .

James said a silent prayer and shoved down the frantic boy trying to bubble to the surface. He gritted his teeth, determined not to succumb to any of those fates.

James *had* to be faster.

He sawed and slashed and cut until his arm ached and his hand bled.

At last, enough of the lines were gone that James could maneuver what was left. George was almost free.

Another thud hit the water, splashing water over George.

James moved to lift his face and noticed not one, but two, gray fins. Closer than before. Probably their blood wasn't helping matters.

James tugged at the loose rope, but a wave pushed him back, causing him to lose his grip on his brother.

He stretched his arms, trying to swim back to George. But his safety line yanked against his waist, tethering him like a mooring line and preventing him from going any farther.

No! He was just out of reach. "George! You have to move!"

George blinked and coughed as the last of the ripples splashed over his face.

The ship was getting farther. The fins were getting closer.

"George! You can do it!"

James watched, helpless, as he was slowly pulled away from his brother. If George couldn't free himself the rest of the way . . . James had no choice, he'd have to untie himself.

But as James placed a hand on the knot around his middle, George wriggled. He kicked. He forced himself free from the last loop of line. "I'm coming, James." His voice was a weak croak, but the boy was moving! Grabbing onto a broken length of floating mast, George flailed and splashed towards James with everything he had.

"Yes! Come on, George. You're almost here." James reached out as far as he could.

George's head lolled to the side, and he slipped off the wood keeping him afloat. He grasped for it, but that only pushed it farther out of reach.

"Keep going!" James stretched so far it felt like his arm would pull off his body.

George thrashed through the water, barely keeping his head up, pulling the sharks in even closer.

With a gurgling plop George was within reach, but just as James tried to grab him, George disappeared beneath the water.

James dove.

Just as the line around his waist went taut, James snatched a fistful of George's red hair.

George went limp.

No! James couldn't lose him now. They were so close!

James kicked for the surface, pushing George above the water ahead of him.

James splashed into the air, gasping and gagging, blinking salt from his eyes. "George?" He pulled the unconscious boy onto his back and slapped his face. "George!"

George blinked, slowly at first. Then his eyes went wide. "I'm alive?"

James's vision blurred as tears filled his eyelids. "Yeah, I *saved* you."

George grinned drowsily. "I saved you first."

James laughed and squeezed his brother. "It only counts if we get out of here." His momentary relief faded at the sight of the circling fins.

James grabbed a floating piece of driftwood and shoved it under his brother's armpits. "Hold this." He placed George's hands around the line at his waist. "Ready?"

George nodded, tightening his grip on the rope.

James took a deep breath, put his knife between his teeth, and began pulling them back towards their ship.

His arms were already tired from hacking George's bonds, but he couldn't stop to rest. Not with those sharks looming nearby. They had to get out of here, fast.

One hand over the other, he pulled them along the rough, wet rope. His hands were red and bleeding, and his entire upper body was on fire.

They left the wreckage behind, moving into open water. The ship was growing closer.

"James! Look out!"

The nearest shark had finally grown brave enough to investigate.

James was already gasping for breath, but the slick gray body caused him to pant quicker, biting into the knife with his teeth. The animal wasn't as big as he'd feared, only barely matching his size, but it still had a mouth full of razor-sharp daggers that could kill him in an instant.

He readied his knife as the shark approached, staring at James as if measuring him with its cold, unblinking black eyes.

The ridge of the handle dug into his palm as he gripped the weapon like he was choking it. As soon as the shark was close enough, he stabbed at the water.

The shark jerked away, startled. Then it veered back, closer this time.

From behind him, George yelled and splashed at the water, distracting the shark.

This time, the shark didn't see it coming.

James stabbed and felt the knife sink into the animal's side.

He got it!

His knife yanked free of his hand as the shark panicked, splashing away as fast as it could, a small trail of blood streaming behind it.

He watched as the knife his father had given him disappeared with the shark—lost to the sea, just like his father. A pang of loss hit him, but it was fitting that the knife had saved his life, as Father had. He shoved his feelings about the knife aside, dwarfed by the fear of his situation and his determination to survive.

James held back the laugh of a crazy person. He'd fought off a shark! Well, he hoped he had. With the knife gone, if the shark came back for revenge . . . They needed to be out of this water before that happened.

His body was exhausted, but James reached, pulled, yanked, and dug his fingernails into the line. And then, suddenly, it was pulling against him. He glanced up at the nearing ship to see a blood-smeared Charlie and soot-faced Kip at the gunnel hauling them in.

"George! We're saved!" James cried and hugged his brother. He'd done it. *They'd* done it. Together.

James stood at attention as the captain paced before him. Behind Hargood, a flock of white flags fluttered in the breeze. It had been a day since they'd won, but James had lost.

"You abandoned your post and disobeyed a direct order." The captain jerked off his hat and shoved a hand through his disheveled hair.

James nodded, accepting the charges. "My brother was in danger, sir. I did what my conscience required of me."

By the time George fell overboard, another British ship had pulled along the other side of the enemy. Pounded from both sides, it didn't last long. Smith should have known that one gun wouldn't make much difference. Smith *should* have given James permission to save his brother. James knew it. The captain knew it. But, rules were rules. Without obedience, there would be anarchy and mutiny. It was a serious offense. And now James would pay the price. He'd probably be discharged from His Majesty's service and would be lucky not to end up in the brig.

Captain Hargood stopped pacing and pinched his nose. "I

understand why you did it. Had I been in your shoes, I might have done the same thing." He let out a sigh. "You're an exceptional officer with much potential, Mr. Evans. A hero, as far as I'm concerned. You risked your life to save one of our crew. Despite that, your actions require disciplinary action." Captain Hargood shook his head, as if sorry he was in this position. "You will receive a formal reprimand which will be placed in your service file. I'm afraid the promotion you seek won't be happening any time soon."

James felt his eyebrows raise involuntarily. *That's it?* It was basically a slap on the wrist. Sure, he would have to put off applying for lieutenant for the near future, but he wasn't being discharged. He wasn't being arrested. "Understood, sir." Trafalgar had given him a new perspective, and this was a price he was happy to pay to have his brother alive. Promotion opportunities might come again in the future, but they'd never be as important as his family.

Captain Hargood repositioned his hat and gave a curt nod. "Dismissed."

James saluted, still shocked at his good fortune. His brother was alive, James only had minor injuries, he hadn't been arrested or sacked, and even his best friend had survived. Well…mostly. All things considered, it was a good day.

Heading below deck, James ducked under a beam and made his way to the sickbay.

"How'd it go, mate?" Charlie reached his good arm to grasp James by the shoulder. "Ya still a member 'a the Royal Navy?"

James grinned. "You were right. Just a reprimand. No promotion for a while, so I guess you're stuck with me." Charlie had been furious at Smith when James told him what happened. His friend seemed certain the captain wouldn't discharge James, but *he* hadn't been so sure.

"I guess that means I can continue to rob ya at the dice table." Charlie laughed, but it turned into a raspy cough. His right arm was wrapped in a bandage, and his face was pale. He'd lost a lot of blood, but the surgeon said he would recover. His right arm may never be quite as good as before, but he'd live and still be able to serve. One arm or two, it didn't matter—as far as James was concerned, Charlie was a hero. Even injured, he'd managed to help rescue James and George before collapsing. James couldn't have asked for a better friend.

"Indeed. But my odds may be better if I play you in this condition." James gave him a friendly pat on the shoulder.

Charlie chuckled, leading to another cough.

James helped his friend sit up a bit.

"Thanks, that's better." Charlie took a deep breath. "So, how many ships did we get?"

"We captured 18 vessels. Those that weren't captured or destroyed fled. We dealt a heavy blow to Napoleon."

"Poor old Boney," Charlie said in a mocking tone. "I can't wait to see what Lord Nelson does next. Think he'll come congratulate us in person?"

James bit his lip. "Unfortunately, Lord Nelson was injured during the battle. He . . . died shortly before the victory."

Charlie's face fell. "That's a blow, that is. He was a grand leader."

"He was. He led us to victory. I think he died knowing he kept England safe."

"Aye."

"Rest up. I'll check on you later."

Charlie nodded, closing his eyes.

James could hear him snoring before he reached the wooden steps to the deck above.

"Tim, you have to hold still." It was George's voice.

James followed it to find Timothy once again tangled in Smith's log-line, with George trying to get him out.

Smith stood nearby, tapping his foot and glaring.

James pressed his lips together, holding in a laugh.

With deft hands, George had the line untangled in moments. As if he'd been a sailor handling rope for years.

James felt a glow of pride. Despite his minor injuries, George had demanded to get back to work the moment he was cleared by the doctor. He could have decided enough was enough, but he was more determined than ever to be a sailor. And that was alright.

Walking up to his brother, James realized the boy had never once seemed sick. "Hey, when you first boarded, weren't you seasick?"

George tilted his head, puzzled. "No? Why?"

It wasn't fair. "No reason. You're just born to be a sailor, I guess."

"We both were." George's smile reminded him of their games as children. The fun and excitement came back to the surface, tinged with a bit of worry and fear, yes, but together they could manage it.

"Come on, sailor. There's still a lot I need to teach you." James patted his brother on the back as they walked across the damaged deck. "Time to get to work."

Harmony's Melody

Skye Rosey

The SS Baltic
En route from Liverpool to New York
August 15, 1851

Mrs. Charity rapped the high F key on the Grand Saloon's piano three more times in violent succession. "This is the note, Harmony. Can't you reach it for once, you imbecile? Or must Melody always do the hard work?"

The insults on Mrs. Charity's lips—for this wasn't the first—pounded in Harmony's ears like the waves battering the ship below their feet. Both things upturned her stomach. She was already motion sick, but if she had to listen for one more minute to Mrs. Charity's reprimands, she'd vomit all over the woman's mustard-colored dress.

"Mrs. Charity, please." Harmony's older sister Melody cut in, her voice sweet with the British accent Mrs. Charity always made her use in public. "Harmony doesn't need to sing the high notes. She sings alto, and she can improvise. She finds the lower notes to complement my higher ones and is quite good at it, if you give her a chance. Allow us to sing this part together."

Melody's fist was clasped around the locket that hung above her chest, no doubt calling on the spirits of Ma and Da for help. Dear Ma and Da, who had music in their blood. They named their two daughters in the Gaelic language—Séis for Melody, and Armóin for Harmony. The first, they'd said, strikes the song into the heart. The second breathes it to life.

After Ma and Da died, and the potato farm fell to ruin, the girls went to an orphanage, where only their English pronunciations stuck. But the meaning of their names continued to define them, both in their voices and in life. Like the melody of a song, Melody's beauty and charm left an unforgettable imprint on everyone she met. Harmony was more reserved, less inclined to ask for attention. But like a harmonizing chord, she supported her sister in perfect compatibility.

As such, Melody was the soloist. Harmony sang the accompanying notes. She could never sing the melody herself, nor did she want to.

Yet here was Mrs. Charity, their wretched adopted mother, forcing Harmony to do just that. The horrid old widow raised an eyebrow. "I'm your mother, your composer, your elder and your boss"—she pursed her lips in a self-satisfied manner—"and I didn't adopt the pair of you, out of the goodness of my heart, to discover that only one of you could sing like an angel."

Adopt. Hardly. A memory surfaced in Harmony's mind of Mrs. Charity's eager face, her eyes gleaming as she inquired of their orphanage matron, *"What is their asking price?"* Whatever term she used for it, it was clear Mrs. Charity had purchased the girls like a pair of Thoroughbreds, hoping to exploit their talents to make a new life in America.

But Harmony didn't dare correct Mrs. Charity. She stayed silent, looking down at the safety of the rugs.

Mrs. Charity plowed on in a hideous whisper as to not attract the attention of passengers relaxing nearby. "I will take nothing short of brilliance today. It's your final performance for the first-class passengers. Once we dock tomorrow, word of your talent will spread. Our reputations depend on this if we are ever going to catch the eye of an influential patron." She glared. "And so, Harmony will hit all the notes, or she will go again without supper."

Harmony blanched. No supper again. Her stomach lurched. Didn't Mrs. Charity realize that the longer she went without adequate food, the sicker she would be, and the worse she would sing, not better?

The air in the Grand Saloon was muggy and hot. As the main indoor lounging area for the first-class passengers, the room was crafted with the finest luxuries possible, including two large columns of glass windows that reached from floor to ceiling. The windows acted as vertical skylights, drinking in the ocean sun and casting its rays sideways, bathing the saloon in a warm, lazy glow.

But the windows also sucked in the sun's heat, and the room was stifling. Sweat beaded on Harmony's brow. Her motion sickness peaked when she couldn't take in the fresh air that the decks of the ship provided. That, and the lack of food, were a treacherous combination.

"But Mrs. Charity—" Melody stepped forward, reaching out as if she could physically stop Mrs. Charity's verbal abuse with her hand. The other gripped the locket around her neck like a lifeline, the only sign to Harmony that her sister had any fear beneath her aura of confidence.

"Silence." Mrs. Charity pointed her finger first at Melody, who stopped in an instant, and then at Harmony. "What a shame to have acquired a pair of singing daughters only to find that one of them is insolent, and the other isn't right in the head." Mrs. Charity rapped Harmony upside the back of her skull, so quickly that no one in the saloon noticed except Melody. Harmony reached up to rub the spot, refusing to make eye contact with her abuser.

Melody's face reddened; her hands balled into fists. Her voice took on a dangerous edge. "Keep your hands off my sister. If you do that again, mark my words, you'll rue the day."

Mrs. Charity turned up her nose and sniffed, ignoring Melody's threatening tone. "You unlearned creatures. Where are your manners?" She emphasized her stuffy British accent. "You'll start etiquette school as soon as we land in America, while I set up recital opportunities. Someone needs to strip that Irish brogue from your tongues."

Melody's face turned downward, her cheeks still flushed. Harmony knew she was sensitive about their accent, but she was better at faking British than Harmony was—another reason Mrs. Charity preferred Melody over her.

"That's right, Melody. Silence is better." Mrs. Charity's index finger slid down to a lower note, a treble C, and rapped it with the same brisk force as her glare. "Now, Harmony, sing this note." Her voice dripped with venom. "If you can."

Harmony bit down a retort. Mrs. Charity was a terrible woman. She deserved nothing but a hundred failed performances and a chorus of boos to haunt her the rest of her days. But singing was the girls' only way to make a living, and if Harmony did anything to ruin this final performance on the ship, the tongue-lashing Mrs. Charity would give her later that night would be worse than any motion sickness. Harmony took a deep breath, forcing all the air into her diaphragm, and delivered a treble C.

To her relief, the note rang out in perfect pitch. But then the ship rocked, and a wave of motion sickness overtook her. She stumbled and groaned, cutting off her note too early.

"What on earth was that supposed to be?" Mrs. Charity smacked the piano keys with both hands, the cacophony of sound startling several passengers lounging nearby. "Do it again, and this time properly."

"Please, Mrs. Charity," Melody begged.

Mrs. Charity ignored her, leaning in close enough to Harmony for no onlookers to overhear. "From now on, every mistake you make is one less meal you get to eat. Now sing."

Harmony forced her eyes to meet Mrs. Charity's aged face. Cruelty made her wrinkles look disgusting. The lines were tightened around those pursed lips, the creases between her eyes as deep as caverns. The sight made Harmony's motion sickness so much worse.

She opened her mouth to sing, but the nausea overwhelmed her. She hadn't eaten since breakfast, and that was six hours ago. Since the voyage to America was almost complete, the food stocks were getting low. All she'd been given to eat were beets.

And now those beets danced a merciless waltz in her stomach.

"I said sing!" Mrs. Charity demanded.

Another wave of nausea coursed through her, and this time, it could not be contained. The beets resurfaced like little red army men surging to fight. They launched, splattering Mrs. Charity's pale face, round spectacles, and yellow bodice with an onslaught of crimson.

Melody gasped. Mrs. Charity cried out in disgust. "You little brat!" She gurgled, then gagged as vomit dripped into her mouth.

Harmony stepped back, wiping her lips with her sleeve and looking to Melody with frightened uncertainty.

Melody's green eyes were round as saucers. *Run*, she mouthed.

Harmony weaved through the onlookers, dodging their shocked, frozen limbs and gaping faces, and ran.

"There you are!" Melody's voice rang out as lovely as a bell. Her face appeared between two pulley ropes strung between the crates Harmony hid behind. "Is this where you've been all afternoon and evening?"

Harmony nodded. The sight of her sister brought a prickle of tears to her eyes after hours of hiding next to the taffrail with nothing but solitude and worried thoughts. Outside on the deck, the setting sun caught Melody's strawberry-blonde hair, lighting it up like strands of copper. Harmony took in a shuddering breath. *She is like an angel.*

Melody stepped into the tiny alcove, hidden away between crates and barrels, to join Harmony at the taffrail. There was hardly enough room for both thin girls, but it was a place one robust Mrs. Charity would never fit.

Melody's eyes were gentle as she looked over Harmony's face. "Have you been crying, lass?" Her British dialect was gone, replaced by her Irish roots.

Harmony lost it then. Tears rolled down her face as Melody swept her into her arms.

"There, there. It's alright, don't you worry now. You've found yourself a nice place, haven't you? No one knows you're here from the other side of these crates, and meanwhile you've got the perfect view." Melody crammed herself in next to Harmony, keeping her arm around her as they leaned against the railing, side by side.

Harmony brought her gaze back over the ocean. The sun dipped below the horizon, casting its last golden-hued rays across the entire sky. It reflected over the face of the water, a double dose of beauty.

Melody's breath caught in awe. "Lovely." She squeezed Harmony against her side and started to hum.

It was a tune Harmony loved; one their mother had taught them. She joined in, like she had so many times before, and on the second stanza, they both sang the words.

Come over the land,
Come over the sea.
Ten thousand landmarks
Keeps not my love from me.

Come in through the veil,
From ending to start.
Death 'tis but new life
When you're safe in my heart.

Their voices entwined in perfect harmony, the notes wrapping around each other like ribbons in the air before being whipped away by the wind. If only music could be harnessed and kept forever. Like a painting, or a locket—because oh, how Melody sang! Harmony yearned to bottle up Melody's voice and keep it with her always.

They sang until they grew tired of it. Afterwards, they watched the sun disappear, and soon twilight bathed the ocean.. Harmony snuck a peek at her sister. Melody's hair was pulled back in an elegant bun, a few loose strands blowing in the breeze. Even in the waning light, her green eyes picked up the hues of the ocean in a way that Harmony's dark brown ones never would. Melody had rosy cheeks, a smattering of freckles, delicate features. Harmony's face was longer, narrower and caved in slightly on one side, an asymmetrical look that she feared put people off. That, combined with her shy, taciturn nature, was surely why Mrs. Charity labeled her things like imbecile and slow of thought.

How lucky she was to have a sister like Melody, who was not only beautiful and captivating, but who also looked out for her, protected her, treasured her. They were, after all, the only blood relation they each had left in the world. Perhaps by the time she was fourteen, Harmony might be as beautiful and confident as her older sister.

"It's a good thing you hid all day," Melody said. "Mrs. Charity's in a right state, to be sure. She said not only did you embarrass her, but you dirtied her last clean traveling dress, and above all, we weren't able to perform."

Harmony's gut clenched. She brushed a loose strand of dark hair from her face. "I'm not as sick up here, where I can feel the breeze on my face."

"Aye, that's clear to me. But Mrs. Charity doesn't care. She's been scouring every nook and cranny for you, and when she lays eyes on you, who knows what devilment she'll unleash. I'm fair worried about your safety." Melody took a large intake of breath. "Which is why you best keep yourself hidden."

Harmony's heart dropped. "You think so?" She'd spent the majority of the day sitting behind the crates. Her knees were stiff from being tucked against her chest, and her hindquarters hurt from sitting on the wooden deck. Besides, soon the sea would turn dark. She didn't want to hide here all night.

"Now, don't fret. I had a chat with Miss Mary earlier. You know, the kind-hearted soul who shared her tea biscuits with you the other day? She's well aware of how Mrs. Charity carries on in the Grand

Saloon, and she witnessed what transpired today, with the beets and all. She's offered to lodge you in her cabin tonight and stand as one of our witnesses tomorrow when the ship docks."

"Witnesses?" Harmony swallowed hard. "I don't know, Melody. Mrs. Charity's always putting on a fine show of manners with the other grown-ups. Why would anyone lend an ear to some stranger's tale against hers? She's our guardian, after all."

Melody's posture straightened. "It matters not what she says. All Miss Mary needs to be is a distraction."

Harmony stilled. "What do you mean?"

"We'll have to bide our time until we disembark, and make sure that Miss Mary holds her tongue until the patrol officers onboard can get a police chief from the mainland. Once they are all gathered and beckon Mrs. Charity over for a chat, we'll both vanish into thin air."

Harmony's eyes widened. "Vanish?"

"Aye, Armóin. We'll slip off the boat with the rest of the folk. We'll tell them a fib, giving them false names, and say our ma was up ahead and forgot to show our papers. And once we are off the ship, we'll run to the nearest orphanage."

"An orphanage." Harmony closed her eyes and smiled at the thought. She never would have imagined she'd be excited to go back to an orphanage. But at the orphanage, they fed the children three meals a day, and sometimes even a square of chocolate afterwards. That was more than Harmony ever got from Mrs. Charity.

Melody's voice hardened. "I've had my fill of watching Mrs. Charity scold you and neglect your every need. She'll never be a mother to us, and I'd sooner go back to an orphanage than remain under her roof." She sighed, her voice taking on a dreamy quality. "And once I come of age, I'll take on the role of your guardian, and then we'll be off. We'll have the freedom to do whatever we please, roam wherever our hearts desire. We can still pursue our dreams of being the renowned singer sisters"—she gave Harmony's shoulders a squeeze—"only *we'd* be calling the shots. Planning our own tours. Seeking out our own snobby patrons." She grinned. "But of course, that's only if we fancy it. If we don't, we're not obliged. We'll have absolute freedom."

Freedom. The most beautiful word ever uttered. Melody's face glinted with the same joy that fluttered through Harmony's heart at the sound of it. What must freedom be like? Better than chocolate. Better than butterflies. Better than song.

Harmony sighed. "I want freedom."

Melody gripped the rail. "As do I." She winked and quirked her token smile, a familiar expression she gave every time she wanted to ensure her sister that all would be well. "And I promise you, we will have it. Together."

The ship rocked then, knocking Harmony off balance. She fell backwards, tripping over a rope on the ground, then careened back toward the railing. Melody caught her around the elbows.

"Mind yourself, Armóin." Melody laughed. "You don't want freedom so badly that you'd fly off the ship for it." She made sure Harmony was steady, then gave her shoulder a reassuring pat. "I want to give you something before I hand you off to Miss Mary." Melody's fingers trembled as she reached around the back of her neck. "I'd like you to have this."

Harmony's eyes grew wide. "The locket?"

"Aye, it's your turn to wear it. Ma and Da would want me to share." Melody unclasped the heart-shaped pendant that hung below her collar bone. "You were but a wee one and don't remember them as clear as I do. But they're your true parents, no matter what Mrs. Charity spouts. Though they've passed on, their love for you is eternal. And so is mine."

She leaned toward Harmony with the two ends of the necklace, bracing her hip against the rail to keep herself balanced.

Harmony's breath shuddered as the warmth of the locket touched her skin. Perhaps it came from the remnant of her parents' souls, nestled inside the locket, giving it its own kind of life. "Do you think Ma and Da's spirits are really inside?" Harmony's voice was hushed. Reverent.

Melody laughed once as she fiddled with the clasp behind Harmony's neck. "I'm too old to be putting stock in such nonsense anymore. However"—her eyes twinkled—"I never open it, just in case. Wouldn't want their spirits taking flight from us now, would we?"

"Never," Harmony breathed. "Thank you, Séis."

The ship rocked again, worse than before. Harmony reached up to grab the locket, worried the movement would make it fall as it wasn't yet clasped around her neck. Her arm knocked Melody, whose hip slid off the railing. She stumbled, letting go of the locket, then hit a crate with her shoulder, which knocked her back towards the rail.

Her fumbling hands missed the railing.

Her green eyes flashed once in surprise, once in fear, as the upper half of her body flew over the rail first, and her legs, for one terrible instant, flipped up toward the sky.

"No!" Harmony shouted, trying to grab on to her sister—her dress, her ankle, her boot, anything—but it all happened so fast, and Harmony's hands could not establish a hold.

Melody slipped through her fingers.

One instant she was there. The next, she was nothing but an array of petticoats flying downward. She screamed for a moment, then her body hit the side of the ship and, rolling twice, was silent.

Melody, a girl who loved to talk and sing, made no more sound as she fell. Within seconds, her body disappeared, sucked into the hungry seam between the metal hull of the ship and the white crest of water racing past.

She did not resurface.

Harmony sat on the ruffles of Melody's bed. A new wave of tears poured down her cheeks, salty on her lips like the sea that was now her sister's resting place. She had not gone to Miss Mary, or to the patrol officers on the ship. She had certainly not gone to seek out Mrs. Charity. Instead, she'd snuck down to the second-class cabin she shared with her sister, sticking to the shadows and moving with the rock of the ship to avoid being heard or seen. But it was only a matter of time before Mrs. Charity would find her here.

Harmony needed to move, to hide, like Melody had told her to. But her treasured hiding spot on the deck was a place she never wanted to see again. Not when the vision of her sister cartwheeling over the rail was ingrained in her memory, replaying over and over like a churn of butter gone spoiled.

She needed a new place to hide, yet her body wouldn't budge. It was paralyzed there, on her sister's bed across from her own, with Melody's dresses in the trunk at its foot and the rest of her belongings—all that was left of her—close by. Stroking the cotton of Melody's quilt with her fingers, she traced the embroidery on its ruffles, wiping snot off her nose with her sleeve and trying to squelch the ache in her head, the pain in her chest, the anguish in her heart.

In her other hand, she caressed the hard, heart-shaped lines of the locket. Somehow, she had held onto it through the whole torturous affair, refusing to let it go even as her sister fell. If she had just dropped it, would that have been enough to have gotten a better hold on

Melody's ankle?

Perhaps she should go the way of the sea and join Melody. It would be what she deserved. Oh, why did she move her arm to grab hold of the locket when she should have grabbed hold of her sister instead?

Harmony threw the locket across the room in disgust. It banged against the wall, then landed with a metallic thud on her own bed.

Her disgust fled, a wave of panic taking its place. The locket! The last thing her sister ever gave her. Melody's last act of kindness. How could Harmony be so thoughtless?

"I'm sorry!" She wailed, her voice thick with tears. "Melody! I'm so sorry!" She scrambled onto her bed, digging through her bedsheets until she felt the gold chain entangle itself with her fingers. Shaking, she lifted the necklace, fumbled until she found the lock of the chain, and clasped it around her neck.

Within moments, the skin on her chest where the locket touched grew so warm, it was almost itchy. She took the locket into her palm. It buzzed with tingling, inexplicable heat.

Perhaps Melody has joined Ma and Da, and the warmth is their embrace. Harmony's heart wrenched at the thought of her family reuniting without her. She had never been more alone in her life. And yet….

She squinted at the vanity on the opposing wall, the only piece of furniture in the room besides the two small beds. Though her eyes had adjusted to the dark, she could still hardly see it. Mrs. Charity had taken the first-class cabin for herself, assigning her so-called daughters to the cheaper class. The vanity, consisting of four modest drawers, was crowned with a simple mirror tacked to the wall above it. Its curled, brass frame, crested with an angel in the middle, was the only embellishment in the room.

Harmony approached the vanity and, after lighting the oil lamp on it, looked into the mirror. Her face was swollen and patchy with red marks from crying, her dark eyes bloodshot. Pieces of her mousy brown hair stuck to the sides of her face with sweat and tears. She briefly registered the fact that she was no longer motion sick. Perhaps the sickness of loss and guilt outweighed it. She sniffled, pushing a particularly ugly-looking strand of hair back from her face with her palm, and then her eyes fell to the locket.

It was glowing.

The glow was faint, to be sure, but definitely there, a yellow tint that brightened the gold heart and sallowed the skin of her chest around it. She snuffed out her lamp. The locket seemed to float in the darkness. *It is definitely glowing,* she thought, lighting the lamp once more. She reached for the locket, looking at it through the mirror, and held it between her index finger and thumb.

Zeal laced through her heart as a thought intrigued her mind. What if Melody were truly here, with her still, inside her locket?

She was told to never open it. But now, there was no one left to stop her. Her reflection stared back at her, fierce and determined. *I want my sister back.*

She dug her fingernail between the two delicate halves of the locket and forced it open with a feverish click.

Harmony gazed into the locket.

It was empty.

She stared at it long enough for the disappointment to settle deep into her bones. Then she grimaced, slick anger overtaking her as she grabbed the locket with both hands and pulled. "Wicked, fake trinket!" She let out a strangled cry. "How could I have been so infernally stupid? No one lives in a locket." She pulled harder, determined to snap the chain no matter how hard it bit into the back of her neck.

"Don't break it," a voice cried out.

A familiar voice that wasn't hers.

She froze, the locket still intact around her throat. She couldn't believe what she had heard. "Melody?"

"Yes, Armóin." The voice was thin, as if trapped behind a barrier. "Look up."

She looked into the mirror.

Melody stood behind her.

Harmony gasped, elation trilling through her. Her sister was here! She wheeled around to hug her. "Séis! Séis, how —?"

But no one was there. She was alone in the room. A chill crept over her.

Slowly, she turned again to the mirror. Melody stood behind her. She laughed, her green eyes twinkling. "How did you not see me?"

Harmony looked behind her again. There were only two empty beds behind her, flickering in the lamp light. She swept her hand through the air but felt nothing. When she peeked back into the mirror, Melody was standing next to her. This time with her arms crossed.

Harmony paled.

"Armóin, why do you have such a fright in your eyes?"

Harmony tried to calm her breathing as she looked her sister over in the reflection. Had grief driven Harmony to madness? Or was her sister's image really there, talking to her in the mirror?

Harmony inspected Melody's face. Her perfect cheekbones, smooth jawline, the smattering of freckles across her cheeks in all the right places. It was definitely Melody. But on closer inspection, there were new things about her. Her hair was wet, tangled, the bun long undone. Her clothes dripped; her skin was three shades paler than normal. And the worst part, the most sickening change—her neck was cocked at an unnatural angle, the skin around the break a bulbous shade of purple.

Harmony's breath caught in her throat as realization dawned on her. "You're a ghost."

Melody's eyes narrowed. "Don't be spouting that word to me." Her voice was sharp, and Harmony flinched in surprise. "I'm here, aren't I? And that's what counts. Would you rather have me lying at the bottom of the ocean floor, my petticoats tangled in coral?"

Harmony gulped. "No. Of—of course not."

"Good." Melody's eyes glinted. Perhaps it was the reflection of the mirror, but Harmony thought they might have changed color for a moment. Grown brighter. Her gaze darted around the room, recognizing it. "You didn't go to Miss Mary like I told you to. Did Mrs. Charity find you?"

Harmony shook her head.

"Good. There is still time. You must—"

A key turned in the door of the cabin, the noise like nails scraping up Harmony's spine. She looked in time to see it pop open. There stood Mrs. Charity, in a nightgown, wearing her spectacles and holding a long, silver ladle.

She seethed, saliva spurting through her clenched teeth. "There you are, you delinquent. Oh, how I have been dying to get my hands on you."

Mrs. Charity stepped into the room, shutting the door behind her and, using the same key from before, locking it tight. She turned to face Harmony, her features like stone, her eyes flickering with anger in the glow of the oil lamp. She dropped the key back into her pocket.

Harmony gasped, her eyes roaming over the giant spoon in her guardian's hand, unsure what to make of it. "Melody, help me!"

Mrs. Charity barked out an ill-humored laugh. "Why, Melody isn't here, don't you see? That's half the problem."

Harmony's eyes darted to the mirror. "But—"

Mrs. Charity interrupted, looming over Harmony. "Melody isn't anywhere. She left five hours ago to find you and never returned. I was beginning to think you had both jumped ship. And yet, here you are. And she is not." Her eyes bore holes into Harmony. "The last person who told me they saw Melody claimed she was walking the deck near the back of the ship, calling your name." She leaned in, her breath reeking of fish and old cabbage. "Did you hear her calling you? Or can your small Irish brain not process your own name?"

Harmony shrunk back. She peeked again at the mirror, needing the mainstay of her sister now more than ever. But she and Mrs. Charity were the only reflections.

Perhaps she had hallucinated Melody after all.

Mrs. Charity growled. "I say, look at me when I'm speaking to you!" She grabbed Harmony's jaw and jerked her face to look at her. "Where is your sister?" Mrs. Charity's voice was high pitched and dangerous. "What did you do with her? I know you've always been jealous, but to stoop as low as to hide her somewhere…."

Harmony didn't answer. Even if she wanted to, she couldn't speak. Her jaw was being clenched too tight.

Mrs. Charity gasped in realization. "That's it, isn't it. You've done something horrible to your sister. You couldn't stand to see her raised to stardom when you yourself could never cut it." Mrs. Charity's spit sprayed across Harmony's nose. "I never should have bought the pair of you. I should have taken her and let you rot in that orphanage."

Harmony didn't answer. She squeezed her eyes shut, tried to still her breathing, but it didn't work. Mrs. Charity was right. She did do something horrible to her sister. She was the reason Melody was dead. If she had never boarded this ship, Melody would be alive.

But she was never jealous of Melody. She was proud of her. She loved her.

"Well, child? Where is Melody? Answer me!" Mrs. Charity's voice thundered.

Harmony didn't answer.

"You know I despise it when you don't answer my questions." Mrs. Charity shoved Harmony onto the bed and pulled a coil of twine from her pocket. She wrapped Harmony's wrists together, then attached them to the bed post with several tight knots. "You have truly outdone yourself today. I thought your embarrassing spectacle with the beets was bad enough. But no. Now you have gone and done something truly wicked." She towered over her, grabbing the ladle, which had been discarded on Melody's bed, and lifting it over her head with both hands like a golf club. "Tell me where Melody is, or, as you Irish brats put it, *you shall rue the day.*"

Harmony's stomach sickened. She knew the ladle's purpose now. She envisioned all the places Mrs. Charity might hit her. The ankles and knees would be first. But if not there, anywhere under her dress, where the bruises would be hidden, was fair game. Mrs. Charity would probably avoid her face, under the pretense that the girls always needed to look performance-ready. With a jolt to her stomach, she remembered that Melody was gone, and there would be no more performances. Harmony swallowed down a lump in her throat. Once Mrs. Charity knew that with a surety, she would preserve Harmony's face no longer.

Mrs. Charity advanced. The ladle glinted in the lamplight. Harmony shut her eyes.

But then, Mrs. Charity gasped. Harmony cracked an eye open to see her guardian with a quizzical look on her face, staring at Harmony's throat.

At the same moment, the locket around Harmony's neck, still open, started to burn.

"Is that…Melody's necklace?" Mrs. Charity's face scrunched in confusion. "Why is it…glowing?"

The locket burned worse now. Harmony groaned, trying to shake it off her skin, but without use of her hands, it was futile.

"Quiet." Mrs. Charity whispered, a new edge to her voice. "Do not muster a sound."

Harmony held her breath to keep from whimpering.

That was when she heard it.

Ding, ding, ding.

The sound of someone tapping.

Ding.

Mrs. Charity lowered the ladle. She looked toward the door. "Who might that be?" Her voice shook. She dropped the ladle to her side and held a giant spoon over her head with her so-called daughter crouched helplessly before her.

But Harmony knew the sound was not coming from the door. She looked at the mirror.

"Melody," she breathed.

Melody was inside, knocking on the glass, as if standing on the other side and asking politely to come in. The mirror plinked at her touch like bells made of glass.

Ding, ding, ding.

Mrs. Charity, still not seeing, stepped toward the door. Her voice took on a falsely cheerful tone that twisted through the tense air like a broken rag doll. "Who is it?"

Melody's eyes shone bright with a mix of amusement and irritation toward Mrs. Charity. But at her sister, she winked. "It's me, Mother," she called out. Then she quirked her token smile, the one that told Harmony she had everything under control.

Mrs. Charity froze at the sound of Melody's voice. "Melody?" She turned back toward the room. "Melody dear?"

"In here, Mother." Melody's voice had a gentile tone, the kind she used in Mrs. Charity's presence when she'd mimic a British accent in hopes of melting the woman's wicked edge. "I'm sorry I'm late."

Mrs. Charity looked around. "Where are you hidi—?" Her eyes fell on the mirror. She drew in a quick breath, her eyes widening.

Melody's smile stretched across her face. "Yes, Mother. Here I am. Were you worried about me?"

Mrs. Charity's mouth tried to form words, but only silence protruded from her lips.

Melody continued, her neck sickly bent, her head protruding to the side like a puppy with her head permanently cocked. "I have never seen you hit my sister with a weapon before." Her tongue clicked. "Is this a new idea of yours?"

Mrs. Charity gaped. "M-Melody," she mustered. "Your clothes. Your hair. Your…neck."

Melody's composure faltered. "Never mind those things!" Her voice rose. She dropped the accent. "Who cares about my neck. You should care more about my sister's fate. And your own."

Mrs. Charity's eyes stood transfixed on Melody. "W-whatever do you m-mean?" She stammered.

Melody now had both hands on her side of the mirror, her fingers splayed as if she were looking through a window and wanted a taste of the delicious, steaming pie on the other side. "Didn't I tell you in the Grand Saloon that if you ever raised a hand to my sister again, *you'd* be the one to rue the day?"

Harmony shivered. Mrs. Charity let out a strangled sound halfway between a moan and a shriek.

"It looks like that day has already arrived." The glass underneath Melody's fingers started to crack. "You are no longer our guardian.

And you shall never lay a hand on my sister again."

And with that, Melody sang.

It was a loud, high-pitched note, so high it could shatter glass. And shatter it did. The mirror exploded.

Harmony ducked her face between her tied-up arms, squeezing her eyes shut and plugging her ears with her biceps. Glass shards blew past her as a terrible, unearthly wind suddenly whipped around the room.

Through the chaos and the wind, she could still make out Mrs. Charity's screams once, twice, three times. Then the wind ceased.

A fourth scream never came.

She felt a gentle tap on her shoulder. Her heart quickened, fearing some kind of bloody scene to have unfolded before her.

She forced herself to look up, then tilted her head in confusion.

The mirror's shards were scattered across the floor, the vanity, and the beds, but she herself was unscathed. In the middle of it all stood Mrs. Charity, her face flecked with tiny beads of blood where glass fragments had hit her.

The blood wasn't the only thing off about her. She gazed down at Harmony, but instead of scowling at her with pursed lips, she was...smiling.

When Mrs. Charity spoke, her voice was kind, a startling dissonance from the woman's cold features. "I promised you freedom, Armóin."

Harmony's jaw went slack. There was no mistaking Mrs. Charity's Irish accent. And her eyes. Her beady eyes. Were they always so...green?

"And now, sure as the dawn, I can deliver that freedom to you." Mrs. Charity winked. "Hold tight, and don't make a sound. I'll be right back."

Mrs. Charity turned heel, unlocked the door, and left it gaping open behind her without a backward glance.

Bundled up in a light cotton blanket, she sat on the sunny deck of the ship the next day, a cup of ginger tea warming her hands. Her wrists were wrapped in cloth bandages to protect her skin as it scabbed over. At least the twine cuts weren't bleeding through the bandages any longer.

She sipped her tea, wincing at the sharp, bitter tang. The ginger was supposed to calm her stomach, but she no longer needed it. The ship was docked, and her motion sickness was practically nonexistent.

She did, however, have a pounding headache. Peppermint tea would have been more useful. Still, it was nice to be taken care of.

Her mind fell back to last night. Such a change, to go from enduring an abusive guardian who was supposed to love her, to being pampered by strangers who shouldn't have cared a whit. Perhaps they felt sorry for her. Perhaps they were afraid. Whatever the reason, it didn't matter. Crew members who had found her and cut her bonds, nurses who tended her wounds, the cook who fed her and made the tea—so far, they were all kinder than Mrs. Charity.

Her lips quirked to the side. Freedom was every bit as good as promised. And yet, at what cost? Her smile faltered, then faded, as guilt and regret took hold.

The SS Baltic had spotted land in the early morning hours and docked at half past noon. The captain announced that the ship had broken a record for fastest transatlantic passageway ever recorded at only nine days, thirteen hours. It was enough to win the coveted Blue Riband of the Atlantic, he'd said.

However, as she watched the passengers exit the ship, she mused that the speed in which they disembarked put such a record to shame. She'd never known a large crowd to move so quickly, and she did not blame them. Surely, they were anxious to get off the ship and away from the garish crime scene they had all been privy to last night.

Many of them had witnessed it. But for those who didn't, word of the disturbing story had spread like wildfire.

Passengers she recognized from the past nine and a half days hurried past with their suitcases, steam trunks and hatboxes, donning their best traveling overclothes. She smiled at them, but they gave her a wide berth, looks of pity on their faces. Some of the ladies spoke low to their companions about *the poor girl*, *"that horrible woman,"* and how it was all *"such a shame that she took her own life instead of dealing with the consequences of her actions."*

"Miss Mary!" She smiled, catching the eye of the familiar woman passing by with her fashionable travel bag. Miss Mary had been so kind before. Perhaps she might be kind again. "Oh Miss Mary! Might I have a word?"

Miss Mary's brow creased, and her eyes darted from side to side as if looking for an escape route.

"I just wanted to say thank you one more time, for your benevolence in offering to help last night. And for the biscuits the other day. You were very kind."

Miss Mary's face was drawn, her cheeks blotchy. She leaned in so no one else around them could hear. "Please, I cannot be mixed up in such a grizzly affair. I have a reputation to uphold. As far as I am concerned, we have never met." She sniffed, raised her nose, and left without another word.

As she watched Miss Mary go, her fists clenched with a mixture of betrayal and confusion. She was not used to anyone treating her in such a way—at least, no one besides Mrs. Charity. Perhaps it would have been easier with freckles, strawberry-blonde hair, and a voice like silver bells.

She stopped herself. No, don't think that way. Things certainly were different now, but it would be alright. Soon, she would never see these people again. It would be a fresh start.

She kept her back straight and her shoulders pulled back, inviting the bright sun to shine down on her face as she sipped her tea and eavesdropped on the three men speaking nearby.

Two were patrol officers from the ship who had been collecting information all night; the other the local Chief of Police who had just stepped on board, sent to investigate the moment the ship docked.

"Glad you could come, Chief." One of the patrol officers dabbed sweat from his temple, his face as serious as a battleground. "Here is the story, according to the witnesses." He peeked at his notepad to make sure he got all the details correct. "The deceased—Charity Bingham, so they say—came screaming down the hallway from the cabin of her two adopted daughters, where she had allegedly tied her younger daughter to a bedpost and broke a mirror during an emotional outburst. Then she scrambled up onto the deck and announced to all who stood within hearing range that she had thrown the older daughter—Melody Bell, the other deceased—overboard hours before in an angry fit, and she was now so broken up about it that she couldn't fathom living another moment. What did she say again, Madsen?"

"I believe her exact last words were, 'Melody didn't deserve to die, Harmony deserves far better, and I don't deserve another breath of life'," the other patrol officer replied, looking off his own notepad.

"Right. And then, before anyone could stop her, she slit her throat with some kind of sharp object in her hand—likely a glass shard from the mirror she broke in the girls' cabin—and flung herself off the taffrail of the ship."

The Chief grunted. "Did you collect a body?"

"No sir. We stopped the ship and tried to look, but she never resurfaced. Since her death was self-inflicted, and due to the nature of it, we presumed there was no chance of her survival. We had no choice but to move on."

The Chief stared off into the ocean, deep in thought. "As for the girl…Melody Bell, is it?"

"We searched the ship. There was no sign of her. Assuming she had been thrown from the ship hours before as reported, there was no sense in going back to look for her."

The Chief nodded. "Anything else I should know?"

Officer Madsen jumped in. "There is one strange thing about it, sir. Witnesses claimed that Mrs. Charity Bingham was British. However, when she spoke her final words, she seemed to have acquired…." Madsen paused, his voice taking an incredulous tone.

"Yes, well, spit it out, man."

"It sounds bizarre…but they claimed she had switched to an Irish accent, sir. Like that of her daughters."

Silence for a moment.

"That is strange. In fact, I don't have an answer for it. Perhaps the woman had gone a little mad, or she was simply racked with guilt over the heinous way she murdered her adopted child."

"Yes, sir. I suppose you're right." Madsen paused and wrote something down on his notepad.

Melody, Harmony whispered into her mind, *do you think they'll ever find out?*

Melody smirked. *No, lass. There is no evidence.*

Do you think she could ever return? The way you did?

Never. She'd have to have a magic locket, wouldn't she now?

Her free hand reached up and fisted the locket around her neck. It was closed again and warm like candlelight.

Melody continued. *I didn't like being inside that awful woman. It was needful, but mighty uncomfortable. Do you know the strain it took to toss so much weight from a ship's deck?*

Harmony giggled, a twinkling sound inside her mind.

Melody went on, delighted to make her sister laugh. *Mrs. Charity, what a bossy old cod. I'm far pleased she's gone.*

Harmony's laugh trailed away, replaced by something more serious. *Do you not feel any remorse for her death?*

The living spend their days fearing death. But once you've faced it, it loses its sting. Still, there are some things you long for. Melody flinched at the wistfulness of her own tone. *As for Mrs. Charity, she deserved what she got. And I'd do it again, if it meant saving you.*

Harmony warmed with joy. Melody could feel her smile. *I'm much happier just the two of us.*

Aye to that. Melody returned the glowing feeling.

I hope the orphanage in America has chocolate.

Melody chuckled. *It had better. But if it falls short, don't worry. We'll go somewhere else. Together.*

Aye, together. Harmony's voice was relieved, content. Secure. *Thank you, Séis, for helping me be free.*

And you, Armóin. Thank you as well.

"What about the other girl—Harmony, is it?" Madsen enquired, the name grabbing the girls' attention. "She's only eleven years old. Where will she go?"

"I suppose she'll go to an orphanage. From what I've gathered, it won't be her first time." The Chief sighed. "One of you can escort her off the ship to the police station. She'll be watched over until we find her a permanent solution."

"Yes, sir." Footsteps came closer, plunking on the wooden deck, until Officer Madsen was right in front of her. "Hullo there." He looked down, smiled at her. He was younger than his large mustache and imposing uniform painted him to be. And he was cute. "Are you Harmony?"

She whirled her smile at him, batting her lashes, pushing a lock of mousy brown hair from her face so he could see both her eyes.

His brow raised, taken aback, as if he didn't expect such bold body language from a traumatized child.

She cringed. She had forgotten things were different now. She scrunched her shoulders to look timid, determined to act the way an eleven-year-old should when addressed by a police officer. "No, Harmony is my sister, the one who is...gone." She frowned. "You've gotten our names mixed up. My name is Melody."

Officer Madsen raised his eyebrows, then nodded and looked down at his notepad. "I see, well...I will make sure to correct that in the police record."

Melody smiled, satisfied. Then she paused. *It's kind of you.* She thought. *Sharing with me. Letting me take the lead.*

It was the least I could do after you freed me from Mrs. Charity. Besides, you are better at making our way in this world than I. Harmony gave her an inner squeeze. The sensation tickled. *I need you, Melody. You are the song that strikes my heart.*

Melody grinned. *Aye, and you, Harmony, are the one who breathes me to life.*

Harmony was quiet for a moment, settling deep into their bones. Finally, she spoke again. *Make me another pledge.*

Anything.

Promise we'll still sing together.

Aye, forever and a day.

As Madsen escorted her off the ship, Melody couldn't help but hum to herself. Inside her mind, Harmony sang along, the alto to her soprano, supporting her melody with harmonizing notes.

Come over the land,
Come over the sea.
Ten thousand landmarks
Keeps not my love from me.

Come in through the veil,
From ending to start.
Death 'tis but new life
When you're safe in my heart.

Officer Madsen stopped mid-step, giving her an odd look.

"Beg your pardon," Melody said, blushing. "I hadn't realized my singing had gotten so loud."

The officer shook his head, then stuck his pinky in his ear as if trying to clean it out. "It's not that, Miss Melody. You have a voice like an angel. It's just"—he gave her a discomfited look—"it's been a strange day, that's all."

"Oh? And why is that?"

"I could have sworn for a moment that you were singing two different notes at the same time." He gave an embarrassed laugh. "My ears must be playing tricks on me. Either that, or I'm just very tired."

"Indeed. It was a long night for us all." Melody looked at him and, using her sister's lips, quirked her token smile.

Drinking Water From the Sea

H. Linn Murphy

Jake Stone had come back to Strawbeach. Jake, my long-ago sweetheart—the beau who had turned Miss Charlotte Benson's girlish heart to marshmallows. He was going to walk up to the window at the Ice Shack and ask me to rent him a bathing machine. Who even used those anymore? One simply donned one's bathing costume and trotted out into the briny waves and dove in. Unless, of course, you were chicken.

The funny thing was, I knew Jake Stone wasn't. Chicken, that is. He was a great many things, but chicken he was not. He might break a girl's heart into a billion tiny shards and leave her bleeding on the shore, but he'd do it up right, if there was such a thing as breaking a girl's heart right.

I sat in my shack and moped. Jake may have come back, but he brought someone with him. She reminded me of a princess, all pink and black satin and the grandest hat a girl could imagine—all bobbing feathers and billowed netting. What a silly thing to wear on one's head at the beach. Still, it had cost a bundle. No need to even try to measure up. I wore my old straw boater. People always told me I looked like a man in it.

I saw the two of them on the boardwalk, strolling down the way, she with a parasol hiding that perfectly smooth, white face with scarlet lips, her hair cut in the perfect bob and topped with a stylish cloche. I would think those feathers would make her sneeze. I'd forever be batting them away from my face. The two of them spoke in giggly whispers, he, squiring her across the sand, his gorgeous chocolate eyes riveted to hers. He sported a mustache, now. I wasn't sure how to think of that. But his girl seemed to endure it quite well.

Was I jealous? You bet. Seemed extremely unfair. I wanted to be at the end of those lips of his, if not the fuzz on his lip. Just not out where people could see me. I'd gladly meet him under the water, even. Or back behind the shed. I wasn't overly particular, as long as he stuck to a few sweet little kisses.

I had half a mind to ignore the man for the whole time he and that slinking cat walked the beach together. Only who was I kidding? Grandfather needed the money. I couldn't afford to turn anyone away. Still, I wouldn't make it fun for Jake the Snake. He already had someone for that anyway.

I had just talked myself out of the whole service with a smile thing, when a shadow darkened the large open window behind which I sat. For some reason, Jake's arm candy had disappeared somewhere. I mourned her loss for maybe a half second.

"I'd like to rent a bathing machine, miss." *Miss.* Like he'd forgotten my name. Perhaps he had after stuffing his head with all that book learnin.' Or maybe someone had hit him really hard over the head. Now where was that flyswatter I'd been using?

I tried mightily to hide my smirk. Jake Stone. How was it he forced me to smile when I had just sworn to make him pay? "We don't rent those here. They finally went the way of the dodo last year." I kept my eyes plastered to the book I'd brought, only peeking at him from the edge.

"Charlotte? Charley? Over here." He rudely waved his hand in front of my face. "Nice boater, by the by. Isn't that a man's hat?"

"I see you. I already told you, sir. We don't rent bathing machines. And my hat is perfectly fine for the discerning young woman to wear in the blazing sun. Bonnets are for old ladies."

He quirked an eyebrow as he reached across, lifting my chin. His silky brown eyes beneath those silky brown lashes roved over my face, his smile playing Hide and Seek. "I've missed you, Miss Benson. It's why I've come to see what you had on offer." On offer? Such as charms? Bahahaha.

"Have you now? I rather think not, since you're here with a girl." I wasn't going to look up and let him see how he had destroyed me last summer.

From the corner of my eye, though, I watched Jake's cheeks turn crimson. "I didn't bring her. She's just someone who appeared. She won't leave me be, you see. I thought I'd get her involved in something and—well—evade her. Maybe come here and be with you."

I couldn't stop the guffaw from bursting from my lips. "My, Mr. Stone, you've learned something at that fancy college of yours. You've gone right past my small town ways, right to the rank sophistication of the occasional tourist." Could he tell some of the shards from my broken heart had washed out to sea along with the tide or lay like sea glass in the shallows?

I must have given him pause. He closed those lips of his over any words he might have uttered. I suddenly found his hand on mine as it rested on the ledge between us. Lightning played across my fingers in the strangest way. I looked up, and he trapped my eyes with his. I loved how his large warm hand felt, covering my smaller, cooler one. His eyes searched mine. He almost had me feeling breathless again. Almost. Until I remembered how enthralled he'd looked with Miss Sophisticated on his arm. How could he bring a girl to my beach town?

I pulled my hand from beneath his. It instantly felt bereft. I couldn't let it. Not at all. Must remember how Dapper Jake had shaken me off like the sand between his toes and left me at the beach to run off to the big city—off to sell books for a fancy big city bookstore.

I stuck the postcard back in my book to hold the place and drew in a deep breath. "I can offer you a frankfurter in a bun, your choice of seaside sand globes, or our newest modern invention, a pair of goggles with which to peer under the water. The glass allows one to clearly see what lies beneath."

Jake rallied. "I'll take a pair of goggles. I'd like to see beneath the water. What a capital idea. You still rent changing bells, do you not?"

"At two bits per half day." I presented Jake with the silly-looking goggles and a key to his dressing bell. "Be careful. There's a pretty steep drop-off about twenty-five feet out. And at times there's a strong rip that'll snatch you away before you can say Jack Robinson."

"I remember from last time. You swim sideways to escape the tide."

I nodded. He left, glancing back at me now and then. Last summer, I'd closed up the shack a few times so I could play in the waves with him. I already knew all the ins and outs of the beach and cove. No prissy sitting on the beach for me. Who did he think had tested the goggles grandpa had made?

This year? Maybe I'd think about rescuing him if a rip swept him out toward the reef. Maybe. I had a little two man ketch moored at the next dock over. I'd have to think real hard about it. Maybe he deserved to have to work his way back under his own steam. After all, he always told me *I* was the damsel, not he.

I cooked myself a frankfurter and put it to bed in its bread nest of mustard and dill relish. I sat chewing on it as I watched Jake emerge from his changing bell in his striped bathing costume.

On seeing that chest of his in its rippling stripes, my throat dried up like the Sahara at mid-day. If I really had to be honest with myself—not a big hobby of mine but occasionally necessary—I'd have to say that I sure did miss Jake Stone as he'd been at the beginning of last summer, when he hadn't been boasting about all the sweet young things he'd meet at college, as if I were his backward little sister or a dog-licked cookie. Before then, he'd sped my pulse like I'd been tacking through a particularly difficult reef or something. I couldn't wait to see him stride over the dunes. Now? Humph.

I ogled him from beneath my hat. That mustache must be a college man idea. I wondered what it might have felt like to kiss such a spiny thing--like kissing a star fish. I imagined Miss Snooty Patooty could tell me. Only I didn't see her on the beach. Perhaps the woman didn't like sand between her toes, or the feel of saltwater on her delicate cream o' wheat skin. I finished my frankfurter and had nearly decided I might save Jake after all, should a roller take him, when She pranced up, already dressed in the strangest bathing ensemble I'd ever seen. No dark cotton swim dress for her, no bloomers with black stockings, such as normal girls wore.

This woman managed what looked like a second skin, sleek and iridescent. The deep blues played into purples and grass greens. She gave me a smile that might have been saucy if I'd been a man. I didn't know what to make of it at all. Not her or her strange costume.

"May I help you?" I asked, not wanting to help the woman.

She missed the tartness in my voice, it seemed. "Do you sell towels, miss? I may have left mine at home."

"No, but I may have one you might borrow somewhere around here, Miss—"

She glanced at me from under her cloche. "It's just Mera. Like the ocean. And you are Jakey's little friend?"

I wanted to close the flap and come around and kick Uppity Mera in the shins until she couldn't prance around in her so stylish shoes and her short skirts and her skin-tight bathing costume ever again. I settled for clenching my teeth over my answer. I could just about hear Grandmother saying in that wavery old voice how swearing *"is unladylike and indicates a small mind."* In my head I was rather an atrocious hoyden.

"Here's your towel, Mirror. Have it back by two o'clock on the dot." I would give her a half an hour to enjoy herself. She clearly wanted to correct my pronunciation of her name, but I closed the hatch right in her face. Luckily there were no other bathers nearby, it being a rather windy day.

I wore my bathing costume beneath my shirtwaist and skirt. It was nothing to tear them off and run out into the sparkling water. Instead of daintily stepping through the tiny wavelets on the shore, I leaped through the initial waves and dove beneath a roller. The O's of Jake's and his girl's mouths gratified me as I stroked past them, my arms flashing in the sun, droplets flying like diamond strands.

I could see Jake's face in the distance. He looked unhappy, as if he'd rather not spend his time prancing through the wavelets like a gamboling lamb. Hah. I couldn't abide it. I dove beneath another wave and waited for another larger set. Making myself as flat as an ironing board, I rode the wave in, nearly to the sand.

Take that, Miss Mera. I bet you can't do that. Nor would you want to ruin your coiffure.

Jake wanted to try it. I saw it in his eyes. He watched me cut through the waves like we used to do together last summer. I hoped he'd enjoy his calm prancing. Only I didn't. I wanted him to be so miserable he'd leave that boy-snatching hussy and come back to me.

Would I take him back? Probably not. Grandma would have kittens if I did.

I spent the next hour or so riding the waves, until my soul had filled with sunshine and the rush of the water. I looked back at the shore. Only one form stepped through the waves there. Mr. Stone had lost his 'tail.' Mera must have gone into his bell to change so she could return the towel. I hoped she might tire of waiting for him and go away. Perhaps I could ride the last wave clear in and be there to accept the returned towel, late though smirking.

I kicked to turn myself toward shore. Something caught my foot. Must've been seaweed. I kicked out, but the weed only tightened around my ankle. I kicked and thrashed again to no avail. Nothing released the clenching weeds entrapping me. I splashed and jammed my other foot at the tightening plants. I took a deep breath and bent my body into the wave as it rolled over.

It wasn't a weed.

The wave had roiled a bunch of silt through the water, making it difficult to see, but I was fairly certain something big and more alive had me. I glimpsed a huge tail the size of a shark's, though it looked nothing like one. I tried to beat on whatever had me in its grip. It felt like—a hand. I couldn't get it to let go, and I *needed* air. *Craved* it. Had to reach the surface.

What to use? At last, I spotted a jagged rock. I swept it up and ran it across what gripped my ankle. Something shrieked. The noise traveled through the water faster than anything I'd heard before. I dropped the rock and clapped my hands to my ears. A massive fish tail slapped at me, narrowly missing my face.

The fish thing disappeared. I sprang to the surface and heaved a huge gulp of air into my aching lungs. I wiped the salt from my eyes and glanced around.

No large fin cut the water. No fish breached. Land, however, lay more than a mile away! I'd either fallen prey to the riptide, or that fish thing had yanked me out and away from shore. I turned and swam parallel to the beach for a bit to escape the current, then started the long haul back to safety.

Stroke after stroke. Soon my arms and legs ached with a fierceness I'd never experienced before. Though a strong swimmer, I'd never had such a long way to go to reach shore. I never seemed to make headway. Something seemed to tug me backward. I took a deep breath and plunged my head beneath the water, only to see that something large did indeed have me by the swim dress, pulling me backward against my strokes!

Why hadn't I kept the sharp rock? I took another huge breath and looked at what entrapped me. Fingers clutched at my skirt—fingers sporting sharp red talons. Nail lacquer? Such as the type Jake's Mera wore? No one else I knew wore that sort of thing. Jake's girl had flaunted her nails.

My astonishment nearly had me gasping in sea water. I took another breath and looked below again, only to see a pair of wide eyes rising from the waves just in front of me. Her head broke the water near my face. I wanted to check her legs but didn't dare break the stare with which Mera fixed me.

"I suppose I've got your attention, now," she said as she bobbed in front of me.

I nodded, unable to form coherent words. What did one say to a myth? My breath came in snatches, while hers issued calmly from wherever it originated.

"Jake Stone is a feckless young man, unfaithful to any mate. You can take that as the honest truth from one who knows."

"Why are you telling me this? Seems like you're just playing with him. Goodness. If I didn't know any better, I'd think you want me out of the way so you can have the man to yourself."

"I thought I did—for a little while. But games lose their luster for me at the swish of a tail, especially if he's all beauty and no mind." Mera dove and came up on the other side of me.

She, however, went on. "I take it you enjoyed his company up until the last day of summer, last year."

I nodded, amazed at her knowledge. I wiped the salt water from my eyes, the better to see her.

"I watched you both from afar. I decided I must test him. You saw the results. When I'm near, he enjoys my company. When he's with you, I'm the unwanted one. I'm not the only other. You must see it. He's fixed to break your heart all over again. You humans put such store by this love you speak of."

"Then why do *you* want him?" I asked.

"I don't." Her face broke into a wide grin. She looked nothing like the lady of fashion I'd envied. In fact, I wondered where all her fine feathers had gone. She almost seemed friendly. Except there was just a little something fey about her. Something Other that couldn't be trusted.

"What *do* you want?" I asked, suddenly a little worried she'd haul me farther out and leave me.

She surprised me. "I want something from you."

"Something? What, may I ask? What can I offer the girl who apparently has it all?"

"I want a friend—one who will guard this beach from people who would spoil it."

"Friendship? I should do things for you and you for me? Braid each other's hair and the like?"

"Of course. Passes the time, one might say."

She had a strange way of showing it. I could barely keep myself afloat, the fatigue so thick about me. "You pulled me under and out to sea. You were going to drown me."

Her smile changed to something much less friendly and more predatory, somehow, her voice harsh. "I'd not have let you die. Just needed you to pay attention." That last bit she said with a musical lilt to her voice that should have entranced me. Her face begged to differ. There was something about her eyes that wouldn't let trust bloom. Her hair fanned around her, suddenly long and greenish, like seaweed, instead of the stylish bob from the boardwalk. The urge to yank it out by the roots died down a little. Maybe I needed to wait until I wasn't in the water anymore. Let her prove she could be trusted by pulling me back to shore. Maybe I'd have to do my Grandmother proud and act like a lady, for once.

"You forgot the other part where you protect this place from other humans."

"A guard. I suppose I can do that. We do own this little chunk of land, Papa and I." I stared out at the tiny slice of beach with the shabby little shack on it.

Relief seemed to paint her face in a much kindlier light.

I smiled at her. "Very well, Mera. We'll be friends. And what about Jake?" I immediately regretted bringing him back to the conversation. Why did I have to open my fat mouth and remind her of the man we 'shared?' I roundly scolded myself for my very loose lips.

"What about him? Shall I drown him for you? He isn't worth much to either of us."

The shock of such a cavalier announcement sealed my lips for a time. I silently trod water until I could say something. With a shock, I realized there were things I liked about the man. Good things that I'd forgotten for a time. I couldn't obviously spout them off for her, or I'd spill this wobbly basket of friendship we'd caught. I bobbed beneath the water for a second, the fatigue creeping into my sinews. Then up again toward the light. "I hardly think he needs to lose his life. He might be good for holding a girl's parasol now and then." I fixed my eyes longingly towards shore, wiping the salt from my stinging eyes. Each minute I spent out there bobbing with the waves so far from the beach taught me to like swimming in the open water less.

Mera made a moue as she thought about my words. "I suppose I won't. For now. Human men might have their uses, though you don't seem like the type who needs someone to hold things for you." Her smile seemed alien to me, the whites of her eyes nearly covered in pitchy black tar. Had her teeth grown sharper? How casually she spoke of taking a life. Jake might be a cad and a bounder and a Jumping Johnny, but I couldn't help wanting his company just a little. Well, perhaps more than a little.

"Please take me back to shore. I'm growing quite exhausted."

Mera lay back in the water as if it were her favorite place to be. It had previously been my own. "If I must. Wouldn't you rather stay out here with me?"

Her question chilled me to the bone. How could I answer and not find myself being dragged to the bottom of the ocean? Couldn't she at least let go of me? I noticed we'd strayed even farther from shore. Subtle. Frightening. I felt as if my blood turned to jagged shards in my veins. Her eyes examined me like some dainty gobbet of food from which she contemplated sucking the juice until it turned to dust.

Around and around she circled. Waiting. Watching me.

I gulped. "I've enjoyed my swim, but now I must return to the shop. And guarding the beach."

"Where you rent towels by the half hour."

Adrenaline thundered through me, pricking me with worry. "I was teasing you." I laughed a little pathetic laugh. Mera's eyes narrowed. She knew.

Her smile froze my backbone solid. "As am I." She reached out and pushed down on my shoulder. My head bobbed under. I shot back out of the water, brine streaming from my hair and into my eyes. I wanted to shout at her, but what, then, would she do next?

"You can keep the towel." I'd bring another from home and hope grandma wouldn't wonder why all her towels were disappearing. "Present from me."

Mera raised a brow. Her smile did nothing to warm my blood. "I never needed it. I just wanted to see up close what sort of human you were." She snorted, her eyes telling me I'd failed her little test.

At last, she sighed and began tugging me closer to shore. I helped by swimming as much as my exhausted limbs could manage. The thin line of soft purple hills grew and coalesced into the palisades surrounding my tiny thread of beach. Perhaps there wasn't really such a strong riptide at Strawbeach after all. Perhaps it was more of something tugging people out to sea without them noticing. Perhaps I wouldn't go out so far anymore. The thought of staying out of the sea cut at my heart a little, though it would be some time before I was ready to come back.

A shadow crept up behind me. At the same time, something yanked me downward. I kicked and thrashed to stay above the waves. The tugging strengthened. Something caught at me from behind. I turned to find a sailboat, in which crouched Jake Stone. He had me under the arms, trying to lift me into the boat, which yawed frighteningly to the side. I stamped my foot into Mera's gut. She let go long enough for Jake to lift me into the boat. We fell backward, nearly hitting our heads on the mainsail mast.

"It took me forever to find a boat I could sail out to fetch you," Jake said when he caught his breath. "I thought you knew what to do in a rip."

"I do. That was no—" I broke off. He'd never believe me. Not when I'd been so jealous of Mera and him. "Never mind. Thank you for the rescue. And tell Spenser Farnsworth thank you for the use of his ketch." I sat gasping, every muscle aching with fatigue. He set the sail, the wind bellying out the canvas. We should have made great time, but we couldn't seemed to go anywhere.

I knew who was behind it. Mera probably thought I'd placed my trust in the wrong person. Now we would pay for it.

The tiller yanked itself out of Jake's hands. I hadn't thought his strong grip could lose against Mera's more dainty fingers. It seemed she had only grown stronger, more powerful as soon as she met the water. Vengeful. Jake lunged for the tiller and wrapped himself around it. A cracking sound ripped through the air. The tiller broke while Jake fell hard against the gunwale. His swearing punctuated the wind as he tried to make something of the mess before them.

"The tiller must be fouled by seaweed. I'll need to clear it."

"No! You can't go down there." Mera would kill him. She might already have lost patience with my fickle human friendship if human games bored her. I, however, didn't consider it very sporting to drown people if they made you angry.

Jake stared at me like I'd lost my mind. "If I can't free us, we'll go over as soon as the wind fills the sail again."

I sprang to drop the canvas. He scowled at me. "What's going on? Is this some sort of trick to get me out here and into your clutches? Because now we'll not go anywhere. Not unless we've oars."

My laughter sounded manic even to me. "My clutches? Preposterous. How can you think such a thing when you just mentioned how we'd go over if I hadn't dropped the sail. Besides, what makes you think I want you in my clutches? Maybe I want someone who can be loyal for longer than a month. Maybe I've learned my lesson about summer loves."

Jake scowled and mumbled something about women, causing him to drop another few points in my esteem.

"If you don't stop muttering about the helplessness of women, I'll go overboard and swim to shore, leaving you out here alone. What of that, oh lover of many women?"

Jake's brows crashed down over his piercing eyes. "What makes you think that of me?"

"Mera told me."

"When? She's been with me."

"Except when she wasn't."

"So you two engaged in a little light gossip at your Ice Shack? How do you know she can be trusted?"

"About some matters she's quite staunch. And well, she doesn't like you. Now that I've taken up with you, she's angry with me as well."

He snorted at me as if I should sign myself into Belview hospital for the insane as soon as we made shore. "You girls don't know what you're talking about. Believe me. I came back for you, Charlotte Benson. That Mera girl was just a flash in the pan."

"Like all the rest."

"Of course. They mean nothing when I'm waiting for you, Miss Charlotte. Not a thing."

Waiting? I wondered casually what constituted 'waiting' and whether those details canceled out the good things I knew about him.

He knelt at the side and tried to see what had happened to the tiller. A sickly white hand emerged from the water behind him. I screamed and yanked Jake back into the boat. The hand disappeared.

Now his anger lashed out at me. "Why did you do that? I nearly fell out of the boat."

"Something is after us, Mr. Stone. Something quite vicious. Call it a shark if you wish. If you insist on putting your head in the water, you'll lose it."

"I saw no shark." He rubbed his neck, the confusion showing in his face. Clearly he thought I had lost my senses.

"It was coming at you from behind. Perhaps you saw the tail. Or maybe that big, black dorsal fin."

"Charlotte, I used to think of you fondly, back when you impressed me with your knowledge of the ocean."

"It's been some time since I thought fondly of you, too, Jake," I muttered. "That ended back when I found out you were a flopnoggin and a cheat." I had about decided to push him overboard to deal with the vengeful mermaid when I heard laughter. Something clattered into the boat. I bent and picked up a pearl bracelet. Good night. The mermaid just gave me a present after I kicked her in the stomach. Maybe she wasn't such an odd fish after all. Maybe. I slipped my hand into the ring of iridescent orbs, admiring its beauty in the afternoon sun. What was I to make of it? Had she given me pearls to remind me of my part of the bargain?

Suddenly the boat began to make wonderful time returning to shore, though we had trimmed the sail and the tiller lay somewhere on the bottom of the sea. Another gift.

We docked around the cape and trudged back to Strawbeach, both of us silently muttering to ourselves. I noticed Jake examining Mera's gift like he hadn't heard it hit the deck. Where did he think I'd gotten it? Perhaps it might serve him right to think another man had given it to me. I would have to think about the uses for such a present. Maybe if Jake thought he had some rivalry he might not think of me as rank chum. I grinned to myself at the idea. Yes. No more shark bait.

As I stepped over the dune to the boardwalk, I looked out at the beach and burst into laughter. In huge, scrolling letters lay this message in the sand:

Jake Stone is a flopnoggin and a cheat.

He came up behind me and, upon seeing the message, burst into his own bout of chortling. "When did you have time to write that?"

I merely shrugged, still going off into gales of giggling.

"You must give me marks for a sense of humor."

"I don't know. You wanted to ship me off to an insane asylum. I don't think you deserve marks just yet. I'll reserve the right to award or withhold them later. For now, you have some explanations and a few apologies to make."

"According to whom?"

"Your friend Mera. You see her work before you."

Jake glanced back at the words gracing the beach, the edges of his mouth tilting upward. He lowered his brows over the question. "How would she know whether I've cheated or not? I only met her on the boardwalk last week."

I shrugged again, unwilling to try Jake's imagination with my experience in the sea.

"I suppose I do owe you an apology. I think you were hoping for more last summer—more than I could have offered back then."

"I only hoped for what you actually were willing to give, Mr. Stone. But no matter. I've gotten over my silly juvenile wants of last summer. Besides, what do you have now that you didn't have then?"

"Gainful employment. I've passed my first year of college."

I wondered how many girls he had stuffed away with his pin on their sweaters. "That's all very well and good, but how many young ladies would I have to share you with? According to Mera, there are lines."

"Goodness. I wonder how I could have kept such an army fed and entertained on my meager salary."

We'd reached the shed by then. I unlocked the door and went in to lift the window. Jake camped out as if he thought of staying forever.

"Say. Won't you come out with me tonight?"

"Pretty sure you'll need to offer old man Farnsworth something for ruining his tiller. I'd rather you spent your huge piles of money on that than on me. Besides, won't Mera be jealous? I definitely don't want to cross her."

"You." He fell silent for a few yards. Then he stopped and turned.

"You want to put that in writing?" With my chin, I indicated the message the wind was scouring off the beach. I couldn't hear him say I was right enough times to satisfy me.

He tipped his head as he examined my face. "I *have* been rather a bounder, haven't I? As I stand here, I can't quite understand why you would give me the time of day. You were so patient when I went on and on about other opportunities. You must have thought very little of me."

"Ah. Then you *have* been paying attention. Opportunities. Is that what we're calling them these days? Well then. I've only now decided you're worth another two minutes because of your apology. It's rather thin, though."

"If you really must know, I felt that you were so far beyond my reach, last summer, that I simply gave up and caved in to my baser instincts."

I raised my brow at his easy words. I was no longer the same rube who'd cavorted in the waves with him last summer. "One would hope you might, instead, hoist yourself up the old mast and be worth something, instead of falling in a heap."

Jake looked, at first, as though I'd hit him with a sand globe. Then he laughed, his voice carrying out over the cliffs and whitecaps. "I deserved that. I did. I suppose it'll take some time to prove my point."

"It will indeed. Eons. You'll have to spend the rest of your time here dealing with the consequences, or lose me forever. We'll soon see if you think I'm worth the trouble."

"You're definitely worth every penny and minute and thought I spend on you."

I laughed. He certainly kept me hopping wit-wise. By that time we'd returned to the beach. Jake reached down and, with a grunt, picked up a star fish and tossed it into the water. And another, and another, until the beach was swept clean of the spiny little creatures. The act reminded me of other kindnesses he'd performed, which, in my mind, his fickleness had previously overshadowed, to my shame. So many such acts now returned easily to my memory—Jake staying to help me close the shack, bringing me an occasional picnic, lifting my spirits at the end of a long day with his silly jokes. How easily I'd forgotten those acts, locked away in that tiny shack as I was. Perhaps I should cut him some slack line. Give his sails a chance to belly out again. Perhaps, in spite of his kind gesture, I couldn't let him off just yet. "You believe that?"

He nodded, the sun burnishing the creases at the edges of his eyes.

I smiled to ease the tension that question brought. Though it seemed true, I didn't want to completely scare the man away. I gave him a saucy wink. That might give me just enough credence. "Very well, then. I'll wait."

Jake lost his smile. "If you really must know, I told Mera a lot of hogwash about calling on multiple young ladies so she wouldn't get too attached. I actually didn't court much at school. You see, there's someone I'm already gone on, and it's not Mera or any other. She's much too mercenary for me."

I lifted my brows at him. Did I have to drag it out of him? I'm ashamed to say I snorted at him. Grandmother would be apoplectic.

"It's you, if you must know. I couldn't get you out of my mind. I tried mightily. I wanted to concentrate on work and school so I could make us a nest egg, you see."

Could I trust him? Everything in me yearned to do so. I gazed into his eyes. It must have been all that saltwater or something, but I felt I could see him clearer. His eyes told me in no uncertain terms that he was mine. Truth gleamed from their depths. I thought back on other things I'd seen him do. I'd watched him fix a child's kite and pay for an ice cream to stanch the little boy's tears when the kite went down in the ocean and got stuck on some underwater outcropping. I'd witnessed the way he treated little old ladies and grumpy old grandpas. He'd brought me food and listened to me go on and on about my parents and their fights. He'd been so kind to only offer suggestions when I'd already exhausted every avenue.

And then he'd gone away.

But here he was again, saying he'd gone to make us a place. Not only that, but he had something else to offer.

"I want you to go to college as well, Charlotte."

I widened my eyes at him. It seemed preposterous. Girls didn't go to college. They met a man and got married. "I don't have a red cent for college."

"I think we can figure something out. I want you to go and study marine life."

"You mean fish?"

"That and other ocean phenomena. I think you could be a dab hand at it. I'd help you. I've got a trust fund, you see."

"Supposing I were to—er—find myself expecting after we married? How would I study marine biology then? How would we even support ourselves?"

"I imagine you'd simply keep going. We both would. We'd have so many reasons."

Another snort. Any more of them and grandmother would have a fit and keel over in shame. "Reasons? What reasons?"

"You're a wonderful, understanding, forgiving person. And we'll find more reasons this summer. Together. Also, I believe the ocean would still be big enough to fit you." He laughed and ran away while I chased him, caught him, and rubbed a handful of sand in his hair. I might have scrubbed extra vigorously.

He turned and caught me around the waist. All at once his lips claimed mine. I wasn't going to allow it. But my knees went lax, and I forgot to breathe. Softly at first, then firmer his lips pressed mine. His hand tightened, drawing me closer. I was fleetingly glad I'd wrapped a towel around my waist, or I might have melted into a pile of slag and bathing costume right there on the beach. "You have the rest of the summer to convince me, Jake Stone. I came at last up for air and whispered, "So far, so good, but I'll be watching you."

A roly-poly man with hair combed to the front over his bald spot stepped up to the window, then. I hadn't even seen him making his way across the sand. He smiled like a snake ready to take a chunk out of my leg. "Excuse me. Do you know who owns this stretch of land."

"I might, sir."

"I represent the firm of Rawlins and Stuckey. We'd like to offer the owners a rather lovely nest egg to relieve them of this dreadful little shack and tiny bit of sand. Could you take them a message? I assume you know at least who pays your—er—salary."

Jake's eyebrows lifted and he fixed me with a meaningful stare. His eyes said, *"This is our chance, Charley.*

The man showed me a piece of paper containing a one and several zeros. That money could make all my dreams come true. I wouldn't have to sit in this steamy little shack anymore. I'd have all the beautiful dresses money could buy. The zeros tempted me for another ten seconds.

I heard a squeal of rage echo across the sand. Then, out of the corner of my eye I saw a large fish tail slap the water, then disappear beneath the waves.

This was what Mera meant. How had she known? I turned my gaze from the waves back to the slimy walrus of a man leaning on my window sill. "Sir, I and my family own this beach and this dreadful little shack. We wouldn't sell to a sock full of sand burrs like you if you were the last snake into the ark. Sorry, Grandma. I just couldn't do it."

"Couldn't do what, miss?"

"Be more ladylike. And keep to one analogy." I gave him a smile that could singe off his eyebrows.

The man smirked. "I'd like to speak to someone with more authority, please."

I opened my mouth to tear the beefy man's head off, but Jake beat me to the punch. "Sir, she *is* the authority. This plot of land is not for sale. Neither is the bay in front of it. Rawlins and Stuckey must go elsewhere to look for an easy sale. And you may put that in writing. We have."

As the beached whale lumbered back across the beach, I fixed Jake with a steely stare. "You'll do."

His laughter burst from him in waves that filled me with happiness of my own.

Something told me I'd enjoy one blissful summer torturing Jake until I said yes and finding out what it meant to be the best friend of a mermaid. Something told me it could be dangerous, but interesting. The tide was still out. Maybe, by the end of the summer Jake wouldn't have proved constant and Mera would. Might having a mermaid for a friend sell more sand globes? Or would she scare people away from the beach? What if I could scrape together just enough money to go away to college and find my *own* place. Maybe. There seemed a good too many bathing bell rentals in my future.

How long could Mera possibly hold a grudge anyway?

Furthermore, how long would it take me to urge Jake to shave off his wretched mustache?

Stoneheart's Soul

C R Simper

No one disturbed Captain Reginald "Stoneheart" Loften during a meal unless the matter was life or death important.

Thus, as his ship cabin door opened, Loften glared at his cowering first lieutenant. He set down his mug of ale.

"Captain Stoneheart, sir, forgive me. There is a strange cloud on the horizon."

"Strange, *how*?" Loften half-scoffed.

"Dark, moving fast." First Lieutenant John Everett grimaced, perhaps recognizing how unremarkable he'd made it sound so far. "The shapes it makes…some of the men are saying it seems unnatural. It's causing a stir."

Loften rose.

In his twenty-plus years at sea, Loften had seen it all, or so he believed. He stood on the bow of *HMS Hephaestus* and pulled out his brass spyglass. The cloud on the horizon grew ever nearer, its shape shifting in ebbs and flows.

"Sir, what is it? A cyclone?" Second Lieutenant John Downs, asked.

"Smoke?" a nearby seaman suggested.

Loften waited until he could see more detail through his glass. The cloud was strange, yes, but not unnatural.

"Birds," Captain Loften replied. "A flock of birds. Maybe thousands of them."

"Birds?" Downs sounded skeptical.

But shortly, a thousand birds of a hundred varieties circled above. Some landed on the masts and rails. Some of the birds fell to the deck, panting and barely alive.

The ship rang with their chatter like an untuned orchestra. Seamen emerged from below deck, no doubt drawn by the racket. Some came pulling on their uniforms and others still in sleepwear.

"The islanders would call this a bad omen, sir," his shipmaster declared.

"I would call it dinner," replied the cook, invoking cheers.

Before the crew could move to gather the exhausted birds, however, the ship rocked on a sudden wave and the sails filled with the strength of an equally sudden gust of wind.

The birds flew on as one to get ahead of it.

Omen, indeed.

"Batten down the hatches, men," Loften ordered. "A storm is coming."

As the men scrambled to their posts, Loften looked to the horizon with his spyglass and measured what he could see of the monster storm driving the birds. A circular ridge of white clouds rose above a dense darkness that reached from horizon to horizon. Loften had survived many tempests, but he had never seen one so vast.

And they, not being birds, had no chance of outrunning it.

"Put on your full uniforms, men. Today we battle the sea," he added, to encourage the greener officers and seamen who looked to him in hope.

"If we're headed down to meet Davy Jones in his locker, might as well dress for the occasion," Downs remarked, too loudly, and some of the younger officers exchanged nervous glances.

"Thank you for your unsolicited interpretation of my remarks, Mr. Downs," Loften growled, dripping sarcasm, then drew the lieutenant aside. "Fear is the exact opposite of what I hoped to inspire. Do not do it again."

"Yes, Captain Stoneheart, sir."

The crew of the *HMS Hephaestus* had fought together many times, against the French, the Spanish, the Egyptians, the Danish, and pirates of various nations. The sea was a foe that could not be outgunned, but it could be out-maneuvered and outlasted. Every storm had an end.

Once the ship was secured, most of the crew took shelter below. They would rotate in turn as men fought to keep the ship upright with the increasing waves. It fell to the helmsmen—two at a time—to keep the ship facing the waves and ride them.

Up and down.

Up and down.

Clouds covered the sun. The sea boiled. Winds whipped and ripped at the riggings. Lightning struck in the distance and thunder rolled.

Steeper and steeper the waves came, for hours on end. Six helmsmen exhausted themselves in turn to keep their shipmates alive. Captain Loften, having spent time as a helmsman in his younger years, chose to assist with the fourth rotation. He took the helm, along with another experienced seaman, eight hours in, watching the sea with the aid of lanterns and the perpetual lightning, to predict the angle of the next incoming wave. The directions shifted in ways that did seem somewhat unnatural, but the size of the storm must have caused it.

Amidst the tempest, lightning flashed and revealed the shadow of another ship off to the side, in Loften's peripheral vision. But when he purposefully glanced aside to find it, he saw nothing but water.

Loften blinked and turned his focus ahead again, cursing his foolishness. To lose sight of the squall, while trying to steer into it, would mean death.

A glow pulled his gaze again, not one from the sky, but below the water, as if lightning had become trapped within the rising waves.

There he saw the shadow ship a second time.

Beneath the sea.

Loften's grip on the helm slackened as his blood ran cold. "What in the name of —?"

The huge wave crashed over the top of the deck and struck Loften a blow as solidly as if the wall of water had been stone. It tore him away from the helm and sent him careening across the deck. The railing broke with the force of impact.

Loften could have thought he'd turned into a bird, the way he flew. He felt the wind around him, carrying him in a slow arc away from safety.

Then, he struck the water and went under.

Captain Loften hadn't lived much of a life, having spent almost all of it on the sea, yet it was a life worth fighting for. He swam, unsure of his direction, but he had to try.

He saw a light ahead, a dim glow, and within it, the shadow of a ship that must be his own. He swam towards it until his lungs burned. He had mere seconds left before he would be forced to gulp in water and drown.

The ship, thankfully, drew nearer as well. It rose, not with wind in its sails, as it had nothing but shredded rags and hanging lines. A gaping hole in its side glowed orange as if aflame. Multiple smaller holes speckled the siding.

With such damage, the ship should not be afloat, Loften realized. Nor should he be alive still to observe its rise from the dark depths. Swirling clouds of birds and epic storms paled to the unholy and unnatural spectacle before him.

As his feet touched down on the deck, Loften fell to his knees and breathed in…

Air.

A bubble of air had formed around him, circular, and walled by water. Outside it, an abomination approached, dressed in what had once been a fine captain's coat and tri-fold hat. The man might once have been a fine gentleman as well, but his skin was sallow, gray, flaking. The man's eyes were so pale that the line between blue and white was nearly impossible to distinguish in the glow of orange light.

The crew of the ship gathered also, just outside the bubble of air. The ghastly seamen wore the tattered uniforms of a dozen nations, over bodies half-decayed. They stared at Loften like a caged animal—curious, perhaps, or waiting to devour him.

Captain Loften had a heart of stone, but even so, in that moment it began to fail him. He set both hands on the grimy floor to keep from collapsing.

He was done for.

The shadow ship's captain stepped out of the ocean and into the bubble of air. The stench nearly gagged Loften, but he controlled the urge to retch.

Except that he had to.

Water spewed from his throat and burned. He didn't recall having swallowed any water, but now it came up in violent heaves, pooling around the feet of the captain of the ghostly ship.

"Who…?" Loften choked. "Who…are you?"

"Have ye not guessed?" The corpse smiled broadly with a mouth full of decayed or gold teeth, some missing.

"Davy Jones. You're Davy Jones." Loften gasped. "You…trap the souls of those who die beneath the waters, from whence there is no…" his voice failed, and he cleared his throat, "…*escape*."

"Aye," said Davy Jones, his smile fading. "Excepting that last bit. Escape there is, for some. For you, apparently. I cannot take you today, and I would like to know why."

Hope came like a beacon from above, literal, and bright. The crew of the shadow ship cowed and shrunk back from it. Davy Jones squinted and scowled.

"I will have you, soon enough, Captain Stoneheart. You won't escape me forever," Davy called out loudly, and then withdrew into the darkness.

Loften sucked in a last gulp of air just before the ship descended rapidly. The bubble collapsed. He again swam for his life, and for his soul this time, towards the golden light above.

Reginald Loften had never seen a beach more beautiful. White sands, turquoise water, blue sky.

And air.

He filled his lungs with it thirstily. Why? Hadn't he just been…?

"Drowning. Yes, you were drowning," said a voice.

Loften turned to see a man, similar to Davy Jones, but different in all the ways that made him look normal and whole. This gentleman's uniform coat was white, his tri-fold hat, also white.

"You…you must be. Saint Peter?"

"Jones," said the man, with a hint of mirth in his dark-blue eyes. "Peter Jones. Not *Saint* Peter. He greets only the dead, and you're not. Not yet."

"Why?" Loften asked. Even Davy Jones had wondered.

"You are protected."

"How?"

The gentleman smiled, no gold teeth, no gaps. "By the prayers of one Frederick Loften."

The name brought images to Captain Loften's mind, memories of his childhood he didn't want to revisit.

"My cowardly brother?"

"*And…*" Peter Jones trailed in without acknowledging the interruption, "…because of the sacrifice you made which started you into this life of hardheartedness."

"Frederick was afraid," Loften spat. "I wasn't afraid. I stepped up when he refused. He was weak."

"It is sad that that is how you choose to remember it," said Peter Jones, shaking his head. "Your brother *was* afraid. *You* were afraid.

You stepped up because you loved him. You cut yourself off from every opportunity to feel anything in order to survive. They came to call you Captain Stoneheart. That is the sacrifice that has earned you this second chance."

"But Davy said he'll take me soon. There is no escape."

"Oh, Davy, such pride." Peter glanced away at the sea. "Of course there is escape, even for him if he would seek it. I can offer you a way forward, but you have to accept the opportunity."

"Yes, I accept!" Loften replied, remembering the crowd of fallen onlookers. "No matter the terms."

"Ah." Peter smiled and took out a scroll. "First, you must say an 'Ave' for every man, woman, or child who died because of your actions or orders."

"But they were my king's orders," Loften protested.

"Yes, and they were not altogether unjustified, but this is your path forward, not his."

Loften thought of the stench and the eternal orange flames. "Fine. I will do what you ask, but how will I…?" The scroll grew longer, infinitely almost. Loften's eyes widened at the addition of thousands of names. "So many?"

"Twenty-six years of wars and rumors of wars. Against countries, rebels, and pirates—"

"Even the pirates?" Loften asked.

"*Especially* the pirates."

"Fine. Fine," Loften agreed.

"Second," said Peter.

"That's not enough?"

"For your *soul*?" Peter replied skeptically.

Loften shrank and shook his head. What were words, really? Just words. "What, then?"

"One hundred British pounds, or the equivalent in silver, to any woman you've ever used and left behind."

Loften felt a flush fill his cheeks. Most of those indiscretions were from his younger years when he'd let the fear of ridicule from other seamen drive him to make poor choices.

"Yes, yes, of course, as I deserve," Loften replied. "But how?"

The names were added to the scroll, this time in rose red. Not so many, but still too many, and spread among the others, perhaps all in timeline order. It would take most of what money he had set aside for retirement.

"As I deserve," he said again.

He hadn't cared then. He didn't care now, but it was a path away from the terrors he had seen below.

"Is that…everything, then?"

"Is it?" Peter asked.

"No," Loften presumed. "Go on."

"You must forgive your father."

"My father?"

"*And…*" Peter led, ignoring him again. "Your brother."

"Never."

"Your choice." Peter shrugged; his expression fell. "My brother cannot forgive me, either. You've witnessed what's become of him because of his choice."

Loften frowned. He had met Davy Jones, face to face, and yet…

"I don't know if I ever can. I don't know how."

Peter handed him the scroll. "There are many ways to break a heart of stone, Captain. One is fear. One is loss. One is love. Choose well. You have three months."

"I'll die in three months?" Loften tucked the scroll inside his coat, where there was a tear in the lining that worked for a pocket. "Or is it that my brother, who prays for me, will die?"

"Your choice to forgive may yet be a deciding factor in your benefactor's long-term fate," Peter replied. "But, more certainly, your own. Good luck."

"But—"

Even as he tried to ask, the beach blurred and the light grew brighter, right before everything went dark.

"Captain Stoneheart—I mean, Loften. Reginald. Wake up."

Loften slowly opened his eyelids; they felt heavy. His entire body ached.

Somehow, he had awakened in his own hanging platform bed. Across the small sleeping cabin, his blue uniform coat hung in its usual place.

"Mr. Everett?" he croaked.

"Captain!" his first lieutenant gasped. "You're alive…and you know my name, sir. It's a blessed miracle!"

"What happened?"

"The waves, sir. They came from every direction, and you kept us upright. You did it, sir, but then…"

"Woosh!" said Lieutenant Downs. "A wave went over the deck and took you right with it. You were lost."

"But the storm, it ended as suddenly as it came, sir, and there you were, floating on a crossbeam, not even from our ship," Everett continued. "We thought you were drowned, but then you retched up seawater and breathed."

It sounded familiar. Loften reached up to determine the source of his colossal headache and found a large bump beneath his thick hair. "I hit my head."

"That's what the surgeon said," Downs replied. "He stepped out to go ashore to get herbs."

"Ashore?" Loften tried to sit up and winced. His head hurt worse trying to move. "But we were days away from land."

"Three days." Everett reached out to assist Loften in sitting up. "The storm drove us most of the way to British Honduras, so we made for it. You've been asleep, all that time."

"I see." Loften almost laughed. "I hit my head and nearly drowned…and dreamed the rest."

Downs smirked. "Good dreams, I hope."

No, Loften did not say aloud. *Nightmares.* But that was all they'd been, right?

"You didn't…You didn't find a scroll in my coat?" he asked.

"A what, sir?" Everett replied.

"Never mind." Loften breathed out a long sigh of relief.

He'd dreamed it all.

Captain Loften stayed in bed another three days. Surgeon's orders. He was in no state to disobey. The light hurt, and he could hardly stand without his head spinning.

Finally, the fourth day, he withdrew from the cabin, a blanket around his shoulders, as unsteady as a toddler learning to walk.

The crew clapped and cheered for him, however. It felt…

It *felt.*

He looked at his men one by one. He didn't even know some of their names. That was his fault. But they were his crew. One or more of them had risked their lives fishing him out of the ocean, then carried him to bed and kept him alive.

"Thank you, all," he said quietly, as gratitude overwhelmed him.

"Captain says 'thank you, all!'" Everett repeated double volume.

And they clapped again.

Loften almost smiled.

But a shadow crossed the sky off to the side, shaped like a large three-masted ship without sails.

Loften gasped and stepped backwards, losing balance. Everett was close by and caught him. When he looked again, there was nothing but sea and sky, not even a cloud.

"You'll get your sea legs back soon, Captain," Everett said.

"Thank you," Loften replied.

"Might need a cane," said Downs.

"Aye, perhaps so," Loften replied.

And within an hour, the ship's carpenter had carved one.

"From a piece of the very beam that rescued you," Everett declared.

Loften walked the deck with it later that evening. He hated the feeling of unsteadiness. He could accept it more from his body, under the circumstances, than from his mind.

As the sun set, the sea below continued to glow, orange and red, like fire.

Then, it moved.

Alarmed, Loften stepped back from the railing. He sucked in a breath and stepped forward again. The sea had gone dark.

"A trick of the light," he said aloud, and he went to bed.

The shadow ship invaded his dreams, but so did the white island and the scroll of names. Within the dream, he saw himself placing it in the lining of his uniform coat.

The next morning, he finally dared approach his dress coat, hoping to find nothing. But a corner of brown peeked out from the torn inner seam. He touched it, feeling the texture of the aged paper as proof that the scroll, indeed, existed.

He left it there, for now.

It couldn't help him yet.

Instead, Loften dressed in his day-to-day uniform and walked more decidedly with the aid of the cane to find a man he had mostly avoided.

The *HMS Hephaestus,* formerly christened *Serpiente,* had been built in Havana in the mid-1700s by the Spanish, then captured for England in the Battle of Cape St. Vincent. She carried an impressive 80 guns, classed as 3rd rate because of having only two decks. She was old and small compared to other British Naval vessels but was still considered a ship of the line. 400 men served aboard, yet with no official chaplain among them.

But there was Seaman James Prior.

Loften found Seaman Prior, as expected, kneeling beneath his hammock on the lower gundeck, mumbling quietly. Prior did not pray aloud anymore because of the teasing of the crew—which was how Captain Loften had been made aware that the seaman was devout. Not Anglican, but something.

Several men slept nearby; the collective snoring drowned out any external noise while he waited.

"Oh, Cap'n, forgive me," Prior spoke quietly and rose. "I di'na see ye waitin' there."

"You're fine, Mr. Prior. I had no wish to interrupt. May I have a word?" He drew in a breath. "I have a question."

"Of a course, sir." Prior frowned. "Ask on."

"What does it mean to 'speak an Ave' over the dead?"

"*An* Ave, or *The Ave*?" Prior asked.

"An. *An* Ave," he recalled.

"'Tis a prayer, then. A hope for their eternal soul to be guided back to God, their maker."

"How…do you do it?"

"How do *I* do it?" Prior frowned again. "When I see the man is dead, I speak a prayer. My mother taught me it is not good to use the name of deity in vain repetitious phrases, so I speak around it. I say: 'Hail to you, creator of the ocean, land, and sky, and lord of man. Please guide the soul of —I would say the name here if I know it—to dwell with you forever. Amen.'"

"It sounds…familiar," Loften admitted.

"I said it for you, when we pulled you from the sea." Prior's brow furrowed. "We all thought you were done for."

"Thank you," Loften replied. "Can you write it down for me?"

"I do not know letters, but you could write it after my shift."

"Come find me in my cabin after second mess, then."

"Yes, sir," Prior said, and Loften departed.

It felt ridiculous to be so afraid. Loften kept his head down as he crossed the quarterdeck and entered his cabin. He closed the door and moved to draw the curtains over the rear-facing windows—a luxury born of his ship's Spanish origins.

A cluster of decaying faces flashed into his mind, staring at him through the windows just as they had watched him from the edges of the bubble of air.

But when he blinked, the windows were empty.

He drew the curtains closed and sat alone in the near-dark, trying to draw in deep enough breaths to calm the rapid beating of his heart.

"Hail to you, creator," he whispered. Shadows crossed the room where cracks of light still shown around the curtains' edges. "Hail…to you…creator of…oceans…"

A loud thump on the deck above caused him to jump. Just the men, *his* men, not mournful crowds of rotting corpses waiting for him to join them beneath the waves.

Being alone in his cabin wasn't helping his anxiety. He rose and picked up the first thing within his reach—a wooden box.

"Lieutenant Everett," he called, exiting his cabin. "Care for a game of chess?"

"Certainly, sir," Everett replied. "Should we take it inside?"

"No. We'll sit right here on the stairs." Loften set out the board. The game proved to be a decent distraction, as Everett was quite good at chess, and in fact better to the point of trying to lose.

"Mr. Everett, you have my permission to win, if you need it," Loften said.

"But…"

"My ego is not fragile. I want to lose. It'll make me better next time."

So, Everett moved his queen. "Checkmate."

"Excellent." Captain Loften studied the board a long moment. "Another?"

Everett agreed, and they played for hours, until the second mess bell rang. Loften had seen nothing unusual during that time and was able to finally relax.

But as he rose from the game, Loften caught a hint of movement out of the corner of his eyes, of a large and looming dark shadow.

And when he dared look, nothing.

"Stop it," he muttered. "Leave me alone."

"Sir?" Everett asked.

"Nothing," he replied. Not a lie, exactly. "Call the men to eat. I'll be in my cabin."

"I'll have your meal brought to you there, then?" Everett asked.

"Yes. Have Seaman Prior bring it. He wanted a word with me."

"He should take any words he wants to have with you, through me," Everett replied.

"No, sorry. I first wanted a word with him." Loften couldn't admit the actual truth to his first officer, and so kept it vague. "And he has the time to bring it to me now."

"I see, sir." Everett grimaced. "I will send him, then."

Loften returned to his dark room. He squared his shoulders and opened the curtains with a jerk, expecting faces, but finding only sea and sky.

What if it was all just a trick of his mind, brought on by his near-drowning and subsequent nightmares?

Still, if it turned out to be nothing, learning an Ave prayer from Prior would be completely harmless.

Over dinner, Seaman Prior talked about how his mother had come from a small Lutheran revivalist community offshoot that had never gained a name. It had since disbanded, and most members of the community had emigrated to America. Prior's mother had remained behind to assist her ailing grandmother and fallen in love with a local boy and stayed in England, raising her family outside the Anglican tenants, but with no organized formal religion.

Loften found the exchange of personal stories to be uplifting and distracting, as much as the chess match, if not more.

He told Prior about how he had been the eldest son of a former military officer, retired to a small estate near Margate, in charge of a small parsonage. When military friends had insisted the senior Loften recommend one of his boys as a Boy Third Class to assist in the war effort, Loften's twelve-year-old brother Frederick had been their father's choice.

But upon finding his brother weeping, terrified at the thought of going to war, fourteen-year-old Reginald had offered to go in Frederick's stead. Unwilling to back out of the agreement, their father had agreed.

The first year at sea had been miserable. Stationed aboard the *HMS Monmouth*, he had witnessed multiple skirmishes, most notably the Battle of Providien. Since then, he'd worked his way up through the ranks, serving on various ships, passing the lieutenant exam with ease, and eventually earning his way to Captain.

"Ye've had a good life, then," Prior observed. "Albeit a lonely one."

"Yes," Loften agreed. "I would appreciate your discretion. Shall we proceed?"

Loften took out a blank ledger book and wrote Prior's Ave on the first page as the seaman carefully dictated it.

He then spent the remaining daylight hours memorizing every word.

This time when night fell—as Loften found himself alone in his quarters, surrounded by darkness, listening to the splashing of water, creaking of wood, the skitter of footsteps above and below—he had a weapon.

He went to his coat, opened the seam, and took out the scroll. He read the first name then closed his eyes.

"Hail to you, creator of the ocean, land, and sky, and lord of man. Please guide the soul of —William Williamson—to dwell with you forever. Amen."

A quiet sound called him to open his eyes. A glowing white line crossed through the name of William Williamson, and then it disappeared from the scroll.

But there was more.

Loften saw, outside his window, the black ship rise from the deep with fire in its belly. This time it did not hide from his gaze.

A white light, fleeting, beautiful, rose from the ship into the sky like a shooting star until it blended with the night.

Loften did not know how or when or where Mr. William Williamson had died, but the spirit of the man was now free.

Davy Jones paced along the crumbled railing on his decrepit ship, ranting at his men and at the sky, and shaking his fist.

The desire to cause further spite to Davy Jones brought a wild sort of courage back to Loften's heart. He left his quarters, climbed up to the poop deck, and read the next name aloud and there offered another Ave.

The night became a light show as the sea gave up her dead.

The shadow ship drew in, closer than ever. Its gunports were open—permanently. Most of the guns were rusted over and barnacle covered. Loften suspected they might still be able to fire under the right circumstances. He didn't dare provoke Davy Jones by ordering a practice volley of shots off starboard.

Though the thought made him smile.

Loften prayed aloud until his voice went hoarse, and he finally collapsed to the deck in exhaustion.

The vision of white shores had changed. The beach was no longer lonely but filled with reunions. Fathers embracing sons. Wives embracing husbands. Children...

It turned out William Williamson was a mere boy, and Loften

watched the child embrace an old man who must have been a grandparent. The boy turned and smiled.

At him.

Loften's heart warmed a little as he smiled back.

"I think the captain has a touch of madness in him," Lieutenant Downs' voice interrupted the dream.

"Do not say such things!" Everett hissed back quietly. "He took a blow. Surgeon says it can rattle a man for weeks. Keep judgment to yourself. Our job is to protect him from speculation, see?"

"If you say so," Downs reluctantly agreed.

Loften kept his eyes closed until they had gone. Obviously, they'd found him unconscious and carried him again to his own bed.

He climbed down, picked up his scroll, and unrolled it a fair stretch. He'd crossed off nearly a hundred names last night, but at the top now, the first woman's name had appeared: Eulalia, no last name. He could connect a face with her name, at least. He knew where to find her, and it wasn't far.

Loften rose and dressed. Everett wanted to protect him from speculation, but he could also help by dressing and acting the part of 'all is well.'

Even if it wasn't, entirely.

"Jamaica," he said. "Turn us and head for the island."

"The men were looking forward to heading home," Downs protested.

"I-I know. Our orders have changed. We have a few stops to make first."

He returned to his cabin and Everett followed.

"Sir, when did we receive new orders?" the lieutenant asked.

"Recently. I forgot to say so, then the storm hit."

Everett nodded. "I see, sir. I'll spread the word."

"Thank you, Mr. Everett. You're a good man," Loften replied. "A good second-in-command. I appreciate your loyalty."

"Oh, uh, thank you, sir." Everett stumbled over the words and departed.

Loften decided he would need to express his gratitude more readily in the future.

They arrived at Kingston, Jamaica without incident. Here, Loften had spent multiple nights on the few occasions his orders had brought him to the Caribbean, but always with the same woman. Loften had controlled himself on that point, at least.

He sought out Eulalia in the daylight hours, so as not to confuse her with the purpose of his visit. Fortunately, the scroll provided a tiny map of her location, or he might have had to ask around for days. It was a needed mercy considering he had so little time to complete his list of soul-saving tasks.

Loften discovered her washing clothes, dressed in a ragged cotton slip, white in contrast to her freckled, sun-kissed skin. She'd told him once she was Scot-Irish, descended from a combination of indentured servants and criminals. Loften had no feelings for her—that was never the point. He'd shut down those caring parts of himself long before they'd met.

"Ms. Eulalia."

She gasped. "Cap'n Stoneheart?"

"It's *Loften*, ma'am," he corrected quietly. "I am here to give you something I owe you, then I will depart."

"You owe me nothing, sir. You were always…a safe companion and paid better than most."

It struck him to hear that "safe" was the quality Ms. Eulalia most admired in a man.

He held out the bag of coins, a hundred pounds worth, in small denominations for her sake, and his. She wouldn't need to exchange them and explain the circumstances of her coming into fortune.

"Here," he said. No other words.

"So much?"

"Is it enough…to buy yourself out of this life you lead?"

Her green eyes lit as she laughed. "You offering?"

"No…no." He grimaced. "I make no offer except my apology. Is a hundred pounds enough? Can you get out?"

"I'll have to leave Jamaica. Start a new life somewhere. But yes."

"Good." Loften wondered if that had been Peter Jones' intention all along. "Where would you go?"

"Boston, perhaps." She threw her arms around him and kissed his cheek. "Oh, thank you, Cap'n."

Loften only nodded. He didn't deserve her gratitude when his motives were entirely self-centered. He returned to the *Hephaestus*, turning neither right nor left before going into his cabin to reopen the scroll.

Eulalia's name had disappeared. A small weight lifted from his heart.

Captain Loften spent the evening offering more Aves for the men on his list. He read each name, then prayed, and watched their names get crossed off by the dozens.

He stopped at the next woman's name, this one from Ireland. He was walking backward through time, to revisit his sins. Loften opened the scroll further to find all of the women on the list and confirm their current locations on the tiny maps, so he could visit them in a logical order and not need to backtrack.

The crew would not argue if they stopped first in Ireland, then Scotland, then Margate, his childhood home, before hitting a few more English ports.

Too many.

He didn't want to think that far ahead.

Once again, in open sea, Captain Loften caught occasional glimpses of the shadow ship in his peripheral vision. It had ceased to startle him, though the deep sense of foreboding remained. He'd entered a race against time.

The images of faces in the window had become less gruesome and more pitiable. Loften began to hope that their names might show up somewhere on his scroll so he might release them, too.

The nightly dreams of happy reunions spurred that hope.

He hadn't cared about the welfare of other people in a very long time, but he was relearning the skill. When saying the Aves became too rote, he stopped for the night. He wanted to consider them each a little more closely.

Englishmen, Frenchmen, Spaniards, Americans, Danes, Egyptians…all deaths that had come by his government's wars. The nameless crews of ships were named now to him, and him alone.

With each prayer, the scroll shortened, and he took hope in it.

His seemingly endless task might have an ending, after all.

Upon reaching Ireland, Loften followed the scroll's tiny map to locate Catherine Michaels. He recalled her face once they met. She was older, her beauty fading beneath the paint and creams meant to maintain it.

She eyed him suspiciously as he asked her to walk with him away from the small stone home she shared with several other women.

"I am out of that business, Lieutenant Stoneheart," she said. "Or is it Captain now?"

"Yes, ma'am." He offered the bag of coins, same as before. "This is for you."

Her eyes widened. "Why?"

"Penance. Mine."

"Ye found God."

"Not yet," Loften admitted. "Trying to."

She accepted the bag. "Thank ye. I will be able to set up a small shop with your penance and keep those other young girls out of the business. We will weave hats and sell flowers."

"That is…very kind," he replied, surprised by her generosity.

What the women chose to do with his offered penance was not his to dictate. He had been asked only to give them the money, and then move on.

As they set sail that evening, Loften confirmed that Catherine Michaels' name had disappeared from the scroll, then continued down his still-long list of Aves before going to bed.

Upon docking in Edinburgh, Scotland, a uniformed messenger came aboard. All British Naval vessels were being ordered to gather and sail for Copenhagen, Denmark. The main fleet had departed Portsmouth ten days ago.

"Why Copenhagen?" Loften asked. "Have they not claimed neutrality in Napoleon's war?"

"Napoleon declared a Continental Blockade against Britain, and we are responding," the messenger replied. "All ships of the line are being ordered to join—along with any merchant ships able to be conscripted for the cause."

"I see." Loften sighed. His list of Aves for the Battle of Trafalgar alone had been exhaustingly long, and now another battle might soon be added. "Hopefully it will only be a short blockade."

The messenger shrugged. "You could still catch up—in fact, you are obligated to try, now that you are aware. You and your crew will be well compensated for it."

"Aye. We must refill our supplies first, in any case," Loften said, to give reason to go ashore that would make sense to a military messenger. "We will set sail tomorrow at dawn."

That should give him enough time.

The most awkward of all his meetings thus far happened in the late afternoon. A man answered the door, covered in soot from the mine.

"Is Ms. Susannah MacLaine in?" Loften asked.

"That'd be Mrs. Susannah MacDougal to you," the man replied. "My wife."

Loften met the gaze of the woman standing behind Mr. MacDougal and saw a spark of recognition shift suddenly to alarm.

"An inheritance, ma'am, from your great uncle Peter," Loften lied, so that the secrets of her former life would remain up to her to keep or reveal. Susannah stepped forward, and he handed her the bag. "To do with as you will. I am sorry it took so long to find you. Please forgive my indiscretion."

"I forgive you, sir," she replied. "Thank you so much."

The couple embraced, whispering of future hopes as Loften departed.

What would he do if one of the women remaining on his list died, or suddenly decided to emigrate to America before he could reach them, now that he'd been ordered to join the navy fleet in Denmark?

Anticipation of failure was a captain's worst enemy, he knew, yet he couldn't quell the fear.

He returned to the ship, impressed by his crew's efficiency. Their business resembled that of an ant hill, with an obvious rhythm to their work, as well as a fierce dedication to a singular cause.

"The crew picked up some rumors about town, sir. Is it true the fleet is headed to Denmark?" Everett asked.

"Aye." Loften frowned. It was the sort of news that shouldn't have gotten out, but then, not all the ships receiving the orders had been military. "We have received orders to join them."

"Should we not have set out immediately?" Downs asked.

"I felt the men would appreciate sufficient rations if it becomes a month-long blockade, or more," Loften replied. "You do like your salt pork and ale, Mr. Downs, do you not?" Downs smirked and nodded. "We will leave at dawn."

"Aye, sir," both Downs and Everett agreed.

The *HMS Hephaestus* set sail for Denmark. The late summer winds were favorable, and they soon joined two other ships headed north.

Their small fleet neared the Danish capital city near sunset. Smoke rose from the city.

Loften's heart fell. Dozens of Royal Navy ships were lined up ahead, bow to stern across the bay, firing broadside towards Copenhagen.

"They are bombarding the city," he said to Everett, who stood by him, awaiting orders. Downs approached as well.

"Are we to join in?" Everett asked.

Through his spyglass, Loften watched the flag signals being passed on from the nearest ship. They were, in fact, being asked to fire upon the city, as well as the Danish ships in the harbor—what was left of them.

Had the civilians been evacuated, or were they murdering innocents? Fire raged through the already-battered structures. The bombardment had been going on for hours already, perhaps days. Adding his forty starboard guns to it would be overkill.

The Danish ships were mangled, some wrecked, some captured, some sinking. One or two were firing back with all their might. If Loften could justify any action, it would be to defend Royal Navy ships from being fired upon, but the Danish ships were not within range.

Suddenly, multiple projectiles launched from the lead British ships, arching up and flying farther than any cannonball Loften had ever seen, into the city.

"Congreve rockets," Everett said. "I heard about them. They can fly 3000 yards."

"They don't need our help, then," Loften decided.

"But what are our orders, Captain Stoneheart?" Lieutenant Downs asked with impatience.

Loften looked away. A shadowy form rose from the deep, between the *HMS Hephaestus* and the shoreline. Of course, Davy Jones would be here, collecting the souls of the newly dead, and hoping for more.

Loften vowed not to provide them.

He recalled a story he'd been told of the first Battle of Copenhagen, a few years back, when Captain Horatio Nelson—rest his soul—had received an order to retreat, but in holding his spyglass up to his blind eye, had claimed not to have seen it, and gone on to win the battle.

Loften did not have such a convenient excuse.

"I cannot tell for certain. There's something wrong with my glass," Loften lied—for now. "We will stand by."

"Sir?" Downs asked.

"You heard the captain's order," Everett said, firmly. "We are standing by."

Night fell, and the hovering smoke, combined with low clouds, created an orange glow across the entire sky, bright enough to see the deck without the aid of lanterns.

In the near dark, a semi-crippled Danish ship attempted to flee as the shift of the night winds off the coast filled its remaining sails. Its angle of departure could put the *HMS Hephaestus* in range of its guns, and the other way around.

"We can take them out, Captain," Downs said with an excitement Loften used to feel.

"Only if they fire on us," he replied.

"Sir?" Downs asked.

As if on cue, the Danish ship did fire on the *HMS Hephaestus*. Their volley fell well short, but Loften had already given his word. Lieutenant Everett and Lieutenant Downs both looked at him expectantly.

"No," he said. "I will not send any more men to Davy Jones today."

The officer's objections were held back by a sudden explosion aboard the Danish ship. It was followed by a second explosion one deck lower, and finally the hold blew in a massive fireball that tore the ship in two.

His seamen cheered, but Loften mourned. Davy Jones's great ship had already closed in to gather what he'd come for. Through his spyglass, Loften could see many injured men in the water struggling to stay above the waves.

They didn't have to die today.

"Take us alongside to assist," Loften ordered. "Does anyone on board speak Danish?"

Downs huffed.

"I'll find someone, sir," Everett said, with a sigh.

They spent the entire night rescuing injured Danish seamen. By morning light, the bombardment ended. The Dane ships had raised flags of surrender. Their nation was suing for peace.

Loften looked over his quarterdeck, filled with prisoners of war. He had saved as many as he could, yet hundreds of bodies still floated in the bay, ignominiously buried at sea.

Loften pulled out his scroll, but no new names had been added.

"Give me their names," he demanded and looked skyward. These dead had not happened under his own orders, but it didn't matter. He felt obligated to free their souls from the abyss. "Peter Jones, do you hear me?"

He received no answer.

Instead, with the help of a translator, Loften located the highest-ranking Danish officer left alive among the prisoners. He took the despondent young officer to his cabin, brought out his ledger and quill, and asked the boy to list the names of all the Danish seamen who had died so his Lutheran-trained chaplain could pray over them.

It was not even that much of a lie.

A more battle hardy man might never have believed him, but the staggering losses had clearly shaken this younger one. The officer added several dozen names to Loften's list, amid tears.

Loften wanted to reassure the boy he'd be all right, but wasn't that the biggest lie of all? The scenes of death young Reginald Loften had witnessed at a too-young age were the very reason why he had turned his heart to stone.

So, he let the boy weep.

Lieutenant Everett arrived as the Danish officer was taken back to join the other prisoners.

"Sir, we have received a message." Everett handed him a tied parchment.

"Admiral Gambier of the fleet flagship *Prince of Wales* is congratulating the fleet on our success," Loften said after reading it over. "And requesting immediate field promotion to Commander for any lieutenant capable of captaining a captured Danish ship back to England." He handed the parchment back to Everett. "Would you like me to recommend you?"

"No, sir," Everett replied without hesitation.

Loften frowned. "Whyever not, Mr. Everett?"

"Speaking freely, sir?"

"Aye.

"I would rather remain your second in command, for however long you choose to continue and eventually captain the *Hephaestus.*"

"Very well, Mr. Everett." Loften picked up the ledger. He hoped to pray over a few of the Danish names before exhaustion overcame him, considering he'd been up all night.

But Everett did not leave.

"Was there more, Lieutenant?"

"Only that you could recommend Lieutenant Downs for the promotion, and I would not consider it an insult," Everett said.

"Any particular reason?"

"No, sir." Everett grimaced. "But I can give you a list of other seamen and junior officers who might work well with him in his new command, if you'd like."

"Of course." Loften nodded. If Downs had been spreading seeds of mutiny aboard the *Hephaestus,* Everett would most likely know of it. "Thank you again."

Still, Everett did not depart.

"Lieutenant?"

"Sir, forgive me. If you find you cannot bring yourself to fire upon an enemy ship any longer, you may want to consider retirement. It is an opinion, not a hope, sir. You've been unwell."

"Thank you once again, Mr. Everett, for your honesty," he replied. "I will take it into consideration."

Everett finally departed.

By midday, the newly-minted Commander Downs left the ship a happy man and two dozen men went with him.

The Danish prisoners were taken ashore to join their captured countrymen. It turned out that the city had been evacuated before the bombardment, but without sufficient manpower to put out the fires, much of the city had burned. Better to be displaced than dead, Loften supposed. The Danes would rebuild.

The *HMS Hephaestus'* orders were to escort the captured ships back to Portsmouth for refurbishing and repairs. The planned route would take them past Liverpool—another stop Loften needed to make.

He gave the orders to set sail, then went to bed.

His dreams were only nightmares of men drowning and him not

being able to reach them. He awakened near dawn, unrested. He picked up his scroll and ledger book and walked up to the poop deck where he could be alone to pray.

Except he wasn't alone.

Among the seven ships in the fleet—four formerly Danish and three English—sailed the shadow ship of Davy Jones.

Loften opened the ledger and read the first name: Johan Sorensen.

"Hail to you, creator…" he prayed aloud, until he saw a bright light launch from Davy Jones' ship.

Within a blink, Davy Jones stood beside Loften on the deck. Loften stepped back, startled, but far less afraid since they were above the water, this time.

"I know what ye are doing, Captain Stoneheart," Davy spat.

"What am I doing?" Loften challenged, despite his fear.

"Taking souls that belong to me."

"I can't take souls." Loften tucked the ledger inside the lining of his coat alongside the scroll. "I can only offer them a path to take themselves."

"You will stop." Davy stepped closer.

This time Loften stood his ground. "I won't stop. Not until I've said an Ave for them all."

"For them *all?*" Davy Jones motioned to the sea.

Thousands of shadow ships emerged from beneath the ocean, each with hundreds of crewmen. There might have been millions of men whose names had been lost to time.

Loften dropped to his knees, overwhelmed by the task. He took off his hat, in deference to the dead. "I'll do it."

"You could give your entire life, every moment left of it, and even if you live to be a hundred it would never be enough time to release them all, not even close." Davy laughed and stepped nearer. "Foolish mortal."

"Then I'll free all the ones I can before I die," Loften promised.

"Not many, then." Davy touched Loften's forehead with a bony finger before Loften could draw back.

Then, in another blink, Davy Jones returned to his shadow ship. It disappeared again beneath the waves, along with the unnumbered dead.

"Put their names on my list, Peter Jones." Loften took out the scroll and held it up to the sky. "All of them. Are you listening?"

But again, nothing changed. Except his head hurt, right where Davy had touched him.

"Captain!" Everett called from the stairs. The ship's surgeon, Dr. Matthew Maxwell, was right behind. "Are ye all right? The watchman saw you fall and called for aid."

"I—lost my balance, is all." Loften stumbled to his feet as the sun broke over the horizon like a refiner's fire. "I should have brought the cane."

"May I look at your eyes, Captain?" the surgeon asked. "Since we are out in the light."

"Yes," Loften said, agreeing to the brief examination. Surgeon Maxwell was an actual trained physician; unlike some other ship's surgeons he'd previously dealt with. "Well?"

"Nothing amiss," Maxwell replied. "Other than…you've lost color. And may I ask, who were you yelling at?"

"Oh." Loften frowned. "I cracked my knees so hard, I had to curse old Davy Jones for the pain. That's all."

He crossed the deck with Everett's assistance, and then returned to his bed.

Within the hour, a fever struck. Loften didn't have the strength to rise, so no one knew he'd fallen ill until Everett finally came in to check on him and sent for the surgeon.

The sickness quickly passed from man to man on board the *Hephaestus.* Captain Loften endured it better than some and on the third day found himself helping to cook soup and delivering it to the sick.

In the night, he rested and watched with a deep sense of regret as the names added to the bottom of the scroll were names of men who served him, whom he knew.

Did it mean their deaths were his fault? He'd dared challenge Davy Jones, and they'd all lost.

One particular name broke his heart more than the rest.

Loften rose and went to the infirmary. As he looked down at the body of Seaman James Prior, his new friend, he came to understand that the names on his scroll had each been someone cared for and real, and he felt for them.

All of them.

Especially this one.

"Hail to you, creator of the ocean, land, and sky, and lord of man…." Lofton spoke the Ave in front of the sick men, and as sad as it was, a sense of peace came into the room. "Please guide the soul of Seaman James Prior to dwell with you forever. Amen."

"Kind of you, sir," the surgeon croaked.

"The least I could do."

"You'll be saying it for all of us, seems," said Everett, from his sickbed.

"We'll get through it," Loften replied, with hope.

And for the first time in his life, Captain Stoneheart prayed for the living.

They reached Liverpool with their quarantine flag still raised. Dr. Maxwell went ashore and returned with news that they were not alone. 'Nervous fever' had spread through the city and killed many otherwise healthy adults, but no children. The disease was running rampant across all of Europe.

Fortunately, it seemed that those who had once suffered it and lived did not catch it again.

Loften took that as permission to leave the ship—with Dr. Maxwell in tow just in case—claiming he'd promised to track down the errant daughter of a friend who preferred to remain anonymous. He followed his map to locate a woman named Elizabeth Irving, and sadly found her quite ill with the fever. Two other women shared the room and were attending to her.

"What can we do?" he asked Maxwell.

"To survive, she will need the long-term care of a doctor and medicines she cannot afford, and even then..." Dr. Maxwell trailed off.

"Money is not an issue," Loften replied. "Her father sent me with plenty. Do you know a local physician?"

"I do." Maxwell furrowed his brow. "But you will need to move her out of this *place* before he would be willing to treat her."

Loften looked at the other two women. They were clearly loyal enough to help their friend, Ms. Irving.

With the 100 pounds, Loften arranged for the three women to rent a small home—paid a year in advance—and assisted them in moving the sick woman. Loften left them another fifty pounds each for food, new clothes, new lives, in case it wasn't enough.

Once safely settled, Dr. Maxwell called in his local colleague to assist.

"Sir, I had no idea you were such a charitable man," Maxwell remarked as they returned to the ship.

"Neither did I," Loften replied. "I wish I could do more."

It surprised him how much he meant it.

Captain Loften reached Portsmouth a changed man—or so he hoped. He checked in with his superiors and requested a leave of absence: a month to visit his former home, check in on his family and his inheritance.

They granted the leave.

Lieutenant Everett was left in charge while the *Hephaestus* was to be put in dry dock for minor repairs. Loften walked her decks and said farewell to his men, honestly unsure if he would see them again.

His three months were drawing to a close.

As Loften left the ship, out of the corner of his eye, he caught a glimpse of Davy Jones' ruined hulk, waiting.

Would he be able to do what was yet required to save his soul?

Loften afforded a carriage ride to Margate through London rather than traveling by sea. To avoid Davy Jones, in part, and to visit the last two women on his list in the city. They proved easy to find and happily received his penance. Loften continued on toward his home, feeling relieved. The scroll was finally empty but for the names of his father and brother.

The seaside village of Margate had grown into a resort town. His father's estate stood a few miles down the coast—or, rather, had once stood.

The only letter Loften had received from his brother, ten years ago, had been sent to inform him of the death of their father. It detailed their father's mismanagement of his estate and the subsequent sale of everything upon his death. Loften's inheritance—as the eldest son— had come down to a small parsonage he had allowed Frederick to move into.

That would be where Loften would face his brother.

The parsonage stood next to the parish church, surrounded by a graveyard. He found his father's headstone beside his mother's, as expected.

His father had folded to the pressure of friends who had expected him to send a too-young son off to war and then mismanaged an estate he'd purchased and knew nothing about running, leaving his sons next to nothing. Both were mistakes, not unforgivable sins.

"I forgive you, Father." He breathed out disappointment and anger and let it go.

Now the hard part.

He walked up to the parsonage door and knocked.

A stranger answered. "May I help you?"

"Mr. Loften...the parson, is he not in?"

"Mr. Loften passed away, sir."

"You mean the old man, Mr. Reginald Loften Senior?" Loften waved his hand dismissively. "I know."

"No, I mean Frederick Loften, the parson. He died of lung fever three months ago. Buried over by the tallest tree, overlooking the ocean."

The news came as a blow. Loften's quest to forgive had ended before it ever began. He could not redeem himself any further. Peter Jones had sent him on a fool's errand from the start. But why?

"Are you all right, sir?" the stranger asked.

Loften managed only to shrug, before he turned and walked away.

A stranger resided in his home. That meant his brother must have died intestate—with no will. No one had let him know. He hadn't been here to fight for his inheritance. He didn't want it, anyway. A parsonage came with a job title he had not earned.

Loften walked to the tree. A wooden cross marked the spot, along with a wreath of dried flowers. No stone yet. He could see the ocean from here in what might have been a beautiful vista, had Davy Jones' shadow ship not been waiting there, in the distance.

"How am I supposed to forgive you, brother?" Loften asked aloud. "We cannot speak of our rift and resolve it."

"Forgiveness isn't about what he did." Peter Jones stepped up beside him. He wasn't surprised—could no longer be surprised—to find them both standing on white shores together, overlooking the sea. "It's about you. Who you are. Who you want to be, moving forward."

Loften took from his coat the near-empty scroll.

"I don't suppose you'll let me add the names of Davy Jones' unnumbered dead to my scroll."

"They will rise in their due time," Peter replied. "By some other voice. It speaks well of your new heart, though, that you would be willing. Let your part in it be done."

Loften nodded. He'd be a fool to leave his brother's name on the scroll, to hold a grudge and lose his soul. He looked inside his heart, and the last of the stone finally crumbled.

"Frederick Edward Loften, I forgive you." As he brought to mind his long-forgotten memories of his younger brother, Loften bowed his head. Years of unspoken pain escaped him through wracking sobs. He didn't hate his brother, entirely the opposite. "Please forgive me."

As simple as that, the name disappeared, and the scroll with it. Loften looked for a long time at his empty hands.

"How do you feel?" Peter asked.

"I...*feel*," he replied. "Thanks to you and to my dead brother. Didn't you say I received this chance because of his prayers?"

"Did I?" Peter asked.

Loften frowned. What had Peter Jones said, exactly?

"A half-truth," Peter replied. "Your brother never forgot your sacrifice and spoke of it often. In every prayer, he prayed for you. And now, so does his son, Frederick *Reginald* Loften."

The scales of anger, doubt, and fear fell from Loften's eyes, and he saw Peter Jones for who he really was: Frederick Edward Loften, his younger brother all grown up, but now dead.

"I am so, so sorry," Frederick said, then gasped as Loften embraced him wholeheartedly. They both wept.

"Peter Jones," Loften muttered while still in the embrace. "Why did it only now occur to me how ridiculous that is?"

"You have no sense of humor, big brother." Frederick drew back. "You never did."

"Thank you, for sparing me that awful fate."

"Thank you for sparing yourself," Frederick replied. "You must keep that stone heart soft from now on."

"I...will try."

"I recommend option three." Frederick smiled. "Worth it."

Fear. Loss. Love.

Loften nodded. "I'll have to find someone to love."

"No worries, brother. Your first opportunity is coming right now to find you, and they have so much love to give." Frederick's eyes filled with tears. "Take care of them for me."

"But I'm—dying. Isn't that what you said?"

"Is it?" Frederick shrugged.

The white shores faded, and Loften found himself standing alone again in front of his brother's grave.

Four people were approaching. The stranger from the parsonage, along with a woman, a boy about six-years-old, and a toddler girl. The woman was lovely but dressed all in black. Mourning.

"Forgive me. Are you Captain Reginald Loften?" the woman

asked. "Oh my, you must be. You look like your brother."

"Yes, ma'am." Loften removed his hat.

"I am...was...his wife, Priscilla. This is our son, Frederick, and daughter, Louisa, and my brother, Parson Galbreath. Frederick, this is your uncle, Reg—"

"Uncle Reginald!" the young boy cried, and rushed forward to embrace Captain Loften. "Have you come here to stay?"

"This is rightly your home," the boy's mother said. "We've tried to reach you. My brother and I will move out as soon as you require it."

Three months ago, Captain "Stoneheart" Loften might have received word of his brother's death and kicked Frederick's family out of his inheritance from afar, too angry still to think of them as people he should care about.

But now he would do better.

"That is unnecessary." Loften looked from Priscilla to Parson Galbraith, her brother. "I am still a commissioned officer and have no need for a permanent home yet. Please stay. I will make all the legal arrangements."

Priscilla smiled warmly, with gratitude and relief.

"Will you join us for dinner, Captain Loften?" Mr. Galbreath asked.

"You must stay with us while you're in town," Priscilla added. "We have a spare room next to Frederick's."

"I would be honored," Loften replied, imagining a lovely dinner and a warm bed, right next door to the small boy who prayed aloud with great fervor and gratitude.

For him.

Loften turned to follow and caught movement in his peripheral vision. Davy Jones' black shadow ship slipped beneath the waves, not to be seen again.

Pearl Island

Erin Mindes

Erin Mindes

1908-Portugal

Oliver Redstone unfolded the handkerchief for the fourth time that day just to see the iridescent blue pearl. His buddy Crispin whistled in admiration.

"It's a rare sight," Crispin said. "But you're borderline obsessed."

"It's hard to believe it's real. But if I can find the source, I'll have it made."

"My fiancée would love a pair of pearl earrings if you *do* find more." Crispin winked.

"Before you know it, we'll have handfuls of pearls just like this one and your sweet Annie can have an entire necklace of them." Oliver chuckled and tucked the pearl safely inside his pants pocket. "First, we need a boat and a captain."

The friends began their travels from Britain less than a week ago, taking a ferry across the channel, many trains through France and Spain, down into Portugal. There they rode in a buggy to a seaside village, Figueira da Foz.

After a day's rest, Oliver and Crispin walked to the pier where a few men, brown from regular sun, were dangling their bare feet off the wooden dock.

"Excuse me, Senhores," Oliver announced. "We need a boat captain familiar with a small island nearby."

One man raised his hand. "Which island?"

"Pearl Island," Oliver said.

Heads darted to the water lapping against the boats, along with a mumbling hum.

Oliver tried again. "No one knows how to get to Pearl Island? Not even for a thousand English pounds?"

Crispin leaned over and whispered, "Are you asking to get robbed?"

"Don't worry, they just need a little incentive," Oliver whispered back.

A man sitting on a modest boat called out gravelly, "You've got a thousand pounds for the boat that takes you to Pearl Island?"

"That's right. Are you up for the challenge, Senhor?"

"A regular ole' captain would be crazy not to take it, but a man would also be crazy to go to Pearl." The man shook his head. The others on the dock pounded the wood slats in agreement.

"And what kind are you?" Oliver had set the hook; now he wanted to reel him in.

The man slapped his hands down on the boat and pushed himself up, sturdy and solid as the boat rocked slightly beneath him. He turned his head, showing Oliver and Crispin a ragged scar that ran from his left temple down to his collarbone. Then he stepped off the boat and onto the dock. "Why Pearl?" he asked. "Where'd you even hear about that island from?"

"A distant relative mentioned it in a journal. I'd like to retrace his life, go where he went." That *was* part of the reason Oliver wanted to go there. The pearl was the other, which he found tucked in the spine of the handmade journal from long ago.

The man stuck out his hand. "Meu nome é Mateo. I'll take half the money now and half if we survive. Give me two days to get supplies and then be ready to leave by dawn."

Oliver and Crispin arrived before sunrise. Mateo was already there loading a crate of fresh fruit onto the boat.

Oliver couldn't believe how close they were to finding Pearl Island. His ancestor would be so proud of him for following in his footsteps and discovering a treasure of pearls, and on a humble fishing boat no less. The boat was only about six meters, the length of two novelty automobiles he'd seen on the streets of London. Inside were two benches at the stern and a mast with a larger area to sit near the bow. He figured a sail must be tucked away in the front.

Mateo gestured to the other crates sitting on the dock. "Grab one. Bring it aboard." Oliver and Crispin tossed their packs onto the boat and each picked up a crate. One with dried fish and bread and the other with bottles of wine.

"You are well-prepared," Oliver said.

Mateo grunted. "I'll need help with the oars and sails when the time calls for it." He moved around the boat checking knots and ropes.

Oliver picked up his bag. "Where shall we keep these?"

"Those benches are available. Stow your packs underneath. There's plenty of space."

Crispin pointed to a steel blade near some fishing rods after he secured his pack. "He's not planning to rob you and throw us overboard, is he?"

Oliver eyed the blade with a small worry in his gut. "Mateo, is this necessary?"

"I always keep my machete onboard in case of danger. You never know what's lurking out there."

Oliver looked at Crispin and shrugged his shoulders. He was glad that someone was prepared, though he silently wished he'd thought to bring a dagger or club. A true adventurer would have.

They traveled all day and into the night, and Mateo took advantage of every breeze no matter how slight by putting up the sail. Other than that, the three of them rowed. When Crispin's turn came, Oliver took his ancestor's journal from his bag. He flipped to the last entry, about Pearl Island, so it would be fresh in his mind when they arrived.

Mateo came over to sit next to him. "What's that?"

"It's a journal."

"Oh, the distant relative's journal. About Pearl," Mateo said. "And when did this relative go to Pearl?"

"He was on board the Julia in 1586," Oliver said.

"That journal alone would be worth a pretty pound."

Oliver closed the journal and tucked it back in his bag, away from Mateo's gaze. "Is money all you care about?"

Mateo rubbed his thick dry fingers along the side of his boat. "I've had this boat for a long time. She could use some extra care. My earnings will go a long way for that." Then he nodded and stood. "I've got to check my compass."

After some time, Mateo took over the rowing, and Crispin and Oliver sat across one another on the benches, ripping pieces of bread off a loaf to eat. Crispin was staring back the way they had come.

"Looking back isn't a good sign," Oliver said.

"Being away from Annie, I'm realizing how much I want the adventure of building a family," Crispin said.

"Soon enough." Then Oliver leaned in close. "Once we find the pearls, you'll be home and married before you know it."

The next afternoon, the wind picked up, so Mateo put up the sail.

"We're moving even faster than before!" Oliver clapped Mateo's back. "The gods are favoring us today."

"Or cursing us," Mateo mumbled.

"How could this generous wind be a curse?" Oliver stood and grabbed hold of the mast, letting the wind blow his light brown hair back.

"My apologies, the wind is a blessing upon the waters. I only mean that Pearl Island is not a place I'd want the winds to take me normally."

"And why wouldn't you want to go to Pearl? Is there something you're not telling us?" Oliver asked.

Mateo stared into the distance, his eyes squinting from the sunlight. "You say you're interested in this relative's life, and that may be, but if you're seeking treasure, it'll be a lost cause on Pearl because there's no gold. The sailors from long ago didn't trust the island so they never buried their gold there."

"And why didn't they trust the island?" Oliver asked.

"They all believed it was a cursed island."

"Cursed?"

"Cursed as in the island takes but does not give. But I don't believe it's cursed as much as it is dangerous, and I know about danger."

"Look there," Crispin said. Up ahead, a lone island revealed itself on the horizon, floating like a ship in the vast ocean. A steep mountain shot up to the heavens in the center. From the shore to the mountain, it was all green, most likely thick with trees and bushes. From this side of the island, it was like seeing an untouched, undiscovered piece of the map. Oliver's heart leapt.

"There's Pearl," Mateo said.

"It's magnificent." Oliver sat at the bow, studying every bit he could see.

"There's so much contrast," Crispin said. "The sharp mountain against the lush greenery and the clear water. Like we're going to an unexplored land."

"My thoughts exactly." Oliver smiled. "Didn't I tell you we were going on an adventure? We're like Louis and Clark or David Livingstone."

As they got closer to the island, the wind died down and Mateo packed away the sail. "Grab those oars. Take us in."

Oliver and Crispin took turns rowing for about half an hour until they were close enough to shore. Mateo jumped out and dragged the boat the rest of the way by rope. Oliver and Crispin cinched up their boots and hopped out, splashing into the shallow water to help Mateo pull the boat up on the sand.

Once the boat was secure, Oliver and Crispin grabbed their packs, and Mateo took hold of his machete.

"You're coming with us?" Oliver asked. "Though I'm not complaining. Your sense of direction could be of great use to us, but that wasn't part of the agreement."

"I know you're only paying me to sail, but I can't in good conscience bring you to Pearl and let you loose," Mateo said. "Oh, and we leave before sunset. I won't be staying here when it's dark."

"We're leaving tonight? That doesn't give us much time," Oliver said.

"It's okay." Crispin put his hand on Oliver's shoulder. "We'll find it quickly, and I'll get back in time for my wedding."

Oliver sighed. "Very well. At least the island is small." He also had the journal so he knew what he was looking for. "Let's get started while the sun is high."

Mateo shifted his eyes to the tree line. "Which way did you want to go?"

"The journal mentioned a pool of water. I'd like to find it. I'm betting the pool was made from rain runoff. Let's move towards the mountain." Oliver pointed to the peak of the mountain through the trees. "I think that's our best chance to find it."

Mateo agreed and walked toward the vegetation. They hurried behind. The first whack with the machete, and Oliver knew Mateo was the best captain for the job. He cut a path quickly and easily.

The terrain was more rugged than it first appeared. They climbed over boulders and broken tree limbs. They passed by evergreens and cut through the waxy green leaves of the thick holly. They only stopped a couple of times to rest under a canopy of trees where shrubs with dark pink flowers grew and where the sea breeze blew in scents of salt and sweet earth. It didn't take long for them to reach the center of the island where the slope of the mountain began.

There they stopped, and Mateo wiped the machete blade against the side of a tree to clean off the buildup. In the moment of quiet, they heard a trickle of water and looked at each other.

Crispin cocked his ear to the sound. "It's coming from over there."

There were overgrown branches blocking the path to the water. Mateo cut them down and stepped through.

Oliver and Crispin were right behind him and froze when they came into a mystical clearing. The trickling of water ran from the mountain into a pool of glistening water, creating a sound that reminded Oliver of soft music playing. Sunbeams stretched through the treetops making everything sparkle. Giant hibiscus blossoms surrounded the pool and vibrant butterflies danced from one flower to the next.

Then Oliver saw colorful pearls scattered on the ground around the pool like decorated confections he'd once seen in France. He was drawn to them immediately. He knelt and grabbed a handful of pearls, letting them cascade over his palm. "Have you ever seen anything like it?"

Mateo picked one pearl up and held it up to the light before setting it back down. "I guess you found what you were looking for. We shouldn't linger though."

Crispin also knelt to touch the pearls. "There's plenty of time before the sun sets."

With his free hand, Oliver reached into his pocket and pulled out the cloth to reveal the pearl he carried. He held out his palms to compare them. "This pearl was with the journal. I hoped that if I found Pearl Island, I'd also find more just like it. And I have, thanks to you, Mateo. Thank you for bringing us here." Oliver set the handful of pearls into Mateo's hand.

Mateo offered them back, then shook his head. "I can't take these, but I will take the rest of the cash you owe me."

"As soon as we're back in Portugal, it's yours." Oliver wrapped his single pearl back up and returned it to his pocket. Then he opened the flap to his bag and dropped handfuls of pearls inside.

Crispin set his bag on the ground and made a pile of pearls next to it. Then he gazed at the water. "If only my Annie were here to see this. She'd probably be the first to dip her toes in the water."

"I'd advise against that," Mateo said, and he found a log to sit on several feet from the pool, gripping his machete.

"Don't worry, I'm not planning to get in," Crispin said.

Oliver continued to fill his bag with pearls, making sure to scoop up every last one.

"Haven't you got enough, Senhores?" Mateo stood.

"Are you that anxious to get back to your boat that you can't wait a few more minutes? Especially when we've just made the discovery of a lifetime," Oliver said.

"Look," Crispin interrupted. "There are gobs of pearls just under the surface."

"My bag is just about full. Do you have room in yours?" Oliver asked. He hadn't expected to find this many. He should have prepared better.

Oliver waited for Crispin to respond but his friend leaned over the water with more curiosity.

"What do you see there?" Oliver asked.

"I don't know," Crispin replied. His face was mere centimeters from the water.

There was a slight ripple on the surface. Oliver focused on it, expecting a watersnake to pop up.

Crispin extended his hand. He lowered it into the water so that his fingertips were barely covered.

"Crispin, what is it?" Oliver asked. "Have you found the mother pearl or some watersnake?"

Before Crispin could answer, a scaly, blue hand burst out of the pool.

It grabbed Crispin's arm and yanked him in before he had a chance to yell. His limbs struggled and splashed only for a moment. The top of Crispin's dark hair floated on top before sinking.

Gone.

"Crispin!" Oliver yelled. He ran to the edge but stumbled back when a human-like face appeared below the surface with glowing eyes and full lips stretched into a smile, revealing pointed teeth. Tiny fins stuck out along the cheekbones and slits, like fish gills, and scales ran down the neck.

Oliver's heart seized. Fear rose through his body. The creature's hands came out of the water, ready to grab him next.

Mateo jerked him out of the way and sliced at the water with his machete. Oliver stared, paralyzed as the creature disappeared underneath the water before Mateo could injure it.

Oliver's heart pounded inside his chest. He blinked over and over, trying to make sense of what happened. "What in tarnation was that?"

Sweat ran down Mateo's pallid face as he struggled to catch his breath.

"My friend. He's gone?" Oliver couldn't blink anymore. He stared at the pool until his eyes burned. *Was Crispin really gone?*

He looked up at Mateo, overcome with fear and shock. "What do you know about this place?"

Mateo shook his head. "I told you a man would be crazy to come here. I told you it was dangerous."

Oliver stumbled over to a hibiscus bush and vomited.

But Mateo didn't stop. "Didn't you wonder why no one wanted the job? No one outside of Portugal has ever heard of Pearl Island."

Oliver tried to process everything from the journal to the pearl and everything Mateo had said. "What happened to Crispin?"

"You saw. That creature took him."

"What kind of creature?" He asked the question, but he wasn't sure he wanted to know.

"Uma sereia, or in English: a mermaid. The Portuguese sailors called her Sharbella and claimed she was a blue-tailed predator." Mateo breathed deeply and let it out, shaking his head.

"Aren't we safe as long as we stay away from the pool of water?" Oliver asked.

"Don't underestimate the mermaids."

"Mermaids? There's more than one?" Oliver groaned. "I think I'm going to be sick again."

"Sailors long ago also spoke of a golden mermaid or golden beauty. Beleza Dourada.

But Sharbella, the blue one, seemed to be the fiercest, which is why we need to move," Mateo said.

But Oliver didn't move. He'd just watched as his friend was attacked and drowned by a creature he didn't even know existed. He didn't want to leave yet. "We can't leave. You have a machete. We'll wait til it comes back, and you can kill it."

"Like I said, don't underestimate them."

"But what are we supposed to do now?" Oliver and Crispin were supposed to be explorers. They were going to pour out the pearls from their bags. There would be flashbulbs and smiles. They'd be in the paper. They'd be in history books.

Mateo stepped up to Oliver. "If we don't move, we're the next ones that get pulled into that pool. Now come on."

Oliver had a brief moment of clarity. Just enough to pick up his and Crispin's bags and follow Mateo back through the brush.

He tried to push away thoughts of Crispin, but their friendship flashed in his mind as he stumbled behind Mateo. They were schoolmates, football mates, and Crispin had just asked for advice on proposing to Annie.

Oh, Annie. She would be devastated. How could he tell her he'd brought her future husband on an adventure and gotten him killed? Tears rolled down Oliver's cheeks, but he kept walking. He had to think about surviving, and Mateo was his only hope.

As they continued, a few small birds flew ahead of them and landed in the trees. Oliver didn't think much of it. But then a few turned into twenty, which turned into a hundred.

When Oliver and Mateo stopped to get their bearings, the birds flew in circles around them and chirped constantly, making it difficult to talk over the chatter. Mateo sliced more branches to get away. The birds chased them for a few minutes and then settled in the trees, quietly chirping to one another.

"What are they?" Oliver asked.

"Grey wagtails," Mateo called over his shoulder. "I've seen these birds on the Canary Islands. I don't like them watching us."

"I don't trust anything here," Oliver stammered. "Maybe it *is* cursed."

Mateo stopped and examined the branches. "I think those birds have got us all turned around."

"Why do you say that?"

Mateo held a group of branches to the side. "Another pool."

"It's smaller than the other one. Do you think they're connected, like a system of tunnels under the island?"

"Possibly. They might even connect to the open ocean." Mateo stepped through the branches but kept a safe distance between himself and the water. A rock ledge hung out over the pool a couple of stories high. "Let's climb up there to see where my boat is."

They hiked the rocky terrain, Mateo in front. Oliver had both his and Crispin's bag hanging off each shoulder. The weight was nothing compared to the heaviness he felt about Crispin. But if he was going to survive, he needed to keep climbing.

They reached the ledge. The top of the mountain was quite a ways away still, but at least they were able to see the ocean surrounding them.

But no boat.

Mateo pointed southeast. "From where the sun is going, my boat should be there."

"Now we just need to get there before the light's gone." Oliver hadn't had a desire to pry into Mateo's personal affairs, but with the killer mermaid and this island, his curiosity about the man's scar nagged at him.

"Mateo, you obviously have faced danger before. Where did that scar come from?" Oliver wasn't sure Mateo would tell him but in light of what happened, they were bonded now. A bond that unfortunately came from immense fear and tragedy.

Mateo sighed and became solemn. "I was a young man, like yourself. Thirsty for adventure and treasure. I'd heard the stories and warnings of Pearl, but I didn't care. So with a new boat, my boat, I made my way here. After finding the pearls and nothing else, I went back to shore, thinking the stories were made-up sea tales." Mateo paused and his eyes were wet.

"You don't have to tell me," Oliver said.

"Sharbella came out of the water so quickly. Her razor-sharp nail caught the side of my face. I dropped the bag of pearls I'd taken."

Oliver's heart pounded. He couldn't help but remember how the mermaid took hold of Crispin.

"Luckily, I had my knife. I fought her, stabbed her fin, scaring her off. I rowed as hard as I'd ever rowed before and didn't sleep for days after. She let me go. I don't know why, but I think it had something to do with the pearls."

"What do you mean?"

"I've never seen one of those pearls outside of this island. It's their treasure, and they don't let anyone take it."

Oliver reached into his pocket and pulled out the handkerchief holding his ancestor's pearl. "This pearl was hidden inside the journal."

Could it be the only pearl that had left the island?

Mateo looked at the pearl lying in Oliver's hand and shook his head. "I swore I'd never come back here again."

"Why did you then?"

"I don't know. I saw my younger self in you young men. And while I knew the danger, I convinced myself that I needed that money and if I had escaped before, then I could do it again." Mateo turned away from the pearl and stared at the ground. "We should never have come here."

They stood on the ledge gazing at the ocean in the distance. Oliver longed to be on it, rowing back to Portugal where he could be safe. Even though the only sound up there were the leaves making tiny whispers in the breeze, he was nervous. Then he froze when a soft melody floated up to his ears. The notes were entrancing as they smoothly blended together, drawing him in.

Mateo nudged Oliver and mouthed, "Beleza Dourada."

Down at the pool, a golden mermaid emerged. Her beauty mesmerized the men as she hummed a tune. The grey wagtails began gathering around the edge of the pool to sing with her.

The mermaid floated on her back, her golden hair spread along the surface of the water like tree roots, reaching. Her tail gently waved. She held her hand out for a bird to land on and it chirped to her. Then the mermaid swam to the edge of the pool and lifted herself onto land. She flipped her tail faster and faster bringing tiny fish to the top. Some fish even jumped out onto the edge of the pool and the birds snatched them up.

It appeared the mermaid and the birds had a system. She provided them with fish, but for what?

Then, she tilted her head and glared up at Mateo and Oliver. The beautiful mermaid turned hideous as she snarled at them, showing her pointed teeth. A snake-like tongue whipped out of her mouth.

Oliver flinched. "At least we're up where she can't get us," he said but quickly regretted it when the mermaid crawled out of the pool and began climbing the mountain. Her nails gripped dirt and rock like a lizard. Her biceps bulged as she pulled herself up. He couldn't believe her strength or her speed.

"We won't be able to out-climb her. I'll use the machete. Grab a rock or stick, something to fight her off." Mateo's eyes were glued to the creature, ready to fight.

The monster would reach them in no time. The best he could find was a rock, which didn't give him much confidence.

"Don't let her get a hold of you. Try to stay back against the wall." Mateo's stance was firm as he held the machete out ready to swing.

The mermaid came up over the ledge, creeping closer, eying the men. The gills on her neck opened and closed. She stretched her mouth open and let out a miserable screech.

Mateo didn't waste any time. He stepped forward and swung, cutting the mermaid and knocking her off the mountain. She hissed, deep and low from her throat at first then shrieked with each strike against the rocks as she fell. They hurried over to the edge to see what had become of the creature.

She lay motionless on the ground a few feet from the water. The birds chirped endlessly in a hum of commotion until the blue-tailed mermaid surfaced.

Sharbella crawled over to her lifeless companion, patted her face, and smoothed back her hair. The humanity of her gestures shocked Oliver. Then she moaned. Tears flowed from her eyes. When they hit the ground, they hardened into pearls.

"We need to move now," Mateo whispered.

Oliver nodded.

As quietly as possible, they worked their way down the mountain. If they could just get out of the trees and down to the sand, they'd have a better chance of getting to the boat.

The grey wagtails were nowhere in sight, but Mateo and Oliver were on high alert and figured the birds were still watching them even if they couldn't see them.

Mateo slashed at the tree limbs blocking their path, and they finally broke free from the dense vegetation. The sand and ocean were before them, yet there was no boat.

There were, however, broken pieces of a ship scattered on the beach. Upon closer inspection, they found bones and a few skulls in the mess.

Neither spoke as they walked through the graveyard. Oliver bent down to pick up a metal plate. "Julia 1586," he read. "My ancestor was on the Julia. I thought he survived. But perhaps only his journal did."

"No one escapes Pearl Island," Mateo said.

"You did."

"Not really. It pulled me back, didn't it? Besides, I could never escape what's haunted my nightmares."

Matco had a point, but Oliver was determined to get home. He took the bags off his shoulders and jingled them, feeling the weight of the pearls. He got what he came for—just not the way he thought. He tipped each bag upside down and shook all the pearls out onto the sand, except for the one wrapped in the handkerchief. That one, he couldn't let go of. It would be his reminder of what he lost on Pearl Island. He vowed to get home for Crispin.

"We can't waste any more time. We've got to find the boat." Mateo walked a safe distance from the water but decided the only way to find the boat was to walk around the island's edge. Oliver followed behind and even began running when Mateo picked up the pace.

Finally, the boat came into view. As they ran, the grey wagtails emerged from the trees, heading for the vessel too.

"The birds," Oliver called out.

"I'm more worried about the mermaid." Mateo sprinted.

They reached the boat panting. Mateo set the machete inside and began to push the boat off the sand. Oliver quickly joined him. The birds flew in and landed on the rim.

"Get in," Mateo commanded.

Oliver climbed in, threw the now-empty bags, except for the journal, toward the front of the boat, and positioned the oars.

As Mateo gave another push off the sand, he jumped into the boat and took hold of the machete. He swung at the birds which hopped off and spread their wings just quick enough to not get hit. Oliver rowed and the boat began to move at a steady pace while his arms burned with each pull. But he couldn't stop. He looked over his shoulder. Mateo watched the water for Sharbella. It appeared quiet. Perhaps she was letting them go. Perhaps she was appeased with him leaving the pearls.

He continued rowing towards safety, until Mateo growled.

Oliver turned around, just as Sharbella launched herself out of the water. She sunk her claws into Mateo's back. His growl turned into a howl from the sudden pain. He tried to fight by swinging the blade overhead, but he lost his balance and toppled into the side of the boat, dropping the machete behind Oliver. Though he managed to pull himself up, Sharbella emerged and gripped his arm. "Oliver," Mateo grunted.

Oliver dropped the oars and tried to pry the mermaid's nails from Mateo's shoulders. Blood seeped through his shirt, as she dug her claws in deeper.

"She won't let go," Oliver yelled. He tried to kick her, but she dodged and sunk her teeth into his shin. His curdling scream filled the air. Mateo grabbed hold of Oliver's shirt, pulling him to his face.

"If. I. Don't. make it." Mateo forced out the words. "Leave the pearl. Get. Home."

"No. If we leave, it's together. Come on." Oliver grunted and kicked hard enough that the mermaid released Mateo's leg, allowing Oliver to twist around and grab the machete.

When he turned around, Mateo's fingers barely held on. Sharbella flipped her tail with enough power to pull Mateo down. They fell with a splash into the icy water.

Oliver froze.

He waited.

Nothing.

It was just like with Crispin. He hadn't come back. Now Mateo wouldn't either. A sob tore from Oliver's throat. How was he ever going to make it? He didn't know but he had to try. He had to row as fast as he'd ever rowed before. He had to get away from Pearl Island.

Oliver gripped the oars' handles and pulled the water with all his might. The boat was moving. Perhaps there was still hope.

"Don't look back," he said over and over. "Don't look back. Keep moving forward." If he maintained a decent speed, perhaps he could get to safety. *Yes, keep going.*

Oliver considered the pearl in his pocket. Had his ancestor actually made it off the island? He wished he'd never found the journal or pearl, but he couldn't toss it away so easily. He'd keep it as a reminder—yes, that would do. And he'd stop anyone from ever coming here. No, he'd stop them from even talking about this place.

Why hadn't Mateo done that for him?

The sun was setting. His muscles began to cramp but he had to keep rowing. It was the only way to get home. Just in front of the boat, a slight ripple caught his eye. A tear seeped out.

Sharbella sprung from the depths of the ocean and landed on the boat. Oliver jumped back and reached for the machete, but it was too late.

With impossible speed, she grabbed the weapon and flung it into the ocean. Then she gripped Oliver's arm. He was inches away from her face. Her mouth slowly grew into a smile revealing the jagged teeth. His head shook with horror before she flung him out of the boat. His body slapped the water. She dove in after him and pulled him farther into the dark abyss with the pearl still in his pocket.

Love, Lies, and Pirate Allies

Amy Trent

Charles was not an emotional man but a gentleman of principle and reason. He did not panic nor did he rage when problems arose. Instead, he set calmly to work on solutions. It was principle, reason, and the urgency of his current predicament that compelled Charles to seek the company of Miss Molly Penbrooke on his last morning in Jamaica, and nothing more.

Molly Penbrooke sat at a café table framed by boughs of magenta bougainvillea. Charles hadn't frequented this café during his stay in Kingston but wished he had. The view from the terrace of the harbor below was enchanting. Sparkling cerulean blue waters, billowing sails of Spanish galleons, merchant vessels, frigates and schooners—it was all so picturesque under the flowering vines. A warm breeze carried the scent of sugar and jasmine, and the only sound, apart from birdsong, on the terrace was the demure clink of teacups meeting their saucers.

It was hardly the place Charles expected to find a captain for hire. As such, he was more than a little muddled when he introduced himself to Ms. Penbrooke and explained his predicament.

"My old captain has left for a posting on a merchant vessel bound for New Orleans." He blew on his cup of hibiscus tea. "Better money. Shorter passage. Completely understandable."

"If inconvenient." Molly did not look up from the leatherbound book she was reading.

Charles understood better than most the necessity of seizing opportunities. He just wished he had more time and more options when it came to finding a replacement. Molly Penbrooke was hardly the chap he'd have picked for the job of manning his crew and steering his yacht safely across the open ocean, but she came highly recommended by the locals. Charles, having an estimable mother and sisters, was above small-minded prejudice against the fairer sex.

He was not above noticing that Molly was his peer in age and education.

"Not so loud," Molly hissed when Charles questioned her about her time with the continent's finest scholars. "I've managed to keep such scandals quiet for years and will not have some starched-laced dandy disseminating my lurid past."

Charles frowned as he never wore lace. He did insist on clean cravats, an accessory that most deemed unnecessary in the West Indies. "If an education is synonymous with scandal and a lurid past, then perhaps one should not read the ancient poets in public."

Molly smiled and snapped her book shut. "I can't promise we'll see mermaids. So many men want to find them. Selkies and sea serpents are rare too. I saw a unicorn once at sea, though. Pods of leviathans are fairly common. Their fluted tails, dappled and glistening in the sunshine, are easy to spot."

She was teasing him. It had been so long since any woman had, Charles had nearly mistaken the droll delivery for sincerity. "I just need to safely ferry my cargo back to England." Charles sipped his tea, but grimaced. It was still too hot.

"What is it you are carrying?"

"I'd prefer not to say."

"Fine. The less I know the better. Makes all the port documents easier to navigate. I'm ferrying eccentric clients and their personal effects across the Atlantic." She winked at Charles. "None of my business if you've packed illicit love potions and plunder from some ancient burial ground."

She should be warned against winking at strangers. Men who were not Charles and who did not have his discipline would get ideas. Easy to do with Molly's bright eyes and the splash of freckles across the bridge of her pert nose.

Molly smiled. "When do we sail?"

Ms. Penbrooke's affability put Charles in mind of glasshouse violets—dependable and cultivated for universal appeal. He recognized that these were useful traits in a trade where professional reputation depended on customer satisfaction in addition to the ability to manage a crew and steer a ship safely to port. Charles also recognized that he'd always been fond of violets.

"As soon as possible." Charles sipped his tea.

"Then we should leave with the tide," Molly said, rising from the café table.

"You…" Charles' cheeks went pink, noticing for the first time that the linen of Molly's day dress did not extend to her ankles, but stopped only inches past her cinched waist. The good captain had replaced full skirts with trousers. Unusual, but not unheard of for ladies in the West Indies.

"Something wrong?" Molly asked, bracing a hand on the curve of her hip.

Charles cleared his throat. "You do not need to make other arrangements? We can leave tomorrow if necessary."

"I'm ready." Molly heaved a carpet bag onto her shoulder.

"You're packed?"

"Of course. Grandmama always said to have a bag packed before chance encounters with strange gentleman."

She was teasing again, and Charles would match her dry humor. "Your grandmother? Really?"

"Oh, she was a fount of wisdom." Molly kept score on her fingers as she spoke. "'Always bring a packed bag. Never keep a monkey for a pet. My firstborn will be a daughter. And cream goes with everything." Molly reached for her teacup and took a final sip.

Charles folded the napkin in his lap into a tidy square, before placing it on the table. "Was your grandmother talking about menus or trousseaux with that last one?"

Molly grinned. "I don't think we'll ever know, Mr. Charles."

"It's Mr. Fitzgerald."

"Of course, my mistake. Shall we?"

"A moment please, Ms. Penbrooke. Five weeks is a long time to be at sea, and I have no intention of chartering a return voyage for quite some time. It could be ten weeks at best, before you could even hope to return to this island. Honor compels me to ask if you are attached to a household, a husband, or…"

She was smiling again. Beaming, really. "Or jealous lover? The kind that would send an armada after me?"

Charles tugged at his cravat. "I believe the words I was searching for were 'parent' or 'relative.'"

"I am unattached, and you appear to be charmingly flushed, Mr. Fitzgerald."

"Charmingly flushed?" Charles repeated, grabbing his black silk top hat and leaving a handful of silver shillings on the table.

"Really sets off your brown eyes." She winked again and headed for the docks. "Do you make a habit of asking all your captains if they are romantically involved?"

Just the pretty blonde ones. Maybe Charles wasn't above small-minded prejudice after all. The thought nauseated him. "I hated to ask, but I'd rather avoid entanglements at sea. They can be messy, and you seem like the sort…"

"Who would have entanglements?" There was that impish smile again. "I won't hold it against you, Mr. Fitzgerald. There's enough mischief on the open water as is."

Charles held his handkerchief to his nose when they arrived at the docks. "The smell is unpleasant."

Molly bit her lip, no doubt to suppress a snicker. "And you have a delicate constitution."

It was a better assumption than that he was desperate not to be recognized by any of the passersby. "Precisely. You may not see much of me once we set sail."

"Do you have the crew manifest?"

"On the ship, if you please." He quickly outpaced her, even if it was ungentlemanly, and all but ran to his yacht.

Molly whistled low when she saw the ship, and Charles, too, took a moment to appreciate the clean lines, trio of trim masts, and elegance of his vessel.

"Pretty, isn't she?" he said.

"Never seen the like. She's like a tiny frigate." Molly ran her tan hands along the brightly polished taffrail. "Or the pretty little sister of a frigate."

Charles coughed, bringing the handkerchief closer to his nose. The sooner they left Kingston, the better. "Welcome aboard, the *Adelaide*, captain," he said. "If you'll excuse me, I have matters to attend to below decks."

Charles had claimed his usual cabin and the adjoining stateroom for this voyage. He instructed all to leave him be for the entirety of the passage, not wanting to risk exposure from a curious crew.

So he was shocked the next morning to hear a knock on his door.

"What is it?" he called from his desk.

"Porpoises off the starboard bow." Molly's cheerful voice was muffled through the closed door. "I thought you might enjoy the spectacle."

"Thank you. No."

Charles continued his work until he was interrupted the following evening by another knock.

"Beautiful sunset." It was Captain Molly again.

The corner of Charles' mouth twitched upward despite himself. "I've seen my fair share, thank you."

Two days later another knock rattled his concentration and nerves.

"Dinner?" Molly's voice was chipper as always.

Charles had enjoyed a late lunch, and so was surprised by his interest in the invitation. Cabin fever must be upon him. It was the only reason for explaining why his mind, with alarming frequency, stumbled into thoughts of the captain. He'd not even been with the woman long enough to mark the color of her eyes but was caught in a storm of distraction all the same. It would blow over in another day or two of uninterrupted study. It had to. "I have no appetite at present, thank you," Charles said, with perhaps more force than was necessary.

When the next knock came at noon the following day, Charles almost expected it.

"Mermaids!" Molly said.

"There is no such thing."

Molly brayed—at least it sounded like a bray—outside his door. "Says you!"

Was she laughing at him? Is that what all these interruptions had been about? Charles opened his door a crack.

Molly jumped but recovered, smiling brightly. "The ocean is vast, her waters deep. Are you telling me you've explored every meter, every cavern?"

"No," Charles conceded, noting that the freckles across Molly's nose had grown more striking in the days since they'd set sail.

Molly stood on tiptoe, no doubt trying to see over Charles' shoulder into his cabin. "Then how would you know?"

"I wouldn't." Were Molly's eyes truly green or was it a trick of the dim light?

"Then join me."

Sunshine would put the question of the color of Molly's eyes to rest, but the captain was most certainly making sport of Charles for purposes no sane gentleman would ever understand. "Good day, captain." With as much politeness as he could muster, he shut the door in the woman's face.

The sun had completely set, and the only light in Charles' cabin was that of the single lantern over his desk, when Molly knocked again.

Charles threw down his pen and journal and opened his cabin door an inch.

"Good evening. I wondered if you might care to join me for some stargazing?" She stood in the narrow passage, arms braced on either side of his door. "I'm beginning to worry about you, Mr. Fitzgerald. Even the most seasick of passengers benefit from going topside."

"Thank you for your concern, captain." Charles had a pile of notes to make sense of before he retired, and a night littered with starlight would not settle his mind regarding the color of Molly's eyes. And contemplating the heavens would only lead to more irksome questions about the captain. "But I have all the fresh air I need."

"Exercise, then. It isn't healthy to stay cramped in close quarters."

"I assure you, I adhere to a strict regime of calisthenics. Good evening." With considerably less politeness than before, Charles shut the door.

Charles woke the next morning to frantic knocking.

"I'm quite indisposed to whatever it is you propose," he yelled.

"Pirates!" The panic in the captain's voice was unmistakable. "They've fired warning shots along our portside."

Charles flung open his door to see Molly, pale and shaken, outside. "We've had no choice but to drop sail," she said.

"Why pirates? Why this vessel and not bigger prey?"

Molly braced her hands on either side of Charles' door. "Perhaps they heard about the hoards of saffron, vanilla, and green cardamom you keep locked in your chamber."

Charles closed his eyes, holding them shut a fraction too long for the gesture to be mistaken for anything but annoyance.

Molly licked her parted lips. "If you have something of value in there–"

"It is all of value."

"—to a pirate, I suggest you hide it or work out what you're willing to pay for its ransom."

"That's it? That's all the speech you have for me? Hide. Haggle. Am I to prepare for battle? Bloodshed?"

"What seas have you been traveling on? These are pirates. They will board our ship, make pretty speeches, and then take what they want... Unless they are plotting something more sinister."

"More sinister than absconding with whatever they please?"

Molly ran a trembling hand through her golden curls. "I don't suppose you have…insurance for this sort of thing?"

"Meaning do I have a trunk of gold to pay them off?"

"They take silver too."

"No. I do not."

"Pity. Well. We'll hope for the best. I'll see you topside. Most pirates get snippy when the full manifest of passengers and crew is not on deck to greet them."

The sunshine was blinding after being below decks for days.

"Nice to see you out of doors, Mr. Fitzgerald." The nerves Molly had struggled with below deck were completely gone.

Charles noted with an odd mixture of satisfaction and dismay that Molly's eyes were indeed green. Not the searing green of the ever-sweltering tropical jungles and not the brilliant green of the June leaves in Hyde Park. Her eyes were the green of fresh mint undeterred by a winter's worth of snow. The same green as the shaded juniper branches that he'd laid under on the hottest of summer days in Gothenburg, when his tutors badgered him with pointless recitations of the law. It was the soft, gentle green that had accompanied a simple life and uncomplicated future. A green Charles believed would always be familiar…until everything changed that fateful night last summer. The one night Charles had let his emotions get the better of him. "How long will this take?"

A man a good score of years older than Charles, vaulted over the railing from the jolly boat. He was dressed in an incarnadine coat and carried himself with a knave's dashing arrogance. "In a hurry to die, are we?" the man said in a jovial tone.

A bosun whistle sounded from one of the men that accompanied this ne'er-do-well.

Molly stepped forward. "Welcome aboard, captain…"

"Pirate, if you please. Pirate Phillips, master and commander of the *Embarazada*, at your service." The man swept into an elegant, if ostentatious, bow. "And to whom do I have the pleasure?"

"Captain Molly Penbrooke."

"Molly Penbrooke. Something tells me we've met before, Captain Molly."

Molly smiled and winked. "I should be so lucky."

Pirate Phillips tittered into an absurd peal of laughter, while Charles quietly berated himself for hiring a captain who winked at strangers and pirates indiscriminately.

"May I offer you a tour of the ship?" Molly gestured to the bridge.

"Yes, let's start with this gentleman's stateroom." The pirate paused in front of Charles, looking him up and down the way one might appraise a banquet table.

Molly laughed. "I'm afraid you'll be terribly disappointed. Nothing but a lot of dusty books and silly journals in that one's stateroom. The galley, however, boasts an inordinate collection of Jamaica's finest pastries and an impressive selection of rum."

It was a good bluff, Charles thought, followed by a tempting offer. He'd make a note to tell his steward to add a pretty bonus to the captain's commission for such quick thinking. Charles cleared his throat. "Yes, why don't you discuss matters over a spread. I'm sure there is more than enough rum to share with your men."

Pirate Phillips unsheathed his saber and pointed it at Charles' throat. "The gentleman's stateroom, then the rum and pastries."

"If you insist." Molly pushed the blade away from Charles' throat. "This way, gentleman."

Molly led them below deck to Charles' cabin. "If you'd be so kind, Mr. Fitzgerald, as to show our guest inside. I will wait out here."

"Aren't you at all curious what Mr. Fitzgerald has risked your life and everyone's life on board for?" the pirate asked.

Charles' temper roiled. He was a gentleman, and no gentleman ever knowingly endangered a lady. This was ridiculous. He would not be cowed by a man who wore more lace than his mother and sailed on a ship named the *Embarazada*. "Don't be absurd," Charles snapped. "What could you possibly do to any of us? Bore us to death with your foppishness?"

The pirate leaned against the bulkhead, crossing his feet at the ankles. "To death? Never. Why kill when you can maim and leave a legacy? Tell him, captain."

Molly met Charles' eye with grim determination. "Pirate Phillips is fond of eyepatches."

"More dashing than peg legs and hooks, but needs must. Particularly when the seas are full of so many deceitful scoundrels."

Charles couldn't believe the implication. "I am a gentleman, sir. I have nothing to hide."

Pirate Phillips laughed. "You have everything to hide, *Mr. Charles Fitzgerald*."

"Oh, for goodness' sake, get inside both of you," Molly ordered.

"Fine," Charles said, throwing open his cabin door. "Just don't touch anything."

Charles did not have time or means to do anything about the

collection in his state room before the pirates boarded the ship. Not that it mattered. A botanist could not hide twelve hundred exotic specimens, even if he tried.

"Plants," Molly murmured. "You've been hoarding…plants."

"Not hoarding," Charles said. "Collecting. Cataloging."

"Yes, Charles has spent the summer collecting for the royal arboretum and garden." The pirate ran a finger across the purple spathe of a rare speckled anthurium.

"I said don't touch anything," Charles snapped. "I haven't yet cataloged the pollen from that specimen, and I can't have you contaminating– What are you doing?" Charles watched in horror as the pirate snapped the bloom of the tiger orchid off its node. "That orchid would have bloomed for three months!" It was a present for his little sister, Drina. A peace offering of sorts.

"But now it looks incredibly fetching in my buttonhole." The pirate patted the orchid into place on his lapel. "Does it not, Captain Molly?"

Molly winked at Charles. "Absolutely."

"So many pretty little plants? Do they know there is a bounty on your head?" Pirate Phillips asked, taking a seat at Charles' desk.

"Bounty?" Molly's brow furrowed, and her eyes narrowed before she smoothed her expression with a smile. "What's this about a bounty?" she asked with a teasing voice, taking a perch on the arm of Charles' desk chair. Was she flirting with the pirate?

"Mr. Charles Fitzgerald isn't at all what he seems, dear captain." The pirate clucked his tongue. "He is, in fact, the long-lost brother of Her Majesty, Queen Victoria."

Charles rolled his eyes, pinching off a curled, dried leaf from the marmalade hued hibiscus.

"No!" Molly gasped. "Stodgy Mr. Charles Fitzgerald—a prince?" She ran her finger along the petals of the tiger orchid at the pirate's chest. "Impossible."

"Do you deny that you are Karl Friedrich Wilhelm Emich, Prince of Leiningen and brother to Her Majesty, the queen?" The pirate waggled his eyebrows. Not exactly a menacing gesture, but nothing about this pirate was. If Molly hadn't gone pale when she mentioned the eyepatches, he would have believed this was all one enormous joke.

But she had. Just as the pirate had thrust his sword in Charles' face. He had brandished a weapon, which meant he might do it again to worse effect.

"I am but a half-brother; I hardly count." Charles pushed the pirate's boots off his desk. "And 'long-lost' seems a bit unfair for one summer in the West Indies."

"Tell that to Her Majesty," Phillips said with a snort. "This is her yacht, the *HMY Royal Adelaide*. He stole it the same night she became queen. Scrape the new splotch of paint off the bow if you don't believe me." Phillips twisted and twirled Charles' penknife the way ladies twirled fans. "I think the only reason the bounty explicitly states you be left unharmed is so she can kill you herself when you are returned to her court."

"Is this true?" Molly asked, her green eyes wide and welling with tears. "You're a prince, and you didn't tell me?"

Tears? Now? Not when she was shaking with fear as she told him to prepare to be boarded? Not with talk of maiming? Charles would never understand women.

"I say." Pirate Phillips dropped the knife and was on his feet, brandishing his handkerchief and offering it to the captain with a felicitous bow.

"Thank you," Molly stammered before blotting her eyes with the monogramed hankie. Charles watched as she swooned, truly swooned, into Pirate Phillips' open arms.

"My dear lady?"

"Forgive me. I'm stronger than this. But seeing you again and then learning Charles is a prince all before breakfast—it's overwhelming."

"Naturally."

"Might I prevail upon your chivalry and beg a glass of spirits?"

"But of course, dear captain." Pirate Phillips took each of Molly's hands in his. "I'll fetch a glass and tray from the galley, posthaste. Oh." He patted her cheek. "You mustn't internalize this as a weakness of character. Everyone is overwhelmed when confronted with ghosts from their past."

"Especially handsome ghosts."

Pirate Phillips clicked his tongue. "None of that. I'm old enough to be your father, dear captain." Pirate Phillips' eyes narrowed on Charles. "Can I leave you locked in here with the likes of him while I fetch victuals?"

"I think so." Molly leaned in and whispered. "He doesn't scare me."

The pirate helped Molly sit at Charles' desk. "Well, he should. Hoarding this many plants should be enough to scare anyone."

Charles glowered. "Collecting specimens for the royal gardens is not hoarding."

"I'll be fine." Molly batted her eyes. "I'm glad it was you, Phillips, that found us."

He patted her hand, a smug smile plastered across his face. "I'll leave my best man outside the cabin."

"Hurry," Molly said weakly.

"I'm sorry," Charles said after the pirate left. "Would you like me to step out when he returns."

Molly rose fluidly, angrily. "I just bought us time to figure out a plan, and you're going to hiss like a jealous tomcat?"

"Oh, that's what all that flirting and simpering was for?"

Molly rested a fist on her hip. "Phillips has an ego to rival yours, Charles, and he lives for intrigue."

"And you are saying you would know?"

"No, no of course not. Maybe. It was a long time ago." Molly pulled her blonde curls away from her face. "Listen. He's going to spend the rest of the day peacocking, strutting about, telling stories, and then at sundown he's going to take you and sail off for London on his much larger, faster ship."

Not without Charles' collection. "It will take two days at least to transfer my specimens to his ship. Longer if he doesn't have a cabin capable of maintaining the optimal heat and humidity levels."

Molly snapped her fingers in Charles' face. "No one cares about your plants. The only way to ensure their safety is for you to stay aboard this ship."

She had a point. "Why do you care if I stay aboard? Is this a ploy to keep you closer to your pirate lover?"

Molly gagged and shivered. "He's old enough to be my father."

"Didn't stop you from fawning all over him during the tour."

Molly rolled her eyes. "I need to get paid. If I am part of the envoy that delivers you to the queen, I get a raise."

"Enterprising of you to see it that way," Charles mumbled.

"And my reputation grows as a captain that successfully held her own with one of the more notorious pirates known on the high seas."

Of course. "That's why you were in such a hurry to leave Kingston. You knew who I was from the beginning!"

"I had a hunch. There are only so many men in the Indies who insist on wearing a cravat."

Charles reflexively tugged at the linen around his neck.

"My suspicions were confirmed when you hid behind handkerchiefs and were preoccupied with *my* presumed entanglements."

"Then you coordinated with that pirate. Admit it."

"So that I could risk losing all my profits and my right eye? Don't be ridiculous."

"If you knew there was a bounty on my head and that something like this was possible, why did you agree to sail with me?"

"I needed the coin. And…" She dogeared a page of Charles' notes, worrying the fold up and down as a sheepish smile graced her face. "I was curious… There were many rumors swirling about what exactly it was you were smuggling."

That explained the near nightly badgering. To think Charles had entertained for even a moment a…*different* possibility. He closed his journal, lest she tear it apart. "Not smuggling. Collecting. I secured permits, worked with the local naturalists, and…" None of it mattered. Not even Molly's amused pout. "Fine, I accept that our interests align. How do we convince Pirate Phillips to let me stay aboard with my plants?"

"Tell him you're in love with me."

Charles brayed in Molly's face but stopped when she crossed her arms defiantly. "You're serious?"

"It's worked before," Molly said.

Charles was too disciplined to consider how Molly had come by this knowledge and with whom. "And if it doesn't work now, one of us could lose an eye." Or a hand. Or a leg.

"Star-crossed lovers who have only their weeks together at sea before they must part ways forever? No pirate could resist such a story."

When did pirates become melodramatic, sentimental sops?

"Tell him at sunset. Sell him the story."

"How? I barely know you."

Molly turned a small potted fern and frowned when several dry leaves dropped from its fronds. "You spent a lot of time gathering these specimens. It'd be a shame to lose them all at sea."

Charles stooped to collect the fallen leaves. "Are you threatening to throw them overboard?"

"No, I am honestly telling you that I've never been able to keep any plant alive for more than forty-eight hours."

Charles twitched. "You can't be serious."

"Violets from the deserts of Africa: drowned and dead after a single day in my care. Vines from India that were said to be indestructible: withered in my room overnight when I left a window open. Seedlings that were gifted to me every spring: planted too early or forgotten and planted too late."

"Stop. Stop. I'll do it." Charles had come this far. What did it matter if shredding his pride was necessary to see the journey through to the end?

Charles found the pirate that evening polishing his saber. "Ah, fair Prince, I thought we'd watch the sunset before bidding the dear captain adieu." Pirate Phillips waved gallantly to Molly at the helm of the ship.

Charles cleared his throat. "May I have a word? It is a matter of great importance."

"By all means." Phillips' smile rivaled the gleam of the sun on his sword.

"In private, if you please. Matters of the *heart* are difficult to discuss, particularly in public."

"Oh, *oh*, of course. Oh, I say. Completely." Phillips ushered Charles onto the bridge, sending his men scattering to below deck. "You would not *believe* the drama that goes on at sea and how quickly gossip spreads on open waters."

"I…" Charles took a deep breath. How had protecting his research come to this? "I am in love with Molly."

"You are! Oh, but of course you are! I knew it!" Phillips reclined on the window seat against a great many cushions, more than Charles remembered there being when they departed from Kingston. "That's why you've holed yourself up in that damp little room. You are too besotted to trust yourself to even be in her presence."

Charles squeezed his eyes shut. Did pride make mewling pleas when it was being ripped so thoroughly from a chap? "Exactly. It doesn't take much to distract me…"

"A whiff of perfume, an errant curl, a view of her backside in those marvelous trousers."

Charles cleared his throat, loudly. "And I am overwhelmed."

Pirate Phillips sighed, pressing his hands to his heart. "Yes?"

"Yes…" Good heavens, the pirate was waiting for Charles to elaborate. "Her striking beauty is a terrible distraction to my research, which you understand is of the utmost importance to me and my country. My legacy depends upon creating a collection at the royal botanic gardens—"

"Enough of that." Pirate Phillips waved his hand dismissively. "Tell me more about how you feel. How love unbraids your scruples, rips up your morals, and would have you barging into the captain's quarters every night."

"Uh... Yes... Well, you see," Charles sighed before quietly swearing. This was far more difficult than he anticipated. What had the captain been thinking? "To tell you the truth, there are times when I can't stand the woman."

Pirate Phillips winced.

"To be near the woman, I mean. I feel as if I'm losing my mind."

The pirate smiled and fluttered his hands excitedly, sending his cuffs of lace wagging.

"It's her voice, I think, that is the worst. I hear it, and suddenly all I can think of is strawberries and sweet cream." Or an eternity of sunny afternoons and clear nights. Charles was a terrible liar, something Drina and Feodora were always quick to point out, but these sentiments came surprisingly easily. "A single word is enough to make me want to run for half a mile, but of course there is nowhere to run."

"Of course! The forced proximity of this ship must be tantalizing."

Charles could wholeheartedly agree to that. "It's agony!"

Pirate Phillips clapped his hands before clasping them under his chin.

"I can feel her everywhere on this ship. I knew that if she were to step one foot into my cabin, I'd...uh... I'd lose control. Years of research out the porthole. None of it would matter because all I'd want was her..."

"A passion that was instant then?"

"Oh no." Charles cleared his throat. He unraveled a tassel of the nearest cushion. "It started as a slow ember."

"Oh!" Pirate Phillips hugged a cushion to his chest.

"A spark in the back of my mind when we first met that whispered, *she's trouble*. Far too smart. Far too..." His mind stumbled over curves that men often contemplated when they were smitten, but he was a gentleman and a prince. "Capable. Far too capable. I'm not making sense."

"You are making perfect sense!" Phillips rolled onto his back and tossed the cushion in the air and caught it.

"That spark grew into an ember when I saw her commanding the crew today."

Phillips frowned.

"And every day. She's very...capable."

"A capable woman is a desirable woman."

Charles coughed. "Yes, well. The ember grew brighter, stronger every day. This may be my ship, but she is the captain. And while I pretended to bristle at her every command, the truth was, *is…*" Charles smiled in spite of himself. "…I am amused. Intrigued."

"Attraction is a confounding trait among us men. Nature demands that visual stimulus should be enough, and yet there is something unexpected added to the formula every time."

"For Molly's sake, I had to stay away, despite my attraction."

"Yes of course! The struggle of decency versus animal lust."

Charles whimpered. "My identity, I could not share for fear of this very predicament we find ourselves in."

"Completely understandable. Noble."

"But it was a struggle, you understand."

"And when you touched her…" The pirate brought his hand to his own face, closed his eyes, and pursed his lips. "The urge to tell her everything and bear your soul was overwhelming."

"Yes…uh… Well…"

Phillips straightened and strode to the mirror. "You have kissed her?"

Silence in which the only sound was the ship creaking.

Phillips gasped. "It's worse than I feared."

"I'm a gentleman! With familial obligations."

"That you've been happy to shirk, ergo the bounty on your unharmed head." Phillips undid a button of his billowing shirt and continued to primp in front of the mirror.

"She is the captain. I hired her. I cannot just steal kisses as we stargaze. Or smile and flirt with her, hold her hand casually on the top deck as porpoises frolic in the waves below."

Phillips undid another button but paused his preening to consider Charles. "This isn't some indulgent dalliance."

Charles tugged at his cravat. "I am incapable of both indulging and dallying."

Phillips tapped a finger to his lips. "Then if you truly care for Captain Molly, this is, in fact, a case of genuine love."

"Of course it is! You don't find a woman like Molly ever. Not in this lifetime. Not in fiction. Not in the worlds beyond. She is a mermaid princess that eschewed her underwater kingdom for one incredible pair of legs."

Now Pirate Phillips cleared his throat.

"The point being that she is remarkable," Charles continued. "The wellspring of all my desires, and I am completely, irrevocably destined to never see her again once you take me back to London. This voyage is all the time I have to win her heart and forge my future with hers."

Pirate Phillips sniffed, his eyes red and wet, before he stormed out of the room.

Charles held his head in his hands and groaned.

"You oversold it!" an irate and feminine voice hissed.

He startled before crossing over to the passthrough door to the galley. "Molly?" Did she hear every word?

"You should have quit before the mermaid allusion." She groaned. "Completely unbelievable."

"Well, I'm sorry." Charles was grateful she could not see his red face. "I'm a botanist. Not an actor."

"You are a cosseted prince who better make peace with parting with his collection of plants because no pirate alive would have believed that bilge-sucking load of–"

Pirate Phillips stormed back into the room, eyes still moist and nose red. He brandished his saber before swiping it through the air—all too close to Charles' eyes. "I will help you," he said, sheathing his weapon with great flourish. "You will have your Molly. You will have your heart's desire."

Pirate Phillips agreed that Charles had to stay aboard the *Adelaide*, and that the *Embarazada* would escort them by sea to London. Furthermore, he insisted on tutoring Charles in matters of the heart, and after six days, insisted the time had come for a proper date with the captain.

"Dancing! Music!" Phillips plucked yet another orchid from its stem and added it to the lapel of his frock coat. "No man or woman can resist such magic."

"Where is music to be had on the open ocean?" Charles asked, scribbling notes in his journal.

"Never fear, my boy. I am quite a hand at the violin. We keep a complement of them on board, and Pedro and I have been practicing."

"Of course you have," Charles said through gritted teeth.

"Now, I have arranged everything. Tonight at sunset, we will strike up the violins and you will ask Molly to dance." Phillips undid the cravat around Charles' neck before he could stop him. "You must tell her how you feel. How your soul burns to be united with hers!"

Charles could think of nothing he wanted to do less.

"And when the music comes to its climax, when the strings vibrate at the height of all that is beauty and romance, kiss her."

Charles whimpered.

"I know you are scared. Honor and all that nonsense about gentlemanly this and that is clouding what is straightforward." Phillips clapped Charles on the shoulder. "Trust a pirate in this."

"Must I?"

"If you don't, I see no reason to keep you in abject misery on this ship. We can transfer you to the *Embarazada* and be back in England in a matter of days."

And all his specimens and carefully collected seeds would be lost to the elements or the captain's well meaning, if inept, efforts. Who knew if they'd ever be found again? So Charles, dressed in a borrowed and outrageous dinner jacket, approached the captain at sunset.

"This is awkward," Charles said by way of greeting.

"You are very red, Charles. Did you get too much sun during your lessons with Pirate Phillips today?" Molly's eyes sparkled and teased. Like her voice. Like everything about her.

The violins started playing.

"I'm to tell you how passionately I love you, and then kiss you when the music climaxes. Don't laugh."

"But I have to. Just a little bit," Molly said and her mirth was threaded through her words, threatening to spill over in her eyes. But she bobbed a curtsey when Charles bowed and accepted his hand.

"Pirates are watching," Charles scolded, when she giggled. He enjoyed how the roll of the ship allowed him to hold Molly tighter as they swayed to the violins. "Your favorite pirate in particular."

"Then you better get this right."

Charles brought a tentative hand to Molly's cheek. He'd wondered in the quieter moments of the voyage how her skin might feel, how his palm would fit against the hollow and high cheekbones. The ocean breeze tickled her soft golden curls against his hand.

Pirate Phillips' bow growled into the strings of his violin.

"Is this the crescendo?" Charles asked.

"I think it must be," she said.

Charles took a bracing breath. One kiss, and this would be over. He'd be able to return to his specimens for the rest of the voyage, ensuring their safe arrival. All would proceed as planned.

Molly quirked an eyebrow. "Less calculation, Charles, and more acting."

Very well. Charles leaned in and brushed his lips against Molly's, but as he pulled away, he made a curious connection. Molly's lips were soft like rose petals but tasted sweeter…like honeysuckle. He kissed her again to make sure. Rose and honeysuckle once more, but also barefoot afternoons of sunshine and shared laughter. He drew her closer, noting the pleasant comfort of her weight against his chest. His hands drifted back to her face. Another kiss, this one lingering, sparked the memory of each of Molly's smiles, illuminating them in Charles' brain as a constellation.

Molly grabbed onto Charles' lapels, and the gentle kiss turned into something shimmering. Dark nights with brilliant stars, waves crashing on the shore, moon flowers blossoming on warm summer nights.

Dimly, Charles took note that the violins were still playing, and more kissing was warranted. Was Molly's neck as soft as her lips? It merited investigation. Charles brushed his lips against the space above her collar bone. Soft, yes, but delicate like the lobelia of the English countryside.

Molly laughed, but also wrapped her arms tightly around Charles' middle.

Charles groaned. "Really? This is still funny to you?" He pressed a kiss to her collar bone.

"I'm ticklish, I'll have you know."

"Below your ear?" Charles asked before kissing her there too. She was the milky smoothness of daisy petals.

"Yes," Molly murmured, before she caught Charles' earlobe in her teeth.

His knees buckled, and he nearly lost his footing. He stumbled against the roll of the waves, nearly dropping the captain. "Forgive me," he stammered, feeling his face flush crimson. The music had stopped. No further acting was required. He cleared his throat. "I think we convinced Pirate Phillips."

Molly's eyes sparkled. "Are you sure?"

Charles was as unsure as he had ever been. The world was upside down. They were sailing through the skies. "Thank you for your help, captain. I will…be in my cabin should you need…" Presumptuous of him to even entertain thoughts of her need.

The next morning, Molly knocked on his cabin door. Charles opened it a fraction of an inch.

Molly leaned against the frame. "Really? We're back to speaking through cracked doors?"

"I don't want the moisture and heat for my plants to escape." And

Charles thought it wouldn't be right to invite the captain in after last night's performance. He stepped out of the door and into the hallway, his hand still on the handle.

"It worked. Pirate Phillips has agreed not to separate us." Molly picked at a chip of paint on the door jamb. "They'll escort us for the remainder of the voyage, but you are free to remain on my ship. Your ship." Molly straightened. "On the *Adelaide*."

"Will further acting be necessary for Pirate Phillips' benefit?"

Molly brushed a dried bit of peat moss from Charles' shoulder. "The good pirate wishes to grant us as much privacy as is possible, considering how ours is a doomed attachment."

"Doomed?" Charles swatted his sleeves and trousers of dirt.

"Star-crossed lovers, remember?" Some of the twinkle had dimmed in Molly's eyes. "Phillips suspects Her Majesty will have you on a very short leash when we arrive. And even so, princes do not cavort with sea captains."

"I never cavort with anyone."

Molly nearly laughed at that. "If you say so. Good day to you, Mr. Fitzgerald."

Charles lost track of the days, his nights too. But after more than a dozen suppers in his cabin, he was relieved to hear the familiar rap on his door. The work of cataloging his samples was mostly complete, and his specimens were still alive. He could spare a moment for the good captain. He could thank her for her service and inquire after her plans once they'd reached London.

Charles stuffed the flame tree seed pod he'd been studying into the breast pocket of his vest and swung open the cabin door. He was shocked to see a vice admiral of Drina's navy in the hallway.

"Your Royal Highness," the military man saluted and then launched into his orders.

"Yes, I have no doubt my sister wishes to see me, but where is Captain Penbrooke?"

The decorated officer smoothed his enormous mustache. "Captain Penbrooke, sir?"

"Yes, Captain Molly Penbrooke."

"Ah, yes. The young lady is conducting business with your steward now."

Charles shoved his way past the vice admiral and bolted for the upper deck. He found Molly lingering at the bow of the ship as midshipmen bustled about with the business of docking.

"You've managed to decorate yourself with dirt again." Molly dusted his shoulders. "An impressive feat after thirty-six days at sea." Her hand lingered on Charles' chest. "Your steward paid me."

"Did he?" Charles covered Molly's hand with his own, for the simple reason that he wanted to keep it there, close to his heart.

"Handsomely. He then asked if I wanted to claim a share of the bounty for your safe return at Her Majesty's court."

"Do you?" If he had known how, Charles would have pulled her closer, not just because pirates were watching, but because he enjoyed holding her.

Molly's nose wrinkled. "Heavens no. Too messy." Molly frowned and patted Charles' waistcoat before she fished out the seed pod from his breast pocket.

"What will you do now?" Charles asked.

Molly twisted the open and empty seed pod in her hands. "Buy a dress; trousers aren't exactly fashionable in London." Her smile was shy, fragile, a spring shoot in danger of withering without proper attention.

He tucked one of her golden curls behind her ear. "And after?"

She shrugged. "Book passage back to Kingston. Check in on old friends. Maybe buy a new volume of poetry." She winked at Charles.

"You wink often, captain." Charles couldn't bring himself to explain that he enjoyed this quirk.

Molly blushed. "Nervous habit." She bent the dry seed pod in her hands but did not snap it in two. "Better than brandishing a sword."

The gulls shrieked and circled above, and on the docks below were an awful lot of soldiers and officers.

Molly donned her tricorne hat. "I believe this is where you shake hands with me and bid me farewell."

Charles hesitated. "Wouldn't a goodbye kiss be more appropriate, considering our, well...ruse?"

Molly grinned, but Charles noticed her cheeks were still pink. "That depends. Do you want to kiss me goodbye?"

"No." Charles hated goodbyes. One of many reasons he left for the West Indies in the dead of night when he panicked last June.

Molly flinched before shifting her carpet bag to her shoulder.

"But that's not to say I don't enjoy or didn't enjoy–"

"Quite alright, Mr. Fitzgerald." Molly extended her hand.

Charles grasped it. "Molly."

She raised her eyebrows, maybe at Charles' pleading tone, maybe at how he was pressing her hand between both of his own. "Captain," he amended. "This can't be goodbye."

"Perhaps you'll spot me one day in your famed arboretum."

Thick gray clouds that promised nothing but months of dreary wet loomed overhead. Charles dropped Molly's hand. "The royal gardens are not open to the public."

"My mistake." She handed the seed pod back to Charles. "Good day, Your Royal Highness." She touched her hat and departed. A bosun's whistle sounded, and below the soldiers saluted. Whereas on the ship, a pirate tutted.

"She would have been decorated for her service to the crown," Charles said, not caring if speaking of such matters was ungentlemanly.

Pirate Phillips eagerly took a perch next to Charles at the railing. "Come again?"

"Captain Penbrooke refused her share of the bounty."

Phillips smoothed the extraordinary amount of lace at his throat. "And why was that?"

Charles twisted the flame tree seed pod in his hands. He felt like that seed pod, hallowed out and spent. "Too messy... What the devil does 'too messy' mean?"

Phillips stared at Charles nonplussed. "My dear boy. Have you really learned nothing from my lessons?"

"Sir." The vice admiral saluted Charles. "We must escort you to the palace at once."

"Not without my specimens. They must be safely brought to the palace immediately."

"Her Majesty will not tolerate any further delay."

"I will not leave this ship without my collection or my notes."
"Oh come on, governor," Pirate Phillips roared. "Let the boy bring Her Majesty a literal olive branch."

"Well, I suppose if it matters that much to His Royal Highness," the vice admiral said.

"It is the only thing that matters to His Royal Highness," Pirate Phillips jeered, and his men laughed.

Drina did not smile when Charles returned to the palace. Not over his specimens or the vast array of collected seeds. Had Phillips not pilfered the orchid blooms, things might have been different. But after many long speeches about duty and national security, his half-sister was at least willing to listen.

"I'm ill-suited to this." Charles gestured to the finery of Buckingham Palace as they inspected his journals and sketchbooks. "I'm a botanist. I don't have the mind for any of your politics or palace intrigue."

"But you are my brother, Chuck." The queen paused to consider his detailed watercolor of the tiger orchid. "And as such, galivanting in the West Indies alone is a national liability."

Charles flipped to another watercolor of a bat flower with unusually elongated stamens. "There were two varieties on the islands north of Jamaica. This one here and another with shorter, yellow stamens."

The queen ran her finger across the sketch. "You brought back a specimen?"

"Yes, although I'd be shocked if it flowered again this year."

The queen nodded and considered one of Charles' data tables. "Next time you set sail across the Atlantic, it will be with my approval and the appropriate complement of naval officers and royal guards. We can't have pirates plucking you out of the ocean again."

"Pirates that were searching for me because you put a bounty on my head."

The queen examined another series of sketches. "I was being resourceful. What's a monarch to do when her brother steals her royal yacht, hires a mercenary crew, and disappears for an entire summer?"

"They are building you a better yacht, a bigger yacht, and you have been so preoccupied with your coronation and what's his name–"

"Albert," Drina said sharply.

"Yes, Albert, that I thought you'd hardly notice. I did write to Albert." The chap had a passion for exotic specimens that rivaled Charles' own.

"And then ceased all correspondence when I told him to tell you to come straight home." Drina snapped his sketchbook shut.

"I am sorry."

"I don't need apologies; I need answers. Why did you do it, Chuck?"

"You're queen now." Eighteen, a full fourteen years younger than Charles, and half his size to be sure, and still ruling the greatest empire in the world. "You don't need some stodgy, old half-brother besmirching your court, dulling the bright promise of your reign."

Charles swallowed past the ache he'd carried since the day his sister's ascendancy was declared and all their lives had changed. Even though it had loomed before the family for years, it was still a terrible shock. Little Drina, lost in an instant to the majesty of Queen Victoria, inseparable from the history and fate of an entire empire forevermore. Rather than witness the erasure of the sister he knew and loved, he panicked and ran away, succumbing to the only thing he dared to still care about: botany.

"No." Drina's voice softened. "But I desperately need my dear, dear brother."

Tears pricked Charles' eyes, but a smile tugged at the corner of his mouth. "Whom you declare vexes you at every opportunity?"

"Because it's true!" Drina laughed. "Did you or did you not steal my yacht?"

"I didn't think anyone would notice, seeing as how you had just become queen."

"I noticed." Drina rose, which meant Charles must stand as well. "You are my brother, Charles. The only brother I have. It was a wicked thing to do, sailing out of town, right when I needed you most."

Charles beamed but had the good sense to look down at his boots. "Right when you needed someone to tell you that you are still the shortest person in every room, and that if you were any more besotted with Albert–"

"Albert thinks you met someone." Drina poured herself a cup of tea from the sideboard. "Did you? A baron's daughter or some such in the West Indies?"

"No…" A constellation of smiles twinkled in his mind, and the memory of rose and honeysuckle brought a flush to Charles' cheeks.

"Because allowances could be made if you had…"

"It was my research alone that held my interest. Nothing more."

But in the days that followed, Charles was increasingly distracted by the same memories. He went through his days in a rose and honeysuckle scented fog, until one afternoon outside the royal arboretum at Kew Palace, when he stumbled straight into Pirate Phillips.

"Sir Pirate Phillips. Your sister had me knighted for my service to Merrie Olde." The man touched the emblems of the crown that now decorated his shoulder. "Turns out bringing you back in one piece was more important than any of us thought."

"Jolly good," Charles said, before thrusting his hands back in his pockets and wandering to the glasshouses. The autumn rains had started in earnest, and the glasshouses with their abundance of lamps would be the only warm spot in the capital for the next six months.

"I say, Charles, what's this all about?" Sir Pirate Phillips said, entering the glasshouse after him.

"I beg your pardon?" Charles tied the raceme of a red desert aloe to a stake.

"Your sister is determined to keep me landlocked until your hangdog moping resolves."

Charles grabbed a paintbrush and began pollinating the yellow and red flowers. "I am sullen by nature."

"You are pining for a pretty sea captain and entertaining thoughts of heartbreak instead of action." Phillips grabbed the brush from Charles' hand and threw it on the gravel floor. "You told me, 'You don't find a woman like Molly ever. Not in this lifetime. Not in fiction. Not in the worlds beyond.' Those were your words."

"Yes, but I didn't mean them!" And yet Charles felt the loss of the good captain keenly. "It was a plot to keep me with my plants and seeds for the remainder of the voyage."

Sir Pirate Phillips bent with a flourish and retrieved the pollination brush. "I may be an old romantic, but I am no fool." He handed the brush back to Charles.

"You knew it was a ruse?"

"I knew you believed it was a ruse. But I also know truth and passion when I see it. I know the difference between two people putting on a show and two people being swept up in a moment."

"It's easy to be swept up in many moments at sea," Charles said.

"It is. But that's not what I saw when I played my fiddle and you and Molly danced." Sir Pirate Phillips brushed his finger against the inflorescence of the plant. "I didn't watch your first kiss, much as I wanted to."

Charles raised his eyebrows.

Phillips shrugged with a smile. "Even pirates have their modesty. I did see your faces afterward. You may have thought you were playing a part, but your hearts did not."

Though it was a relief to make sense of the internal mess that had taken residence in his heart, it was no solution. "Phillips, I'm a fool. But I'm also an obligated fool. Pleasure cruises and warm sunny afternoons on white sand beaches are not part of my future." Drina wouldn't stand for it.

"As fond as both you and the good captain are of the aforementioned, you may be surprised to discover that Molly is keener on something else entirely."

"What's that?"

"A happily-ever-after with you."

Charles burst into tears. "I love her."

"Of course you do."

"Everything I told you on the *Adelaide* was true!"

"Of course it was."

"Phillips, I need to beg a favor."

"The *Embarazada* will always set sail for the right price."

"We have to find Molly and bring her back. I'll import white sand, make a swimming hole in the middle of this glasshouse—anything to make her happy."

"Why don't you start with the words, 'I love you. Marry me.'?"

"Yes, good. Very good! Phillips you deserve a peerage."

"I'm counting on it," the pirate smiled. "In addition to a lot of coin."

It was four months and two transatlantic voyages later before they found Molly captaining a Portugues barque two-hundred miles off the coast of Lisbon. Charles was so overjoyed to be reunited with the good captain that he fell promptly to his knees, declared his love, and proposed. When Molly agreed, Charles begged Sir Pirate Phillips to officiate the nuptials on the deck of the *Embarazada* that very day.

"My dear boy, this is *simply* not the thing." Sir Pirate Phillips splayed a hand across the froth of lace at his throat. "What's more, Her Majesty would have our heads if she were excluded from this happy event." Phillips brandished his saber, swiping it through the air thrice for effect. "A pretty chapel, a big dress, Her Majesty's approval, and a crown of orange blossoms in the fair captain's hair are the barest minimum for me to even *consider* officiating this union."

Molly smiled before squeezing Charles' hand. "I am fond of orange blossoms."

In the end, Drina insisted the Archbishop of Canterbury perform the marriage rights. Just as well, Charles was sure Phillips would have charged an exorbitant fee for the service. The man was a pirate after all.

The happy couple spent their honeymoon sailing around the Mediterranean, and when they returned to London that spring, Drina had a surprise wedding gift for them. A sleek, new yacht of their very own.

"What should we name her?" Molly asked, adjusting the bouquet of roses, honeysuckles, and violets they had picked together from the royal arboretum that morning.

Charles sat on their bed with legs crossed at the ankle, sketching the blossoms of the potted orange tree they had brought back from Sicily. "I was thinking the *Embarazada II.*"

Molly laughed. "Not the yacht, dear."

Charles charcoal pencil broke in two. He looked up from his sketch and found Molly beaming. "You mean…" Charles was on his feet, overwhelmed with love and hopeful joy. He embraced his wife and kissed her breathless, before sweeping her off her feet and depositing her gently on their bed. "My darling captain, are you saying we'll need to add a crib to our stateroom?"

"My dear prince," Molly brushed a kiss to Charles' lips. "That is exactly what I am saying."

Keep Your Blade Sharp

Michelle Dennis Christensen

Alec held his gaze on the dock as the small skiff pulled away from the edge, eyes alert for a watchman that might catch him. The boat slid forward and ducked into the shadows of the big merchant vessel, *The Monarch*.

Just in time.

The night watchman's footsteps thudded on the boardwalk and stopped. The bright moon reflected off the water. Alec shot a fervent glance at his brother William. Both men froze. Ten agonizing seconds later, the footsteps clunked on the boardwalk again, growing fainter with each step.

"That was close," said William. "Now, we'd better get moving before he comes back." William dipped the oars into the water and gave a hard tug and smiled.

Alec only shook his head. The knot in his stomach tightened. His feet shifted back and forth as he gazed across the pier into the oven black night. He dropped his head, chin resting on his chest.

"Cheer up, Alec. Soon ye'll be a free man." William's voice held a lot more confidence than Alec felt.

"I don't know. Maybe I could..."

"We've been over this more times than a baker's dozen. Ye can't go back to Scotland. Ye can't go to England. Ye can't go to any of Her Majesty's colonies. The Craigs are too powerful. Ye have to get to America."

"But stowing away?"

"Can ye go home?"

"No." Alec paused. "Well, maybe I could lay low. I shouldn't have to leave. I did nothing wrong." He huffed. An explosion of noise bounced off the rippling water and skittered across the surface. Both Alec and William froze, oars resting in the water. Nothing broke the stillness, and the brothers let out a sigh of relief.

"Maybe not if ye were in America. But in Scotland ye can't hit yer betters. Even when they're wrong."

"They're not better than me."

"Here they are. Can't ye get it through yer thick skull? That's why yer leaving. Once ye are on the boat, ye'll be safe."

"Safe?" Alec guffawed. "Safe? Are ye out of yer mind? What if I get caught?"

William shrugged. "Truth be known, stowaways always get caught. Once the ship's at sea, they won't turn back. They'll put ye to work. Mind yer manners, and ye'll be fine."

Alec sobered and squinted at his brother. "What if ye get caught, aiding a stowaway? Ye'll lose yer situation on the wharf."

"I'll be careful." William shrugged and pulled the small boat to the side of the large schooner. "It's time for ye to get on with yer life. Time to make something of yersel, break free from the Craigs."

"But what about Ann?"

"Ann's not in as much trouble as ye are. Our sister was handling herself until ye interfered. She'll be fine, especially now she's in Liverpool with Jane and me. Now, go."

Alec stood, naturally adjusted his balance as the boat rocked, and faced his brother. "Thanks." His voice was husky as he clutched the bundle that contained all he now owned in the world.

The skiff sloshed when the two men broke apart. Alec stumbled. Arms flailing, he plopped onto the seat. The bundle flew open and contents tumbled everywhere. His dagger thudded on the bottom of the boat. A pair of socks plopped in the dark water of the River Mersey.

Alec leaned over the rowboat. It tilted closer to the water as he stretched, and his fingers brushed the wool as they started sinking. Only an inch more. He reached farther.

A hand grabbed the back of his shirt and yanked him back. "It's a good thing yer a baker and not a sailor. Ye would drown at the first gale."

The small craft wobbled from side to side, and Alec gripped the edges. "Not so. I can handle the waves. Ye know I've never been seasick a day in my life."

"Riding canals doesn't count." With one swoop, William maneuvered an oar under the socks before they disappeared, lifted them out of the water, and swung the dripping mess to his brother.

Alec shoved the socks into the bundle and retrieved his knife–soon to be his only friend.

"Is that the blade Da gave ye?"

"Aye, the very one from dear Athair, God rest his soul." Alec pulled the sheath off and ran his thumb along the steel blade from his father. "Sharp as ever. The way Athair taught."

William nodded. "Ye have the land of opportunity before ye. With yer lucky blade ye can have yer own bakery. No boss. I can see it now, 'Warnock's Bakery,' just like Da's." William's voice was wistful. "Now, go seize the moments. Goodbye and Godspeed." William stuck his hand out.

Alec stared at his brother. William may long to go to America, but he wanted to stay. With a swallow, he pushed past the hand and wrapped his brother in a tight hug. "Godspeed." A minute later he reached for the rope ladder dangling on the edge of *The Monarch* and pulled himself onto the ratlines.

"And Alec—" William called after him.

"I know. I know. 'Keep a sharp blade but a sharper eye.'"

William snorted. "Aye that. But I was going to warn ye not to show off on that ladder. The night watch might spot ye."

"Ye mean, not do this?" Alec climbed a few rungs, wrapped his legs in the rope, dropped his body and flipped backwards, feet landing on the line they had vacated seconds ago.

"No one would ever know yer twenty-five." William shook his head, waved, and paddled away.

Alec sucked in a deep breath. Without his brother as witness, he let his face and body sag against the ropes. What was he doing here? Echoes of past conversations tumbled around and around, each vying for dominance, each growing louder, more urgent, demanding to be listened to, dealt with.

"Alec, ye can't leave."

"What will we do without ye?"

"Are ye sure this is what ye want?"

No. This isn't what he wanted. He didn't want to leave his family, especially his little sister. No telling what the high and mighty Lord Craig would do once Alec was gone. His hands clenched around the woven rope. He should have taken out the pompous dolt when he first noticed the man's interest in Ann. A lot of good his sharp eyes did him and his sister.

The thought of Ann made him turn toward the oily black water lapping the edge of the schooner. Maybe he could stay. Disappear. It wasn't too late. He could find employment in London where Craig would never find him in the midst of the stink of English factories. Alec took a step down and searched the water for his brother's boat. Gone.

Before he could take another step, rhythmic thumping returned to the boardwalk. The noise stopped. The echoes died off the ship. Alec froze, suspended in midair, hoping his brown wool clothes would blend in with the ship enough to disguise him. He could picture the watchman leaning forward and peering into the dark, trying to detect the slightest movement.

If Alec called out, if he even moved, the night watch would catch him and then catch William. He wouldn't let his brother get caught because of his cowardice.

A cloud drifted across the moon, and the footsteps resumed, growing fainter with each second until they disappeared.

Alec held his body taut for another two minutes. At length he turned back toward the ship, and his face brushed the rough planks on the side. With clenched teeth, he climbed up and hoisted himself over the starboard rail. The wet socks dripped onto his clothes and ran down to the small of his back. Like it or not, he was here. Now he had to hide before anyone caught him.

Alec landed with a quiet thud on the wooden deck and looked around to gain his bearings. William had told him about a hidden crevice between two nooks against the side of the ship. "The hole is so small no one would think of searching there."

Alec picked his way across the main deck to the central hatch, turned, and plunged deep into the dark hold. He moved past crates, barrels, long wooden containers, trunks, and metal chests until he found the nook.

"Ye've got to be kidding me. He expects me to hide here?" Alec's whisper bounced around the dark space, louder than intended.

He shoved his bundle in first and slid sideways into the cranny. The rough, wooden beams brushed against his face and snagged the back of his wool shirt below the shoulders. He pushed deeper into the recess where the space opened a few inches and allowed him to slide his back down the side of the ship. With only enough room to sit with knees bent and hugged next to his chest, Alec tucked the bundle on his lap and waited.

And waited.

Alec shifted between sitting with cramped legs and standing hunched over with the back of his neck scraping the wood above him. He peered through the dark hold and tried to gauge the time. Muffled sounds of the wharf reached his ears, the rhythmic thump of carts being pushed across boardwalks, the clanking of metal against metal as warehouse doors opened and closed, the thudding of footsteps walking, scurrying, strolling.

It must've been morning, though no light penetrated the dark prison that was sealed tight against the waves and water. Each thump, clank, and thud from the pier shouted into his heart that he was a prisoner. He shifted again. Shouldn't *The Monarch* have departed by now? But it sat as if becalmed on the ocean without the privilege of greeting the empty horizon.

A rat ran across his foot. Alec retrieved his dagger and swiped at the vermin with the sharp blade. Da would roll over in his grave if he knew Alec had used the prized knife on a rodent: the very knife Athair had built his trade with, the one he'd insisted on giving Alec.

"But Athair," Alec had protested. "Ye can't give this to me. It belonged to yer athair."

"Yer a man now, Lad. Ye need it. Me? I've had me a good life, and yer at the beginning of yours. Take it. Do something with it. Make me proud."

With a sigh, Alec cursed Lord Craig who'd forced him to abandon his father's bakery after Athair had died. His da had made the best bread in the county. Now he was dead, Alec was gone, and Ann was alone.

Alec's stomach rumbled at the thought of food. He scowled, dug into his bundle, and pulled out some stale bread. They said America was the land of opportunity. Could he really start over with Da's blade? Da's lessons? Aither had taught him the value of a sharp blade.

"Dull blades harm ye faster than ye can cut off a chicken's head. Keep her sharp, and she'll serve ye well." Athair had paused, lifted his prized knife and jabbed it in Alec's direction. "Ye are like this knife. When ye push and saw and jam yer way through life, it harms you like a dull blade."

"But Lord Craig, Aither, he's no good. I dinna like the way he leers at Ann."

"Maybe not. But," Da had jabbed the blade again in Alec's

direction, "watch yerself. Keep your eyes sharp and your wits about ye. Then ye can cut through problems with ease like this here knife when it's sharp." The sharp chopping sound of a blade slicing carrots with ease had filled the air.

Now Alec dropped his head onto his knees, glad his father couldn't see him.

The increased noise from the wharf told Alec the day was progressing. That and how the heat in his dark prison intensified like an oven. Alec licked his chapped lips. The inside of his mouth was coated like he'd sucked on dry flour. He licked his lips again and dug for a scarf to wipe his brow. His hand brushed against his socks, still holding a small amount of river water. Desperate, he grabbed the socks and shoved them into his mouth. The putrid flavor of the Mersey quenched his parched mouth.

"Heave ho!"

The ships' anchor chain tumbled and clanged somewhere close behind him. Heavy thuds echoed through the hold as the heavy anchor struck the side of the ship, bounced, and was cinched into place.

A wave of relief rushed out of Alec's chest. Time to get out and stretch. And find something to eat. He pushed one foot out of the nook and shook the tingly appendage as blood rushed back toward it.

A dim light appeared and drew closer to Alec.

"Alright, men. Scour this hold for thieving stowaways."

Alec halted, foot suspended in midair.

"When ya find them, bring them to the main deck."

"Yes, sir." The voices of a dozen men bounced around the hold.

Alec gulped, clenched his teeth, and eased his foot back into the nook seconds before a heavy thud passed near the opening.

"If they cause ya trouble, clobber them with your loggerhead. It's good for more than smearing tar on the deck." The man chuckled.

Alec's foot twitched. He couldn't hold the awkward angle a second longer and kicked against the beam next to him.

"Check out that sound over there."

Frantic, Alec slid deeper into this hiding place, hoping the scuffle of men and creaking timbers masked his hurried noise. Through a knot hole he spied a bearded sailor saunter toward him with a spike. The sailor stopped and shoved it through an opening in a large crate pushed against the beams of Alec's prison. A scream followed.

"Get out ya thieving stowaway. On top."

A scrawny fellow popped up. "But sir. The ship. It's done left port.

I cannot swim."

"Thank your patron saint there's a tug down below waiting to haul you worthless criminals back to land. Move. Afore I clobber you."

A yelp was followed by running footsteps.

Alec tensed, squeezing tighter and smaller into his hiding spot, bulging eyes staring at the tiny opening in front of him. He couldn't get caught. Not now. Why hadn't he remembered the tugs? He dropped his head back against the timbers and shook it in disgust. What a dolt. He knew better. The ship wouldn't be out to sea for ten miles. And even then, it would be too close to the port to be safe. He had to stay put.

A spike with a sharp nail on the tip thrust through the opening with force. The sharp point scraped the side of Alec's cheek and nicked his ear before it clunked into the wood behind him. Alec gasped. Another passenger grunted at the same time. A sailor cursed, and the whimper of a child filled the air. Blood trickled down his neck from the pike's scratch. Alec clamped his teeth onto his tongue.

The spike withdrew, and a dagger sliced through the open space where Alec had been minutes before. It stabbed again and again each time at a different height and angle.

Alec's shoulder tensed and his stomach tumbled. Maybe he should give up. Not be caught in shame. It would be better that way. Like he told William, he could lay low. Find employ beyond the reaches of the Craigs.

The knife pulled away.

"Men, haul these prisoners upstairs. Be quick about it. Irvin, find anyone else over there?"

"Nay, sir. Ye want me to keep searching?" a young Scottish brogue asked.

"No. Good search. Head up top."

Dozens of footsteps clattered across the hold and up the stairs. Alec held his breath until the last sound departed. He counted to a hundred before he dared let his body sag against the side of the ship. Still, he didn't dare move.

That was close, too close. His hand slid to the dagger in his bundle; there he was again, caught as a dull blade with dull wits and dull eyes. If they found him now, they'd learn William helped him, and they'd find Ann. The best thing he could do for his family was avoid getting discovered. Maybe his brother was right. Maybe it was time to start over. Not that he had much of a choice.

Two days passed, and with it Alec's meager bread ration. His socks had long since lost their small relief from the Mersey water. At least the rocking of the ship was natural and soothing, and his stomach hadn't relinquished the paltry nourishment. As he'd told William, seasickness wasn't an issue. Alec had never thought it would be, not with the way he spun and twirled on the dance floor, or the way he swung and flipped on the big tree outside the Craig's house after tricking him. No, movement wasn't his enemy. Lack of food was.

Darkness cloaked the hold, and he figured sneaking out from his shelter under the cover of night gave him the best opportunity to find food and get back to his hiding place without getting caught. Tongue parched and stomach growling, Alec crawled out of the tight prison. Tingles flooded cramped muscles as the blood began to flow. With the bundle slung over a shoulder, he bumped and shuffled his way through the hold toward a faint light coming from the open hatch.

He climbed the stairs, the scent of seawater growing stronger with each step. On deck, Alec paused, grinned, and turned a complete circle, all hunger forgotten at the expanse that greeted him. Four bells chimed with a small pause in the middle. The clean tone resonated and lifted to greet a sliver of the moon that peeked over the horizon. Thousands of stars winked down at him, more stars than he saw in the countryside of Scotland.

"Hey, sir?"

Alec jerked at the sound of the young Scottish brogue. He shot a furtive look at the sailor as his mind raced.

"What're ye doing here? Curfew was two bells. Ye should be below deck."

"Breath of fresh air." Alec gulped. "Tis bad below. The smells. Might ye have some fresh water?"

"Irvin?" The same gravelly voice Alec heard below thundered across the deck. Alec spied a stocky, weathered sailor making his way toward them and inched toward the open hatch.

"Mr. Patton." The lad stiffened to attention as he turned toward the man. "This here passenger is above deck after curfew. I'm about to escort him below."

"Passenger? Not likely." The man snarled, his putrid breath assaulting Alec. He grabbed the front of Alec's shirt and jerked him closer until the sailor's whiskers brushed Alec's face. A fat scar above the captor's eye pulsed as the man stared Alec down. "Their leader told me they was all accounted for."

Alec couldn't break his gaze from the hard, cold eyes. He swallowed hard. "I—"

"You're a stowaway." He spat on Alec's face.

Alec's fist clenched. How dare he? "I demand to see the captain."

"He don't have nothing to do with the likes of you."

"Then take me to the first mate."

"Yer a looking at him." The man shoved Alec as hard as a dull cleaver cutting frozen meat. Alec flew across the deck. The man charged across the boards and yanked him up.

"Irvin?" The mate growled and shifted his attention to the lad standing next to them. "How did ya miss this one?" The mate clapped the boy on the side of the head.

Alec bristled and doubled his fist as he watched the boy wince and bite his lip. It was just like back home with those in charge beating on those under their control. He wanted to deck the man, like he had done after Lord Craig kissed his sister. He needed to show this brute that he couldn't treat people that way.

"I don't know, sir. I did what ye told me to do. Searched with me knife and spike."

The lad's brogue reached Alec's ears, soft and young, yet confident, and Alec shifted his gaze to the boy. The boy's hands flexed, conflict on his face. Then his fist relaxed, and the young sailor stood straight and tall with submission but without weakness.

"Keep your eyes sharper." Da's voice echoed in his brain. If he defended this boy, the lad would suffer, just like his sister had after he'd belted Craig. Alec forced his fist to relax.

The mate turned back to Alec.

"How did ya get on board?" the man growled.

Calmer, Alec thought about William. He couldn't get William into trouble. He straightened and met the gaze of the first mate. "Alec Warnock, Sir. I'd like to offer my services with your crew."

The mate shook him. "Who helped ya?"

Alec stood mute. The man shook him again. Alec clenched his teeth together and kept silent.

"No matter. We canna turn back. You will work for your passage, by Jove and rue the day you boarded this ship without passage."

"Aye, sir." Alec looked him straight in the eye.

"Irvin, take this man below where he can pay the devil." The mate shoved Alec away from him and started toward the forecastle. Alec tumbled onto the deck.

"Aye, aye, sir." Irvin strode toward Alec.

"Devil, sir?" Alec scrambled to his feet before the lad could reach him. Alec's brother, often complained about how hard it was to pay and pitch the longest seam in the hull. And that was at low tide when the boats could be tipped on their side. But when the ship was at sea? Alec wanted nothing to do with the back-breaking work that would dangle him over the edge of the ship and dip him below the water level to seal the seam.

Alec protested. "Please sir, not the devil."

Patton kept walking and hollered over his shoulder. "Irvin, grab some pay on your way down. He can at least start with hot pitch."

"Sir, please don't send me to the devil."

Patton stopped and turned around. A cranky smile spread across his face. "Ya don't want to pay the devil? Can't blame ya. Irvin, take him to the bilge. He can clean and pay that."

The young lad, much fiercer now, approached him with the force of a dull blade. Alec backed away and shot frantic looks around the deck. There had to be something else. There was no place worse than the bilge, hunched over the boards in the hull, shoving oakum between the cracks, then sealing them with hot tar. Thirty-four days in the bilge before they reached New York might ruin his hands—hands a baker needed. Then what? He'd have nothing. No money. No trade. No means of starting one. Nothing. Why couldn't he have stayed in Scotland? Why did he have to take out the monster Craig?

"Wait, sir, isn't there anything else? Let me help in the galley." Alec clamored to face the first mate and clutched the man's arms.

The stocky man shoved Alec away and turned his back on Alec's desperate plea. "Now, Irvin."

Irvin grabbed Alec by the arm with a steel grip and wrenched him toward the main hatch. A wiry sailor shoved past them before the two could descend.

"Mr. Patton, sir. The cook's drunk again, and Captain wants to eat."

Alec halted their progress and studied the mate, his eyes sharper than before. The cook was indisposed. He could do it. He could cook in his sleep. The only problem was to convince the overbearing first mate.

"Let the galley hand take care of it." Patton growled as he stalked away from the interruption.

"But sir, the hand was conscripted for the war in America." The old sailor looked down at his bare feet while he talked.

"I'll skin that cook alive if I catch—" The mate let out an oath Alec had never heard before.

Alec jerked his arm out of Irvin's grip and turned to face Mr. Patton. He lifted his chin and looked him straight in the eye. "Might I offer my services as a cook?

Mr. Patton shot a nasty look at Irvin. "Irvin, get him below—"

Irvin's tough fingers dug into Alec's arm again. Larger than the lad, Alec pushed toward the mate.

"Wait, sir. I'm a baker by trade. I even have me own baker's knife." Alec shrugged off the young Scot and retrieved Athair's blade.

"A baker? Bah. What do we want with a fancy baker?" Patton's face clouded with anger.

"Sir, Captain needs his food, and ye are looking at the man who can deliver it for ye." He took a breath and noticed the mate pause. He pushed on. "I can help."

The burly man paused, shook his head, and scowled. "Blast it all. Irvin, drag this thieving rat to the galley and let him begin earning his passage." He turned to Alec and stared at him with fierce eyes. "When ya are done with breakfast, I'll personally escort you to the hull where there'll be nothing but the devil between you and the deep blue sea."

Irvin opened the galley door and shoved Alec inside. What gave that wee lad the right to treat him that way? Alec clenched his fist, his hand brushing against his blade.

He paused. Again he heard Da's voice. "Be sharp like this blade." Alec had scraped his way out of the bilge. He didn't want to end up there. He couldn't force his way through like a dull blade. That would only harm him. With a deep breath, he entered the galley.

The large cook lay sprawled across the tables. A mouse ran up his arm, but the drunk didn't move. The mouse scurried onto the table, nibbled some crumbs, and disappeared when Irvin approached the bench. Alec's stomach rumbled at the sight of food.

"Mr. Frye!" Irvin called out. "I brought ye some help." He shook the cook's shoulder. The lad grabbed a lock of hair, lifted the head, and stared at eyes closed above a bulbous red nose. When he let go,

Cook's head thumped back onto the rough table.

With a shrug, he turned to Alec. "Fix a platter for the captain."

Alec gaped at him.

Irvin scowled and shoved Alec toward the storage area.

Alec grabbed a platter and scrounged through the pantry until he found cheese and fruit and thrust it into Irvin's hands.

Irvin pushed the tray against the door. "Someone will pick up the captain's breakfast at four bells into morning watch. If Cook's not awake, ye'd better have it ready."

"Wait, what time? I heard four bells on deck before we came down."

"Ye heard the first watch bells. Breakfast is during morning watch." Irvin's tone sounded as if he was talking to a small child rather than an adult. "That's about six. Sun's up at one bell into morning watch, and ye best be getting breakfast ready by then."

"One bell?"

"Half past four in the morning." Irvin's words were faint, swallowed by the coal blackness of the hallway

The ship swayed and slammed the door shut with a crack. Bowls slid across the dirty table. Water from the heavy pots sloshed onto the metal surface of the stove and sizzled before it ran down the side onto the sand-covered brick platform underneath the huge free-standing camboose.

The cook snored.

Now what?

Alec's stomach gurgled as he moved to the camboose. Water boiled, and the steam carried the stench of old pudding. Alec wrinkled his nose. He could do better than that, but his stomach demanded to be fed first.

After devouring stale food, he searched the galley. Stashed in various sizes and shapes of bowls and barrels he discovered all manner of dried meats, fruits, and baking staples. It wouldn't be fancy, leastways not as fine as he was used to, but he could make do. There appeared to be plenty of suet for the voyage. He'd start with suet pudding to go along with the morning meal. He pulled Athair's steel blade out of his bundle and set to work slicing, dicing, chopping, and mixing. Once a mixture was simmering on the camboose, Alec dropped onto a bench by the table and let his head drop onto his arms. Sleep claimed him within minutes.

Alec was jolted awake when the bench he rested on upended, crashing him to the floor.

"Who are you and what are you doing in my kitchen?"

Alec scrambled to his feet, fists ready to defend himself.

Cook shoved his bulk toward Alec. The door slammed open, and Irvin along with ten men piled into the kitchen blocking the cook's path. The bulky man lost his balance, crashed backward onto a bench, and sat stunned. Hungry sailors grabbed wooden plates and sat down.

A steward made his way across the room and over to Alec. "Captain's breakfast ready?"

"Aye." Alec straightened himself and tugged his dirty waistcoat down. He put meat on a tray and added another dish with a savory aroma that wafted toward the steward.

"Mmm. Smells like this ain't come out of this kitchen in a while."

Alec smiled, giving the man a jaunty bow. When he straightened, his chest pushed out a fraction, and he sauntered toward the camboose to serve the men.

The cook scowled as the steward picked up the tray and left.

"Gentlemen." Alec smiled and placed two dishes on the table with all the flourish of a manor's head footman. "Your breakfast. Boiled pork and a little something I cooked up."

"Suet pudding? Is that what we smelled coming down the passage?" The men dove into the dish and heaped large portions onto their plates.

"Hey, Cook," an old wiry sailor called out. "Why can't you cook like this?" He pushed a wooden platter in front of Cook. Cook shoved it away.

Between the cries of pleasure from the men who rotated in and out during the different messes, Frye glared at Alec. The door swung shut with a final thud when the last group left.

Alone with the cook, Alec watched the burly man with a wary eye as he cleared and straightened the table.

Unencumbered, Cook stormed toward Alec. He rammed Alec backwards into the barrels tucked underneath a counter.

Alec's blood boiled and simmered. "Take yer filthy hands off me." He shoved the bulky man. Frye staggered backwards, regained his balance and hunched down with shoulders forward as if he was about to charge.

Patton entered. "Mr. Warnock, sir."

Cook straightened and busied himself at the table.

Patton addressed Alec instead. "Captain sends his compliments and requests another such delicacy for supper. Want to avoid the bilge for another day?" The faintest hint of a smile lit the man's face and disappeared.

"Aye, aye, sir." Alec stood tall and saluted the first mate. This was so much better than the wet, putrid bilge. He shot a wary glance at the burly man glowering at him and then shrugged. He could take care of that oaf.

"As the galley hand, Warnock. The galley hand." Patton's voice held a warning, all friendliness gone.

Alec shrunk his posture a fraction and nodded at the first mate.

"Cook?" Mr. Patton hollered. "This man is to help you." He paused and eyed down the bulky man. "Unharmed."

Frye growled and gave a curt nod. As soon as the officer left, he grabbed a ladle and slammed it on the table.

"Let's get one thing straight. I'm the boss here. You do what I say, and we'll have no trouble."

Alec eyed his opponent up and down. He ought to deck the man right now and give him a lesson. He was like Lord Craig. They were all like Craig. Yet, he was still a stowaway. One bad move, and he'd end up in the keel before supper, never to come out again. He would toe the line, and if he kept his eyes as sharp as his blade, he might find the opportunity to stay right where he was for the next seven weeks.

Alec forced the blunt edge of pride back into its sheath and nodded. "Aye, aye."

Two days passed with Cook barking orders and Alec obeying. He'd had plenty of practice back in Scotland. He didn't like it, but he knew how.

Cook snapped out orders. Alec chopped and diced and paired. Men came and went, rejoicing over spiced and savory dishes. Cook glowered, took a swig from his bottle, shouted commands, and swallowed more rum. One by one, the bells chimed from one to eight and started over again with a new watch and then another. Time passed with the flimsiness of rising dough where one wrong move could collapse the whole thing.

"*Mr.* Warnock." Cook snarled and pointed his knife under Alec's nose at the start of the second dog watch the second day. "Get the meat out of the larder. That's the only thing we'll be serving for dinner."

"Sir? I could make some more pudding. The captain—"

Cook slammed his cleaver onto the cutting board. "Let's get one thing straight, *Mr.* Warnock. In this kitchen, I'm the law, the judge, and the executioner. Now, get that meat."

Alec lowered his head to hide the anger firing in his eyes. He yanked the larder open and gagged on the stench of rotten meat.

"Cook. The meat is bad. Ye can't serve it." He paused. "Sir."

"You know nothing. It's fine." The burly man's words slurred together.

"It's bad. Ye can't serve this." Alec gagged again and slammed the larder door shut.

"You'll do what I say, and I say get that meat out."

Frye's bloodshot eyes focused on Alec. His words were slurred, but his voice was deep and threatening. He shoved at Alec with the brunt force of a dull blade. The simmering tension of the past two days was a full boil.

The food was spoiled. Alec knew it, and Alec knew Frye knew it. The cook had been waiting for this opportunity. Maybe the man's wits weren't as gone as Alec had believed. If Alec disobeyed a direct order, he'd end up in the keel doing backbreaking, filthy work.

But if he served bad food, and the men got sick he'd take the fall and end up in the bilge anyway. He knew the effects of bad meat. More than one sailor would wind up in the infirmary, sick for days. Some might die. He wouldn't serve the bad meat. Regardless of the outcome. Alec squared his shoulders and faced Frye.

"I will not. It'll cripple the men."

Cook picked up his cleaver and charged. Alec ducked under Cook's arm and grabbed his newly sharpened knife off the cutting board. He whirled around and faced the cook, dagger in front of him.

"Ye can't serve that meat."

Eyes wild with anger, Frye lunged toward Alec. Cook's cleaver glinted in the dim light as he slammed the metal down. The dull blade embedded in the wooden counter with a thud. Alec spun out of the way and grunted. In one quick movement, he slashed his dagger at the meaty hand tugging on the handle.

Frye howled as blood dripped from his hand. "You'll pay for that." With a shriek he flung his arm backwards, connecting with Alec's head.

Alec sprawled on the ground. His dagger clattered onto the bricks where the camboose stood and slid on the sand underneath the heated stove. Alec dove for his knife and knocked it further out of reach.

"No!" Alec plunged his arm under the scorching metal toward his knife. Heat singed his hand and forced him back. Panting, he rolled as the drunk man barreled after him. Heart pounding, he scooted backward on all fours and searched for a weapon. The poker. He seized the metal spike, scrambled to his feet, and charged.

The man barreled through Alec's defense like it was a toothpick. The poker clattered to the floor. Frye's meaty paws wrapped around Alec's throat and squeezed.

"You will do as I say," he bellowed.

Black spots danced in Alec's vision, and he choked and sputtered. He batted his arms against Frye's large back. The man squeezed tighter. Alec flung his hands wildly around, searching for something, anything. His fingers brushed the cast iron skillet near the camboose. Alec swung it at the cook's arm. The man loosened his grip. Alec swung again, harder and harder, the skillet slamming onto Cook's his neck, back, arm.

A sickening thud connected with the man's shoulder. Frye yowled and dropped Alec who lay in a heap, panting. Head down, the burly man heaved his bulk toward Alec's stomach. Alec forced his bruised body to roll out of the way. The heavy man's momentum propelled him forward where his head crashed into the hot camboose with a crack. Cook dropped to the floor, motionless.

"What the tarnation is going on here?" Mr. Patton charged into the room. Several sailors piled in behind him. Patton looked from Alec, slumped against a wall, to the Frye, crumpled on the floor.

Alec staggered to his feet, panting and sweating. He wiped his brow with the back of his hand. "The meat, sir," he said between gasps of air. "It's rotten. He was going to serve it anyway."

Patton's face darkened. "Warnock, you'd better be right."

"I am, sir. See for yerself." Alec leaned against the wall.

Patton jerked the larder open. The reek from the rotten meat filled the room.

"There's not enough lard in that bin to keep it fresh," Alec explained between heavy breaths.

Mr. Patton slammed the door shut. He turned to the men crowding in the room. "Back to your watch," he barked. "Irvin."

The lad stopped his retreat. "Aye, sir?"

"Get the second mate, and tell him to round up a few sailors to help him take Frye to the brig." He turned to Alec shaking his head. "Warnock, it looks like you find yourself as a cook after all."

Alec tried to hide a shaky smile. Patton glared at Alec. "Frye's a good man. Your blunt force may have cost him his position."

Alec winced. "He charged first, sir. It was self-defense. He tried to kill me. I rolled out of the way, and he slammed into the stove."

Patton grunted then looked at Irvin still standing in the doorway.

"Irvin, you're now the galley hand to this man. And keep an eye on him."

Irvin shot Alec a nasty glare before he disappeared out of the galley behind the first mate.

A trial commenced the next day. Alec recounted the events that took place in the galley, including the problem with the rotten meat. As the details came out, the sailors awarded Alec grudging approval. Frye did nothing to defend himself and only glared at Alec. The cook was found guilty and sentenced to confinement in the brig the rest of the voyage.

Alec settled into a routine of cooking and making dishes that pleased the men. As he taught Irvin everything his athair had taught him, the lad's wary distance thawed and disappeared with the steam rising from the black pots on the old camboose.

At the end of each shift, the two would saunter to the top deck and catch the breeze. The two Scots whiled away the evening hours talking about their home and all they'd left behind. Alec never tired of staring at the never-ending expanse.

"Have ye ever seen so many stars?" Irvin spotted a shooting star and pointed out the good luck sign to Alec.

"They make me feel so small, powerless."

"Nay, Alec. The heavens are yer friend. Stars tell you how to get where ye go. The moon? She whispers the weather to ye. The wind? He's yer enemy."

Irvin raised his arm and pointed out the constellations one by one.

The scent of pipe smoke filled the air as Mr. Patton strolled toward them.

Alec jumped up. "Beg pardon, sir. Irvin was teaching me to navigate. I'll scurry back to the galley." Alec turned on his heel and moved toward the hatch.

"Warnock."

Alec stopped, pivoted, and faced the first mate. "Beg pardon, sir. I didn't mean—"

"Warnock, as an idler you don't have a watch. You may proceed."

"Sir? I don't idle away my days. I work hard for my passage."

"Stand down, sailor. An idler is a crew member without a watch, like a ship's surgeon or cook. Aren't you the cook?"

Alec swallowed hard. "Aye, sir."

Mr. Patton chuckled, shook his head, and offered a plea to the heavens. "St. Nicholas, give me patience, or I shall surely hurl this man overboard into the sea. That is if a storm doesn't do it first."

"Mr. Patton," Irvin caught the mate's attention. "The moon. There's a ring."

Alec turned and saw what Irvin was pointing at. A large ring encircled the moon in the cloudless night.

"That's nothing to worry about. I've seen many a ring without a storm. Should a storm come, there's nothing to fear. *The Monarch*. She's seaworthy."

"But, sir, 'tis both Friday and a ring around the moon."

"This is your first voyage, Irvin. You've a lot to learn." Mr. Patton sauntered toward the forecastle, swaying with the motion of the ship, the embers from his pipe glowing in the dark.

Alec looked back at Irvin who was shaking his head.

"Bad sign," the lad said. "Bad sign."

The nerves tightened around Alec's shoulders. He'd come to trust the wee lad and his senses. But the mate was right. This was Irvin's first voyage—his, too. If Mr. Patton wasn't worried, Alec shouldn't be either. Still, something didn't sit right as he made his way below.

Alec fell out of his berth. He'd only been asleep four hours. Crates slid across the floor. Trunks banged into the walls. Personal effects tumbled, rolled, bounced. The passengers moaned and braced their hands on berths or the sides of the ship to maintain balance. Alec strapped his blade to his side and staggered out of steerage. Urgent, clanging bells competed with the howl of a gale.

He headed to the galley. The men might want coffee or tea between storm watches. A log rolled on the kitchen floor. He picked it up and opened the stove, ready to pitch it into the, cold belly of the camboose. Where was Irvin? It was his watch to light the fire that day.

"All hands. All hands." The call echoed down the dark passage and into the room. The bells continued, faster than before.

Alec rushed to the main hatch. Last night Mr. Patton had called him an idler, part of the crew. If the crew needed help, he'd be there. Water sloshed through the opening. Alec gripped the slick stairs with his hands and pulled himself up. Wind pushed against him. Ducking his head and pushing his shoulders forward, Alec made his way upwards.

He poked his head out of the hatch into the very jaws of death. Mountainous waves surged and receded and surged again. Watery fingers clutched at the men, the sales, the rails. Fear and bile crawled up his stomach and to his throat. Alec swallowed both down and straggled toward the crew.

"Get out of here," Patton shouted.

"I'm here with the crew."

"You're not a sailor. Get below deck before they batten down the hatches." The mate hurried to the main mast, shoving Alec aside.

Alec stumbled and slid across the wet boards. Air whooshed out of his lungs. Before he could catch his breath, a wave crashed on deck and hurled Alec to the starboard rail with a painful thud. Patton was right. Alec didn't belong with the crew. He had to get below deck.

Alec fought against the driving rain, clenching his teeth and forcing his body to move through the formidable tempest. Water crashed over the starboard. The ship lurched to the other side. Alec slid, rammed into a jolly boat, and slumped on the deck. Hot pain seared through his back. He had to get up. He had to move. Now. Before it was too late.

"Batten down the hatches." Patton raced past Alec without a glance and hollered the orders again. The wind mourned and howled and swallowed the orders. The mate repeated them again and again. Men rushed past Alec toward the hatch, their faces hard as steel.

A surge flung the men forward to the hatch. Cries of help whipped around with the wind. A sailor yanked on a canvas to force it over the opening. Wind tore it free. More men joined him. Each man clutched one hand on the opening and dragged the canvas against its will with the other. Brute force of six men secured the tarp. Alec watched in horror as they anchored the wooden coverings on top leaving him on the wrong side.

The Monarch tilted again. Angry foam clutched Alec with a wet death grip and propelled him to the edge. He grabbed the rail and clung while his legs flew into the air.

The Monarch righted itself. Alec's legs slammed back against the deck. Pain tore through his thigh where he landed. He had to get to the other hatch. Letting go of the rail, he limped forward, head bowed against the driving rain. Too late. He couldn't go down.

"Heave to! All hands aloft! All hands aloft!"

Alec clung to the edge of the hatch with both hands and tried to stand against the force of the driving rain. Men grabbed the shrouds and pulled themselves onto the ratlines. Alec peered upward through the driving rain. Sails, already shortened and reefed for the storm, ripped and tore. They beat backward and forward with every gust. Terror bubbled through Alec. What more could they do?

In horror, he watched the men climb and furl the sails. Alec squeezed his eyes and prayed to the sailors' patron saint. "St. Nicholas, keep us from the watery grave." He opened his eyes and spied Irvin at the base of the main mast.

"Irvin! Help furl them sails afore we capsize!" the first mate shouted. His palm connected with the lad's back and pushed him forward.

"But I'll die up there."

"If you don't get up there, you'll die here and now."

With shaky hands, Irvin climbed. His foot slipped off the soaked rope. He dangled and swung.

Alec held his breath and stared.

Irvin's foot found the cross rope. He moved upward again. The mighty ocean flung the ship sideways and slammed Alec against the hatch while his young friend forced step after step in his fight with the watery beast. Irvin reached the foreyard and shimmied onto the beam next to a gangly old sailor. Handful after handful, they gathered and cinched the canvas upward. The large sails were almost bound against the yard.

A small sail next to Irvin ripped free of the mast. Within seconds, the heavy canvas was shredded and thrashed with each wind gust. The ship plummeted to the side. The sailor next to Irvin tumbled backwards. He fell into the ratlines and was caught fast. *The Monarch* lurched again, and the tattered canvas wrapped around Irvin's legs.

The wind whipped him off the wooden beam. With a fierce hold, the sails' tentacles yanked the boy's legs and flung him upside down. Irvin dangled and swayed. Wind howled and laughed as the cruel master yanked the lad away, then wrenched him back. The old sailor next to him struggled to free himself, leaving Irvin alone.

"No!" Alec's cry was lost in the tempest. Frantic, he searched side to side. Someone had to help. A man rushed past him. Alec grabbed the man's shoulder. Patton shook him off. "Warnock, what are you doing here?"

"Sir! Irvin needs help." Alec gestured wildly to the mast above.

The mate looked up in the driving rain. The mast swayed. A loud crack filled the air, and the mast tilted to the side. The ship keeled far to the starboard side. Water poured onto the deck, and an angry gust threw Alec into the mate. The old sailor shoved him off and charged toward the front of the ship.

"The wheel!" Mr. Patton hollered at a scrawny sailor, the only one in sight. "Get to the wheel. Help him. Lash your hands to it if needs be. We have to keep this ship aright." He led the way to the wheel. The bony seaman followed.

Alone, Alec peered through the blinding rage. Irvin dangled in the storm's brutal fist. He couldn't let the lad die. Not on his watch.

He grabbed the knife, slipped the sheath between his teeth, and charged for the rigging. The ship pitched him forward, and Alec slammed into the ropes and entangled an arm in two of the ratlines. He tugged and jerked, but the arm wouldn't pull free. In a swift motion, Alec yanked his dagger out of the sheath with his other hand and sliced through the rope as easily as he sliced through hot butter.

The wind whipped and hammered. A large wave dowsed Alec, and he gasped for air. The sheath tumbled out of his mouth and blew into the foamy depths below. With the sheath gone, Alec shoved the cold steel between his teeth, pulled himself past the severed lines, and climbed.

Half of the sail was free and billowed toward the sea, tugging on the mast. Another crack pierced the air above the cacophony. Seconds later, the large canvas slammed against the mast. Alec's legs shook. His fingers tightened around the rope. Not daring to remove his hands from the shrouds, he slid them inch by inch up the sides and moved his feet up the unstable ladder.

Irvin struggled as the ropes sagged. Alec reached the foreyard where the lad dangled. He grunted and wrapped one arm around the shroud. A piercing wind flung the boy toward the mast. Alec grabbed at the tattered canvas. The storm forced the shredded fabric out of his hands and flung the boy outward again. The wind carried Irvin's cries to Alec. A wild swing flung Irvin back to the mast. Alec grabbed and missed. He panted, his shoulders heaving up and down, and watched, helpless, as the boy spun and twirled. He couldn't let this happen.

Alec wrapped an arm and leg around the slick horizontal yard. The weight of his body spun him around, pulling his back downward. With a groan, he pulled himself on top and clenched his stomach muscles for balance. He stretched forward and grabbed the strand of fabric when it swung back. Digging his left fingers in the folds, he heaved it toward the mast and freed the knife from the clench of his teeth with his free hand.

"Irvin!" Alec shouted against the roar.

The lad looked at Alec, his face contorted in fear. "Help me!"

The desperate sound shook Alec to the core. "Irvin. Look at me. Grab the shrouds with yer hands. Hang tight. I'm cutting the sails from the mast afore the storm carries ye away."

Irvin nodded with wide eyes, focused on Alec. Trembling hands clutched the lines. The mast swayed with another gust. Irvin's hands slipped and regained their grip. White knuckles showed as he stared at his hands with gritted teeth.

Alec slashed the canvas. Instantly, Irvin's legs and body tumbled and collided with the shrouds, bouncing outward and back again. Alec shoved the blade back in his mouth, swung his arm, and caught the boy's legs. Irvin wrapped his arms and legs around the shrouds. He clung to the rigging and panted while his feet scrambled onto ratlines. Wind whisked the shredded sail into the angry storm.

The Monarch continued her dance with death. Together, Alec and Irvin furled the sail. The old sailor broke free from the ratlines and helped. Bit by bit, the rest of the sails were furled tight. Free from the billowing drag of canvas, the ship stabilized. Alec and Irvin worked their way back down the ratlines to the deck with the rest of the men.

Feet on the deck once again, Alec collapsed, his legs unable to keep him upright. His heart pounded in his ears, louder than the gale still whipping around the deck. After several gulps of breath, Alec lifted his head. Irvin sat next to him. They smiled at each other.

Alec let out a belly laugh, releasing tension like a pot of stew boiling over. He pulled the lad—no, the man—into his arms. He shook his head and remembered the backflip he'd done on the ropes before his brother left him. William would never believe it. Far from getting him caught, Alec's acrobatic antics had saved a life. He gripped his knife and cast his sharp eyes around to see what was next.

The crew assembled for further instructions. Alec went with Irvin and took his place among them. Mr. Patton barked out assignments, first to one sailor and then another. His eyes locked onto Alec's. He paused, nodded, and continued issuing orders that included Alec.

Just a stowaway baker hoping to escape the past. Alec never felt so alive.

Two watches later, bright sky opened in the west. The waters calmed, and the crew opened the hatches. Alec made his way to the galley and fired up the old camboose for coffee and tea for the men.

In the days that followed, the crew repaired what sails they could, and *The Monarch* limped toward the New York Harbor. Seven weeks after she sailed from Liverpool, the call came from the crow's nest.

"Land ho!"

Alec drank the last of his tea, collected his bundle, patted the black camboose, and walked out of the galley without a backward glance. He climbed the hatch and looked at the bustle of the harbor. Men loaded cargo onto carts. Horses and donkeys clopped on the boardwalk as they pulled creaking wagons. Sailors called. Dock workers hollered back. Gulls screeched up and down the wharf. Sounds that had held him captive seven weeks earlier he now greeted with an eager step.

His new home. Land of opportunity. With his trusty blade, still sharp, and his wits, sharper than before, Alec knew he could be whatever he wanted. He could open his own bakery with no one telling him what to do. The Craigs were gone, gone from this land, gone from his mind.

"Mr. Warnock?"

Alec turned to face the first mate.

"You worked hard. Here are your wages." Mr. Patten pushed a small bag toward Alec.

"Wages?" Alec shook his head. "I worked for my passage."

"That you did. But you also worked as a member of the crew. I'm a fair man, Mr. Warnock. You earned every penny." He grabbed Alec's hand and dropped the bag into his palm.

"I thank ye, Mr. Patton. With this I have more than my wits to use for a new life."

"Sure you don't want to sign on? You took to sea life like I've never seen any man afore. We can always use a good man like you."

Alec looked toward the harbor and back to the mate. Alec surprised even himself on the ship. Truth be told, he liked cooking for the men. He was proud of saving Irvin. But the sea still held men with rank giving orders to others, and he could never be truly free as a sailor.

"I thank ye kindly for your offer. But I fled from Scotland as a wanted man. I was a fugitive on your ship. Even under your command, I was still a bound man. I want to be free."

"Landlubbers. You're all the same." Mr. Patton stuck out his hand, and his grizzled face smiled wide. "If you change your mind, let me know. *The Monarch* will be in port for three weeks."

Alec reached his hand out and shook hands with the mate. He saluted and turned. Alec sauntered off the gangplank, free for the first time in his life with his blade sharp and his eyes even sharper.

Ghost of the Pirate Queen
L.M. Ontiveros

Grace O'Malley had just thrown more turf on the fire, when her father Brian tumbled through the door of the inn and collapsed.

"Da!" Grace ran and dropped to her knees beside him.

Her Uncle Colin appeared behind his brother, breathing heavily. "Old fool'd finished diggin' the grave by the time I got out there."

Together, they lifted Brian to his feet and helped him over to the hearth. They laid him on a straw pallet, then Colin sank to the floor beside him. Grace wet two rags, and after handing Colin one for himself, gently wiped filth and sweat from her father's face.

Brian weakly waved his daughter away. "Stop fussin' over me, girl. You work too hard as it is."

"But haven't I labored here in our family's inn since I was a wean and never complained?"

His eyes filled with sorrow. "We're descendants of the great chieftains, you know, Gracie love. Your ninth great-grandmam, Grania O'Malley, the Pirate Queen, was the greatest of them all. Convinced the queen of England herself to release her sons, who'd been thrown in jail by the evil Sir Richard Bingham."

"Aye, you've told me the story many times." Grace smiled warmly at her father. "She vowed on her deathbed to come back someday and take her revenge on the English."

"Those bloody devils stole our high station from us long ago. 'Tis why we must work our fingers to the bone just to survive." He gently laid a rough hand on her cheek. "Saltwater runs through your veins, as it did hers. When I gaze into those blue eyes of yours, I see the ocean."

"Hush. Lay still, Da," Grace soothed. "Save your strength so you can say a few words when we lay Michael to rest."

His hand dropped to the pallet. "Faith, I've grown so weary of buryin' our friends. Poor old Michael Murphy today, and Heaven only knows who the Banshee'll keen for next." The weariness creasing her father's gaunt face twisted Grace's stomach into knots. They were all growing weaker by the day.

The O'Malleys had been rationing their own food for several weeks now, sharing what little they had with the poor tenant farmers of Kilgeever Parish. After their potato crops failed, the skinny, hollow-eyed beggars, homeless after being evicted by their landlords, had begun showing up at the inn. Her parents took them in and were now doing everything they could to keep them alive, but many still grew weak and died.

Just then, Grace's mother Mary returned from searching the thicket of yew trees beyond the inn for food and dropped her empty basket at the door. "*Arrah*, Brian! What's happened, then?" She ran and knelt by her husband.

"He's after diggin' up Michael's grave by himself," Colin grumbled. "Stubborn eejit."

Brian rose up on the pallet and shook his fist. "Listen, brother, I may be weak, but I can still show you the back of my hand." He lay back down with a groan. "When I've recovered a bit, though."

Mary gave Grace a weak smile, and took the rag from her hand. "I'll take care of this now, *a ghrá*. I see you've put the kettle on. Be a darlin' and bring some tea around to the others."

Their tiny inn was tucked away at the base of Croagh Patrick, the mountain of the saint. Its four guest bedrooms had once been a welcome refuge for travelers on their way to Westport, or for pilgrims of the mountain, devout folk who climbed to the summit yearly to pay their respects to Saint Patrick.

Now, no one came to scale the mountain, and the desperate travelers seeking work in Westport had no extra money for lodging. Instead, the guest rooms were crowded with starving Irish families. Some slept on pallets, others on whatever blankets Grace's parents had been able to gather, but most of them lay on the bare floor.

Grace stepped carefully around their guests now, handing out mugs of tea. It was barely more than hot water, they'd had to steep the leaves so many times over. But it was received with heartfelt gratitude, as weak voices murmured, *"Thank you, child,"* and *"God bless this house."*

If nothing changes, these, too, will join poor old Michael Murphy, Grace thought. *Who will bury the dead when Da and Uncle Colin are too weak from hunger to heft a shovel?*

That afternoon, Michael Murphy was buried among those who'd gone before. Rough wooden crosses marked their graves in the makeshift cemetery behind the inn. Brian said a few words in place of Father Flanders, who'd died of cholera the week before.

Afterward, Grace and Mary baked one small oat cake apiece for their guests. Grace gasped when she went to fetch the oats. Tears sprang to her eyes. There was naught but a few meals' worth of it left in the larder, perhaps enough for a fortnight if they used it sparingly. She trembled at the thought of their food running out. They were all so hungry already.

Wiping her tears away with her sleeve, she straightened her back and held her head high. She'd be serving their guests with a smile tonight, as she always had.

Later that night, under the orange and pink light of the evening's sunset, Grace sat on a patch of grass behind the inn, gazing at the fresh graves. She stroked her long, flaxen braid, a habit she'd pick up as a girleen, in whose wild imagination lurked evil fairies, witches, and púcas.

Most fearsome of all were the Merrow. Fishermen visiting the inn told tales of those man-eating mermaids after consuming too much of her da's home-brewed poteen. Grace had been both enchanted by the descriptions of their beauty, and terrified by stories of whole crews of sailors lured to their deaths by the wicked creatures. In her youth, the feel of her braid's soft, knobby weavings brought her comfort and calmed her fears.

Tonight, though, hopelessness settled over her heart, like mist on the peat bogs. She wondered what a girl of eighteen could do to help her family and the people of Kilgeever Parish, as she lay down on the grass and closed her eyes.

A powerful voice said, "As I see it, you can either curl up in despair, or get up and do something about it."

Grace bolted upright, her heart pumping wildly. She looked around, but saw no one. Shaking her head, she lay back down. *My empty belly must be affecting my mind.*

"You heard me all right, Grace O'Malley. Your great-grandmother, the Pirate Queen, stands before you."

Grace sat up again. Floating in the air above her was the ethereal form of a woman. Trembling, she covered her face.

"Worry not, *a ghrá*," the ghost said more gently. "I'm just a spirit and can do you no harm."

Swallowing hard, Grace uncovered her eyes. The woman, with waves of dark red hair flowing out from under a wide-brimmed, ostrich-plumed hat, smiled down on her. Leather lacings crisscrossed over the bodice of her plain green dress, and hanging from her brown belt was a gleaming brass cutlass on one side, and a silver dueling pistol on the other. The hem of her gown was torn off to just above the knee, and black leather boots covered her legs. Her face mirrored Grace's–blue eyes the color of the sea, high cheekbones slightly ruddy from the harsh Irish weather, and the straight, noble nose of ancient royalty. With the exception of hair color, they could have been twins.

"Are y-you really–" Grace cut herself off, rubbing her eyes with her fists as if that could erase the terrible sight before her.

"Aye, child, your great gramma, Grania O'Malley. 'Grace,' if you like, though I prefer the Gaelic. Sure we've no time for polite introductions, though. As we speak, your British overlords are shipping off Irish grain to feed England. They've stolen our land, our dignity, and now they threaten to take away your very lives. The devil take 'em!" She sneered with disdain and spat. "Filthy pigs!"

"I-I'm afraid 'tis true." Grace said, her voice still quavering. "And most of the Irish simply don't have the strength to fight back anymore."

"'Tis more the pity, indeed." The ghost shook her head. "'Tis why I've come to you. To teach you the old ways of dealin' with those English bilge rats."

Grace calmed her fears, and eyed her great-grandmother with curiosity. "Well, just what did you have in mind, then?"

A smile spread across the specter's face. "Why, piracy, of course."

"Piracy?" Grace exclaimed. "I'm a Christian woman! Besides, we don't even own a boat."

"Ship, child," Grania corrected, then she sighed. "And don't be turnin' your nose up at my chosen profession. 'Twas how I kept the O'Malley clan thriving in my day. Faith, hasn't it broken my heart to watch my descendants slowly lose their relationship with the sea over the centuries? I once commanded a fleet of the finest ships in Ireland, but those grand vessels lie at the bottom of Clew Bay, long forgotten. You've all grown dependent on the land now, and the people perish because of it. Potatoes, bah! What kind of foolish nation relies almost entirely on one bland tuber for their survival?"

Her great-grandmother's words were true. The O'Malleys had once been masters of the sea—fishermen, tradesmen…and pirates. Now, though they lived only a stone's throw from the great waters, the O'Malley descendants might just as well fly as sail a ship.

Grace had tried her entire life to be a peace-loving soul, as the Holy Scriptures taught, and piracy went against everything she stood for, but desperate times called for desperate measures. "And how do you propose we become pirates, then, with no ship and no knowledge of sailing?" Grace asked. "And what bounty would you have us plunder? Silver and gold will do us little good. As you said, anything that might fill Irish bellies is shipped off to England. Gold can't purchase what can't be found."

"We won't be pillagin' gold or silver."

Grace blinked. "I don't understand."

"We'll be pillagin' food! Tomorrow, a merchant ship, loaded to the hilt with Irish goods, sails from Westport. You'll be aboard that ship, Gracie girl, and once put out to sea, we'll take control of it, bring it back to Irish shores, and feed Kilgeever Parish." She rubbed her hands together. "We'll show those English snakes there's still fight left in the Irish!"

"That's daft!" Grace exclaimed. The ghost's eyes flared red with anger. "I-I'm sorry. I only mean…well, I'm only eighteen, and a wee thing at that. Even Mam's taller than I am." She dropped her gaze to the ground. "My parents would have been better off if they'd been blessed with a strappin' son instead of a scrawny daughter."

The Pirate Queen smiled warmly at Grace. "Ah now, love, you're stronger than you know. And a true blessing to your poor old parents, who were childless until it was almost too late. How glad they were to have their baby girl, and happy they are still."

"Aye, maybe they don't think upon a son, but Da and Uncle Colin are old men now. Who'll take care of the inn when they're gone? Surely not me."

"Whyever not? Women can do many hard things, you know." Grania held her head high. "I was chieftess of my clan, and a pirate of the seas."

"But you're...you."

"And you're my great-granddaughter. My blood flows through your veins, child."

The sky had grown dark over the course of their conversation, and Grace heard her mother's voice in the distance, calling for her to come inside.

"Go to your mother now, *a ghrá*. Once your parents are abed, pack a bag and meet me back here."

After listing off the items Grace would need to bring, the spirit shimmered out of sight, and Grace was once again alone.

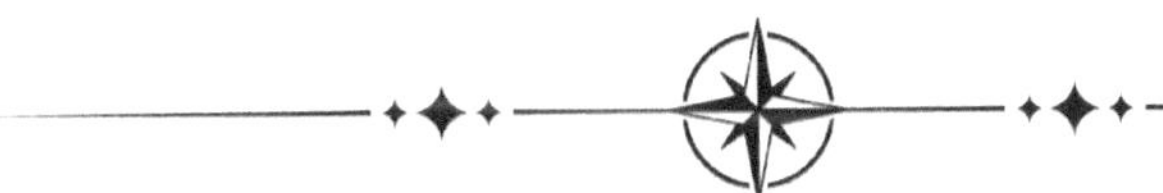

Grace stood by the wagon and waited for the ghost to show herself once more.

The minutes ticked by. Had she imagined the encounter after all? Eventually, she scoffed, turned the donkey around, then headed for the stable.

"And just where d'ya think your goin', granddaughter?"

"Go away," Grace said into the dark night. "You're just the hunger giving me nightmares."

"I'm real as you are, Grace." Grania appeared before her.

Grace groaned. "Faith, I hoped I'd imagined you. Then I could go back inside and go to sleep."

"Afraid not, love. We've work to do."

"I feared you'd say that." Grace climbed up in the wagon and flicked the reins.

"Did you leave a note?" the Pirate Queen asked.

"I wrote I was going to find food in Westport." It was close to the truth. "'Twon't keep them from worryin' though."

"'Twill have to do."

They rode along in silence for a while, then Grace said, "Mind you, I'll not be party to murder."

"What?"

"I know your reputation, Gramma. 'The terror of the high seas.' I'll only do this if you promise me you won't use that cutlass of yours. Or the pistol." She pulled up on the reins and turned to face Grania. "This isn't negotiable. We won't be murderin' anyone, and if that's what you're expectin', I'll just turn this cart around."

"'Tis true I killed many an Englishman in my day, all deserving of it, too. If only I could've brought down that vile bilge rat, Sir Richard Bingham. Would've truly enjoyed runnin' that one through."

"He died centuries ago, Gramma." Grace leveled her with a stare. "Promise me."

"These weapons I wear are just shadows of those I used to carry. I can't kill anyone." Grania sighed. "But this isn't a game, love. You'll be at sea with men that'd just as soon shoot you as look at you. You may need to defend yourself."

Grace flicked the reins again. "I won't let it come to that, then."

"We'll see."

As they drew closer to Westport, a thrill shivered through Grace. Her apprehension and fear were pushed aside by…what? Excitement? Anticipation? In a few hours, she'd be sailing the ocean!

Perhaps piracy still flowed through her veins after all.

They reached Westport Quay, and Grace parked the wagon.

"We must work quickly," the Pirate Queen said. "Hop down, and bring your bag with you.

Grace grabbed her mother's old carpet bag and climbed down from the wagon.

"Change out of your dress quickly, and put on young Aidan's shirt and breeches."

Grace hid behind the wagon and undressed, wondering if it was disrespectful to wear the clothes of a dead boy. Aidan Flanders, just fourteen years old, was the first to perish at the inn.

Grace wasn't particularly buxom, but she wrapped her chest tightly in strips torn from an old sheet, just to be sure, then put on Aidan's shirt.

She pulled her mother's sewing scissors from the bag, and held them uncertainly. "Is there no other way?"

"Is the story told of when I, being just a girleen, asked my father, Owen, if I might go with him on his ship?"

"All of Ireland knows that tale. He told you no, that your long locks would get tangled in the ship's rigging. To show him you meant to have your way, you cut your hair and told him he'd no excuse to leave you home."

"Believe it or not, 'twas just as much of a sacrifice for me as it is for you. I was burdened with the nickname Bald Grace for years after. But that first expedition was the beginning of my reign as queen of the sea. When Owen was killed, I was prepared to take his place."

Tears stung Grace's eyes. Losing her braid, her source of comfort from the time she was a wee girl, seemed almost as tragic as losing a limb. Grania gave her a soft smile. "'Twill grow back faster than you can imagine, *a ghrá*. One day you'll have your long locks again, I promise."

With determination, Grace swallowed her tears, and grabbed hold of her hair. Cutting through the thick plait was slow work, and by the time it came loose from the rest of her hair, her fingers ached. She coiled up the braid and put it in the carpetbag. *Perhaps someday, if I survive, I'll tell this tale to my grandchildren. And won't they be surprised when I show them the very braid I cut from my head?*

The Pirate Queen grinned. "Now your parents have the son you wished upon them!"

Grace shook her head. "What shall we do next, then?"

"Stay here. I must go search the ship for a suitable place for you to hide." With that, Grania disappeared.

"Well, good bye to you too," Grace muttered, rolling her eyes. The docks were nearby, and she grew curious to see the ship that would take her to sea. She crept away until she was in sight of it, and gaped. What a grand vessel! Three masts towered along the length of it. What a fearsome sight it must be once the sails were unfurled. On the side, in gold letters, was printed the words *Fair Maiden*.

"*Fair Maiden*," she whispered to herself. "What a lovely name for a ship."

The gangplank was down, and dockworkers carted crates and barrels up the length of it, disappearing into the ship once they reached the top. A tall man wearing a blue tailcoat, gray trousers and a black peaked cap marched down the gangplank, a sack thrown over one shoulder. He waved to the dockworkers and saluted the guards at the bottom, then headed toward the city.

Emaciated children, just skin and bones really, crept out of the shadows and staggered toward him. He reached into the sack, pulling out loaf after loaf of bread and handing it to each child. He walked to the side of the path, giving out more to those who must have been too weak or too afraid to venture out from the brambles.

Grace blinked hard. The last time she'd been to Westport with her father, she'd seen droves of English soldiers and sailors pass by beggars as if they were invisible. Children who'd approached too closely were kicked out of the way like garbage, but this man treated them kindly. He moved from person to person, speaking to them in hushed tones. Then he nodded farewell and marched on toward the city.

Grace shook her head. An Englishman with a heart? Surely her eyes had tricked her!

"Why did you not stay by the wagon, *a ghrá*?" Grace jumped at the sound of Grania's voice.

"Forgive me, Gramma. I grew curious. Did you see that man?"

"What man? We've no time for games, love. We must get you aboard that ship. Naught but a skeleton crew remains on board. The rest are spending their last night in town at the pubs. When the dockworkers are finished loadin' her, I'll make some noise in the bushes to distract the guards, then you'll sneak aboard while they're distracted."

They walked back to the wagon. "We can't just leave this here," Grace said. "'Twill be stolen for sure, and the donkey will need tendin'."

Grania whispered something in the donkey's ear, and gave it a slap on the rump. It took off with the wagon. "Funny thing about animals and ghosts. Seems once a soul's out of its corporeal body, the barrier between animal and human is gone, and we can communicate."

Grace shook her head. "Given the fact I'm talking to a ghost, nothing should surprise me anymore."

"We can't have her returnin' to the inn pullin' an empty cart, though—your parents will panic for sure. I've sent her to a hermit that lives upon the mountain. He'll take good care of her until we return. Now, let's get you aboard the *Fair Maiden*."

After half a day's journey out to sea, Grace climbed out of the jollyboat in which she'd been hiding, and staggered onto the deck. The rise and fall of the ship sent waves of nausea through her body, and she swallowed back the bile that rose in her throat. Sailors swarmed the deck, all busily working in some capacity. The sails she'd imagined before were fully unfurled now, billowing in the wind. They were just as impressive as she'd thought they'd be.

"Boy!" someone shouted. A pair of meaty hands grabbed her by the scruff of her collar.

"What're you doing here?" a sailor asked in a gruff voice.

Grace stared at him with wide eyes. He was massive, as round as he was tall. His shirt buttons gapped along his broad chest and protruding belly, and a pair of light green eyes glared at her from a round, ginger-whiskered face.

"So you refuse to talk, do you? Well, let's see what the captain has to say about this." He clamped one large hand around her arm and dragged her across the deck a few feet. They hadn't gotten far when an older man approached them.

"What have we here, Mr. Wilson?" The man narrowed one dark eye at Grace, the other being covered by a shiny black patch. He wore a dark cocked hat, with silver strands of hair peeking out beneath it, black tailcoat and white trousers. His hand rested on the silver handle of a walking stick. On his leathery face, creased with deep lines, there was a look of deep disdain.

The sailor let go of Grace, dropping her to the deck, and saluted the other man. "Stowaway, Mr. Partridge," he shouted.

The man nudged her thin frame with his cane. "I thought as much. Where were you taking him?"

"To the captain, sir!"

The older man's lip curled as he peered down at Grace. "That won't be necessary, Mr. Wilson. As first mate, I'm more than capable of handling matters such as this."

Grace rolled onto her knees and begged in a trembling, high-pitched voice, "Please, sir." She remembered she was meant to be a lad, coughed, and lowered her pitch. "I've no family and no home. Sure I'm a hard worker and wish for a job aboard this fine vessel."

"He appears to be Irish, sir," the sailor yelled. "Says he's an orphan."

"Irish? Gah!" Mr. Partridge sniffed, then pulled a handkerchief from his pocket, lifting it to cover his nose. "It's bad enough he's Irish, but the little maggot stinks, too."

Grace had no doubt she smelled, for she'd vomited in the jollyboat the moment the ship hit deep waters.

"What do you want me to do with him, sir?"

Mr. Partridge glared down at the trembling Grace, considering his answer. "I'm afraid we've no need for another cabin boy aboard the *Fair Maiden.* We already have a fine *English* lad to do the job." Then he called, "Jack!" A boy not more than twelve, with sandy unkempt hair and light hazel eyes, instantly appeared.

"Yes, sir?" he said breathlessly, in a voice higher than Grace's. When he saw her kneeling on the deck, he shot her a glare that rivaled that of the first mate.

"Do you need this piece of Irish filth to aid you in your work?"

"No, sir!"

The first mate smiled at the boy. "Good lad." Then he turned to Mr. Wilson. "Throw the little imp overboard." Grace's heart leapt into her throat.

"Sir?" The sailor's face contorted in confusion.

"Kindly toss this garbage into the sea. Perhaps Davy Jones needs a cabin boy aboard the Flying Dutchman." He chuckled at his own joke, as Grace's eyes stung with tears and her body shook so hard her teeth chattered. When the sailor still hesitated, Mr. Partridge pulled his pistol from its holster and aimed it at Mr. Wilson's foot. "You heard me–into the sea with him straight away, or you'll be walking with a limp the rest of your days." He stared the man down with a look that could melt iron.

Mr. Wilson slowly pulled Grace to her feet. "I'm sorry, boy," he whispered.

Grace blanched. Suddenly, Grania's plan seemed foolhardy. What had possessed her to listen to a ghost? *Sure I'll be joining Michael Murphy and the others now.* She hung her head. Then, sniffing back her tears, she scowled. *I'll not let them see me cry. They'll be takin' no pleasure in my death.*

"What the blazes is happening here?"

Grace jerked her head up and gasped. It was the man from the night before, the one who fed the poor beggars. No longer in uniform, he wore his white shirt tucked into his blue trousers. His head was bare, his long brown hair tied back with a white ribbon. Dark stubble shadowed his masculine features, and his grey eyes, the color of the sky just before a cloudburst, regarded her with interest. Grace blushed, having never seen such a handsome man. The entire crew, including Mr. Wilson, stopped what they were doing and saluted.

"Captain Hawthorne, sir!" Mr. Wilson said.

Mr. Partridge lifted one hand to his forehead in a lazy salute. "Sir."

"Mr. Partridge," Captain Hawthorne said evenly, looking the first mate in the eyes, "was Mr. Wilson about to throw this lad overboard?"

"Just dealing with a stowaway, sir." He gave the captain an oily smile. "It's nothing with which to concern yourself."

"You'd do well to remember that everything that happens aboard the *Fair Maiden* is my concern, Mr. Partridge."

"Yes, sir." He bowed his head in deference, but the expression on his face belied his obvious contempt for the young captain.

The captain turned his attention to Grace. "Who is your new friend, Mr. Wilson?"

"Stowaway, sir. Found him by the jollyboats. Orphan, by the sound of it."

"An Irish maggot," Mr. Partridge added, and the captain shot him a glare.

Captain Hawthorne's eyes traveled up and down her thin frame, and Grace wrapped her arms around herself. "Quite scrawny, isn't he? How long since you've had anything to eat, young man?"

"Don't rightly know." The captain raised one eyebrow. "Sir," she added.

Captain Hawthorne's gaze lingered on her face a moment longer, then he turned to Mr. Wilson. "Take this lad to the galley and find him some food. He looks as if the first high wind we encounter might blow him right off the ship." He smiled warmly at Grace, and her cheeks burned furiously. "Once you've eaten, report back to young Jack here." He patted the cabin boy on the shoulder. "He'll find some work for you, won't you, Jack?"

Jack dropped his gaze to the deck and glowered. "Yes, sir."

"Good lad." He ruffled Jack's hair, then gave Mr. Wilson a dismissive tip of the head. "That will be all, sailor."

"Yes, sir." He saluted the captain, then led Grace down a set of steps until they were below decks. He let out a long breath. "That was close, ah…what did you say your name was, boy?"

"Thomas," Grace replied. "Thomas Leary." It was the name of a boy who'd been sweet on her in primary school.

Mr. Wilson offered her his hand. Grace eyed it suspiciously, but decided the man meant no harm, and shook it. "Glad to meet you, Thomas." He smiled broadly, then his face grew serious. "Here's a bit of advice for you—stay away from Mr. Partridge. The man's trouble, without a doubt. He hates the captain and cares not to hide it. Wouldn't surprise me at all if he decided to mutiny. You seem to have made an enemy of him, too, I'm afraid. He's a vengeful man, Mr. Partridge is. Probably shoot his own mother in the foot if she crossed him."

Grace shuddered, remembering how he'd looked at her, like she was something he'd just scraped off the bottom of his boot. "Thank you, Mr. Wilson. I'll do my best to avoid him."

He patted her head. "Smart lad—you'll do just fine then."

He escorted Grace to the galley. The dry biscuits, salted fish, cabbage, and hard cheese he gave her seemed a feast after weeks of eating tiny oat cakes and thin porridge. But she knew it was nothing compared to what Grania had told her was in the filled storage rooms: barrels of grain, dried peas and beans, along with firkins of butter, jugs of honey, and cases of salted beef and pickled herring. Topside, she'd seen cages upon cages of chickens and rabbits at one end of the ship, and several milk cows tied up. There was enough food on the ship to feed all of Kilgeever Parish for several months, perhaps even a year if they parsed it out carefully.

Hopefully, it would soon be theirs.

Grace awoke to deafening snores, like the grunts of wild boars, rattling the walls around her. The stench of unwashed men assaulted her senses. Her pulse raced as she struggled to remember where she was—certainly not slumbering comfortably on her soft straw pallet in the inn, to be sure. Her thin frame ached from sleeping in a hard, coffin-like bunk, and the rolling and bobbing of the blackened room made her stomach lurch. She instinctively reached for her braid, but her heart sank like a stone—it wasn't there. Her hands flew to her head to find a shock of short, uneven clumps of hair where her waist-length tresses once were.

Finally, she remembered.

It was the night of her second day at sea. She shivered under her thin blanket, recalling that first day. After she'd eaten and reported to Jack, he'd given her every lowly task he could think of: scraping the rust off chain cables, scrubbing the deck. But unraveling old ropes—'picking oakum' they called it—was the worst job of all. After a few hours of that, her fingers were cracked and bleeding. She rubbed her scabbed fingertips in the dark.

Captain Hawthorne made regular rounds of the ship. Though he smiled and nodded when he passed by her, he didn't stop to talk, much to her disappointment. She wondered if he'd seen how difficult Jack made life for her. Did he even care? Then she scoffed. He'd saved her life–she should be grateful enough for that. *He's also an Englishman,* she reminded herself. *The enemy.*

But there's something different about him, she considered now as she lay in the hard bunk. *He fed the poor, treating them like human beings, and showed compassion for me when Mr. Partridge wanted me drowned.* She chuckled quietly. Wouldn't the Pirate Queen be horrified to know of her admiration for the captain, himself being an Englishman and all?

She ran her fingers over her short hair again, and frowned. Faith, who would want her now, though? Surely not a handsome ship's captain.

One of the sailors stirred. "Water, boy," he growled, flinging an arm Grace's direction. "And be quick with you, if you want to avoid a whipping."

"Yeah, boy." Jack sneered in the bunk below her. "Best hurry along now."

Grace sighed. As a new cabin boy, she was at the beck and call of the sailors, day or night. So far she'd avoided the cat o'nine tails, thank goodness. A whip would not only be painful, it would surely tear through the fabric of her shirt, revealing her secret hidden beneath. She could only imagine what they'd do to her if they found out she was a woman.

She climbed stiffly out of her bunk. In the dark, a hand grabbed her ankle, and she fell forward onto the rough floor. *Jack!* She heard him laugh, and rage burned in her like the bonfires on *Samhain.* She got up and stalked away.

Once she reached the upper deck, she breathed in the fresh sea air with pleasure and made her way to one of the water barrels. She grabbed a tin cup from a hook and filled it with water. Looking around first, she spat in the cup, then chuckled at the thought of the lazy sailor drinking it.

"Ah, our new cabin boy," Captain Hawthorne said. Grace gasped.

Where'd he come from? Had he seen her? She turned around, but kept her eyes down. "How do you find my ship, Thomas? Is it to your liking?"

"'Tis a fine vessel, sir," she replied, her heart racing.

"I'm glad you think so. How is the crew treating you?"

She hesitated. "Just grand, sir."

He chuckled. "That well, eh?"

"'Tis more than I deserve." She dared look into his face. His tanned skin crinkled around his grey eyes, and his smile was genuine.

He set a strong hand on her shoulder, and heat traveled down her arm and up her neck at his touch. "I know Jack's working you like a horse, but believe me, it'll build character. I started out as a lowly cabin boy myself, and look where I am today. Perhaps you'll captain a fine ship like the *Fair Maiden* someday." He took one of her work-worn hands and turned it over in his. "Has you picking oakum, has he?"

"Aye." Much to her dismay, a tear rolled down her cheek as she recalled her mistreatment.

"Don't be angry with poor Jack. I found him in a London slum. His family had died of typhus, and he was trying to make his way on his own. I took pity on him and gave him a job as cabin boy. I imagine he was quite jealous when I took you on as well. He has many rough edges after all those years on the streets, but he'll turn out all right in the end. Inside, he has a good heart."

Grace stared at him, feeling her anger toward the boy begin to fade. His situation wasn't much different than the suffering children of her parish. He'd just been lucky enough to have someone rescue him, was all.

He dropped her hand. "Tell you what, Thomas. Meet me at the helm near the end of the morning watch, say, seven bells, and I'll teach you how to man the wheel." She gazed up into his face. "Would you like that?"

She gave him a small smile. "Aye, sir."

He patted her hand. "Good lad."

He gazed at her a moment longer, then turned and walked away. Grace watched him climb the steps to the forecastle deck and gaze out over the bow. Then she headed down the stairwell to the lower decks.

"Grace." The Pirate Queen appeared, motioning for her to follow. They found an empty storage room and ducked inside. "What were you doing with that Englishman?" Grania hissed. "I didn't like the way you were eyein' each other."

"He's the captain, Gramma. If I'm to be on an English ship, I've no choice but to speak to Englishmen." She leaned in close to the ghost. "As part of the act, don't you know?"

"Ah, I almost forgot you were acting." She winked at Grace.

That makes two of us, Grace thought.

"Quite a convincing performance, darlin'." She smiled approvingly, and Grace felt a stab of guilt. She couldn't let Grania know how much she'd enjoyed the captain's attention. "Speaking of performances, how d'ya like your role as cabin boy?"

"Faith, 'tis not an easy task. I'm workin' my fingers to the bone. Truly." She held out her raw fingers for her great-grandmother to see.

"*Arrah!*" The apparition's eyes burned with fire. "The blaggards have you picking oakum, do they? That task's only fit for murderers and thieves! The Lord as my witness, they'll feel the wrath of the Pirate Queen for this!"

"Aye, we'll take their ship–that'll be punishment enough. Remember our agreement."

"Aye...aye...no killin'. Not that I could, anyway," she groused. Then she smiled mischievously. "Doesn't mean I can't give them a good scare, though. Drive them mad with my fearsome presence. I never promised I wouldn't haunt them."

Grace rolled her eyes. "'Twas implied, I believe."

In truth, though, Grace wouldn't mind letting Grania give Mr. Partridge the fright of his life. Of all those aboard the *Fair Maiden,* he'd treated her the worst by far. Since the first day, when he'd ordered her drowned, he'd belittled, shoved, and struck her with his walking stick every time he passed by her. She'd tried to stay out of his way, as Mr. Wilson suggested, but he seemed to go out of *his* way to find her. If anyone deserved the Pirate Queen's wrath, it was him!

I'm a Christian woman, Grace reminded herself, *and vengeance is only for the Lord.* Shame washed over her.

"We'll take our revenge tonight, *a ghrá,*" the Pirate Queen said, as if she could read Grace's mind. "Just after the start of the middle watch."

Grace's heart leapt into her throat, and panic took its place in her chest. It was too soon! "Tonight?"

"Yes, love. Soon this ship will be ours."

"How is this to be, then, seein' as how we're so vastly outnumbered?"

"You must have faith, granddaughter. I'm centuries old, but I still have a few tricks up my sleeve. Meet me under the mainmast just after the beginning of the middle watch. And bring some wax.

Grace blinked. "Wax?"

"Aye, wax, as in candles."

"We're to take over the ship with wax?" Now Grace wondered if all the years of being a ghost had driven her great-grandmother mad.

"Faith, 'tis naught wrong with my head, girl! 'Twill all make sense tonight. Go now, and do your duties as if it's just another day at sea." She began to fade away. "Middle watch," she repeated before leaving Grace alone.

Grace eyed the forgotten cup of water she still held in her hand, and cringed. With any luck, that sailor was sleeping soundly now, his drink forgotten.

Grace lay awake in her bunk, waiting for eight bells to sound, signaling the start of the middle watch. She hadn't been able to go to sleep, for the excitement and worry of it all. She touched the bruise on her cheek. As luck would have it, she'd found the sailor awake in his bunk after all. Triumph filled her, though, remembering how he'd downed the whole cup–the one she'd spit in–after striking her.

A smile came to her lips at the memory of Captain Hawthorne, standing behind her with his hands on hers as she held onto the ship's wheel. As he instructed her, his breath had warmed the back of her neck, and the heat from his body had set hers aflame. Of course it was all innocent on his part—he was simply teaching a boy to sail, but having him so close nearly drove her mad. Mr. Partridge had stood glaring at the two of them, disapproval painted on his pale face like whitewash on a privy wall. He made no secret of his hatred of the Irish, and seemed especially hostile toward her. *We'll see how he feels about the Irish tonight.*

Finally, the signal for the middle watch sounded. She waited a bit for the watches to change hands, then quietly slipped out of her bunk, tiptoed across the floor and out the door, pulling it carefully shut behind her.

Grace stepped out into the night, where a full moon shone brilliantly in the black sky. She crept along the deck, staying undercover in the shadows of the sails, until she paused under the mainmast. The quarterdeck, where the helm was located, was just a few yards away.

The Pirate Queen suddenly appeared. Her wide eyes glowed brighter than the moonlight, her wild red hair danced around her shoulders like Medusa's snakes, and every inch of her seemed to quiver with anticipation. "Make ready, Grace. Time for these English rats to pay their dues."

The sound of singing drifted over the edge of the ship on the evening breeze. It was lovely, like a choir of angels. Grace closed her eyes and drank in the beauty of it.

She felt a tap on her shoulder. "Open your eyes, *a ghrá*, and witness a miracle." Grace looked and saw dozens of pairs of wide set, sparkling eyes set in strikingly beautiful faces rise above the ship's rail.

"The Merrow," Grace breathed, awestruck. "Sirens of the sea."

She covered her ears, but Grania shook her head. "Their song only enchants men." Grace lowered her hands, and gazed at them in fearful wonder. They climbed over the side of the ship, and instantly their tails and fins became human legs. Their long luxurious hair, in every hue of the rainbow, covered most of their nakedness.

"Aye." Her grandmother's face shone with pride. "I made some friends from beneath the waves in my pirate days, you see." Grace followed Grania up the steps to the raised quarterdeck. They found the helmsman in a deep trance, his hands frozen in place on the ship's wheel.

Grace gazed out along the deck. The sailors who'd been on watch were in the same enchanted state as the helmsman. Hatches opened, and members of the crew slowly climbed out, tossing their weapons in a pile, then shuffling toward the sound of the music.

Grace turned to her grandmother, dropping her hands to her hips and scowling. "Do you not remember your promise to me? Won't the Merrow lure all these men to their deaths?"

"They have a taste for human flesh, 'tis true," Grania replied. Grace shuddered at the sight of the ravenous sirens.

The Pirate Queen went on. "But they've agreed to take most of the crew to live with them in their land under the sea."

Grace gasped. "As their slaves?"

"As their husbands."

"They wish to marry them? How can that be?" Grace's eyebrows creased over her nose. "And what of the rest of the men? Are they to be their dinner?"

"No, child. We'll choose a small number to stay and help us guide the boat back to Ireland. That's what the wax is for." She motioned to her ears. "So they are protected from the Merrow's song." She lowered her voice. "The Merrow men are…how can I put this delicately?" She pursed her lips, considering her words. "Ugly as sin. Hideous creatures, all of them. Which is why Merrow women will sometimes take mortal men for their husbands. They were more than happy to agree to keep this lot alive."

"They prefer humans to their own kind?" Grace couldn't believe her ears.

"Aye. 'Tis a blessed life these men will have—they'll be treated like kings—and it pains me to give it to them. If it were up to me, I'd run them all through, but I must keep my word to you." She shook her head. "Sure I've become soft after three centuries on earth."

"Thank you, Gramma," Grace said. She saw the sailor who'd struck her shuffling slowly across the deck, and thought perhaps the Merrow could have one sailor to dine on. Rules were sometimes meant to be broken, after all. *No, you'd never be able to forgive yourself, Grace.*

She peered back out over the main deck of the *Fair Maiden*, gasping when a few sailors took hold of the sirens' hands and were pulled over the side of the ship. "Are you certain they'll be all right, then?"

"We have the word of the Merrow."

Grace thought to argue that taking the word of a man-eating race of sirens might be a bit naive, when she spied Captain Hawthorne slowly crossing the deck. Without another thought, she ran down the steps and stopped in front of him, barring his way. His gray eyes were milky, like a foggy window, and Grace realized with despair he couldn't see her. His long hair fell loose over his shoulders. Grace touched the brown locks, then rested her hand on his cheek. No, the sirens would not have her dear captain, even if, to him, she was but a lowly cabin boy. She slapped his face, but got no response.

Then she remembered the wax in her pocket. She took a piece out, broke it in two, and shoved one piece in each of his ears. After a moment, he blinked, and recognition returned to his eyes.

"Thomas?" He blinked again, then looked around. "My men!"

"I can explain--" Grace's words were cut off by the feel of cold steel at her throat.

Captain Hawthorne glared at the figure behind her. "Partridge, let her go."

Grace's eyes widened at the word 'her.' *Does he know?*

"Her?" The first mate scoffed. "I think you have this Irish maggot confused with someone else. Perhaps one of these lovely sirens? I knew this boy was trouble the moment I laid eyes on him, Captain.

You should have let me toss him in the drink."

Grace struggled against Mr. Partridge's grip, but he only pressed the knife more firmly against her throat. Warm blood trickled down her neck.

"I'll wager you didn't know, boy, that I'm almost completely deaf, though I'm very good at reading lips. An injury sustained in Her Majesty's service, you see, as was the loss of my eye. I used to think I was cursed, but now I see the loss of my hearing was a blessing. Your mermaid whores have no effect on me."

"Let. Her. Go!" Captain Hawthorne repeated.

Mr. Partridge tsked. "I see being under the influence of the sirens has addled your brain, Captain, for you continue to see a woman where I see a maggot. I'm afraid once I've disposed of this filth, it will also be necessary that I take over command of the ship." He chuckled. "That was my intention from the beginning, you know, but now the process has been simplified. When we go back, you'll be raving about sirens taking your men. They'll throw you in the madhouse, while I take over command of the *Fair Maiden*."

"He's a hundred times the captain you could ever be!" Grace cried.

Suddenly, the Ghost of the Pirate Queen appeared behind the captain in terrible splendor, eyes red and flashing, her face contorted like a horrible monster. Partridge screamed in terror, and Grace elbowed him as hard as she could in the ribs, then stomped on his foot. He howled in pain and in fury. Captain Hawthorne grabbed the first mate's pistol from its holster, and clouted him soundly over the head with it. Groaning, he dropped to the deck with a thud.

"St. Patrick be praised," said Grace, her heart thundering. "And St. Brigid, too." *I suppose there really is a time and a place for violence after all.*

Captain Hawthorne ripped off a strip of fabric from the bottom of his shirt, and held it against Grace's bleeding throat. "Are you all right?"

"I-I think so. It's not deep."

All around them, the sailors stood still, shaking their heads in confusion. The sirens had stopped their singing. They peered at the captain, eyes regarding him coolly. Grace shuddered. If they thought he had any notion of denying them their husbands, there was no telling what they might do to him.

Captain Hawthorne pulled the wax plugs from his ears, and folded his arms. "What's the meaning of all this, *Thomas*?" Grace blanched at the way he said the name. *Saints preserve us, he* does *know of my deception!*

"Captain, my people are starving. You walked among them the other night in Westport, so you know what I mean."

"You saw me?"

"Aye, before I boarded your ship."

"I see. And you thought to take over this vessel singlehandedly?"

"I'm not alone, sir," she said quietly.

"Right. You did bring some assistance." He gestured to the Merrow. "How in the world did you form an alliance with them?"

"That was my doin', Captain Hawthorne," The Pirate Queen said, still unseen behind him. He turned around, then gasped and stumbled backward when he saw her. Grace caught him by the arm.

"Ghost," he said, pointing a shaking finger at Grania.

"'Tis nothing to fear, Captain," Grace soothed. "Just the spirit of my dear departed great-grandmother, Grania O'Malley."

Captain Hawthorne stared at the specter in awe. "The Pirate Queen herself," he said reverently. He gave a slight bow. "Your majesty."

Now it was Grace's turn to stare. "You've heard of her, then?"

He smiled, his trembling subsiding. "My mother was Irish but died when I was very young. I was raised by my English father, but he'd loved my mother so much, he made certain I was brought up knowing my Irish history. He hired an Irish nanny to care for me when he went out to sea, and encouraged her to teach me the Irish language, customs, and stories."

"Faith, I don't believe it," Grace said.

The captain chuckled. "Funny, coming from a woman trying to pass herself off as a boy."

Grace lowered her gaze to the ground. How long had he known?

He cocked his head to one side. "Did you really think I was that thick, Thomas…I mean…dash it all, what's your real name?"

"Grace," the Pirate Queen said when her granddaughter couldn't answer.

"Grace," he repeated. "Named after her famous ancestor." Grania nodded her head solemnly. "As I was saying, *Grace*, you may have been able to fool that lot—" he motioned to the stunned sailors all about the deck—"and Partridge." He nudged the unconscious first mate with his foot. "But I knew when I first laid eyes on you that you were a woman."

Grace dropped her hands to her hips. "Then why didn't you say something? And why'd you let Jack make me pick oakum!"

"Aye, I can't abide that, either, though you be half Irish," her great-grandmother agreed.

"I was simply waiting for you to come to me with the truth, Grace," the captain said. "I figured you'd give up and confess after the first hard day, but I was wrong. You're a stronger woman than I thought, as brave and as cunning as the Pirate Queen herself, I see."

"Aye, I like this one," the ghost said. "And I can see you do, too, *a ghrá.*" She winked at Grace, who blushed from the top of her head to her toes. Captain Hawthorne cleared his throat next to her.

"He's a good man, 'tis true," Grace replied. "I greatly admire him…as my captain."

Grania scoffed. "Right, love." Then she turned to the captain. "We seem to be at a bit of an impasse here, Captain." She gestured around them. "We were in the middle of takin' over your ship, but things have gotten…complicated."

The captain scratched his head. "I must say, I was not expecting two mutinies on the same day." He looked around, and shouted, "Is Mr. Wilson on deck?"

"Right here, Captain, sir." The large sailor came trotting over. His hair was disheveled and he was still in his nightshirt, which was a might too short for Grace's liking. She averted her eyes.

"Find a couple able-bodied men to help you carry this blaggard down to the brig immediately." He pointed to Mr. Partridge, still lying unconscious at their feet.

"Right away, sir." Mr. Wilson saluted him, then grabbed the first mate by the ankles and dragged him away.

The captain brushed off his hands. "Now that's taken care of, there's the bigger question of *this* mutiny." He fanned his hand over the ship. The men seemed to be waiting for their captain's orders, or perhaps to see if Grace and her strange ghostly companion were to be their new leaders.

"Captain," said Grace. "With all due respect, we can't let the food aboard this ship go to London when we need it so badly back home. My family's been sharin' what we have with the beggars who come to our door, but we're almost out of food."

"Yes." The captain grew serious. "I'd no idea things were so bad in Ireland until I saw those poor urchins in Westport. All those hungry children!" Grace's heart squeezed when he blinked back tears. "This assignment never sat well with me, but I was at the mercy of my employer."

The sun was just peeking up over the horizon, the moon and stars giving way to the morning light.

"We're nearing London, Captain Hawthorne," the Pirate Queen said. "We'll be turnin' this ship about, with or without your approval. The Merrow will be wantin' their menfolk now, too. We've no more time for talk."

Grace gave him an apologetic look. "I'm sorry. We've buried enough of our friends, and my own family is on the verge of starvation. Could you not find it in your heart to join our cause?"

"I don't seem to have much of a choice."

"There's always a choice, Captain," the Pirate Queen said. "You can join us, or you can join the Merrow."

"Gramma, no!" Grace cried.

"Life in an underwater haven teeming with beautiful sirens? Or help you steal this ship." The captain rubbed his chin. "Those are my choices?"

"Aye." The ghost crossed her arms, waiting for his answer.

Grace's breath caught in her throat.

The captain smiled. "What need have I of enchantresses, your majesty, when I have Grace O'Malley, great-granddaughter of the Pirate Queen, right here beside me? To hell with the shipping company. I'm taking this vessel."

Grace breathed a sigh of relief, and smiled broadly. "I was hopin' you'd stay, Captain Hawthorne."

He wrapped his hand around hers. "My name is William."

"William," she repeated. "A fine, strong name." He kissed her hand, and she felt her legs might give way beneath her.

"We can't return to Westport Quay, though," he said. "Is there another place the *Fair Maiden* can land?"

"I know a hidden cove where you can drop anchor," Grania explained "We'll use the ship's boats to bring the food to shore. From there, we'll cart it to Belclare Castle, the place of my birth and childhood. It stands empty now, but it'll make a grand storehouse and distribution center."

"Well, I guess that's settled, then. Now, what about them?" The captain motioned to the Merrow, who were glaring at him, arms folded across their chests.

"They'll rip your ship apart from bow to stern if they don't get what they want, and dine on you first, then the carcasses of your crew. They'll choose revenge over husbands any day. You've no choice but to let them take your men."

Grace gasped. *What a bloodthirsty race!*

The captain swallowed hard. "I've a few men with families to go home to. Could you ask your friends if they'd kindly let them stay? Plus a small crew to man the rigging and help us sail her back to Ireland."

"We'll need Mr. Wilson," Grace chimed in. "And young Jack."

The Pirate Queen stared at her. "Faith, after the way that young scallawag treated you? Are you certain, granddaughter?"

She smiled at William, recalling Jack's past and how the captain helped him escape London's slums. "I'm certain."

The Pirate Queen rubbed her hands together. "Then, it's settled. Captain Hawthorne, please gather up your crew and the married men and make ready to bring this ship about."

William bowed solemnly. "As you wish." He called out, "Jack!"

Immediately the cabin boy was at his side. "Yes, sir!" He saluted the captain.

"Jack, go find about ten strong men to stay aboard the ship. Make sure to gather the most trustworthy ones."

"You want *me* to gather them, sir?" For once, Jack dropped his tough façade and looked genuinely pleased.

"Are you questioning my orders, son?" William asked, a twinkle in his eye.

Jack blanched. "No, sir! Right away, sir!" He ran off to complete his assignment.

"I'd better go check our heading," William said. "The helmsman still looks pretty dazed." He gave Grace one last lingering gaze, then headed for the helm. Grace blushed furiously.

"So, you greatly admire him as your captain, then. Is that it?" Grania said. "When were you goin' to tell me you'd fallen for an Englishman?"

"Half English," Grace corrected.

"You didn't know that when you fell in love with him, though."

Grace cleared her throat. "Speakin' of fallin' in love, look." The remaining sailors were standing with the sirens, deep in conversation. One by one, the Merrow took them by the hand and together they disappeared into the sea. "They're going with them of their own free will. I must say, I much prefer it this way."

"Aye, 'tis a better fate than many of them deserve. If only this cutlass were real…"

"Gramma." Grace warned.

"Sorry. Maybe not all Englishmen are bad."

"That's better." Grace gazed at her great-grandmother fondly. "Our people will finally have full bellies. How can we ever thank you,

Gramma?"

"I didn't do it alone, Grace darlin'. We did it together." She raised a fist in the air. "The O'Malley's are once again masters of the sea!"

"Well, I wouldn't go that far." Grace laughed. "But I do believe it's high time we returned to our seafarin' roots. Perhaps even a little...piracy? Just think of the people we could feed if we could plunder more English vessels."

Grania leveled her with a stare. "So, my peace-lovin' granddaughter wants to pillage English ships now? For shame!"

Grace shrugged. "I'd still prefer not to kill anyone. But, aye, I suppose a little violence can be justified, given the right cause. After all, the Lord did command the Israelites to invade and take back the lands the wicked Canaanites had stolen, and Jesus turned over the money changers' tables."

The Pirate Queen grinned. "I was just thinkin' what a fine pirate ship this would make. Perhaps you can convince William to let us...borrow it for a while."

"You know, I have a feelin' he'll agree."

"Gramma, show us the braid!"

Grace's ten grandchildren were gathered around her, spellbound by her story. She'd been telling the same tales for two generations now, and the children never seemed to tire of them.

"Be patient. I'm getting to that part." Grace smiled lovingly at each precious little face. "So the Pirate Queen says, 'Grace, love, you must cut off your hair if you're to pass as a cabin boy.' So I take my mother's scissors and...snip! My braid's gone. But it wasn't really gone, you see, because..." She reached into her knitting basket beside her rocking chair. "...here 'tis!" She yanked the plait out quickly. The children—some with flaxen braids, some with Grania's wild red locks, and some with their granddad's brown hair—gasped and clapped their hands.

William, who was building up the fire, grumbled, "We spend years out on the open sea, taking back Irish food from English vessels, fighting storms and cannon fire and dodging the law, and they want to hear about your hair."

Grace snickered. "Now, who wants to hear about the time Grampa sailed the *Fair Maiden* through thirty-foot waves and gale-force winds to board the *Royal George* and recover one hundred and fifty barrels of oats and ninety firkins of butter?"

"Aye!" they shouted in chorus. "Tell us, Grampa!"

William grinned and sat down in his own rocker next to Grace's. "We boarded the *Royal George* in the dead of night, so we might be able to work under cover of darkness—"

"Was Uncle Jack with you?" asked little Mary.

"And Mr. Wilson?" asked her brother Brian.

"Yes, yes, but hush and listen now. Admiral Nottingham was waiting for us, you see…"

Grace patted her husband's shoulder, and got up from her chair. She wandered out back of the inn and sat down in the grass, letting the last of the sun's rays soak into her skin. Croagh Patrick stood like a fortress over Kilgeever Parish, rock-solid and steadfast. It was the end of June, and pilgrims to the mountain would once again arrive to hike to the new chapel, devoted to Ireland's patron saint, on its summit. She and William had built five extra rooms onto the inn after their last ocean voyage. By next week, they'd all be full.

She gazed out over the makeshift cemetery where so many dear ones rested peacefully, her parents and Uncle Colin included. Permanent headstones had been added to many of the graves, replacing the simple wooden crosses they'd so hastily cobbled together long ago. She'd only seen the Pirate Queen a handful of times since their adventure together, and not for many years now. She'd accepted the idea that she might never see her again.

A familiar voice made her smile. *"Grace."*

"Gramma?" The Pirate Queen appeared before her eyes. "I wondered if I'd see you again. What's the occasion?"

"I've missed you, *a ghrá*."

"And I you." Grace thought a moment. "You're not here to take me to Heaven, are you? I'd like to stay a bit longer."

"Oh, no, no, nothing like that."

Grace breathed a sigh of relief, then gasped. "Not William, then!"

"No, dear. You've both a few years left." She hesitated. "I've come to say good bye."

"Good bye?"

"Aye. I've roamed the earth almost four centuries now. I wish to join my husbands—I was widowed three times, you know—and my children, who wait for me in Heaven. 'Tis time I was with them."

"Oh." She'd never told Grace she'd been separated from her family all this time. She must have been more than ready to be with them

again. "I'll always remember you, Gramma."

"And I you, Grace. I'll see you again in a few years, though."

Grace thought she saw a tear roll down the Pirate Queen's cheek, though it was hard to tell through her own misty eyes.

"Thank you, Gramma. For everything."

"No, thank *you*, darlin'. *Grá go deo.*" Grania's spirit transformed into a cloud of dust that sparkled like diamonds, then blew away on the late afternoon breeze.

Grace ran her fingers along her long, gray braid. "*Grá go deo*, Grania O'Malley. Love you forever."

Seaflower

Leah Moyes

Marseille, France 1827

"There is nothing more enticing, disenchanting, and enslaving than the life at sea."
— Joseph Conrad (Polish-British Novelist).

Clutching the weathered oak railing of the *SV Seaflower*—my father's French Maltese ship with impressive masts and stately sails—I inhaled the memorable scents of my childhood, salty sea air, fish, tar, and fire-cured tobacco.

With every intake, a different recollection emerged, nightly revelries beneath a canopy of stars, the rancid scent of salted pork, and my father's smoky wooden pipe. It had been ages since I set foot on board one of his ships, and I savored every single moment.

"Miss Sophia, yer trunk." Shorty dropped my hefty brown chest onto the deck with a thud, and my matching valise tumbled off to the side.

"Careful there, Shorty," I teased and smiled at the man, who spanned nearly as wide as he was tall. "There's precious cargo inside."

Wiping his forehead, he groaned. "What'd yer pack, *little mouse*? Rocks?"

I laughed and wrapped my arms around the dear old man. Shorty's skills in vessel maintenance earned him the title of boatswain for as long as I could remember and, despite his childhood nickname

215

for me, I now stood taller by three inches.

"It's only my books. I couldn't leave them behind."

He wiped his brow a second time and grumbled as he reached for a leather strap on one end and tugged.

"Leave it be." I motioned. "Father hasn't assigned my bunk yet."

"The captain's quarters, Miss Rickaby." A warmth washed over me as a familiar, yet oddly foreign voice rose from behind.

I steeled my posture and circled around to see a man standing in place of a boy I said goodbye to six years ago. My eyes betrayed me as I scanned the length of his torso, from his impressive height, the breadth of his shoulders, and the hint of a shadow on his strong chin. Then, somehow, my eyes fixated on his slightly exposed chest. The precise place his loose-fitting shirtsleeves didn't cover. I held my breath. *Could this be?*

Then he smiled, and the charming dimple that stole my heart so long ago appeared.

Oh.

I swallowed the enormously large lump in my throat.

Freddie Martin.

I pressed one gloved hand to my flushed cheek and the other against my rapidly beating heart.

"Are you well?" The warm timbre of his voice caressed my skin as if I had bathed in the morning sun.

I nodded, still unable to wrap my mind around the healthy physique before me. He was a gangly fifteen-year-old when Father sent me away, having not quite grown into his own. Now, he was… well; I struggled to form words that effectively described this man who stood before me. Flashes of the marble sculptures I'd seen at Versailles came to mind.

"Do you not recognize me?" he whispered as several members of the crew labored around us preparing for our departure from the docks.

I only managed to nod once more, substantiating my inability to find my voice.

"Martin, leave her be!" My father's shouts soared across the deck as he swooped in and took me fully into his arms. The same earthy, musky smell that lulled me to sleep at night in Madame Laurent's *École pour jeunes filles* enveloped me here. I had stolen one of Father's cravats the night before he left me in the school for young misses in Marseille and slept with it under my pillow. The rekindled aroma propelled me to cling lovingly to the lapels of his greatcoat.

"Lud, I missed you," he muttered as he drew back and scanned me from head to toe. "My word, my little girl has grown into quite the lady."

Heat coursed through my cheeks. I could not recall blushing ever being part of my physiology until I went off to finishing school. There, blushing became an art. One that women mechanized into their arsenal used for husband hunting.

Father clasped my gloved hand and raised it up high. Turning me towards his crew, he hollered, "My little Sophia is back!" Thankfully, his men didn't give credence to the superstitious myth of women on board equals bad luck. They boisterously celebrated my return. Many of which knew me from the time I toddled around in leading strings, but as my eyes glazed over the crew, I only truly searched for one.

Freddie Martin.

He stood behind Shorty and Gil, and the moment our eyes collided, I knew, without a doubt, my voyage back to England might be one of the greatest tests of my young life.

Once my father heaved my hefty trunk upon his broad shoulders, I fell in step behind him as we ascended to the quarterdeck and the captain's quarters at the stern.

"Father, the journey to London is less than a week with advantageous weather. I can take my previous cabin. I don't wish to evict you." As the only woman on board, I trusted these men with my life. I never felt unsafe in their company and wasn't about to start now.

"Nonsense." He balanced the load to free one hand for the latch on the door. I promptly swept around him and opened the door in a flash. He placed the trunk at the end of his imposing four-poster bed. "You are a woman now, and it would hardly be proper for you to bunk in the hold."

I knew the maze of corridors below deck no longer held the air of mystery it did in my childhood, but I also didn't feel Father, the captain of the *Sailing Vessel Seaflower,* should bunk with his mates.

"There's the storeroom off the galley. It used to be supplied with a cot."

He shook his head the same moment a knock sounded at the partly open door. With a gentle push, Freddie stepped inside, holding my garment bag. "Your valise, Miss Rickaby."

Once again, I found myself entranced by his very presence and froze. *How did it get so awkward?* He knew me almost as much as I knew myself, and I could not recall a single memory from the age of seven to twelve without Freddie being a part of it.

He held the handle of the valise out to me, and I stepped forward to receive it, brushing lightly against his fingers in the exchange. Tiny sparks shot through my body, and I fought to keep the effect from materializing on my face. *Did he recall his youthful confession to me the day we docked in Marseille? Or did our pending goodbye provoke hollow words of affection?*

Brushing my hand across the elaborate stitching on the satchel, I smiled faintly. Little did Freddie know the very bag he touched carried a collection of unsent letters addressed solely to him. Over the six years of our separation, I wrote him once a month, but without the ability to send them, they became more of a journal of sorts, a heartfelt narrative of my life on land, away from the sea.

Father cleared his voice. "Thank you, Martin." And waved him away. Father always called his men by their surnames, but Martin wasn't truly Freddie's family name. It was the one my mother gave him when we found him adrift on a small boat in the North Sea. With no evidence of a frigate or warship nearby, the mystery of this young boy only mounted when we discovered he suffered injuries that stripped him of his memory. One that never returned to date. So, at the age of nine, he became Freddie Martin, cabin boy on the *SV Seaflower*.

Father's eyes studied me. "You are no longer that little girl roughhousing with the cabin boy below deck." He attempted to hide his frown.

"He appears to no longer be a boy, Father." My lips lifted in a quirky half-smile.

The muscles in his jaw tightened. "No, he is not." Father scratched at one of his long sideburns. "I cannot deny Martin has worked very hard at earning his promotion to first mate. He shall make a fine quartermaster one day."

I clapped my hands. "First mate! Why didn't he tell me?" I smiled over my friend's good fortune. "I knew he would prove himself to you."

"Sophia." Father's authoritarian voice returned. "Your life is altered now." He retrieved his watch from his pocket and glanced at the time. "I daresay, lass, you have a remarkable opportunity... far from the muck of the sea. A season in London awaits you."

My eyebrows furrowed. Pacing in a small circle, I chose my words carefully. I wanted nothing more than to please him. "But, Father, I don't know England any longer. I'm only familiar with life on the ship and France." My memories of Britain included only cursory glimpses of the landscape and occasional docking for supplies. "Why must I return?"

Father tugged uncomfortably at the scarf around his neck. "Come here, lass." He took my hand and led me toward the looking glass in the corner of his cabin. Drawing me in front of him, he gently gripped both of my arms. "Look, Sophia, what do you see?"

I studied my reflection—an eighteen-year-old woman in a pale blue traveling dress, matching spencer jacket, wispy auburn curls styled in the latest fashion, and the same bright blue eyes of my mother. I sighed uneasily, wondering what Father saw. Fearing the resemblance I shared with her only tormented him further.

Father whirled me around to face him. "You don't belong here any longer, lass."

My heart plummeted.

"I wish for your life to be better than mine. Life on the sea can be treacherous…" Father's voice caught. "As you well know." We hadn't spoken of my mother's death since I left for France. He squeezed my arms. "You have been given the occasion to marry well and have a splendid life."

I bit my lip to keep it from trembling. "But you and mother clearly loved each other."

Father turned his head, most likely to hide the unwelcome moisture in his eyes. "Yes, I loved her more than life itself."

"And you were happy together at sea."

He nodded.

"Why would you presume I wouldn't be happy here as well?"

He hesitated, and for a brief moment I believed my pleas had reached him, then he lifted his chin and reiterated his stance. "Your Aunt Helga has offered to be your companion for the season. We go to London." He kissed me on the forehead. "I'll join you for supper this evening. Get some rest." Then he precipitously excused himself, leaving me with the torrent of emotion that reared its ugly head far too often since he sent me away.

Sitting on the bed, I unclasped my valise and retrieved the stack of letters tied with a yellow ribbon. Sliding one out, I unfolded it and read the contents.

18 September 1825

Dearest Freddie,

Oh, how I wish you could be here with me exploring all the sights of this grand city, much like we did in Algiers, Ciutadella, and Palermo. Beyond the Old Marseille Port is St. Victor's Abbey. The stone fortification hides rows and rows of haunting catacombs. We would have a thrilling time with a foot race in the tunnels. There is also an offshore prison island where the most notorious villains are sent. It's called Chateau d'if and I am certain a black cloud resides permanently overhead. The pastries and crepes are divine. You would particularly love the cheese and onion variety with your fondness for such oddities.

I miss you.

I cannot imagine what it shall be like when I see you again. Promise me you won't change. Promise we will still play crown and anchor, blind man's bluff, and dance the night away when I return... and promise me, Freddie, you will never forget me.

All my love, Sophia

Lying back on the coverlet, I let the letter fall from my hands, discouraged. I had returned to the very place I had dreamt of for six years, yet I could not help but feel it slipping through my fingers and disappearing forever.

How might I convince Father my life is here, not in some stuffy drawing room or crushing ballroom, and certainly not entertaining men who strut around like peacocks with their frills and lace and boast of horseflesh and deep coffers?

I longed to be at sea, just like my mother, the daughter of a Royal Navy officer. At the time she met Father, he held the rank of lieutenant, but it didn't take long for him to sweep her off her feet. Within two years, Father sold his commission and obtained a benefactor who helped him purchase one ship, which turned into a fleet of three at the time of their marriage in 1808. But my mother, in her fiercely passionate ways, refused to remain alone on shore in England and insisted she join him at sea. When I came along the following year, the three of us sailed from port to port as a family. I grew up with sea legs, learned to tie the Bowline and Clove Hitch knots, dance a jig while playing the harmonica, and believed for most of my young life that I was a mythological mermaid named Coral.

Only weeks following Mother's tragic death, Father, in his deepest grief, sent me away. He enrolled me in Madame Laurent's school for young mademoiselles in Marseille, France. *Why France? Why not*

England? Though he never fully revealed the reason, aside from my French fluency, I alleged he desired both a place where proper decorum was still necessitated and a far enough place to maintain his distance.

While only my mother had physically died, I lost both my parents that day.

Awaking to the gentle roll of the ship and shouts of the crew members outside of my cabin, I arose and glanced out one of the captain's beveled glass windows as the outline of Marseille faded in the distance. We were fully underway.

The sun now reached midday, and the ruse of a clear sky entranced us into believing King Neptune and his court blessed our departure with a calm passage. I wasn't naïve enough to believe that we would have smooth sailing our entire voyage. In fact, the harshest lesson I learned was that the sea could be your friend one moment and your enemy the next.

Patting my crumpled hair, I recalled how Madame Laurent insisted I hire a companion for the crossing, though I refused, not wanting to subject any young miss to an unaccustomed hardship. Besides, I didn't need my hair fashionably styled and my dresses pressed while en route. I hardly planned to wear the finer gowns I acquired at the modiste, only the plainer ones with a basic corset. I also knew enough to plait my hair or twist it into a simple chignon at the back of my neck.

After replacing some pins that fell out while I rested, I stepped out of Father's cabin and inhaled the briny air as if it were the oxygen I'd been denied for so many years.

I watched the crew as they feverishly worked in their various roles—weighing anchor, navigating, placing oakum on the plank seams, hauling ropes, pulleys, and rigging sails. Much like a well-oiled steam engine piston that moved back and forth in the cylinder, they, too, were synchronized with one purpose. The similarities were staggering. I had the benefit of riding a train for the first time from Marseille to Paris. That was when I visited the majestic palace of Versailles.

Though I was twelve the last time I stood aboard a ship, I had not forgotten how to rig a rope, furl a sail, sift powder, or read the skies; and my fingers ached to engage. Stepping over to the railing, I scanned the curl of the water below, watching the blue-gray waves lap against the wooden sides as if they playfully teased the ship in a game of tick.

As work continued around me, I found comfort in the ship's motions and sounds and remained on deck until the sun began its slow descent to the west. Father taught me rather young how to read a chart and a compass, and I knew from our heading we would reach Gibraltar by morning.

"Are you well, Miss Rickaby?"

Freddie appeared and leaned against the railing beside me.

Wrinkling my nose, I Inwardly groaned. "Freddie, when have you *ever* called me Miss Rickaby?"

He chuckled and pointed to the beige morning dress I changed into. "Since you no longer wear breeches."

I nudged him in the shoulder. Maybe we only needed time together to remember our friendship from before I left. It was so simple back then, so… I needed to be careful where my thoughts wandered off to. If Father forced me to stay in London, I could not bear another heartbreaking goodbye.

When I stole a glance in his direction, his half smile revealed his blasted dimple once more.

Drat it all.

"So, first mate, huh?"

He smiled again and when he lowered his head, one dark curl fell forward onto his forehead. I itched to touch it. I *had* once, though it now seemed ages ago.

"Did you enjoy school?" he asked, still flashing that mesmerizing grin.

"You said you would write me." I folded my arms over my chest, pretending to be cross with him, all the while thrilled to be standing beside him, soaking in his manly evolution.

"I did!" he cried, then mumbled, "Once."

My mother taught both Freddie and me how to read and write at the same time. His ability to absorb knowledge and learn quickly surely became the root of his swift advancements.

"Yes, four years ago, after I had already been there for two." Turning to face the sea again, I lifted my chin to feel the breeze on my face. "I missed this immensely," I said, steadying my emotion. I had learned to tame my sentiments at school, forced to behave in all things proper, and a woman swooning was not considered proper. But my next words slipped out uninhibited. "And you."

Freddie leaned in. The salty scent of his skin filled my senses as he whispered, "I missed you too, Soph." The tenor of his adult voice swept over me and lifted me to heady heights. When shouts from behind us cut the imaginary string that tethered us together, he took a step away, then reached over and squeezed my hand gently. "Meet me at the hatch cove tonight so we can talk."

Chills ran down my spine at the idea of being alone with him, especially in the precise place he kissed me for the first time. Of course, it was only a quick peck on my cheek, but I etched the memory of that moment deeply into my heart.

Supper that night with Father proceeded much like I expected. We engaged in polite conversation with one another. He asked about my accomplishments in French, painting, and the pianoforte, and I asked him about his cargo, the ports, and his men. Despite his attempts at skirting any conversation that centered on his fleet, now totaling six frigates, I found ways to bring it back to all things water. I needed him to see how much I missed this life.

Father spent nearly his entire life at sea. First, as a sailor in the Royal Navy and then as a merchant marine. His hard work earned him a trusted reputation and powerful associations. It was only with pure determination that my mother refused to live on land without him. Therefore, I had been born and raised under similar circumstances and life seemed like it could never be better...at least before the spring of 1821. But fate had a different plan and when a torrential storm claimed the life of my mother, it changed me forever.

Following the tragedy, Father attempted on three different occasions to take me back to England and to my aunt, but each time, I hid within the crevices of the ship until Father's deadlines forced him to set sail again. I knew the secrets of the *SV Seaflower* as well or better than he did. It was, after all, named after me. Shortly before the acquisition of the ship, eleven years ago, I presented Father with a tender gift. Within my tiny seven-year-old fingers lay a slightly wilted sea anemone of purple and green. I had collected the aquatic bloom from the Cubellas tide pools in Barcelona the day before. "A Seaflower from a Seaflower," Father said, smiling down at me with his larger-than-life smile. And shortly thereafter the *SV Seaflower* was christened.

As night fell and Father stood to leave, I felt guilty my arrival forced him into one of the lesser bunks, but he insisted once more on my welfare and safety and advised me to keep the door bolted the entirety of the night. "While my men know a keel hauling awaits them if they so much as lay a hand on you," he spoke of the severe punishment a sailor faced by being dragged beneath the ship. "I refuse to chance a wayward drunken sailor pushing the limits." He kissed me on the cheek. "Sleep well, lass."

Time passed unbearably slowly as I waited for a suitable time to slip out of the cabin. The previous times I met Freddie in our hiding place, I delayed my departure from my quarters until the moon shone brightly above and the majority of sailors slept. This time was no different. Only the night watch remained at the spar high above. And fortunately, I knew how to avoid them.

I dressed in a simple brown dress, the darkest I owned, and in my satin slippers, I tiptoed out of the quarters, down the steps, and to a hidden compartment near the port gangway. Freddie and I found it on one of our many adventures and claimed it as our own.

The door could only be pried open with a knife. I borrowed one of Father's daggers off his coat of arms on his wall for this purpose. Sticking the blade in the crease, I wiggled it until the door finally popped open. From its difficulty, I presumed the hatch remained unused since I left. This brought a smile to my face as I crawled inside and closed the door behind me. Maneuvering to the farthest end of the narrow space, I pulled my knees up to my chin and confirmed my dress covered my ankles. Chuckling, I took a deep breath in the dark. The hatch felt a great deal bigger at twelve.

I waited only a few minutes when the tip of a blade penetrated the crease once more and pried the door open. Freddie dove in.

"Oof," I cried out as he landed on my feet.

"Sorry." He promptly closed the latch and adjusted himself, but now that he was inside, I realized how much tighter the space had become.

He lit a small bronze oil lamp and chuckled as the simple flame lit up the gap. "We might have to look for a bigger place."

My cheeks heated. Did he believe our clandestine tête à têtes would go on forever? Didn't he know as first mate what our heading was? Where my fate lay?

"Yes, I was significantly smaller years ago," I mumbled. Though I truly believed the expansion of Freddie's chest and long legs were the sole reason for the change, I couldn't help but wish to go back to the simplicity of our childhood. The overwhelming trepidations of adulthood weighed heavily on my mind.

He reached for my hand and rubbed his thumb against my palm. The mere touch of his bare fingers on my skin sent a contradiction of sensations racing through me, from alarming chills to soothing placation. I struggled with the effect. When did I start feeling so...*female?*

In the shadows of the dancing flame, Freddie's green eyes sparkled as they followed the contours of my face and left a fluttering in my stomach I had not felt so strongly before. *Strange.* I had spent the last two years in drawing rooms, ballrooms, and music rooms amongst some of the most handsome men of France, and yet none of them caused the stir Freddie did in this one moment. Glancing downward, I chewed my bottom lip. I should not have come. Saying goodbye to him in five days might literally break me.

Freddie seemed entirely unaware of the tempest brewing beneath my skin as he leaned forward, and a faint smell of rum escaped from his lips as he spoke. "Tell me you didn't miss this." Then adjusted himself parallel to me. My body leaned hypnotically toward him, as if an invisible magnet drew us together. Wrapping one arm around my shoulders, he drew me against his chest. The warmth of his body seeped soothingly through my dress. "Yes, I missed this," I whispered.

He squeezed my shoulder. "Soph, seeing you again has been..." his words faded. I felt his heart beat a tick faster. "It's never been the same without you. Promise me you're not going back to school."

I groaned. "You wouldn't believe what they made me do, Freddie, and what they've made me wear, gowns, petticoats...corsets!"

A profound silence hung between us. If he wasn't touching me, I would've thought he simply vanished. "Freddie?"

"You are beautiful, Soph." There was a peculiar desperation in his tone. Was the thickness in the air as palpable for him as it was for me? "No matter your attire, I'm grateful you're still you."

My mind whirled chaotically. What did he mean? I nudged his side. "Did you expect me to return dreadfully plain or become an unsightly spinster at eighteen?"

Freddie's warm exhale tickled my skin. "No, never plain, and you can hardly be a spinster." He took another breath. "I feared you'd be betrothed."

"Betrothed?" I choked out the word, though it was hardly foreign to me. Madame Laurent encouraged several gentlemen to come courting, but my heart never engaged.

I squeezed Freddie's hand. "I'm afraid the only marriage I seek is the one my parents had."

And in that instant, our flirtation subsided. It took only minutes for us to fall back into the playful comfortability of our childhood, and we spent the entirety of the remaining night inside the hatch, speaking of all that had transpired in our years apart.

By the time Freddie exited the compartment and confirmed the coast was clear, the sun initiated its rise on the horizon. I had forgotten how much I loved seeing the splintered orange and yellow rays explode against the blue-green sea. From the narrowing land on both sides, I recognized our location as Gibraltar. The channel, flanked by Spain and Morocco, led directly into the open ocean.

Freddie drew the attention of the night watch over to the starboard side of the ship as I slipped back into the captain's quarters. Though lack of sleep exhausted me, a giddiness stirred my body from the memory of our time together. If only I could convince Father we needn't rush back to England so soon. Then maybe Freddie would make his affections known and ask Father for my hand.

One could only hope.

Turning the latch on the captain's door, I slid inside, clicked it closed, and leaned back against it, relishing in all the highs of the night. Small bursts of light streamed through the rear windows and complemented the lift in my heart.

In a sidelong glance, a subtle movement caught my attention. Then dread swept over me. My father sat in a chair at his dining table. I had forgotten how early he breaks his fast. A bounteous variety of foods sat untouched before him. *Drat.* Obvious disappointment leaked from his eyes.

"Father?" I squeaked. Then calmed my racing heart. "Good morning?"

He cleared his throat. "Is it, Sophia?"

I swallowed hard. "Yes, exceptionally. I—I took an early morning stroll. I couldn't sleep."

The muscles in his jaw twitched. He stood to his full height, and the wrinkles beneath his eyes sagged more than usual. He approached cautiously. "Now, tell me the truth," he said, lifting a parchment up. As my eyes narrowed in for recognition, I felt the blood drain from my cheeks. He held the letter I wrote to Freddie. The one I pulled out of the stack yesterday to read.

"Wh—where did you find that?"

"On your bed… the bed that wasn't slept in last night."

Though I had nothing to be ashamed of outside of the guilt that consumed me from lying, I lowered my head. "Freddie and I were only talking."

Father's face tightened. "What do you think people will say when they see you alone with him? Have you learned nothing about how fragile a woman's reputation is?"

"Father, it was harmless, and no one saw us."

"Has he made his intentions known? Compromised you?"

"Honestly, Father." I scoffed. "It's just Freddie."

He shook the letter. "These are not words for *just* Freddie."

I panicked. "You read my private letter?"

"It was laid out in the open for anyone who entered this room to read," he grumbled. Then rubbed the back of his neck. "You cannot marry him, Sophia."

"Marry?" I chuckled. "Father, we're friends." Even as I spoke those words, I knew they weren't entirely true.

He arched one eyebrow and narrowed his eyes,   just like he used to when he wanted   me to confess as a child. He had perfected the captain's scowl that burrowed into one's soul.

I shifted uncomfortably. *What if I do love Freddie?* I pondered the thought, but remained silent. Though I knew a life at sea with Freddie as my husband would be near perfection, I never allowed myself to hope for fear of his rejection. Now that I knew my dearest friend had a fondness for me, my hope shifted to dreams I now wished to breathe life into.

"You are going to London and will marry a gentleman." Father's imperious voice commanded the room. "You will settle down and have children and live a normal life."

Frustration threaded through my veins. Madame Laurent taught me that a lady never raised her voice, but I constantly wrestled with the person I wanted to be and the person I was forced to be. "That is not the life I desire, Father." Tears bubbled on my lashes. "I want to be on the sea…like my mother."

He went still. He attempted to hide the pain, but I saw glimpses of it. "And what happened to her?"

I glanced away. I didn't want to revisit such agonizing memories.

"Say it, Sophia!" Father demanded.

My heart pounded in my chest.

"Say it!" he repeated.

"She drowned!" I shouted, with little control over my tears. Slumping to the side of the bed, I let my head fall into my hands as my cries came faster. I cried so hard I didn't hear my father's footsteps retreat, or the door close, or the sounds that signaled the day turning to night. At some point, I fell asleep and dreamed of being the mermaid again.

I awoke to utter darkness as it permeated the room. I fumbled around until I located Father's oil lamp and lit it. A meal had been left on the table for me. Touching the cold meat, I shuddered at the time that had passed. Reaching for the bun, I held the soft bread to my lips and replayed the earlier conversation with my father. *How could he not want me to be happy?*

After I ate the bread, I poured water from the pitcher into a basin and removed my dress. Standing in my shift, I moistened a linen and dabbed my skin, desperate to feel fresh and renewed. If I could wash off the dirt, maybe my melancholy would vanish with it.

I struggled through the tightening of my corset, then left the ribbons loosely tied and changed into a light-colored frock. Twisting my wayward curls into a simple chignon, I felt ready to face the others and stepped out of my father's quarters.

The men gathered for their nightly revelries and crowded the deck with their pork knuckle in one hand and a pint of grog in the other. I leaned against the top railing and watched as they joyfully danced and sang amongst themselves. Tears brimmed once more and threatened to fall. I loved this life, but feared I would have to say goodbye to it because I loved my father more.

"How are you feeling, Miss Rickaby?" Freddie's gentle tone emerged from behind me.

I motioned to turn around, but his hand pressed against my lower back and stayed any movement.

"No, don't," he whispered. "Don't turn around."

I faced forward again. *What had my father said to him?*

"I shouldn't be seen talking to you."

"But we're friends, Freddie." I choked out. I didn't want to lose him. "Friends talk."

His hand caressed my back and moved upward underneath my hair. The tingle of his fingers against my neck sent a flurry of emotion bursting out of every limb.

"Not just friends, Soph," he leaned closer until I felt his whispered breath in my ear. I already knew this, but to hear it from his lips made my heart soar.

I bit my inner cheek to keep from crying openly. "Yes, not just friends." My legs trembled beneath my dress and a weakness consumed me. *Don't swoon. Don't swoon,* I repeated in my mind. Circling around, I took three steps in my effort to dart back into the captain's quarters when his hand clasped around my wrist, tugging me to the side with my back against a shroud. The thick netted mesh kept us carefully concealed.

Clutching the gridded rope on both sides of my body, he leaned forward with an expression of torment. "I must tell you at least once, Soph. I have *always* loved you."

I wanted to scream *no, don't say that like it's the only time you ever will,* but my throat constricted at the racing pace of my pulse.

I felt his anguished exhale on my lips and made one final resolution. If I was forced to keep my distance from Freddie from now on, I would first have what I always wanted. My first proper kiss from him. I bolstered my confidence and rose on the tips of my toes, pressing my lips to his. He shook backward, releasing my poor attempt at the act.

I bit my lip, fearing I had overstepped, but there was no mistaking the indisputable yearning that flashed through his eyes. His hands reached out and cupped the back of my neck as his lips met mine once more.

At first our touch came with caution, almost timid exploration, but then the kiss deepened to the raw urgency we both felt. My arms wound around his waist and gripped the back of his shirt, simultaneous to his igniting touch and the guiding movement of his mouth. Exhilaration eased through my body and consumed all logical sense until the threat of finality emerged. I couldn't bring myself to break free. But Freddie did.

With a final squeeze of my hand, he disappeared into the darkness.

I leaned against the shroud and touched my soft and swollen lips, stunned at both the gloriousness and the agony of such a moment, resigned to etch every bit into my heart forever.

The next two days passed by relatively calmly, both above and below the sea. Although dark clouds massed on the horizon, I didn't fear their threats. We had weathered storms before and prepared accordingly.

Once the *Seaflower* reached the open waters of the Atlantic, I spent most of my time gazing over the railings' edge. The draw of the waves hypnotized me as they cut beneath the ship, and occasionally something unusual would catch my eye… like the good luck a pod of dolphins brings, the majestic spout of a gray whale, or the smooth motion of a sea turtle. Once, an enormously large shark shredded our net full of tuna and sent the men scrambling for their harpoons. In the end, the shark disappeared deep beneath the bow and whether he had a metal stick attached to its flesh, we didn't know; but a shark sighting signified a darker superstition, one believed to proceed the death of a crew member.

In these last two days, we passed only three ships, to my knowledge. One, my father identified as a slave ship coming from Ghana or Guinea with its iniquitous merchandise and two East India trading barges. With the constant threat of piracy, some merchants worked in pairs, a practice my father told me he recently adopted. One of his other ships, the *Victoris*, planned to join us as we rounded A Coruña and entered the Bay of Biscay.

For the most part, the trade route remained secure. The Royal Navy policed these waters, and over the years, drove piracy to the Caribbean. However, occasionally some would slip through.

Father never seemed to fret over this with as battle ready the *SV Seaflower* was with her 32-pounder carronades and 24-pounder long guns, but one could never be *too* sure.

Naturally, without Freddie to keep me company, my days passed in unbearably long and dull ways. Even my beloved books could not keep my interest as I tried to occupy my mind with anything other than the man who labored extensively before me. I watched as Freddie worked harder than any other sailor, second to my father. No wonder Father promoted him so quickly.

Other than an occasional stolen look or smile, we never interacted, and it hurt my heart to accept such a miserable end. At night, when I tried to settle my restless mind, I fought the temptation to run to our hiding place just to see if Freddie was there where his arms or lips would find me.

The kiss we shared replicated something from one of my novels... desperate and delicious, and the memory of it nearly drove me mad. I longed to repeat it. In truth, however, I knew Freddie would never disobey a direct command from my father, and if his captain demanded that he stay away from me, he would.

"Sophia, darling." Father wiped his mouth after finishing his evening meal of glazed eel and steamed rice. "Thank you for joining me for dinner. I know this hasn't been an easy voyage for you."

I gazed at him. I'd missed him considerably while at school and had only seen him a few times during that time away. He aged significantly since then. From his gray hair in his sideburns and the deep lines on his face, he had changed, but I believed remnants of the same loving man from my childhood were buried within. I only needed to find them.

"Thank you for inviting me," I said, trying to keep the despair I felt from bleeding through.

"We should make port in two days." He watched me with curious eyes. "Try to be happy about this. It's what your mother would have wanted."

"She wanted me to be sent away?" I choked out, surprised. "To live away from you?"

He shook his head. "She would have wanted to see you married with a family of your own."

"Mother chose you. She chose this life." I waved a hand around me. "Why can't I have that same choice?"

"Because this is not an easy life."

"But isn't life easier when you are with the ones you love?"

Father frowned. Tossing his linen napkin on his plate, he stood up. "Our days of even keel are over, lass. We expect rough seas tonight. Please remain inside." He kissed me on the forehead. "Goodnight." Then departed from the room.

I sat still for an immeasurable amount of time, listening to the gentle patter of raindrops against the windows, trying to strategize anything and everything to stay aboard this ship and not disembark in London. I was no longer a child and able to hide in small compartments or pitch my infantile fits, but I needed to somehow convince my father that this was the future I chose, and Freddie was the man I chose.

Though the rain continued to fall, the ship's sways were not terrible, and falling asleep felt more like being lulled soothingly by a symphonic melody.

I dreamt of days at the sea where I learned to sing, dance, and play. I dreamt of the ports we made and their immersive cultural experiences. Places where vibrant shades of reds, golds, burgundies, and plums inspired me. Places I succumbed to the immersing scents of frankincense, myrrh, saffron, and cinnamon. Places with wonder and delight. Places like India and the Orient, where the sky lit up with exploding, vibrant fire rockets and the most mesmerizing sparks I'd ever seen. My heart pounded in unison with the booms of explosion and the excitement I felt. A tremendous pop and crackle stirred my eyes open. Then a bright light spanned the length of the windows, and a boom rattled the bed. I rubbed my eyes and sat up.

We are not in India. Why do I hear fireworks?

I reached for my dressing gown and tied it over my shift as I tiptoed toward the glass. Pressing my face against the window, I struggled to see through the heavy raindrops. The lightning storm seemed worse than I expected. A sudden squall, perhaps?

Another bright light streaked by, followed by a booming shudder. One that rocked me sideways and onto the floor, smacking my head against the corner post of the bed. Reaching to soothe what might be a bruise, the next tremor jostled me forward. This time, into Father's personal correspondence desk. Though presumed to be bolted down, the small crate that stored his vellum scrolls, stylus, and inkwell crashed to the floor. The bottle shattered, splattering black ink along the floorboards. Another flash of bright lights and another boom sent me scurrying beneath the bed.

Could this storm be more violent than the one that claimed my mother?

The ship creaked and groaned. Despite its hardiness, it had weathered eleven years on the sea. Would it hold up under such dreadful circumstances? When the ship tilted now to the starboard side, I couldn't stop from sliding, and swiftly clutched the base of a bedpost to keep still. Then horror filled my chest as I felt the bed break loose and skid with me. I screamed, but the thundering sounds around me drowned out my voice.

The door flung open. "Sophia!" My father yelled. "Sophia, where are you?"

I caught sight of his black boots as he approached the bed. He moved like a sailor deep in his cups, but I knew my father abstained from spirits as captain.

"Here, under here!" I scrambled out from beneath the bed and lunged into his arms. "Father, the storm! It's frightful!"

His eyes met mine for only a brief second. "It's not a storm, lass." Then he hooked his arm around my waist and led me cautiously toward the door.

"Not a storm?" I struggled to comprehend. What else could cause such a... *Oh. No.* My heart raced. Only one thing brought about such unnatural carnage. We were under attack!

Before we reached the doors, a boom and crack shattered one window. Father dropped me to the floor and hovered over me as glass flew like small daggers in all directions. Piercing shards skidded across my exposed legs, leaving narrow trails of blood from the nicks. Father pulled me upright again, ignoring the two large fragments that lodged in his skin. "It's too dangerous for you to be here!" he shouted above the noise. "I need to get you to the treasury." My father referred to the most secure compartment on the ship. It carried his most precious merchandise. However, getting to it below deck would be nearly impossible.

"Wh—who is attacking?" I attempted to steady my voice. Years in drawing rooms had turned me timid.

Father took a deep breath. "The colors appear to be from..." he paused. "Uh..." He didn't finish his sentence and pulled me toward him as he pressed parallel against the doors.

"P—pirates?" I squeaked out.

"Not precisely." He shook his head. "I believe it's the *Guerrera*."

I pressed my hand over my mouth to keep from crying out. I was certain Father would not have told me if he knew of my familiarity with the name. While many of the pupils of Madame Laurent's school focused on the society columns in the press, I read the periodicals of nautical news. I knew precisely what the ship, *Guerrero*, delved into. They were a slave ship that acquired their slaves by attacking other ships. My heart sped up. I now feared my future choices shifted from marriage and family to enslavement or death.

Cracking the door, father studied the scene.

When another boom blew the door off its hinges and threw us both back onto the table, its legs collapsed, and we rolled to the floor. Bewildered, I attempted to stand, but my senses felt foggy and raw. I shivered from the rain showering through the now glassless windows and doors.

When I realized the body at my side failed to move, I panicked. "Father!" I screamed, but he remained motionless on the floor. Above his brow, a finger length gash bled profusely. I ripped the lace from my dressing gown's hem and wrapped it around his head. It would not stop the bleeding entirely, only slow it down. On my knees, I scrambled for my trunk and sifted through until I found my needlepoint, then secured the needle with its thread to the fabric at my wrist. I returned to my father as another loud boom and crackle connected somewhere on the ship. I felt the vibration keenly from where I knelt.

"Soph!" A shout came from the door.

"Freddie!" I cried. "My father, he's…"

Freddie didn't hesitate. He grabbed the coverlet off the bed and wrapped it around me, and lifted my father up and over his shoulder. With one hand secured on my father, he gripped my hand. "The hatch cove."

My eyes lit up. Yes, it would be the closest and safest place.

"Stay beside me, Soph. Don't hesitate. Once we are outside, we run!"

I nodded, but first rushed over to where my father's coat of arms crashed to the floor and retrieved the remaining dagger. Gripping it at my side, I followed Freddie. The blade would do nothing against a cannonball or musket round, but if the ship was breeched, I would defend it to the very end.

Dashing down the stairs and off to the side opposite of where the enemy ship attacked from, I used the blade to pry the compartment open. I set the quilt inside while Freddie gently laid my father on top. Deep guttural groans were a welcomed sound, though he still hadn't opened his eyes. More explosive sounds rippled around us. We were fighting back. The *Seaflower* maintained more than enough defenses to thwart most attacks, but if it was true and the adversary was indeed the *Guerrero*, this would not be an easy victory.

I once read that the Royal Navy did not label the ship's crew as pirates by the traditional sense, but law breakers of a different kind, slipping out of their hands over a dozen times. They attacked swiftly, strategically, then disappeared south of the equator with their newly acquired human commodities.

"He's breathing." Freddie announced after pressing his ear to my father's chest. "Just keep pressure against the wound to stop the bleeding." He tore off his wet shirt and pushed it into my hands. "Use this for dressing." Freddie pulled me against his bare chest. My heart matched the pace of his as they thumped simultaneously. "And Soph, don't make a sound and do not come out." With a brief kiss, he ushered me inside. The space would be dark without the added lamp from before, but I could feel my way around enough to care for my father.

With a final nod, Freddie sealed the door and despite my desire to weep, I knew I needed to be brave, just like my mother, my father, and Freddie.

"S—sophia?" My father mumbled my name. The few words that followed were incoherent, but the sound of his voice generated some relief.

"Shhh, Father. It's alright. Just rest."

The distressing sounds continued for what seemed like hours, though it surely wasn't. The ship rattled often from the booms of the cannons below and to the crack of the enemy's cannons connecting with yet another portion of the ship.

What would be left when we emerged? *If we emerged.* We could very well meet our fate in a watery grave if they sank the *Seaflower*.

Curiosity inched me forward, and I pressed my hands against the hatch opening. My heart thumped twice as hard as I cracked the door open. One mast collapsed across the quarterdeck, while another exploded in flames. Clamping my palm over my mouth, I fought the scream that sought to come forth. I swiftly secured the hatch in place once more, fearing discovery, and scrambled back to my father.

Feeling around in the dark, I placed my father's head in my lap and removed Freddie's shirt from the wound. He moaned at the movement.

Bringing Freddie's shirt to my nose, I inhaled the musky scent that lingered within its fibers. Mixed with a salty aroma, I recognized it as all Freddie, and I yearned to have him here with me. Yet, with the captain out of commission, Freddie would never submit to cowering away. He would rise to the needs of the ship in the captain's place and defend to the bitter end. And that particular thought carved a hole in my heart. I suddenly realized my life would not be *my life* without him in it. If we survived, I could never leave him.

As the terrifying booms continued to rattle the hatch, I fumbled for the needle at my wrist. Placing it tightly between my lips, I tied the end of the thread into a knot. With my left hand, I removed the lace and gently fingered Father's wound, pinching it tightly together,

Using my thumb and forefinger of my right, I pushed the needle through his flesh, attempting to seal his wound sight unseen. A subtle groan surfaced, but Father's eyes remained closed.

When the cannons finally ceased, my heart seemed to stop beating as well. Shouts were heard, then gunshots, then silence. I gasped, then clamped my lips shut to keep from crying out. Typically, the only reason gunshots would be heard so close was in defense of the deck or to kill the crew. My mind flashed to the men. Men who were like uncles and brothers to me. Men who taught me how to harpoon, spit, sing off tune, and love... like Freddie.

Tears formed in the corners of my eyes. I swiped at them, fighting to keep them from falling. Whatever lay behind that door, I would not let them think I was weak. I was a maiden of the sea, a mermaid named Coral, and a captain's daughter. I would go to the depths of the ocean before I would willingly surrender.

Undecipherable words were exchanged before a scratching sound emerged on the opposite side of the door. I held my breath as a blade entered the crack and popped the door open. A slight streak of sunshine cut through the gray clouds and blinded me. I shielded my eyes but didn't move. Father's head lay cradled in my lap with a needle attached to his brow at the end of a dozen crude stitches. The leftover thread dangled along his cheek while I clutched Freddie's bloodied shirt in my fist.

"You're safe." Freddie appeared on his knees. He then turned to the men behind him. "Assist me with the captain," he shouted. Several hands appeared and tenderly retrieved my father's body.

Once Father was on deck, Freddie reached for my hands and assisted me from the hatch. My body shook from both the thin fabric of my nightclothes and sitting in such an awkward position for so long. Yet, I truly didn't know how much time had passed. I wiped my face with my sleeve and tried to grasp the scene before me. Parts of the ship smoldered, some floated upon the water, and some were missing all together. The extensive damage to the *Seaflower* left us listless, as if the wind failed us, but the fault did not fall to mother nature.

"What of the *Guerrero*?" I whispered.

"Gone," Freddie said. "With a naval fleet on its tail." He pointed to the west. "If it weren't for the *Victoris* arriving when it did, there'd be nothing left of our ship."

I shuddered to think such a grim thought, though it had crossed my mind more than once in the hatch.

"I'll take you to the captain's quarters. Though there isn't much left, maybe you can find something warm and dry to wear." Freddie pointed to the ship parallel to ours. "We'll return to England on the *Victoris*. The *Seaflower* won't make it."

"But it will be rebuilt, won't it? Can't you jury rig the ship?" I referred to the hauling a disabled ship to shore. This boat was as much a part of me as anything else.

Freddie shook his head. "I'm afraid this will be its final resting place, Soph." He took my hand and led me up to the damaged quarterdeck. Half the stairs were missing, and two of the four walls of my father's cabin were destroyed, as well as most of my belongings.

We scoured to find something decent for me to wear. Somehow, in our separation, Freddie located another shirt for himself, but the closest attire I could find was in my father's wardrobe—breeches and shirtsleeves. Pieces of my fine linen gowns were found strewn all around where my trunk should have been. Nothing could be salvaged.

Stepping into the alcove of the two remaining walls, I removed my robe and slid the breeches on, fastening them as best I could. Buttoning up the shirtsleeves, I snickered at how they swallowed me whole. Retrieving a piece of rope, I tied it around my waist, then double knotted it. I then rolled the pant legs up to my ankles and my sleeves to my elbows. It felt ridiculous, but would have to work. I could hardly continue wearing my thin, wet shift. Stepping back out to the deck, Freddie chuckled when he saw me.

I grinned, twirling before him. "It's all I could find."

"It suits you." He placed his hands on my waist and pulled me into an embrace. The safety of his arms around me confirmed the trust I felt in his presence.

When I glanced up, I met Freddie's eyes. He shared a great deal of emotion in that simple look. Finally, he spoke, "Regardless of my desire, Soph, after this attack, I'm certain your father will insist you stay in London."

"After this attack," I paused, then leaned forward and kissed him. "I'm certain I will insist on quite the opposite."

He smiled, and his dimple deepened.

"Miss Rickaby!" A sailor from the *Victoris* shouted. "Your father is asking for you."

I rushed to the wide plank that the crew of the *Victoris* secured between the two ships and, with support from Freddie and another sailor, I crossed without incident.

They led me to the captain's cabin where I found my father resting comfortably on the plush bed, much like the one on the *Seaflower*.

"Father!" I cried as I raced to his side, tears already spilling down my cheeks. A paleness covered his skin, but now that he was conscious with a proper bandage over his wound, nothing else mattered.

"Sophia, lass." He raised one arm and motioned for me to come closer.

Hugging him carefully, I kissed his cheeks. "I'm so thankful you're safe."

"It is your safety I'm grateful for," he said, then glanced past me and motioned toward Freddie. "And I have you to thank for that."

Freddie stepped forward and shook his hand. "I only got you both to the compartment, sir."

Father looked at me with remarkable gentleness. "Forgive me, darling, for my foolish mind."

"There is nothing to forgive."

"We shall have you safely on dry land soon."

I brushed my hand across his forehead and pushed his droopy bangs aside. "Father, the two men I love the most in this world live on the sea, and I wish for nothing more than to be with them."

His eyes widened. "Sophia, you could've been killed just now."

I cupped his jaw in my palm. "But I wasn't." I smiled. "Because of the two men I love the most in this world."

His eyes softened, and he looked past me at Freddie once more. The silence between us amplified until Father spoke. "I have taken this sweet girl for granted." He exhaled. "Don't make the same mistake, Martin."

I held my breath, unsure of where Father was going with this conversation.

"All this time, I commandeered her future and her happiness into what *I* believed was right for her. I was wrong." He looked only at his first mate. "Do you love her?"

I gasped and turned to see Freddie's smile broaden. "Since the moment we met."

"Do you promise to care for her?"

"I promise, sir. Forever."

Father shook his head. "Heaven help you, son," he muttered. "You will find you can never say no to her."

I laughed.

Father squeezed my hand. "If you choose this life, Sophia," he exhaled, "I shall not stop you, for I truly desire nothing more than *your* happiness."

I flung my arms around his neck and kissed him again, nearly forgetting how gentle I needed to be. Jumping to my feet, I reached for Freddie's hand and raced for the door. Though all manner of labor resumed around us, I found a quiet space near the railing and led Freddie right to it.

He placed his hands on my waist, and their warmth seeped through my bulky attire. Then his face grew serious. "You know I would leave this life for you, Soph. I would do anything you asked."

I knew this.

I also knew sailing was as much a part of his soul as breathing. How could I ever ask that of him?

"Then allow me to be on the sea beside you, Freddie, sailing, exploring, and finding new hatches to secret ourselves in." I winked devilishly.

"Well, then, Miss Rickaby..." His half smile teased while his dimple appeared. "Sounds like we have an accord."

My heart skipped a beat at his looming proximity, but managed to smile in return. "We do, Mr. Martin, but only if you are agreeable, posthaste, to such an alliance."

He kissed me tenderly, then whispered against my lips, "Is today too soon?"

I laughed and glanced down at my clothing. "I only need a dress."

One of his eyebrows arched playfully. "I prefer you in breeches, love."

My heart thrummed. "I *prefer* you kiss me soundly, love."

The Mesmerizing S.S. Mesmer

Holly D. Morgan

Arabella Parsons's heartbeat pulsed in her ears. The ribbon that fastened her blue mask against her skin felt as if it'd become a boa constrictor, tightening against her skull. Blaring music and dancing feet were drowned out by the rhythm. As well as the occasional cough from the passengers too weak to participate in the embankment celebration.

None of that mattered. It was her first night on this healing cruise, and she'd seen him.

The man in the black fox mask. Her brother, Lawrence, who'd been missing for six months. The blush on his cheek was pale against the fabric on his face.

He wasn't alone. Two men followed him, casually pushing through the crowd, disrupting the flowing gowns.

Arabella's stomach churned. She wasn't sure if it was due to the swaying of the ship on the sea or the fear sweeping over her. She took a step forward when a hand wrapped around her arm.

"Would you like a drink?" her husband of two months asked. Arabella glanced at his thin face. Her eyebrows narrowed. "Huh?"

"A drink," James repeated. "Would you like one?" He shuffled slightly in place as his gaze moved to where Arabella had been looking moments ago. Only the disturbance had cleared, and she could tell by the way he rubbed his pointed chin he'd missed the suspicious looking men that'd been after her brother.

Her eyes flitted to the upper balcony. If she made her way there, she'd have a better view of the crowd below. A better chance at finding her brother once more.

"Yes, a drink would be wonderful," she said. Although James had agreed to hop on this ship at the last moment before departure, she didn't trust he'd follow her up the closed-off steps. They'd married for money, not for love.

James nodded. "I'll return shortly."

As soon as his lean frame disappeared through the crowd, Arabella seized her opportunity. She searched for Lawrence as she made her way, but she didn't see him within the mass of gowns and dark suits. She slipped under the thick, red ribbon that closed off the upper balcony and took the steps two at a time to the top.

Her arm clutched against her middle as she scanned the ballroom floor, examining the mask of each head with hair that matched the sandy coloring of Lawrence's.

A green one. Another shaped like a bear. Black, but a plain style across the eyes.

This man turned his head with a sharp motion toward another who'd shoved him to the side. Arabella squinted her eyes.

The black fox mask. She knew that mask well. Lawrence had it made after sighting a black fox during the first hunting trip he'd taken after Father died. Its rarity assured him it was a sign from above. Their father was watching over them.

Lawrence ran as if he were the prey instead of the hunter. Behind him the two men from before picked up their pace. They were closing in on her brother.

A light glinted off the giant chandelier hanging above the room—a symbol of the money and prestige that was put into this ship. Arabella didn't let the fact that her new father-in-law was the one who supplied both those things sway her. The rope holding the light in place was nearby. If she could time it right…

Lawrence rushed through the middle of the dance floor. The end of the rope slipped out of Arabella's hands and off the hook.

The crowd screamed as glass shattered across the ballroom floor. It was a shame the manufactured light fixture had met its end on one of its first cruises in 1895. But some sacrifices had to be made for the greater good.

Passengers who had dived out of the way now laid face down on the wooden floor, including the two men that'd been chasing Arabella's brother. Others ran in every direction to avoid the shards.

Lawrence was nowhere to be seen. He'd escaped his assailants.

"Bella!" James's voice soared above the chaos below. He approached Arabella from the side, his breathing rough as he clutched two empty cups with his hands. Liquid glistened across his white knuckles. "What are you doing up here?"

"I could ask you the same question," she said, her head held high.

His eyes moved to the empty hook then returned to her. "Please tell me you didn't…"

"I had to. I saw Lawrence."

James let out a deep breath. "Explain how that justifies vandalizing my father's ship and putting the people below in danger."

"*He* was in danger."

James shook his head, his mouth gaped open. "That explains nothing! We don't even know for sure if it was him. We're on this cruise so you can avoid too much excitement. This is *clearly* the opposite of that."

Arabella paused. Her new husband didn't believe her. "He's out there still, possibly running from them. We need to find him."

"Look," James said, ushering her to the side to be hidden within the shadows. "It might've been him. But until we know for sure, we need to be careful."

A siren filled the room, instructing passengers to assemble onto the deck for an announcement from the captain. Arabella's pulse quickened, worried she'd been seen. Would her connection to the owner of this ship be enough to keep her from facing backlash from her actions?

As they headed out the balcony doors onto the upper deck, James muttered under his breath, "I never should've left you alone to get those drinks."

Light from the waxing moon shone across the dark waters. It would be a few days before it filled its full circle, however, its brightness made up for the missing slices.

Arabella followed James as they headed to the deck. People were scattered across the wooden floor outside. Some clutched fresh wounds whipped upon them by the falling glass. Others were affected by the afflictions that motivated them to step foot on this ship to begin with.

They passed by a man coughing into a blood-soaked handkerchief. A woman lay curled on the ground, muttering to herself as she mimicked the motion of the waves, rocking back and forth. A glint shined from her ruby necklace as it swayed in the moonlight.

Captain Bernheim stood on a platform in the middle of the upper deck. His usually straight and proper blue hat tilted to the side. He shouted above the cries and wails of the passengers. "An accident has occurred in the main ballroom. I apologize for the fright. However, be assured the rest of our journey is expected to be smooth sailing. Tomorrow we have a full itinerary, including our first demonstration of healing."

An accident. His wording calmed Arabella. She hadn't been seen. Her eyes wandered over the crowd, searching for her brother. She saw no one she recognized. On the way back to their cabin—pale faces, sickly faces, ones in pain—but no Lawrence.

The morning breeze sent a chill through Arabella's spine as she stepped onto the upper deck. She wrapped her shawl tighter around her shoulders to keep from shivering.

James placed a hand on the small of her back, his light touch guiding her through the crowd of people that headed toward the ballroom. She wanted to slink away, unused to such forward advances from the man she'd known for only two months. Certainly he was only trying to keep her from making another rash decision. Didn't trust letting her out of his sight.

As they entered, the difference in the room's appearance from last night was drastic. Clearly, workers had stayed up getting it ready. The floor had been cleaned and lined with chairs. A stage had been constructed at the front. The glass from the fallen chandelier was gone. In fact, the entirety of the chandelier was missing, leaving an empty hook in the middle of the ceiling.

James moved his arm to usher her forward as Arabella stared at the empty space above them. She'd been the one to cause the damage, and the truth behind that haunted her. She was raised to be a well-bred woman and meet society's expectation of a lady of excellence. Her dream was to be a wife and a homemaker.

But now that her dream had come true, something was missing. It wasn't enough just to be Mrs. James Parsons. Something was missing, and it had to be her brother.

If she could find him, then she could return back to her new home and become the wife she was meant to be. At least, that's what she told

James when he questioned her state of melancholy. It truly didn't take much convincing for him to agree to this healing cruise.

As she glanced at her husband now, she knew he hoped for a greater outcome from this voyage. She was sure he hoped she found her sanity.

James caught her staring and smiled wearily.

The room was packed. They found seats several rows back from the stage and waited for the production to commence.

It didn't take long before a man in a long coat swept onto the stage. "Greetings all, I'm Doctor Hippolyte Myers." His French accent was strong. "I'll be your guide into the world of healing and peace. I studied at The Nancy School and have worked in this field for over two decades."

The crowd was silent, enthralled by his commanding presence. That is, until a coughing fit echoed through the ballroom. Arabella followed the mass of heads, turning to the back of the room. The woman she saw rocking on the deck last night was hunched over, gasping for breath. She clutched the ruby necklace hanging over her chest.

"I believe we've found our first patient," Dr. Myers said, drawing the attention back to him.

Arabella's gaze, however, lingered on the woman. A man approached her from the sidelines, taking hold of her folded arm to usher her toward the stage as her coughing subsided. Arabella's heart raced. Something about the way this man moved was familiar.

As they neared, the stage cast light onto his face. Arabella suppressed a gasp. This was one of the men she saw chasing Lawrence last night, she was sure of it. A red scratch marred his cheek.

James cast her a worried glance. "Everything alright, darling? You're looking pale."

"Good, then I fit right in," Arabella said. "Everyone here is pale."

James narrowed his eyes but turned his attention to the stage.

"Ladies and Gentleman," Dr. Myers said as he stretched out his arms. "What you are about to see here is a testament to science and the will of survival in the human mind and body. Madame, please, share your name."

"Constance de Puysegur," the woman said in a squeaky voice.

Dr. Myers motioned to a chair sitting in the middle of the stage. "Please, take a seat, Constance."

She listened, her frail body shaking under the full attention of the room.

The doctor pulled a coin out of his pocket and held it about a foot from Constance. "Do not become distracted by the faces around you. Do you desire healing?"

Constance covered her mouth and coughed. Once finished, she lowered her arm and nodded.

The doctor continued, "Are you ready for your pains to be alleviated?"

Again, she nodded. Her eyes shifted to the audience.

"Keep your focus on me," Dr Myers said. "Good. Keep a steady, fixed stare on this coin." He waved toward the man who'd brought the woman onto the stage, who then moved to a phonograph. Soft, soothing music flowed from its horn.

Arabella searched the faces in the crowd. She saw no sign of her brother.

After a few moments, the woman's hand raised. Her body tensed, as if another coughing fit was about to begin.

"Keep your focus…" Dr. Myers stopped her. "Relax your body."

The woman listened, her arm returning to her lap. She began swaying in her seat.

The doctor moved the coin toward her face. Constance's eyelids closed.

"Your mind is clear," Dr. Myers said. "The ailments of your body will heal with rest. Allow your lungs to reach their full potential."

The woman took a large breath in. No rasp was heard. Her breathing was clear. Murmuring waved across the crowd.

Dr. Myers's attention stayed on the woman. "When you wake, your lungs will obey your mind. You will have control over your destiny." He threw the coin into the air and caught it, enclosing it within his palm. With a snap of a finger, the woman's eyes opened, searching for the coin that was in front of her moments ago.

Her face wrinkled. "Where'd it go?"

"Your healing has been completed," Dr. Myers said. "How are you feeling, dear Constance?"

She looked at the audience, their faces wide with anticipation. Then, she turned back to the doctor. Her body relaxed. She took in a deep breath and released it slowly. "I feel well."

The doctor smiled as murmurs of amazement and disbelief burst through the crowd once more.

"Give it time," one man close to Arabella said. "No way this is real."

"Look at the color returning to her face." His female companion pointed at the stage. "She has to be healed."

"I'm not sold," he said in response.

Dr. Myers turned to the audience. "Who would like to be next?"

James gave Arabella a side eye but said nothing. She had no desire to go on stage. Besides, she wasn't on this healing cruise because of an ailment. She had a different mission—one that seemed as if it might be solved as the doctor pointed to someone on the other side of the room.

A man in a wheelchair headed toward the stage. Once he cleared the front seats of the crowd, Arabella stood, her hands covering her mouth.

She knew the man being helped to the stage. Lawrence took shaky steps as he ascended the stairs onto the platform, leaning on the man he'd been trying to escape from the last time Arabella saw him.

She wanted to go to him. Run onto that stage and wrap her arms around his shoulders. It'd been six months since the last time she saw him, other than last night and the time on the dock, which had led her to run onboard, her husband close behind. But even then, there'd been a part of her that wondered if it was simply an illusion. Her brain showed her what she so desperately wanted.

James tugged on the sleeve of her gown, pulling her into her seat. "We need to wait."

Arabella shot him a glare. "You didn't believe he was alive. Yet, there he is."

His cheeks reddened. "I admit, I was mistaken."

"Well, well!" Dr. Myers grabbed the attention in the room once more. "It seems your condition is much more advanced than Ms. Constance's. May I be given a name?"

"Law." Lawrence was lowered into the lone stage chair.

"Law, eh?" Dr. Myers raised an eyebrow. "I can assure you all that is done 'ere is within the legalities of our Royal Highness." The doctor laughed—a slow, unconvincing huff. "All jokes aside, today will be the first day of the rest of your life."

Seeing Lawrence under the stage lights illuminated the state of his health. His face was white, the color gone from his sunken cheeks. His normally thick, blond curls were now thin and straight. He reminded her too much of their father before he passed. Bangs covered his eyes as his hazel gaze fell on the coin in the doctor's hand.

The music played. Lawrence's body swayed. His eyes closed. The same routine that was used on Constance.

"My boy," the doctor said, "we are here today for your healing."

Arabella's hope rose. She'd heard rumors of hypnosis, how the therapy used the mere suggestion of healing to allow the body to right itself. The medical trials done throughout France and England had promising results.

But then, she'd also heard the controversy. Placing people in such a suggestive state led to questions of agency and morality.

That was supposedly the stigma Dr. Myers was hoping to undo. By performing such therapy in the eyes of the public instead of hidden inside a hospital, he could show how truly safe such a practice was.

"This man has now entered a state of sleep," Dr. Myers said. "His will now possesses a stronger and greater mental power than if he were awake. Through this, I shall command his healing."

Lawrence's body continued to sway.

"What ails you?" the doctor asked.

"Consumption." Lawrence's voice was sleepy. Arabella had expected this answer, yet she felt faint at the mention of it.

Dr. Myers's face tightened. "That is a bit tricky."

Arabella knew what that meant. There was no cure. Not for her father. Not for her younger brother, barely at the end of his teenage years.

The doctor bent closer to Lawrence, whispering something in his ear. Moments later, he regained his composure. "It is quite the diagnosis. Your disease has been progressing, has it not?"

Lawrence nodded.

"You are bound to a wheelchair?"

"Yes," Lawrence answered, still in his trance. "The strength of my legs often fails me."

Arabella's face scrunched. Last night her brother had been running on his own, his legs strong.

"I see," Dr. Myers continued. "That shall be no more. The pain walking brings you will be replaced with health. You shall have the ability to run, skip, and hop to your heart's desire. Your strength shall be restored."

He snapped the coin away, bringing Lawrence back to the present. Arabella sat on the edge of her seat, waiting to see her brother's reaction.

Lawrence glanced around, as if exiting a daze.

"It is done," Dr. Myers said. "You may now walk."

Lawrence stretched one leg, then the other. He grasped the chair as he stood, wobbling at first, but then finding his balance. He took one step across the stage, then another, and another. The crowd cheered at his recovery, seemingly won over after such a drastic change in countenance.

Arabella knew it wasn't real. She looked at Dr. Myers as he clapped along with the applause. His face was straight—a stark difference to the smile he wore after Constance's miraculous recovery.

If the walking was a hoax, perhaps the consumption was as well. Arabella had to hold onto some strand of hope, even though something wasn't right. The first step to figuring out what was wrong was talking with Lawrence, who she quickly realized was no longer on stage. She searched frantically through the crowd, her eyes landing by the steps of the stage.

His wheelchair was there. Empty.

"He was here," Arabella said as James's hands held her in place, his palms on the top of each arm.

"I know." James glanced to the back of the ballroom, where the crowd dispersed, heading to experience other activities this cruise offered. Many likely headed to the lounge to listen to relaxing music as they chatted about the miracles they'd witnessed. "But we need to go," James continued, "we've been spotted by—"

"Hello, James," a male voice behind them said. Only the elite of the elite could afford such a leisurely voyage. Those who had more money than they knew what to do with. The kind of people that made the man standing behind Arabella very happy.

Which was the opposite of how he sounded now.

"Hello, Father," James said, lowering his hands. Arabella twisted 'round to face the older, mustache ridden image of her husband: Count Victor Parsons, the owner of the S.S. Mesmer they now sailed on. He held a wooden cane in his hand.

"I expected you to be in London on business." Lord Parsons looked over Arabella's head to speak to James. "You seem to have made a wrong turn."

"I was..." James stammered. He rubbed the side of his face as his brows narrowed, as if trying to think of what to say.

Arabella moved to his side. "It was me, sir. It was my idea. When we were dropping off the last of the supplies for the voyage, I saw the ship and decided I simply must be on it. I'd always dreamed of experiencing the seas up close, and he granted me my wish."

With thin lips, Lord Parsons looked from Arabella to James. "Is this true?"

James nodded.

"I expect to have you dine with me tonight," Lord Parsons said. "We shall discuss this failure of character in more depth." He turned and marched away, his cane tapping on the floor with each step.

Arabella looked to her husband. He'd turned ghostly white.

Dinner was uncomfortable. Not because of the hard dining chairs that lined the private table in the lounge. Not from the smoke that filled the room from the other guests. No, the way Lord Parsons's eye pierced into James in silence throughout the meal was enough to make anyone want to lower a rowboat and paddle home.

Except for Arabella. She wasn't giving up until she could bring her brother with her.

Lord Parsons cleared his throat, and a waiter removed his half empty plate. "I would like to meet with you in the Smoke Room." He didn't specify that the invitation was only meant for James, but Arabella already knew. Men needed their privacy for *important* business a simple woman wouldn't understand.

Arabella didn't protest. In fact, it worked in her favor. She eyed the faces at a neighboring table: Dr. Myers and his crew. The two goons conversed and laughed together while the doctor seemed not to care. He held his coin in his hand, tossing it into the air and catching it repeatedly. The way the light caught on its golden plating drew her attention…

"Shall I accompany you back to our stateroom?" James turned to Arabella.

"What?" Arabella asked, her focus returning to their table.

"Shall I go with you back to our room? You're looking rather tired, Dear." James's term of endearment made her cringe, but it was part of their plan. They needed to convince his father of their deep love for one another. Deep enough for them to make the foolish decision to sneak onto this ship.

"No," she said, rather too quickly, despite her eyes feeling heavy. "I mean, I could use some fresh air and would like to take a walk around the upper deck."

James narrowed his eyes. "Are you sure that's safe, my love?" He was good at playing the lovesick partner.

"We're on a ship in the middle of the ocean," Arabella said. "Certainly no danger could befall me... Dearest." She was not as good at showing her affection. Afterall, this match was made for her societal advantage. Love wasn't a necessity. She batted her eyes, remembering the way her friends back home would earn a man's attention.

James's face scrunched, as if holding back a laugh. He did, however, smirk.

"I can send a maid to accompany her." Lord Parsons raised a hand, motioning at a steward. The young man nodded and left the room.

Arabella knew it wasn't her place to refuse further. He was her father-in-law and, as such, remained in control of her home and fortune.

The steward returned with a young woman. She seemed to be a few years younger than Arabella, likely still in her teenage years.

"Come, James." Lord Parsons ushered her husband through the door on the side of the room. The steward followed, as well as Dr. Myers and his goons, who Arabella had only just realized had joined their group at some point.

Regardless of when, it was now time for her to make her own departure. She headed for the outer doors. If the men were distracted with their smoking and drinking, perhaps now was the time to do a deeper search of the ship.

"Wait for me," the maid called, hustling behind her. "I'm meant to 'company you."

Arabella spun around, causing the maid to take a step back to avoid running into her.

"I'm Lacie, Ma'am" she said.

"No need to 'Ma'am' me. You may call me Arabella."

Lacie's eyes widened. "I'm not sure that I can."

"Oh, parsnips. Yes, you can." Arabella eyed the door on the other side of the room opposite of where the men had disappeared. "What is that room there?"

"That leads into the kitchens, Ma'a—Mrs. Arabella."

Arabella wanted to correct her further, but she'd take a "Mrs" over a "Ma'am" any day. "If I were to, say, want to hide a passenger in a place they couldn't easily escape from, where might that be?"

Lacie's body tensed. "Well, 'tis is a large ship. Many hidden spaces for people to hide, I suppose. But why would a lady like you have a need for such a place?"

"Oh, never mind." Scaring the help wasn't necessarily the best route to go about finding her brother. "Let's head to my room." It seemed she'd need to rid herself of her shadow if she wanted to make any progress.

The full moon shone in all its glory, casting shadows around the fog covered deck. Arabella couldn't help but think the full circle had closed sooner than she'd expected from the night before.

Without much time to ponder on the irregularity, Arabella turned toward the bow of the ship. It would mean a longer route to her room but might as well cover some ground before the night became later. The men would only socialize for so long.

As if on cue, a door from the side opened in their faces. Arabella jumped back against the side of the ship, her hand stretched in front of Lacie.

Male grunts came from the other side as the door slowly closed. "Can this body be any heavier?" a gravelly voice said.

With the door closed, Arabella saw it was the man with the scratched face. The other chaser held the opposite side of what looked to be a large carpet they were lugging. Both were so focused on their task, they didn't seem to notice the girls.

"Over here." Arabella motioned for Lacie to follow her as she hid behind a nearby pillar.

The men continued their task, heading toward the edge of the boat. Arabella's heart raced as she watched. She was sure the sound of it thumping would give their position away.

"On the count of three," the gravelly man said. "One... two..."

"Oof," the other said, the carpet sliding from his hands. It landed on the wooden deck, the cloth unraveling.

Arabella placed a hand over her mouth. The body of a woman rolled onto its side. Her skin was discolored, making it difficult in the moonlight and fog to distinguish her features. However, around her neck a ruby necklace caught the light from above.

The man who'd dropped the body quickly lifted it once more. As they did, her necklace caught on a nail on the floor. It broke apart, landing on the ground. "Let's just get this over with," he said as the two swung the body toward the edge.

Arabella wanted to step out. To yell. To stop the atrocity she was witnessing. And yet, her body was frozen, unable to save the woman as a splash sounded in the water below.

The woman whose skin matched the same tone Arabella's father did after his death.

The woman who was supposed to have been healed that morning but now slept on the bottom of the sea.

The two men wiped their hands. The scratch-faced one retrieved the necklace from the ground. "I'm sure our boss would appreciate this memento," he said as they headed back inside the boat.

As they passed, Arabella sunk into the shadows. Her heartbeat quickened as her thoughts returned to her brother. These were the men who were chasing him that first night. The ones that brought him onto the stage to be "healed" just like this woman. Yet she was dead. Was it because of the healing, or something else? Was her brother also in danger?

Lacie placed a hand on Arabella's arm. "Mrs.," her small voice said. She'd been hiding behind Arabella, and she wasn't sure how much she'd seen.

"Did you see what they threw overboard?"

"It looked like an ol' rug," Lacie said.

Arabella released a breath of relief. At least someone so young hadn't witnessed such a dark event. "Yes… Shall we continue?" Her reserve to search the ship had waned, her mind overcome by the grief she so often held inside. Now, she truly desired her room. To be alone, for just a moment.

However, in her soul hung the truth of what she'd seen. If that woman had been a puppet in the show that morning, Lawrence was likely one as well. Had he already faced the same fate as her?

"Perhaps we should head back in the other direction," Lacie suggested. "I believe it's a quicker route to your room."

Arabella nodded. She didn't want to cross the path the men had taken. Although it wasn't physically tainted with the woman's blood, Arabella couldn't help but imagine it there.

They passed the door to the lounge as they backtracked their journey. The door snapped closed, causing Arabella to jump. "What was that?"

"What do you mean, Ma'am?" Lacie asked.

"*Ma'am?*" Arabella raised a brow. "Don't you mean *Mrs.?*"

Lacie nodded her head. "If that is what you prefer. Shall we continue to your room?"

Arabella felt lightheaded as they walked. As they turned a corner, she bumped into a man.

She took a quick step back. "Oh, I'm sor—" Her words stopped as she gawked at her brother standing in front of her.

"Don't be," he said, his eyes wandering over the people on the deck. "I suppose I'm not good at watching where I'm walking when I'm busy searching for someone."

Arabella's mouth gaped open. "Lawrence! I've been looking for you!" The tightness in her chest moments before lightened, feeling as if she might float away any moment.

She'd found her brother.

His face scrunched as he took a full look at her, then broke into a smile. "Arabella! I knew I saw you that first day at boarding!"

"You did," she confirmed.

He stepped forward and wrapped her in a hug.

Lacie stood slightly behind, her face reddening at their closeness.

"Oh, how I've missed you." Lawrence released her. "Oh, don't cry, Ara."

"These are happy tears," she said, although she knew that wasn't fully true. Seeing the condition of his health so closely confirmed how much it had progressed. "I've been looking for my brother."

"Oh!" Lacie exclaimed, looking relieved. "Your brother, how wonderful."

Arabella turned to her. "Isn't he? It seems I will no longer be in need of your escort. You are free to resume your regular duties."

With hesitancy, Lacie eyed Lawrence. "Are you sure, Mrs.?"

"Yes," Arabella said. "I'm sure Lawrence would be happy to accompany me for the evening. I appreciate your time."

"Yes," Lawrence said, offering his elbow to Arabella. "It would be my pleasure."

Lacie bowed her head slightly, then turned around and headed back in the direction of the lounge.

Arabella slipped her hand into her brother's arm. Before she asked the question on her mind, Lawrence beat her to it.

"What are you doing here?" he asked. They started to walk around the deck.

"As I said before, I've been looking for you." There was a chill in the air. Arabella suppressed a sniffle. "You've been gone for six months!"

Their footsteps thumped on the wooden floor, joining other passengers on their evening strolls, who nodded at them as they passed.

"I've had… business," he said.

So many thoughts ran through her mind, conversations she wanted to discuss. His sickness, and "healing" from yesterday, the scene she'd just seen moments before. But the thought that propelled her on this journey in the first place was the one that popped out. "More important than your older sister's wedding?"

Lawrence halted. He turned his head to look at her. "I never wanted to miss your wedding."

"Well, you did. And it was an awfully unlike-you thing to do."

"I didn't even know it'd gone through until I saw you with James," Lawrence explained. "Don't get much news on the ship. I tried to find you last night, but my *employers* don't like me being out and about using my legs. Regardless of the fact I was wearing a mask."

So that's the story behind last night. He'd been searching for her.

"*I* thought you surely must have died." Arabella moved her arms across her chest. "But instead, you decided it was time to abandon me. Leave me with a wealthy match and go."

The pained expression on Lawrence's thin face caused guilt to ripple through Arabella. "I thought a wealthy match was what you desired."

She placed a hand on his upper arm. "Yes, so that I could best take care of my little brother."

His eyes relaxed. "You wanted to marry for money… for me?"

"We both saw the way father suffered with no care in the end." She took a deep breath. "I will not allow that to happen to you. I simply cannot stand for that. And then you went and ran away."

"I took this job for you," Lawrence said. He ran a hand through his fine hair. "I wanted to make sure *you* were taken care of." His voice was hoarse.

"Oh…" The dots were lining up, connecting. "You agreed to work for Lord Parsons in exchange for my hand in marriage?" She'd wondered how he did it. Sure, Lawrence inherited a title from their father, along with a slew of gambling debts. Didn't exactly make Arabella a top choice for a wife. It seemed her brother found a way around that. Instead of a dowry of money, he'd offered himself as a servant.

"Lord Parsons is the type of man that has more money than he knows what to do with," Lawrence said. "Control, on the other hand, is something he seeks. I gave him that."

Arabella pursed her lips. He was talking about the man that raised her husband. Who taught him what it looked like to be a husband and father.

She shook her head. James wasn't like his father. As much as he tried to maintain being the head of their small household, he also gave

Arabella space to think. If he were more like his father, they never would have stepped foot on this boat in the first place.

Which also meant she wouldn't have seen the woman with the ruby necklace being tossed overboard.

Lawrence pulled a handkerchief out of the pocket of his overcoat, catching a cough. It went on for several seconds before he was able to take a deep breath, silence falling over them once more.

"There's something I'd like to tell you," Arabella said.

"What is it?"

She glanced around, placing a hand on his arm and directing him to the railing of the ship. Her stomach churned with the movement of the dark waters below. The moon quivered across the waves, a small sliver missing from its edge.

"I believe I've witnessed a murder. Or, at least a cover up of a woman's death."

His brows narrowed. "What do you mean?"

"The woman that was *healed* before you at the demonstration this morning. Constance." Arabella looked side to side. No one was near. "I saw the doctor's workers throw her dead body overboard."

Somehow, under the dim lights, Lawrence's skin became whiter. "I was worried something like this would happen. I rather thought it would be me."

Arabella swallowed back bile. "You're in danger. We need to get you off this ship and find you medical care."

"You know," Lawrence said. "When I made this deal, I had hoped Dr. Myers's miraculous treatment would cure me. Turns out, I'm too far gone, even for miracles."

Arabella shook her head. "No, there has to be something we can do."

Knowing dawned on Lawrence's face. "I know something."

"A cure? Is it likely to work?" Arabella knew better than to get her hopes up.

He shook his head. "No, not that. Constance. I think I may have seen something earlier."

She perked up.

"I remember," he continued, "after the demonstration. I saw her. She was talking with Lord Parsons at the time. He didn't look happy."

"He usually doesn't," Arabella said.

"True." Lawrence nodded. "But this was more than usual. He was angry, and Constance looked to be arguing with him."

Arabella knew her father-in-law wouldn't like someone talking back to him, but... "That's not enough to say he's the reason she's dead. Maybe she succumbed to her sickness?"

"She was an actor," Lawrence said. "Like me. Hired, or blackmailed, by the count to make Dr. Myers's act look real."

"So the whole idea of hypnotism is fake?" She'd suspected, but hearing it confirmed brought more bafflement. How could this truly be a debate among medical doctors then?

"Not exactly. Dr. Myers believes in it, but it's not a cure all. It has its uses in the medical arena, not so much on the stage."

Arabella was filled with disgust. Her father-in-law made money off wealthy, unwell people. Did James know? Was he involved?

"How do we find out who killed her?" she asked.

"It seems pretty obvious to me," Lawrence said. "If Lord Parsons didn't deal the final blow, he certainly ordered it done. The question we should be asking is—" He paused to cough once more. This time Arabella caught the bright red in his handkerchief before he tucked it away. He continued, "How do we expose him?"

"There's another healing demonstration tomorrow, correct?"

Lawrence nodded.

"I believe I have an idea."

The next morning, Arabella's head throbbed. After the excitement from the night before, she'd fallen asleep as soon as her head hit the pillow.

She hadn't even roused when James slipped into the twin bed next to hers. He lay with his eyes closed, his chest moving.

Unlike the woman's chest last night, with the ruby necklace attached to her dark, decaying neck.

Arabella shook her head. She needed to be rid of the image.

James rolled over in his bed, his eyes opening to meet hers. Immediately, panic lined his face. "Are you okay? You look like you've seen a ghost."

"I very well may have."

James looked downward and bit his lip but stayed silent.

"What happened last night?" Arabella asked.

James's face widened once more. "Wh—What do you mean?"

Arabella narrowed her eyes. "With your dad. After I left."

He relaxed. "Oh, yeah. That. He's 'deeply disappointed' in me. Says I need to learn to 'control my wife and home' like I had no say in the choice to come on this boat." He sounded angry.

Arabella had never seen him so open about his feelings before. She liked it. However, a part of her was weary; it could all be an act. Just like the one his father performed to attract customers to his ship.

James rubbed the side of his face that wasn't resting on a pillow. "Sorry, I shouldn't be putting this all on you."

"No, it's okay," Arabella said. "Please share it with me. I also do not care much for your father."

James laughed and shook his head. The sound brought warmth to her cheeks, betraying the unease she felt. He rolled over, as if trying to go back to sleep.

Perhaps being married to this man was worth more than just his fortune. She couldn't name one other suitor of hers that would have gone along with her plan. She had a hard time believing he was truly involved in his father's affairs.

Sure, James claimed he agreed to come on the premise she would return home, put her woes for her family behind her, and focus on conceiving an heir. But even then, he could have demanded she do her part for their union.

He never did. Never pressured her and listened when she spoke about losing her father and her fears for Lawrence.

However, she had no idea how he would react to her plan later that day.

"James…"

"Mhmm?"

She wondered how forthcoming she should be about last night, but perhaps his reaction would give away if she could trust him. "Last night, I saw something."

James flipped over to face her. His voice was filled with urgency. "What do you mean?"

His tone scared her. This might be a bad idea. "Well, I went for a walk toward the bow of the ship…"

His face softened. "What did you see?"

"The men who had chased my brother that first night. They threw something overboard."

"Do you know what?" His brows furrowed.

Arabella nodded. "A body."

She'd expected a look of shock to cross his face, however, instead it creased with pain. "Bella, look—"

The ship whistle blew twice. Was breakfast over already? The sun shined through the porthole window, brightening the room with mid-morning light.

"What is it?" Arabella asked. James had been on the verge of sharing something.

He bit his lip. "It's just that it must've been scary, what you saw. I'm sorry you had to experience that."

Arabella shrugged. His response didn't tell her anything. "We need to get to the healing demo." She hopped out of bed. "Lawrence may be there again." She thought about mentioning seeing him last night but didn't want to risk compromising their upcoming plan.

James slowly sat up. "Yes, perhaps he will."

They arrived in time to sit in the third row. Arabella's stomach churned. The last time she was here was the last time she had seen Constance alive.

At least this time she was prepared. She knew what to expect.

Dr. Myers strode onto the stage in his long, black cape. "Welcome passengers, to our second day of healing. I hope you've taken advantage of the fresh air and ocean breeze. It is important to give your worries and cares over to the heavens and allow yourself the space to truly live."

James's eyes were glued on Arabella as she looked around the crowd, pretending to look for her brother even though she knew he wasn't there. The real target of her search stood at the back of the ballroom; his blue captain hat settled on his head. After the confirmation, she met James's gaze. "What?"

With slight movements, he shook his head. He turned his attention to the stage.

"Today I would like to ask for a specific volunteer," Dr. Myers continued his presentation. Arabella sat up. This wasn't quite what she expected from the doctor. "I'm in search of someone who has experienced great loss. Someone who feels as if their life has gotten off track and the things that once brought them excitement and fulfillment, now have dark clouds cast upon them."

His gaze drifted to Arabella, pausing for a moment before moving on. It was eerie how well his description fit her life. Whether it did or not, didn't matter. She planned to be on that stage today.

"Is there anyone here that fits that description?" the doctor asked.

Arabella shot into the air. James gave her a side eye, but he didn't pull her down.

"Yes, the young lady in the lavender dress." Dr. Myers pointed at her. The scratch-faced goon walked toward her to usher her to the stage. She didn't wait. She took long strides and rushed up the stairs, plopping into the chair on stage.

Dr. Myers widened his eyes. "You seem quite eager to be here."

"I am. I've suffered long enough." Her shoulders drooped with the words she truly meant. She wasn't planning on acting today.

"Would you be so kind as to share your woes?" the doctor asked. He held nothing in his hands.

She needed him to complete his act. "I've lost my father."

"I am sorry for your loss. I can see how that's placed you in mourning. Are you ready to find freedom from your pain?"

Arabella nodded. Turned out she did need to act, at least a little bit.

Dr. Myers pulled his coin from his pocket and held it in front of her face. The gentle music played.

She focused her vision past the coin, in the direction of the phonograph. The goon stood there, waiting to stop the music when it was time. Behind him, she made out the figure of Lord Parsons.

"Focus on my coin." Dr. Myers held it a foot from her face. Arabella swayed her body. "Let all your worries and pain float away for this moment," he said.

There was too much on Arabella's mind for that to actually happen, so instead that's what she focused on.

Her father's tragic death. Her brother disappearing, being used to lie and cheat others for her to be wedded into the very family that was misusing him. How all she'd ever wanted was to be a wife and mother, yet the sacrifices that were given to make it happen weren't right. She'd been growing feelings for her husband that she wasn't sure were fully innocent. His response today would make or break their vows.

The doctor moved the coin closer to her. Her eyes closed.

"Tell us," the doctor said, "what ails you?"

This was it. "Not all is what it seems."

"Hmm… How so?"

With her eyes closed, she couldn't see his facial reaction, but his voice sounded intrigued.

"Constance is dead."

A gasp rippled through the audience. Arabella resisted breaking the trance. She needed them to believe she was under hypnosis.

"You saw her die?" Dr. Myers asked.

Slowly, she shook her head no.

"Then how do you know?" he asked.

"I saw her dead body thrown overboard. Fed to the fishes within the sea."

The crowd became noisier.

"Has anyone seen Constance?" one voice shouted.

"This is absurd," said another.

"Now, now," Dr. Myers said, raising his voice. "We must wait to hear the full story. Who did you see do these things?"

"Your attendants," she said.

"Hypnotism killed her!" a woman screamed.

"I knew this was a hoax."

Voices in the crowd grew louder.

They believed Arabella.

Footsteps pounded onto the stage. "Settle down," the voice of Captain Bernheim boomed next to her. The crowd obeyed. "What is the meaning of this commotion? What spell have you put on this woman?"

"A person in a hypnotic trance answers to the truth of their conscious mind," the doctor explained. "That doesn't mean what they say is fact. It merely means it's what *they* believe."

The crowd ramped back up.

"So she truly saw a body thrown overboard?" the captain said.

"It would appear so," the doctor replied.

"By your attendant there?" the captain asked.

Arabella didn't hear the doctor's response over the murmuring.

"I want to speak to her out of this trance," the captain stated.

The crowd quieted. The gentle music had stopped playing. She heard the snap of the doctor's hand and opened her eyes, squinting against the lights.

She glanced around in a dazed state. She caught sight of Lawrence now standing behind Lord Parsons. He nodded his head.

So they were right.

"Young lady, I have some questions for you," the captain said.

"Yes?" Arabella showed confusion.

The captain stood tall with his shoulders square. "Do you wish to make an official accusation of wrongful death? Against that man there?" He pointed at the goon, who had two security officers standing at his sides. The other goon was missing.

She swallowed. "Not exactly. He's involved, but not the murderer."

Her eyes washed over the waiting crowd, landing on James.

"Then who is responsible for Constance's disappearance?"

"Lord Victor Parsons," she said with confidence. James's mouth dropped, his head turning toward his father with the rest of the crowd.

Lord Parsons marched his way onto the stage. "I beg your pardon?" His voice was hard. "You better have evidence for such an outlandish accusation."

"Check his pockets," Lawrence shouted from the sidelines. "I saw him slip her necklace inside them this morning."

Lord Parsons shot him a glare.

"Well," the captain turned to the count, "shall we put an end to this story? Turn your pockets out."

"This is absolute ridiculousness," he said as he moved through each coat pocket. When he placed his hand in the last, he paused.

"Go ahead," the captain encouraged.

Lord Parsons pursed his lips as he pulled out a chain. On the end of it was the ruby pendant. Blood stained the chain.

The captain pulled out his handkerchief, holding it out for Lord Parsons to set the bloodied necklace upon.

"I'm placing you, along with your accomplices, on official ship arrest until this matter is further investigated. You shall remain locked in your quarters until either Constance is found, or we arrive on land. Which then, in case of the latter, the authorities shall take over the matter." The captain motioned for another security guard to approach Lord Parsons.

"This is my ship!" he shouted.

"And *I* am its captain!" Captain Berheim waved for him to be taken away.

"We did it!" Lawrence said, approaching Arabella on stage once the others had left. She was glued to her chair, not sure of what would happen next. "That necklace was covered in blood."

"How did you know it was there?" she asked.

"This morning, as I was looking for evidence, I saw the count talking with Dr. Myers. Lord Parsons reached into his pocket, pulled the necklace out, examined it, then placed it back in. Can you believe my luck?"

Arabella couldn't, but she didn't have much right to complain.

Without that necklace, their whole plan would have failed. But also, wouldn't that mean the doctor knew it was there as well?

She didn't have time to dwell on that. Now that the crowd was dispersing, Arabella searched for her husband. James sat in the same seat, his head crashed in his hands.

Lawrence saw where she looked. "I don't think he's his father."

"But how would you know that for sure?"

"I never would have let him marry my sister if I thought he was." He bumped into her arm.

She smiled. Perhaps he was right.

"Go check on your spouse," he urged.

Arabella approached James slowly. She sat next to him, placing a hand on his back.

"He did it," he said.

"I don't know for sure if he did—" Arabella started.

"If not to her, then he did to others." James raised his gaze to meet her eyes. "He's done it before. Gotten rid of people that stood in his way or angered him. I thought he'd never be caught. Thank you."

Arabella swallowed. She hadn't expected her husband to be grateful that she'd gotten his father arrested.

"What do we do now?" she asked.

James looked behind her, over to where Lawrence stood waiting. "Well, I suppose we make the most of this situation and spend the rest of our time with your brother."

Arabella wrapped James into a hug. He pulled away, and without a care if any lingering passengers saw, he leaned over and kissed her.

Ten days later the S.S. Mesmer pulled into port. Arabella leaned over the side with Lawrence and James next to her. She was glad to have James near, as the rest of the trip he'd been busier than imagined, tending to the affairs his father was responsible for during the voyage.

That left Arabella plenty of time to reconnect with Lawrence. Now that he no longer had the pressure from Lord Parsons hanging over his head, his frail body began to regain some weight. He looked good in the bright morning light. Consumption wasn't going to consume him yet. He had more fight left in him.

An officer approached James as they stepped off the boat. Lord

Parsons had been escorted to the side, waiting with the two goons in the middle of the group of officers.

"We need to have a talk about your father's affairs," the officer said. "It seems his finances are mixed up in more dirt than we'd thought."

"I'll be right back," James said.

"I wish there was more we could've gotten the doctor for," Arabella said as Dr. Myers made his way off the boarding ramp. His demonstrations were scratched off the posted itineraries for the rest of the trip. No one was interested in hypnosis after Constance's death. He passed by the sibling pair.

"Excuse me, Sir." Lawrence called the doctor over.

Arabella wanted to go and hide, but she didn't.

"Yes? You're Law, correct?" Dr. Myers asked.

"Full name's Lawrence."

"Nice to 'officially' meet you, off the stage that is." The doctor shook his hand. "Lord Parsons doesn't like me to converse with those he hired. All those times on stage though... I'm deeply sorry there's not more I could do for you. Hypnosis is not a cure all, as some people think."

Arabella's forehead creased. "What do you mean?"

"Well," Dr. Myers said, "some people think hypnosis is a party trick, or performance. Others believe it's a breakthrough in medical research. A therapy that will revolutionize the treatment of patients. Some want to take advantage of it, while others want to use it to change lives."

"And which are you?" Arabella asked.

Dr. Myers smiled. "Let's just say I'm not the type of man who would provide a loan for another's training, and then turn their education into a game for my own profit. Play along or be completely ruined. I'm the type of man to use science to make the world a better place."

With that, he tipped his hat. His coat swooshed as he turned and headed toward the streets of London.

Arabella watched him go, in awe of the answer he'd given. She turned toward her brother. "But if he's a man of science, why would he perform on actors?"

"As he explained, he had no choice," Lawrence said.

A shiver ran up Arabella's spine as she glanced at the doctor once more. As he approached the nearby buildings, a woman emerged from the shadows, wrapping her arm in his.

Arabella gripped Lawrence's arm.

"Ouch," he complained.

"Look." She pointed at the doctor and his companion. "Isn't that…?"

Even without the ruby necklace, Arabella recognized the petite woman as Constance.

Lawrence squinted his eyes, but shook his head. "No, it must be someone else."

But Arabella had a feeling it wasn't. Had the entire scene of her being thrown overboard been an illusion? An image of the dinner flashed into Arabella's mind.

She glanced in the direction of Lord Parsons, with his hands cuffed in front of him. James was nearby, talking with the officers, likely discussing what was to happen next. He nodded his head and walked back toward Arabella and Lawrence.

As he approached, Arabella asked, "Did you know?" James *had* been elusive after dinner that night, as if something more was bothering him.

He sighed. "I suspected my father was up to something, but didn't know exactly—"

"No, that night at dinner." Arabella saw the realization dawn on James's face.

"What are you talking about?" Lawrence asked, his brows wrinkled.

"Dr. Myers hypnotized Arabella," James answered.

"We all saw that on stage…" Lawrence said.

"No, before then. At dinner."

So she was right. The coin flipping; Lacie resorting back to calling her Ma'am after the incident. The pieces fell into place.

Arabella had been hypnotized into setting up her father-in-law.

"So you knew it was a lie all along." Arabella tried to keep her voice steady to keep from drawing attention from the other departing passengers. "Why would you let me continue on thinking I'd seen a dead woman."

James's eyes widened. "No! No, that's not what happened. At least, as far as I knew. Dr. Myers simply asked you how you felt about… um… me. He had pulled you aside and whispered in your ear for a bit, but I assumed that was part of getting the hypnotism to work. At least, until you started talking about seeing a dead body. I suspected, but wasn't sure."

Arabella's cheeks reddened. "And what did I say?"

"About the dead body?"

"No." Arabella took a step toward James as Lawrence stepped back, giving them space. "About you."

"You said 'love wasn't a necessity' when it came to marrying me," James answered, the side of lip rose into a smirk before falling. "I didn't know the doctor was going to use and manipulate you, I promise," he whispered, his head lowering. "And then when it worked to get my father locked up, I didn't know what to say."

Arabella took a deep breath. James hadn't known for sure, although he suspected the doctor was up to something. If he had told her as much, would they be where they are now? With Lord Parsons's other dastardly deeds about to get him locked up for good?

She looked at her husband. His face was down, his body tense, as if he didn't expect her to believe that he wasn't involved in this whole plot. If he were anything like his father, he very well may have orchestrated it all.

Arabella threw her arms around his neck, causing him to jerk back before wrapping his own arms around her. "Perhaps love has become a necessity," she whispered as his grip tightened. He wasn't like his father—that she was sure of.

One year later, Arabella sat on the porch of their new sea home rubbing her growing belly. After the amount of debt James's father had left them, their best option had been to sell their estate and move into a cottage by the sea.

Arabella didn't mind. She quite enjoyed the homemaking involved in keeping up with a small home. Plus, the fresh air near the sea was best for her brother's condition.

Lawrence joined her on the bench. "Beautiful weather today, isn't it?"

She gave him a smile. "James should be enjoying it on his walk home. He should be finished with the final inspection for the new ship."

"He's adjusted well to having his world turned upside-down."

Arabella nodded.

As if knowing he was being talked about, James's figure appeared on the hill path. Arabella rose from her spot, holding onto it for a second to catch her balance.

"Perhaps it's time you stop running out to greet him, and instead let him come all the way to you?" Lawrence said.

"No way," Arabella answered. "I'm a strong, capable woman, and I can meet my husband halfway."

Lawrence shook his head. "I'd say you do more work than him already, not counting the human you're growing."

She waved him off and waddled down the path. She did keep her pace slower. Meeting him a quarter of the way home was good enough.

James smiled as he approached, dropping his bags and running to her. He wrapped her in his arms, running one hand through her loose hair.

"Welcome home," she said. "How did the inspection go?"

"The S.S. Constance is ready to earn her sea legs," he said. "But I much prefer staying on land to enjoy our new home—together."

Shivers ran down Arabella's spine. "Same. I much prefer being in your arms."

"On the sand or the sea, there's nowhere else I'd rather be." James leaned down, his lips pressing onto hers.

Secrets of the Celtic Sea

Jaclyn Rose

When I was a wee boy, my Da used to tell the story of how my older brother, Thomas, was killed while battling a giant deep-sea creature called the Oillipheist. Even now that I am older and have wee ones of my own, I still remember it as if it were yesterday.

The year was 1847. I was six years old. We lived in the small town of Eyeries, in County Cork, Ireland. Eyeries is nestled closely into the lush green countryside covered in wildflowers, and is best known for its brightly colored buildings, stunning views of the water, and small-town charm.

The day my Da told me the story for the first time was the day my brother died. The somber sun set over Coulagh Bay, saturating the whole sky in a copper, whiskey-like glow, when Da stumbled home from the pub in town with the help of Mr. Maccarthy.

Mr. McCarthy helped Ma carry Da inside the house and got him settled into bed. I peeked in from around the corner. Ma's eyes were red and puffy and she tenderly patted Da's forehead with a washcloth. She thanked Mr. McCarthy, he offered his condolences, and then went on his way.

Da didn't get out of bed for a few hours, but when he did, he wrapped himself in a wool sweater and went out back to watch the waves crash upon the rocks in the moonlight. That's when I joined him.

"Da?" I asked quietly.

"Yes, son?" He asked, without turning to look at me.

"Thomas is'na coming back…is he?"

There was solemnity in his silence as I took a few steps toward him, and then we both watched a wave crescendo in the moonlight.

My heart began beating wildly as I tried to make sense of it. Thomas was a kind soul. We would play together in the yard, he helped Ma cook sometimes, and he always laughed at Da's deep sea fishing stories. He was my best friend. The last time I saw him, he even shared his meal with me. Ma always scolded him for doing that. I wasn't supposed to hear it, but our cottage only had two rooms, so I heard everything.

"Thomas! There's not enough fer one person to have seconds," she'd say in hushed tones.

"I'm okay, Ma! He needs it more than me. He's a growing boy."

"Yer practically skin and bones!" She'd argue. "Look! Yer shirt is falling off of ye!"

"I'm just fine Ma," he'd say, giving her a gentle hug. "Don't ye worry about me."

Suddenly, a snake-like cloud passed in front of the moon, shrouding Da and I in more darkness.

"What happened to him?" I asked, with tears rolling down my cheeks.

My Da stared at me for a long moment, absorbing my pain. Whatever he said next was going to change my life forever.

Da wiped the tears from my face and paused with an unsure look in his eye. "Don't ye cry now, William… yer brother was brave. He went to sea to fight the Oillipheist."

"The Oillipheist?" I asked curiously.

"Yes, son! The Oillipheist is one of the most dangerous beasts in all of Ireland and it dwells in bodies of water just like this one." He pointed to the bay. "It first showed up when St. Patrick tried to drive out the serpents from the land, but was defeated. Now, every forty years it comes to the surface again to destroy ships and even whole towns to get its revenge."

"What does it look like?" I asked, dabbing my eyes with my shirt sleeve.

"Oh, it's a horrible sight. It's a giant winged, fire-breathing beast with yellow eyes, jagged teeth and talons," my father said, pulling his cheek to the side to show his teeth. "But what is especially terrifying about this beast is that when the Earth shook and the sea swallowed up the cavern he lives in, he learned to swim underwater. He has been known to rise to the surface to stalk his prey, before taking down whole ships with one swipe of his tail."

My pulse raced. "How do they know when he's coming?"

"There are signs to watch out fer. First, schools of fish will start splashing like crazy on the surface of the water. Then, ye might hear a low growling start, and right before he strikes, ye'll see his yellow eyes pop out of the water to meet yer gaze."

My eyes got wider, and I think my Da realized his story was too scary for a six-year-old.

"Ye don't need to worry about it anymore, son. Yer brother stopped him from hurting anyone else."

"How?"

"When the Oillipheist snapped the wooden post in half that holds the sails with his teeth, yer brother steered the ship so that it stabbed the beast in the mouth. The beast screeched loudly and flew up high into the air, breathing fire as it thrashed its neck to and fro."

"He *did*?"

"Aye, boyo. Ye see, Thomas was the bravest warrior there e'er was."

"What happened after that?"

"The beast was badly injured and retreated into the water again. Not to return for another forty years."

"And Thomas?"

"A poisonous barb in the Oillipheists' tail stung Thomas."

"What were his last words, Da?" I choked.

My Da stared at me, with tears in his eyes too. "His last words were… Tell William he will be okay."

The worst day of my life was the day that Thomas died, but the second worst was the day I discovered my father had lied to me about it.

Two years after Thomas passed, I came home from the schoolhouse in tears with a bruised eye. When Ma asked what was wrong, I told her a boy from another family said the Oillipheist wasn't real. When I told him it was, because Da told me it killed Thomas, he said Da was a liar.

Ma was sitting at the kitchen table, making dough for pasties, as I paced around telling her what had happened. My face was stained with dirt and tears when I decided to confront her.

Be brave, like Thomas, I told myself.

"What's the truth, Ma? Did the Oillipheist really kill Thomas?"

Ma's eyes were downcast. She took a deep breath in, dusted the flour off her hands onto her dress and patted her knee.

"C'mere love."

It wasn't until that day that I realized the true devastation all of Ireland had faced during the potato famine. Ma told me that Thomas had died from starvation, and I sobbed remembering the times he gave me his portion of food.

"I didn't know, Ma!" I screamed through tears of humiliation.

"I know, William. I know."

Just then, Da came through the door. "What's all the ruckus about?"

"Ye lied!"

Da tried to grab me as I rushed past him, but I broke free from his grasp and busted through the door to the backyard. I ran so fast, neither of them could catch me. I collapsed near the cliff edge and wept until sundown. From that day forward, I made a promise to myself that I wouldn't tolerate lying and I would do whatever it took to make sure my family never went hungry again.

Thirty years later, I still lived in the same cottage I grew up in. I lived there with my wife, Joanna, my two children, and Da. Ma passed on four months earlier. It had been difficult for the whole family, but especially the kids, Tillie and Emmett.

Ma succumbed to a sickness caused by a lump in her breast, and Da had problems with his memory for quite some time, although he would never admit to it. Stubborn as a mule, that one. He kept asking when Ma would be home from town. Every time he asked, I'd tell him the truth, and each time, he'd get more cross with me.

"Ye should just let him think she's at the market," Joanna would softly suggest.

To which I would reply, "I willna' lie about death, Joanna. A man is only as good as his word."

Last week, after one of our ructions about Ma, Da stormed into the shed where he kept his old sailboat that he'd won in a bet with a man at the bar. That boat hadn't set sail in more than a decade, but he wouldn't let it go. Many times, I bargained with my father to sell the boat and fetch us some money for things like shoes for the children or a headstone for Thomas, but he wouldn't budge. Shortly after he stormed out into the shed, I heard a loud clanging and banging in the wee hours of the morning.

"What's that noise?" Joanna asked, startled awake.

"I'll go check," I said, kissing her forehead and getting out of bed.

As I looked out the window, I saw a flickering light in the shed. It was a candle, and through the window, I saw Da working on his old boat.

For the next five days, he worked on that boat tirelessly. Joanna would send the grandchildren in to bring him supper and water.

Good, I thought to myself. *At least he is keeping a hobby and hopefully his mind is off of Ma.*

Some years ago, I got a job working as a teacher at the local school. I enjoyed working with the children and there was a real thirst for knowledge among young people in Ireland. But, according to the principal, the school in Eyeries wasn't doing well.

"I'm real sorry to tell ye this… but there's a lack of money in the school's budget this year," the principal said.

"But… my family, John. How will I feed them?"

He handed me a small stipend— just enough to cover one week's wages. "I understand, and I have this fer ye as a parting gift to help make ends meet. As soon as more money comes available, we'd love to have ye come back, William." His voice was layered with woe. "The children love ye, they really do. It was a hard decision, fer sure."

As I walked home that day, my brain was working like a clock, trying to come up with a solution, but I couldn't see one in sight. Worry and fear quickly settled in my bones like ink on a page.

When I got back home, no sooner did I sit down at the table did Da come through the door babbling on about some nonsensical theory he had.

I usually had more patience with Da's failing memory, but that day had been different. I was already at my wits end.

"What in the good lords' name are ye talkin' bout' now, old man?"

"I *said*, I know what happened to yer Ma, William. It was the Oillipheist again."

"Oh, faith and begorrah, Da! Give it a rest, will ye? The Oillipheist is make-believe. It dinna' take Ma just like it dinna' take Thomas."

But when Da made his mind up about something, there was no reasoning with him.

"My boat is ready, and I'm going to hunt the beast down," he declared.

I let out a hearty chuckle upon hearing his half-cocked plan. "Oh, huntin' the sea dragon are ye, now? Ha! What a knee slapper. Good one, Da." Sarcasm layered my tone like frosting on a cake.

That's when he fixed his steely stare upon me. Da's eyes were the kind of blue that would remind you of the sky after the fog lifts. He was an impressive man, standing as tall as the door frame, but wasn't one for fisticuffs. I raised an eyebrow and met his eye, but to my surprise, there were no signs of playfulness on his face.

His hair, although it had lost some of its luster, was still true Irish red, and his hands were calloused and hardened from many years of manning sails of ships on the Celtic Sea.

"C'mon now. Ye must be jokin' me?" I asked.

The Celtic Sea, although vast and gorgeous, had tested the skills of even the greatest sailors and was one of the most dangerous bodies of water on Earth due to its notoriously rough conditions. The deepest part of the sea, the Celtic Deep, reached depths of more than two hundred seventy-five meters and held many unsettling secrets.

It has been said that the blackened underwater cavity where the Oillipheist lives, lies on the sandy floor in the innermost darkest part of the sea. The cavern is surrounded by the hollow shells of sunken ships this monstrous being has taken captive in its wake on its mission for revenge. Legend goes that other malevolent creatures, such as Merrow, are drawn to the beast and even encircle the giant's home for protection during the daylight hours. Then, at night, they rise to the surface, searching for vulnerable sailors to enchant with their melodic voices only to lure them into a watery grave.

"Quit giving out at yer old man, will ye? I'm no eejit! I worked on boats my whole life."

He was right. He had worked on boats his whole life, however; when Da braved the Celtic Sea before as a boatswain, he was much younger and was on a ship with a full crew of experienced sailors. If he wanted to go out this time, it would be extremely risky, and in his current condition, he'd surely meet his maker.

"I'm just sayin'— only an eijit would attempt such a feat," I retorted.

"He took Nora, William!" Da said, his voice shaking with anger.

I clenched my jaw, wondering for a moment if it was worth the energy it would take to argue my point, but instead I said, "It isna' safe, Da. Ye canna' go."

Da scoffed and sized me up and down. "Well tis' a damn good thing I dinna' need yer permission, boyo. Don't forget who raised yer insolent arse."

"But Da!"

"But nothing!" he shouted, his ears turning redder by the minute. "I leave at first light."

In a fury, I went to talk to Joanna. "I canna' believe him!" I groused.

"I know it's frustrating, love," Joanna said, softly touching my cheek to calm the storm in my soul, "but look at it this way— he may forget all about it in the mornin'."

"Maybe," I said, contemplating the probabilities, "but if na', we will have a different problem."

"Offer to go with him, and just steer him round the bay. You both can be back by dinner time, and he may na' know the difference."

She had a point. In this instance, his memory loss might be an advantage. A sudden thought crossed my mind. If I did go with Da, we could fish. Fish would bring in food and money for the family until I could secure another job.

"Yer right," I said. "Let's just see what the daylight brings."

Da didn't forget in the morning. In fact, he still had a bee in his bonnet. I woke to the sounds of Da and several young men from town helping him get the boat down to shore. I quickly threw together some fishing supplies, kissed Joanna and the kids, grabbed some bread for lunch and headed down the dirt path to the shore. Da and the men were just getting ready to put her in the water when I shouted after them.

"Wait Da!" I said as I hurried down the trail.

"You canna' stop me, son," Da hollered from the boat deck.

"Just wait one minute!" I took a moment to catch my breath from running. "I'm goin' with ye."

Da raised a brow and gave a confident smirk. "Well I'll be! Coming with me, are ye? Yer old Da doesn't sound so crazy after all?"

Down by the water, you could smell the aroma of the bay and feel the spray of the waves hit your face as it was carried in the wind. Seagulls soared overhead, enjoying the weather. Da smiled and thanked the gentlemen who helped him get the boat to shore, before extending a hand down to me.

"Oh hush!" I said, attempting to climb on board with my net and pole.

"I hope yer not expecting to catch him with that net. Yer underestimating him if ye are."

"No, Da" I set down my things. "This is fer fishin'."

"Oh, the fish will come…That's when the real battle begins," he said, referring to the rumored strange behavior of fish near the Oillipheist.

I had a moment of panic when I thought about how long it had been since this ship had seen the waters it was built for, but I brushed the thought away. The boat, although it had sat in a shed for many years, was still in good condition and would do just fine for a day trip around the bay. The boat was just shy of six meters long and was painted red and white. Small patches of rust appeared here and there where it had sat docked in the salt water.

I watched Da go from stern to bow checking off things in his mind, and I was a tad surprised he seemed more aware than usual. He looked good on a ship. He seemed more lucid, almost as if the sea was where he truly belonged. For a moment, it seemed like he was his old self. I offered to help, but Da' reassured me that we were ready.

Da stood at the bow and looked out over the horizon. The sunlight hit the surface just so, and you could see the water shimmering like a polished emerald. I went to join him.

"Do you know which direction we are headed?"

"Follow me," he said, as we walked to the hull to get something. Da unfurled a large map of Ireland, the surrounding bodies of water and Great Britain.

"We are here," he pointed to Coulagh Bay, where the water bordered the coastline around our home of Eyeries. "The Oillipheist lives near here," he then pointed to a section of the map that read *Celtic Deep*.

I took a deep breath inward, wondering how I would convince Da that we were venturing into The Celtic Deep when we were only supposed to stay in Coulagh Bay.

"I'd like to go fishing in the bay first," I said, hoping if some time passed, it would be easier to convince him.

"Aye. That's a fine plan, son."

It seemed that as he got older, there were several different versions of Da. Sometimes he'd be happy and even agreeable, but usually only if you were on his side. Other times, he'd be argumentative and dig his heels deeper than a clam in the sand.

I could probably blame the arguing on his memory, but the truth was that ever since I found out Da lied to me about Thomas, things were never the same between us. There was always one inexcusable falsehood we shared that now caused a great divide between us, much like a gulf that I couldn't get past.

I cast part of the net for fishing over the side of the water when Da interrupted me.

"No, no, no, son! Yer doing it all wrong." He stormed over to haul the net back in.

"I'm only doing it the way YE taught me when I was a boy."

"I wouldna' teach it to ye that way because that's wrong," he said, adamantly.

"Oh yeah? Then who taught me to fish if it wasna' ye, Da?"

"Whoe'er it was, did it wrong. If I taught ye, ye'd know the correct way to secure the net first."

Da continued to mutter things under his breath as he brought the net onto the deck, and I rubbed the sides of my aching head. This was going to be a long day. Da secured the net his way and threw it over again. It splashed a circle in the water, then disappeared as it sunk lower and lower.

"Well, aren't ye a real spitfire this morning!" I said.

"There," Da replied, ignoring my comment. "Now it's right."

Sometimes I wondered if Da cared more about being right than anything or anyone else. At this point, it didn't matter who cast the net, as long as it returned fish to either feed my family or produce enough money to help us get by until I found another job. My main goal was keeping my family fed, Da included.

Da handed me the rope attached to the net after it had been secured. I took it and stared out at the water, thinking about my next move.

"Well, what are ye waitin' fer, William? Haul the net back in. This is called fishin', not waitin'."

"Ye know, Da, sometimes it's better to give it a bit of time and let them come to ye. Instead of forcing it."

"Give it too much time, and ye'll lose them forever."

I looked at Da's eyes and wondered if we were still talking about fish. Just then, I saw two small splashes just below the surface.

"There!" Da shouted.

"I see it!" I said, hauling the net back in.

The rope felt heavy as I dragged it back through the water toward the side of the boat. The sun reflected off of something just below the surface, and my heart was beating loudly in my ears. The net finally surfaced, and I gasped. It was full of herring and mackerel. It was enough fish to feed my family and sell the rest.

"Yes!" I shouted and danced.

Da laughed at my excitement. "If I dinna' know better, I'd say ye were just a wee lad catching his first haul."

"Da, help me pull up the net!"

Da helped, but I had to do the majority of the heavy lifting. As I pulled it out of the water, the net suddenly felt much fuller because it no longer had the buoyancy of the water to help it float. There were so many fish, I nearly fell over the side of the boat, but Da grabbed me by the trousers and pulled me back so I could get my balance again.

"Woah now! Do na' go o'erboard on me, son!"

The net crashed onto the deck and splayed wide, splashing salty sea water with it. Dozens of fish spilled onto the floor. My heart flopped in my chest the way the fish flopped in the net.

"We did it!" I breathed a sigh of relief. This would be a great haul for us to take home.

Da nodded at me and helped put the fish in barrels he had stowed on board for just this type of thing. The sun was high in the sky and the water was fairly smooth, but I knew as soon as it started going down, the windchill was going to turn the water frigid and as we sailed closer to the sea, the waves would get rougher and conditions more treacherous.

Once we got the fish into the barrels, we both sat down to rest for a moment.

"I'm not as young as I once was." I joked.

"How old does that make me, then?"

I chuckled. "Too old."

"Aye," he agreed, and he unfurled the map once more to get his bearings.

"I'm going to shut my eyes fer just a moment." I said. "Do na' forget to set the anchor."

"Ha! Boyo catches some fish and then thinks he can tell me how to man my own boat." He scoffed. "Get yer beauty sleep. The real sailor is in charge now."

I sat there with my eyes closed, listening to the playful sounds of the gulls flying over the bay and feeling the warmth of the sun and being rocked by the gentle sway of the boat on the water. I hadn't planned on truly sleeping, but I didn't realize how tired I was. I thought I only closed my eyes for a moment, but the next thing I knew, I woke up to the sound of waves splashing up against the boat and wind sharply whipping through the sails.

My eyelids fluttered rapidly as I woke and caught a glimpse of the sun on the horizon just before the sea swallowed it whole. I jumped up, wondering how much time had passed.

How long had I been asleep?

I looked around and began to panic, because I couldn't see the coastline anymore.

At the other end of the boat, I noticed Da was still staring at the map, looking concerned and muttering things under his breath.

"Da!" I hollered. "What in the world happened? Where are we?"

"What the devil do ye think I'm trying to do, son? I can't decipher north from south on this map!"

I wondered if that were the truth or if it was that he couldn't remember where we were headed next. I scolded myself. I never should have fallen asleep.

"Did ye not remember to throw down the anchor? Or where we are headed?"

Da shot a sharp look at me, like a knife. Suddenly, all of his frustration went away from the map and was pointed at me instead. "ME throw down the anchor? It was *yer* job to throw down the anchor. Of course I know where we're going." He said, pushing up his sleeves. "I'm no eejit!"

I looked down at Da's arm and saw faded words written in pen under where his sleeve had been. It read *Oillipheist has Nora* and I finally understood.

"Oh, no!" I said, shaking my head. "Yer not pinnin' this one on me, old man. That was *yer* job. Just admit ye were wrong fer once in yer life, Da!"

"I'm not admitting I was wrong because it wasna' my job."

I stormed over and tried to wrestle the map from him. "Now yer away with the fairies if ye think yer right on this one. Just give me the bloomin' map!"

"Let go ye Langer!"

The sea air blustered around the boat and the edges of the map made a snapping sound as they flapped in the wind. It started to rip, so I let go and the map instantly went spiraling through the air in two pieces on a gust of wind. Da and I watched it go far into the distance and I felt heat rise up the back of my neck.

"Now just look what ye did!" He scolded.

I had hit my patience limit with Da. "That's just deadly now, innit, Da? As always, e'rything is my fault, ne'er yers. Ye ne'er think I can do one thing right. Now we're ne'er getting home."

"Maybe if ye hadna' fallen asleep like a wee sissy lassie taking a cat nap, we wouldna' be free floatin' in the ocean right now!"

It was so dark now; the stars had begun to come out and the waves began growing choppy.

"Maybe if ye had any common decency and hadna' lied to me about Thomas and the Oillipheist in the first place, we wouldna' be in this position at all!" My hands shook with anger as I said those last words. Da and I hadn't talked about Thomas in a long time. The wind gave a shrill whistle through the sails, and I wondered if that's what sailors would mistake for the merrow's singing.

"Faith and begorrah! Yer still mad about the lie? Don't ye realize ye were just a boy? I was only trying to protect ye!"

"Ye should have told me the truth!"

"Maybe I should have! But I canna' change it now, can I? Ye can forgive me or hate me. Those are yer only two options. Grow up, son!"

That was the first time Da had taken any sort of responsibility for lying to me, but it wasn't the apology I had hoped for.

For a moment, I felt like throttling Da for making me so angry, and then overhead we both heard an ear splitting sound crack across the sky. It was followed by a bolt of lightning so bright, it lit up the entire sea, before going black again. Seeing the way the weather conditions had turned convinced me we were on The Celtic Sea, and for the first time, I began to grow fearful.

We watched as the surface of the water was unexpectedly disturbed by hundreds of fish flailing as if they were afraid of something coming.

"It's him, William!" Da shouted. "The Oillipheist! He's summoned the storm!"

I looked at Da as lightning flashed in his eyes and knew he believed what he was saying. One by one, raindrops began falling faster and faster. The wind howled so loudly it was hard to hear Da's voice.

"Get to the sails!" Da shouted at me. "We need to secure them! The beast will try to attack the sails first!"

The boat was rocking violently now, tossing me from one side of the deck to the other as I stumbled across to him. Overspray had made the deck so slick it was nearly impossible to navigate. Another flash of lightning went across the sky, and I realized the waves in the distance were taller than the boat.

I thought of my dear Joanna and wondered what would become of her and our children if I died at sea. I was determined not to let that happen. If Da and I were going to make it back alive, we were going to have to work together to get through the storm, whether we believed the same truth or not.

I grabbed the ropes for the sails, but they were soaked in salt water. Despite them being slippery, I gripped as hard as I could.

"We're going to pull hard this way on three!" Da said.

I nodded yes and held on for dear life as the storm tried to lift me up and throw me into the sea.

"ONE...TWO..." Before he could say three, one of the barrels full of fish rolled across the deck with a vengeance, and took Da's legs out from under him. Part of the ships' railing exploded as the barrel made contact, sending splinters of wood through the air.

"Look out!" I shouted in terror.

I released the rope and reached for Da. Nothing mattered more in that moment to me than saving Da's life. Even though the wind was knocked out of him, I was able to catch him before he fell overboard. I helped him to his feet, and squeezed him tight. Although he was dazed, he kept focused.

Da had taught me several commands and safety tips when I was younger from his time as a boatswain, so even though I was a bit rusty, I tried my best to remember what he'd told me. We worked together to make sure the boat was as safe as it could be.

Da steered the ship while I quickly closed all the windows and hatches, stowed away unnecessary gear so it wasn't a hazard, and used a bucket to bail water off of the deck to keep the ship from capsizing. Wave after wave pummeled the boat and tested its ability to stay upright, but we held our ground.

"Don't give up, Thomas!" Da cried, lost in memory. "I won't let the beast take ye!"

It was at that moment that I realized Da needed to believe in the sea dragon, because the truth was a lot scarier than a myth.

All at once, the entire boat rose higher than it had before, being carried by a great force. Up ahead was a jagged rock formation sticking out of the water.

This is it, I thought, bracing myself and holding my breath. I expected the waves to toss the ship, forcing it to crash down and smash into pieces on the rocks, but I was wrong. Instead, it got wedged atop the rock formation and was mostly out of reach from the giant waves.

Sheets of rain continued to make their way across the deck. I hollered for Da to follow me to take cover under the hull. We had done all we could above deck, and now all there was to do was to take cover and wait out the storm. We climbed into the cargo hold and tightly closed the lid. It was so dark you couldn't see the hand in front of your own face, but we were safe. If only for a moment.

Over the next few hours, we listened as the rain lightened up and the lightning and thunder stopped. Da and I talked for a while in the dark, apologizing to one another and sharing stories about Thomas until we fell asleep from pure exhaustion.

When I woke, the sun shone through a couple of cracks in the door to the cargo hold.

"Da!" I shouted. "It's mornin'."

My heart raced in my chest as I felt the ceiling and forced open the door to the cargo hold. I climbed out of that cramped space, and I was never so thankful to see sunshine and blue skies. I could smell the salt in the air and the water was pristine and sparkling.

"Da!" I yelled, running back over to the dark hole we had spent the night in. "We made it Da! Come see fer yerself!"

I went to reach out my hand for his, but it was barely warm. I used all of my strength to pull Da out of the cargo hold and onto the deck, and that's when I noticed his blood-soaked shirt. His body was limp, and I let out a shriek. A shard of wood had splintered off of the ship and lodged itself into the side of his ribcage. He had been bleeding all night, and I hadn't even noticed.

"Stay with me, Da!" I held him in my arms as I thought about what to do next. Suddenly, I felt like the same helpless child as when Ma told me that Thomas died from starvation.

I put my ear near his mouth to check if he was still breathing. He was, but it was very faint. I tried to rip part of my shirt to fasten it around his torso to stop the bleeding, but he had already lost so much blood. I was afraid I'd noticed it far too late.

"C'mon Da! Don't leave me like this. We made it!"

"William, my son," Da whispered weakly.

"Yes Da?"

"You will be okay," he whispered, and then just as quickly as the breeze blew through the sails, he was gone.

I held Da in my arms for a long time, weeping, when suddenly, the ship began to rumble, creak and move. I wondered if the ship had come loose from the rock formation, but to my surprise, the rock formation rose and sank into the water, carefully placing the boat safely back on the surface and guiding it along for a short while. I looked around, stunned, wondering if I had hallucinated.

The boat suddenly came to a gentle stop, and I heard the horn of another ship sound in the distance.

There was hope yet, I thought.

I peered over the side of the boat, trying to make sense of what had happened. The sun cast glistening streaks through the surface of the water, and I swore I saw two large golden colored eyes blinking slowly at me from below.

But when I looked again, they were gone.

The sight took the breath right from my chest. I gasped and scrambled away from the edge, but whatever it was, wasn't interested in hurting me. Instead, light ripples danced across the water, like a trail of breadcrumbs as it gracefully swam away.

The Sirens of Whitby

W. M. Ashley

1 April 1980

The salty scent of the sea filled my nose as I walked the narrow streets of the English seaside village of Whitby. Tiny bells rang as doors to sweet shops and vintage boutiques opened and shut, and the gray gulls that swooped over my head were about twice the size of the seabirds back in the states. All these curiosities lay in the shadow of the ancient ruins of Whitby Abbey, which towered over us atop the tallest cliff that loomed over the bay. I shivered and slid the zipper to my coat up to my chin.

I was one of twelve students on a study abroad trip for English Lit majors at my college. My professor was overly excited about this trip, since it was the setting that inspired Bram Stoker's *Dracula*, on which he had written his dissertation.

As I followed my class toward the ancient steps that led to the infamous graveyard of St. Mary's Church, the setting that inspired Stoker's novel itself, I noticed an old woman preparing a large fishing lure on one of the docks. The lure was unlike any I had ever seen: the fish at the end looked almost like a small human and was about three feet long. I shuddered at the sight.

The woman's eyes met mine, but she said nothing. I glanced back at a couple girls from my class hurrying up the steps to the churchyard. I didn't want to fall too far behind, but my intrigue took over and I sauntered over to the dock where the woman and her strange contraption awaited.

The woman was dressed in a withered green raincoat, rubber boots, and suspenders; her wrinkled hands and face making her age seem almost undeterminable.

"That's a very strange fishing lure," I commented as she lugged the lure over her shoulder.

She grinned at me beneath her white bangs. "If truth be told, it's the fish that sometimes do the luring..." Her voice sounded slightly French, with a hint of a cockney accent. She turned her back to me then and began shuffling down the dock to where a small fishing vessel was docked.

Confused at her words, I followed. "What do you mean?"

She stopped and then turned to me, a thoughtful look in her eye. "You'd better return to your friends. No sense hanging around a crazy old fisherwoman."

"It's just my college class. We're visiting Whitby as part of a literature trip."

She shifted her gaze up towards the churchyard, its crumbling stones and haunting cemetery a lure of its own. "Well, lass, if you really are interested in stories, I have one you may not have heard before..."

15 August 1897

The day was the brightest I had witnessed over my two-week voyage, a good omen for sailors, our captain had said. I was seventeen and finally paying a visit to my cousin Wilhelmina in Whitby who I hadn't seen in over a decade. Mama paid for my passage, and I was more than relieved to see a familiar face after almost a month at sea surrounded by a shipload of strangers.

Crowds of voyagers and unwashed sailors nudged me along as we marched off the boat, and my legs couldn't help but wobble atop the sturdy, unmoving ground.

Suddenly, I was almost toppled over by the mad rush of a violent hug as my cousin swung her arms around me. Shorter than I was, she was also much stockier, her arms nearly squeezing the air out of my lungs in greeting.

"Elizabeth!" She beamed, adjusting the pink shawl she wore around her shoulders. "How long has it been?"

"Too long, Cousin," I managed to squeak out before she finally released me. She weaved her arm through mine as I grabbed my bag and we ambled away from the crowd of deportees.

"Just wait until you see Whitby!"

"It looks like a quaint place." My gaze shifted to the cobblestoned streets lined with stores and window-shoppers. No carriage was in sight, the streets far too narrow for such a bulky contraption, and a white lighthouse beamed at the crest of the horizon.

"Oh, that's only because the sun is out. When the fog rolls up from the ocean and the seagulls stop crying, that's when you must be on your guard." Her expression turned serious. "That's when the *sirens* come out."

"The sirens?" I repeated. "You honestly do not believe in those mythical creatures, do you?" Then I remembered who I was talking to. Wilhelmina had been obsessed with fairy tales ever since we were children, but I had hoped she had grown out of it by now. We were practically adults.

As if confirming my suspicions, she prattled on. "Have you read Mr. Stoker's new book *Dracula* yet? It was inspired by his trip to Whitby, you know. Oh, just wait until you see the churchyard! They say that is where the actual vampire is buried! And Mr. Stoker named his character Mina after me, you know!"

I raised an eyebrow. "But your name is Wilhelmina, *Wilhelmina*," I retorted, wondering if this entire trip would be filled with my cousin gushing about a new gothic romance novel.

She waved off my correction. "I've decided to shorten it. It sounds so much more romantic, don't you think? At any rate, we should give Mr. Stoker some credit for putting Whitby on the map. Local businesses here were faltering before he came, and now tourists cannot get enough of it!"

She babbled on like that for a while as we headed up the cobbled slope to the abbey. An old sailor barked at us as we began our ascent up the 199 steps to the abbey. "Count your steps, or an omen will curse your next ones!"

"Are *all* sailors superstitious?" I found myself asking Wilhelmina—Mina—as I looked out at the harbor and rooftops sinking below us as we inched farther to the top of the cliff.

"When your life is in the hands of the sea, I've known many sailors to fear," she answered as we both arrived breathless at the top steps of the churchyard. Tombstones about as tall as my own petite frame loomed before us, some covered in blurred sandstone where thoughtful epitaphs were once engraved.

"How sad." I pointed to one teetered at the edge of the cliff that faced the ocean.

"They get that way from the salt of the sea." She shrugged, as if everyone was supposed to know that. As we traversed farther down the graveyard's path, Wilhelmina sputtered, "Come, I want to see where Dracula is supposed to be buried."

"How can the undead be buried?" a melodic voice said from behind me.

A young man and his companion bowed and approached us. The one who spoke had skin as fair as a baby's and his tousled hair was streaked with blonde. His eyes were colored a striking blue that reminded me of sapphires. His companion was darker-haired with olive-toned skin and narrow eyes.

"Who are you?" my cousin blurted out, before I had a chance to address them. "I know everyone in Whitby, and I've never seen either of you before."

"We just came off the boat," he answered without hesitation, as if he was ready for the question.

My cousin turned to me, as if to confirm their story.

"Forgive me, but I just came off the boat, and I do not remember seeing either of you… I'm sure I would have remembered," I added with a slight blush. The dark-haired one smiled slightly. There were quite a few passengers on the ship, and I kept to myself for most of the voyage, so they may have been telling the truth. Regardless, why wouldn't they have been truthful?

Just then, a tall man dressed in a long flowing cape and a black top-hat exited the church and headed over to where we all stood.

"I believe they are starting the tour," the blonde-haired boy said as we all walked farther into the cemetery.

The tall man in black's voice quivered over the crowd. "…If you look closely, you can see the mists beginning to creep over the sea…the perfect setting for a vampire to hunt his prey…"

"What a load of codswallop," the dark-haired boy whispered as my cousin and her new beau listened eagerly to the tour-guide. "What do you say we get out of here to somewhere less crowded?" Since I had been around nothing but crowds of people for the past few days, the offer sounded tempting. But I barely knew this boy, and I couldn't leave my cousin.

I glanced at her, her own gaze fixed on the tour guide—a silly smile was plastered on her face, and her eyes gleamed at the tale about her new hero.

"Let us not go *too* far," I responded, and I followed him out of the cemetery. I knew my cousin or I should not have been without a chaperone, but how much danger could I be in with so many people around?

"Are you hungry?" he asked.

My stomach rumbled in answer. It had been a while since my last meal—if one could call a handful of ship's gruel an actual meal. I nodded, and he guided me over to one of the fish shops near the pier.

The sun no longer shined as brightly as it had when I first arrived, and a thick mist drew closer to the shoreline with every lap of the waves against the wooden pillars below our feet.

"So," he began, turning his gray eyes on me, "you are from France?"

I couldn't help but gasp slightly each time this young man spoke. His voice had a sing-song quality to it like his companion, and I couldn't help but desire to hear more.

I nodded between mouthfuls of fresh cod. "Is my accent that noticeable?"

He shrugged and then winked at me. My heart fluttered at his striking gaze. I was never a girl people would describe as pretty; I was too tall for my age and hadn't developed yet in certain areas that dresses would complement. But this boy seemed to like me. And I liked that he liked me.

"Are you from Whitby, originally?" I asked, trying to flutter my eyelashes in a flirtatious manner.

His smile widened. I must have been doing it correctly. "Yes, but farther down the shoreline." He pointed down the pier. "Come, I'll show you."

He grabbed my hand. My heart leaped at his touch. I couldn't discern if it was solely because I was attracted to him or because his touch was coarse, like sand. We walked farther down the pier, and by the time we reached its end, the mist was so thick, I couldn't see much farther than a few feet down.

"Beyond," he pointed out into the mist.

I couldn't help but stifle a laugh. "Your eyesight must be better than mine. All I see is white mist from the sea."

He was no longer smiling. "Precisely."

The next thing I knew, I was falling…plunging…submerging into dark, icy water. I couldn't breathe. I opened my eyes to the murky undercurrent my body had just fallen into and saw traces of green—it must have been seaweed—and something else. A hand reaching for me across the murky green. I reached for it, knowing it to belong to the young man; he must have dived in after me. How gallant!

But as his hand gripped mine once more, I discovered that he was dragging me down farther into the gulf of murky water instead of upwards towards the air.

I tried to recoil my hand, but it was stuck in his sand-papered grasp. I used my other hand to pull his fingers from my skin, but his grip was strong. Doing the only other thing I could think of, I bit his hand as hard as I could.

It worked for a moment. He briefly loosened his grip and let out the strangest sound I had ever heard above or below the ocean's surface. It was a high-pitched screech, almost like a siren.

Down he dragged me until I became so weak from holding my breath I felt my head would explode. But then, right when I was about to give up, the monster's hold on me loosened again. Squinting through the dark water, I could almost make out a set of pale hands grasping the creature's neck.

With one last ounce of adrenaline, I pushed against the salt, seaweed, and murky abyss, leaving my heavy skirt and petticoat behind, and I surfaced. The white mist blowing against my face was as arctic as the water. Which way was the shore? And where was my attacker? Where was my rescuer? Without pausing for further thought, I started swimming, hoping that I was heading in the right direction, until I saw a small light in the corner of my eye. The lighthouse!

I kicked as hard as I could towards the shimmering reflection of its light until I saw a familiar pile of wood marking the pier and heaved onto the rickety ladder at its end. I needed to get out of the water and away from this water demon. As much as it pained me to admit, I thought I would have rather faced off with a vampire. At least it would have been on land.

I shook the irrational thought from my fatigued mind and climbed up the rungs of the ladder until I reached the wooden surface of the pier. I trudged along the dock, shivering in my chemise and bloomers as I looked around for a sign of any living soul, but the wharf was abandoned. The fog must have scared the locals back into their homes, like Wilhelmina had said—and rightly so. Perhaps it *was* safer to be a little superstitious after all.

Wilhelmina. She could be in worse trouble than I was. What if the boy she was with was a monster too? I raced down the pier until I saw the infamous ruins of Whitby Abbey peeking through the mist. I scurried up all 199 steps—not bothering to count each one this time—until I reached St. Mary's Church cemetery where the tour group used to be. All had dispersed except for the black-clad tour guide in his top-hat. My attire (or lack of) must have been quite a shock to him, but this was a matter of life and death!

"Wh-where is my cousin and the boy she was with?" I managed to sputter out between my teeth chattering and gasps for air.

His mouth fell open at the sight of me and his eyes widened. "Madam, are you quite alright? You are soaked to the bone!" He took off his cloak and offered it to me to cover my indecency.

Not needing a reminder about my horrific ideal, instead of accepting the cloak I found myself grabbing his lapels—a very unladylike thing to do—and repeating my question much louder.

"I-I don't know," he responded, a little frightened now. "I finished the tour, and everyone dispersed because of the fog. If it was that know-it-all girl who kept asking where Dracula was buried who you are referring to, she and her blonde companion headed down to the beach about ten minutes ago."

I careened out of his presence down the unsteady terrain of the cliff to the beach below. My heeled boots sank into the sand as my feet pummeled the ground. Desperation rang in my throat as the beach absorbed each of my footsteps. "Wilhelmina! Mina! Where are you?"

Suddenly, right where the surf met the sand, I noticed an abandoned pink shawl. I took it in my hands, and my heartbeat began to speed up again as I realized where my cousin must have gone. Without even thinking, I trudged farther ahead into the crashing surf as it lapped against my already numb legs. Maybe she was still…

But before I could finish my wish, I was distracted by a tangle of light-colored seaweed floating towards me. Horror struck me as I realized that it was not seaweed, but hair.

Wilhelmina's hair.

I lunged for her and burst out into sobs as I flipped her over. Her pale cheeks and opened eyes, glazed over with death, would surely haunt my dreams. Wilhelmina lived in Whitby; she knew how to swim. Someone had drowned her. And I knew who.

I felt myself screaming as I scanned the beach for the blonde-headed boy responsible for her demise but could see no one. He had gone, along with his partner-in-crime, into the abyss from which they came.

20 August 1897

The funeral procession for Wilhelmina was like something out of a dream. The sun shone, the preacher said some things I could not discern through the shock emanating through my body and escaping through my tears. After much hesitation, I realized that I should tell Wilhelmina's parents the truth about how she died. They were Whitby citizens after all. After witnessing the fear grasping the crowds enough to shut them up in their houses, I concluded that they may believe me. They did not.

It was easier for them to agree with the coroner who concluded that their daughter died of a drowning accident. I did not dare tell anyone else about what had really happened, and her parents forbade me from doing so. I knew they blamed me for her death, so the least I could do was obey their wishes.

After Wilhelmina's coffin was laid in the sea-swept earth of St. Mary's churchyard, I could not help but wonder how long the inscription on her own tombstone would last against the relentless salt-filled air. "Here lies Wilhelmina" her epitaph read. "At rest, but not forgotten."

She may have rested, but I knew that my own guilt could not. What if these monsters from the sea drowned another poor soul? How would I prevent it? How *could* I prevent it?

1 April 1980

"And rest in peace she did," the old woman continued, "that was, until her grave was found unearthed and cracked open two days later."

"What? How?" I'd remained silent until she relayed this sudden turn of events.

"The police didn't know what to make of her missing body, other than grave robbers. Was it my monster and his comrade? What more did they want with her? Hope seemed to escape all of us, until something curious washed up on shore a week later. Something with webbed fingers, sharp teeth, and blonde hair. It looked like the boy who had been her companion, but different. Where his hands should have been, was a scaley green webbing of thick skin and teeth sharper than I had remembered. No one could identify who this strange boy was, but they could gather where he had come from. Luckily it gave my own story I told Wilhelmina's parents some credence, but what puzzled the coroner most was the cause of death: drained of blood from two puncture-wounds in his neck..."

I couldn't stop my mouth from hanging open. Perhaps Bram Stoker gained more inspiration from Whitby concerning vampires than had been reported.

"Are you saying that Wilhelmina became a...*vampire*?"

The old woman did not bat an eyelash. "I am simply relating the evidence. But I couldn't help but wonder if the mysterious being who saved me from my own monster had anything to do with it."

I blinked. "How so? Did you ever find out who it was?"

"Or *what* it was."

I shuddered at her inference. Did she believe her attacker was taken down by a *vampire*?

"Do you think," I paused before uttering, *"it* killed your attacker?"

"Alas, his body was never found."

"Is that why you are using that fishing lure?"

"Indeed, I will keep searching until he, too, no longer terrorizes Whitby."

Eager to get back to my class, and a little warier than before, I told her I had better be heading back to them.

"Be careful," she said as she again turned her back and headed towards the edge of the dock. "Sirens like to target foreigners."

With that warning in mind, I made my way off the pier and hurried up the sloping 199 steps to where my class was about to tour St. Mary's churchyard. A calm, eerie fog seemed to follow me, and a strong paranoia that vampires and sirens would follow me in my wake began to settle in the pit of my stomach.

Upon arriving, I noticed the looming grave markers, some of their epitaphs far beyond recognition due to the spray from the sea. A black wooden sign greeted me on a post that looked like it had been erected in a more recent century. It read *Whitby Cathedral 1882* in gold paint, and underneath was a plain white paper taped onto the post that stated in black type: *Please do not ask us where Dracula's grave is located.*

I barely had time to register a smile when a voice came from behind me—a voice that sounded like waves crashing upon a shoreline. "How exactly does someone bury a vampire?"

Almost mechanically, I turned to the mysterious voice, though I had an inkling about who it may have belonged to. "My thoughts exactly," I responded as I gazed upon the fair face, narrow eyes, and dark hair of a young man dressed in jeans and a Whitby t-shirt.

"You're American," he said. "Is this your first time in Whitby?"

I could barely hide the shiver creeping up from my paranoid stomach to my shoulders. This was all starting to sound very familiar. "Yeah, though I find large tour groups boring sometimes."

"Why don't we head farther down the pier, then, away from the madding crowd, so to speak?"

I gulped in answer. "Can we get something to eat first?" I asked, hoping to prolong the sinister design he had in mind.

"Indeed. I know just the place."

I'm sure you do. I followed him down the steps and to the corner fish-shop that also served ice cream and "Welcome to Whitby" stickers. While he waited in line, I took my chance.

"I would like to take some pictures with my new camera," I remarked with a giggle and a smile, so he thought I was a girl interested in his mysterious attractiveness. He responded with one of his own smiles that both allured and frightened me, and I headed further down the pier.

When the fog was thick enough, I sprinted down the dock to where I had left the strange old woman. She had boarded her boat but had not yet set sail. I waved my arms at her, not wanting to shout and draw too much attention to myself. Luckily, she saw me. She turned off the engine and poked her head out the cabin window.

I approached the boat, out of breath. "I think," I began, taking in a few gulps of air, "I think I've found what you're looking for!"

Tail of Rope and Stone
L.P. Masters

The water sucked her down. Deeper and deeper. Darker and darker.

Ana tugged at the ropes around her legs, trying to loosen the sailors' expertly tied knots. The water compressing her chest made it harder to hold her breath, and with the pressure squeezing on her ears, her head felt like it was about to pop.

She managed to wedge her finger into one of the knots and got it to slip ever so slightly. The rope unraveled once, whipping around free, but there wasn't just one knot to release. Every sailor on that ship had added his hands to tie her up. Every sailor on that ship was responsible for the rough stone touching her bare toes.

The stone that dragged her down into the all-consuming depths.

They'd ripped her shirt off, since a woman on board would anger the sea gods, but a naked woman would calm the sea. They'd left her blue skirt on, though, and now it was tied up to her knees with a rope.

Ana's chest burned from the pressure of the ocean and the need for oxygen. As she looked up through the salty water, she barely saw the flashes of lightning and the hints of sunlight filtering down through the breaking clouds. The surface was leagues away. Even if she got the rope and stone off now, she would never make it back to the surface. And if she made it to the surface, what good would it do? She was in the middle of nowhere. If another ship happened to pass by, they wouldn't take her on board. They'd be just as afraid of her "bad luck" as the men who threw her overboard.

Why was she even fighting this?

She closed her eyes, salty tears unnoticed amidst the brine.

She clenched her toes around the stone.

She knew she should just get it over with. Death would be a relief. One breath was all it would take, then the suffering could end.

She was about to take a killing breath when the free end of the rope whipped at her thighs. No! She still had a few seconds of oxygen left in her lungs, and she wouldn't give up until she'd done all that she could.

She reached down again and caught that loose rope. The constricting pressure of the water squeezed the knots tighter into her legs, and the rope was cinched up like rigging in a storm. Despite the futility, she tried to tease apart the ropes, using the piece that had slipped free as leverage. She kicked her feet, trying to unleash the rock tied around her ankles. The added struggle only exhausted her limited supply of oxygen even quicker.

Finality settled within her. She had done everything she could do. Ana closed her eyes and imagined standing on a rock at the edge of the sea, fresh air surrounding her, cool and wet from an evening storm.

She took a breath.

The burn from the salt was the first she noticed. Like breathing in acid instead of air.

The easing of the burn in her chest came next. Like a breath of pure air.

She pushed the water from her lungs and took another breath. It was thick and sluggish. It still burned her throat, but it eased the need to breathe as well.

Her eyes shot open. She looked around the deep water surrounding her. Although still dark, it seemed she could see a little better than she'd been able to earlier.

The water faded into oblivion below her, but the pressure of the ocean had flattened the rock at her feet. Her kicking motions had thinned it out into two points like a tail. The water pressure had fused the ropes to her legs. She looked like…

Like a mermaid.

Stone gray at the tip of the tail, slowly changing to the tan color of the ropes, and finally, the blue of her skirt above her knees. The piece of rope she had untied on her way down still dangled freely from the rope and skirt fused to her knees, a memory of how hard she had fought for freedom.

She kicked again, and the stone propelled her forwards and upwards. She looked around in amazement. *How is this possible?*

"Welcome," came a watery voice. "Congratulations. You made it."

"Hello? Who's there?" Ana twisted around in the water until she spotted something behind her.

Another mermaid.

Her tail was a similar stone gray at the bottom, tan almost all the way to her hips. The very top was a brilliant, bright red. The mermaid had large clamshells covering her chest, and a throat full of necklaces and decorations. A combination of natural and man-made trinkets hung from her neck. Seaweed, shells, fishhooks, lost coins... even a few fish bones made up the decorations.

"My name is Mari," said the mermaid. She smiled. Ana kicked towards her, entranced by her face, drawn in by her voice. "The first mermaid of this place."

"How did this happen?" Ana looked down at her own tail again, feeling a combination of shock and awe. The pressure around her was still tight, almost suffocating, despite the fact that she could breathe the water.

"Magic," Mari said, "and willpower."

"I don't understand."

"This trench has magic in it, but only if you go deep enough while still alive. Most give up before they reach the magic, and if you're dead before you change, nothing can be done for you." Mari gave a little flick of her tail and drifted forward. "What is your name?"

"I'm... Ana."

"Well, Ana. Welcome to the life of a mermaid."

The trench was deep. To Ana, it seemed to go down forever. It was both horrifying and spellbinding. Something about the depths called to her, and she didn't know why. She didn't want to answer that call. The thought of diving deeper into the pit disturbed her.

But the thought of rising any higher in the water was just as uncomfortable. The surface seemed like a curse. She knew what was up there. It called to her, and she knew why.

The sun existed above the surface. But she would never experience the sun again. Not in the way she had done when she was a child. She would never lie on the green grass beneath a tree, stare into the blue skies that were aglow with light. It was one of the first things Mari had warned her about. A mermaid could get out of the water for a few moments, but if she stayed out too long, she would perish.

Mari said that going any closer to the surface would only be torture, so Ana stayed deep enough that all she could see of the sun were the diffused rays clawing their way through the suffocating depths. She promised herself she would never return to the surface; she would never see the sun again. She would forget she'd ever lived a life above.

Because you couldn't miss something if you forgot it ever existed.

Indefinite amounts of time passed. If she had cared to count, Ana could have figured out how many days had gone by, watching the sun and moon filter through the leagues of water above her. But there was no point. What event was she counting from? A bad memory. What did she have to look forward to? Darkness and cold. How many days or years had she been in the water? How many years ahead of her did she have down here, alone, lost in the depths?

"You're not alone," Mari said one day, when Ana had expressed how she felt.

It was true. There were many other women just like her and Mari, who had been tied to a weight and tossed overboard. Women who had fought and struggled to survive, until the rope and stone had fused into a tail, and the magic of the burning, salty brine had given them a new life.

The range of attitudes among those other mermaids varied as much as the types of fish one could encounter. Some mermaids came together in large groups, where they talked and laughed together. Some formed smaller, more intimate groups, and spoke quietly and seriously. And some mermaids were dark and sulky; completely aloof. Ana fit in with the last group.

"You're right," Ana shook her head, and looked toward a group of mermaids that were a little ways away, laughing and joking. "I'm not alone. Thank you." She wasn't officially alone.

But she may as well have been. There was no way she could join those others. Ana turned and swam away.

"Ana," Mari called, but Ana didn't stop. She wanted to go back to her place in the sea. Never would she have called her place home, but it was where she always returned to.

Most of the mermaids stayed on the shelf surrounding the trench.

Some of them had even built homes and buildings on the sea floor. Others remained nomadic, going wherever they wanted and sleeping on the sand, or tucked in a garden of kelp, or simply floating motionless in the water.

Ana's place was right at the edge of the shelf, where the ocean floor cut down sharply into the abyss. Very rarely did any of the other mermaids disturb her there.

"Quickly!"

The word was said with such urgency and haste that it spun Ana around on her tail.

The group of women who had been giggling together just moments ago were suddenly pumping their tails, rushing towards the surface.

"Is it one of your sailors?" asked a mermaid with a wrap of seaweed around her chest.

"Not just one. A lot of them. It's the same ship. I can tell!"

There were already six or seven mermaids, but as they all rushed upwards as one. The one with the seaweed wrap looked around and called out. "Come! Anyone who wants to. Join us! Sophia's ship is here!"

For a moment, Ana kicked her tail, bringing her closer toward the surface. Her heart thundered in her chest as she thought of what she would find up there.

Sunshine. Gentle winds. Memories of grass and trees.

She squeezed her eyes closed, and when she opened them, she saw Mari. "Where are they going?"

"Why, to the surface, of course." Mari reached into a bag that hung from her shoulder and drew out a new necklace she was working on. She was always creating something out of coral or seashells, kelp or bones.

Confusion swirled inside of Mari like a whirlpool. "Why? What's there for them?"

"What's there?" Mari watched as the group of mermaids grew smaller in the distance. At last she said, "The taste of revenge."

That pressure in Ana's chest tightened. "What do you mean?"

"The sailors have always spoken fearfully of mermaids, of sirens. Of women able to call them into the depths with nothing but their voices. What they don't realize… is that they are a siren to us. We are drawn to our sailors as strongly as they are drawn to us."

Mari put a hand on Ana's shoulder. "One day you'll understand," Mari continued. "One day, a man who threw you into these depths will pass above you, and you will want to go and call to him. He won't be able to resist you, just as you won't be able to resist him. Once you have him in the water… Well, it's up to you how gently or harshly you deal with him. But you must know—revenge tastes sweet. Sweeter than any candy; stronger than any drug. It's an addiction."

Ana clenched her teeth.

Mari's voice was deep and rich, her words a warning. "There are many mermaids who have dragged down the last of the men who wronged them, yet they go on. Some mermaids will drag down any man they can sink their voices into. To them, *all* men have wronged them, and the revenge will never end. I have seen this happen to many mermaids in my years here. My advice to you is that you never start. Never taste that revenge."

Ana shivered as the cold of the ocean waters seeped into her bones. That pressure in her chest—it wasn't the weight of the ocean; it was the need for revenge. The names of the men who had wronged her poured into her brain. *Devon. Asher. Lucius…*

Trent…

She closed her eyes. She had worked so hard to forget all of it; the men and what they had done. The sun and what it had felt like. But why was that burden of forgetting laid on her? Because of them.

The men had wronged her. And if she had a chance to set that right, wasn't that, in a sense, her obligation? To make sure that what happened to her wouldn't happen again?

"If I taste revenge once, will I ever be able to forget the flavor?"

Mari smiled sadly and strung a fishhook on the necklace. "You never forget the flavor of revenge."

Every time a mermaid raced to the surface, Ana vowed she would never go up there. Mari's warnings about the taste of revenge tormented Ana.

She had been fairly successful in forgetting the most painful memories, but some memories are so intricately weaved into our lives that it's impossible to forget them.

Her father's addiction was as strong of a memory as the sun flitting through the leaves.

When her brother finally admitted that he had succumbed to the same compulsion their father had, his warning became a song she could never forget. *"Don't start, Mari. Just don't ever even touch it. We got da's blood in us, sis. One drop of that stuff and we're hooked. For life."*

Would the dependency on revenge be the same as alcohol? She didn't know, but she refused to find out. Ana kept a sharp shell with her, and anytime she considered tasting revenge, she clenched her hand into a fist and let the shell bite into her palm.

But when her time came, she was not as strong as she believed she would be.

It was like a fishhook had pierced her heart. A strong hand and a rod on a boat pulled and pulled. The more she fought to swim the other way, the more she struggled against it, the more that hook set in her flesh and dragged her onward, upward constantly.

Ana swam up, then managed to stop herself, aim her body for the depths and dive. But moments later she was headed for the surface again. Over and over this dance played on, until she was too fatigued to fight it anymore. She gave in, letting that sensation drag her upward.

Even before she broke the surface of the water, the light became blinding. The sun was glaring and garish, and she closed her eyes and pretended she hadn't missed it.

At last, her head popped up above the water and she drew in a deep breath. Her throat burned from the saltwater, but the air in her lungs was intoxicating. The weights on her chest had all but fallen away.

And yet there was still that fishing hook in her heart. She searched through the choppy waves until she spotted the ship. She kicked the stony end of her tail, and it propelled her forward to the hull. She reached out and grabbed a rope hanging over the side, letting the ship pull her through the waves.

Who was on board? She felt him. She knew him.

She called to him. "Devon."

Her voice was hoarse and raw from the saltwater, but it only brought her tone down to a deeper, enticing register.

"De-von," she called again.

Her heart was racing, waiting for him to appear.

One more call. "Devon!"

A face peeked over the edge of the deck, covered in a black, wiry beard. He leered at her, eyes wide, intoxicated, enchanted.

"Devon," Ana whispered hoarsely. She reached out the hand that wasn't holding the rope. "Come to me."

He gazed into her eyes and smiled.

"Come to me, Devon. Take my hand."

He reached over the edge. A voice from farther up on deck yelled, "Devon! What are you…"

The moment his fingertips touched her palm, Ana pulled hard and yanked him into the water. He fell in, still entranced by her. She released the rope, wrapped her arms around him, and dove under the surface just as a cry from above called, "Man overboard!"

And then… the memories. As she inhaled the briny saltwater, the memories flooded in like the ocean did …

Ana had legs again. Or… still.

The memory was almost painful, looking down at her feet peeking out beneath her blue skirt and realizing just what she had lost.

She clenched her toes on the sodden wood. And then she nearly lost her footing.

Men yelled, and water flooded the deck, nearly pulling her feet straight out from under her. She yelped and gripped the handrail tighter, but continued her treacherous journey to the bridge.

She went up the stairs, one step at a time, as men cursed and screamed, and the deluge attempted to tear her from the ship. Finally, she reached the wheel.

"Is there anything I can do to help?" she yelled above the gale.

Two sets of eyes looked back at her; one pair shocked and afraid; the other pair angry. The man with the angry eyes spoke first. "You!" he hissed. "You're responsible for this cyclone."

"Devon, no," said the other man.

But in a move as sudden as a flash of lightning, Devon gripped Ana by the throat. She gasped and choked.

"This is all her fault! I knew we should never have allowed a woman to stay on board once we found her. Bad luck. Bad luck this entire trip, and now we're about to get ripped in two…"

She kicked him, and she got enough purchase that he lost his grip on her throat. She stumbled backward and threw her hands up to stop him. "Stay away from me!"

Ana tried to back up, but she'd reached the end of the bridge. There was nowhere else to go except over the edge, and it was too far down to the deck below. She'd break a bone if she jumped, and that wouldn't help her.

Devon walked toward her slowly. Movement behind him

distracted her for a moment; he lunged out and snatched her by the wrist. She screamed and tried twisting away, but his grip was crushingly tight.

"You know what we have to do, men!" Devon yelled above the roar of the storm. "We have to sacrifice her if we'll have any hope at all of surviving this cursed trip."

"No! No! Stay away!"

Desire and excitement filled his eyes as he said devilishly, "We'll have to drown her."

Ana realized she was still dragging Devon through the water. Already a fair distance away from the ship, Ana rose to the surface again before Devon had a chance to drown. That was too good for him.

He gasped, either unaware or uncaring that she could have left him down there until he'd had no air left.

"Look how beautiful you are," Devon said, and reached out to brush her hair behind her ear.

"Don't you touch me," she snapped. He jerked back in surprise and moved away from her, treading water a few feet from where she floated effortlessly.

"I told you on the boat to stay away from me. You didn't listen then, and now you get to pay for it."

She twisted at her hips, bringing the stony end of her tail up out of the water and slamming it against his body. He was launched out of the water and landed some distance from her, screaming and trying to swim away.

One flick of her tail brought her to his side again. She performed the same movement, throwing him the other direction instead.

"You say it's bad luck to have a woman on board?" Ana growled at him. "Well, it was worse luck to throw her into the sea."

She brought her tail up one last time, smashing the gray stone against his head.

Saltwater mixed with red splashed into her mouth, tasting of iron and brine. Like an anchor. And just like an anchor, it crushed into the seafloor of her heart.

Ana stayed on the surface and watched the body drift slowly down into the depths.

She took another breath of air and looked up at the glorious shining sun.

Mari was right.

She would never forget the taste of revenge.

The first time she'd felt the pull, it was a fisherman's hook. Ever after that, the anchor had been set.

Mari probably was right. If Ana had fought hard enough, she could have snapped that fishing line that had pulled her up there the first time. But she'd given up partway through the fight. She'd found Devon, and she'd killed him.

Now, it was impossible. The next few times it happened, she fought and struggled against the pull, but instead of a hook and fishing line, it was an anchor and chain—strong and unbreakable.

Again and again, Ana went to the surface, haunted by the sailors that had stripped her, tied a stone to her feet, and threw her over the edge of the ship. She repeatedly dragged them under the water and relived that nightmare, watching the faces of the guilty sailors as they lent their hands to tie her ropes.

After all that, she brought the men to justice. Every time she tasted that revenge, she loved it and craved it more. And she hated it.

"I am not my father," she would whisper to herself, and grasp her sharp seashell until she bled.

Yet, as she waited uncounted days and months for the next ship to pass overhead, she was impatient. It was a sickening feeling; to hope above all else to taste that one thing again... and to hate herself to the core for needing to taste it.

But eventually, she fought less and less against the draw of the anchor. Eventually, she went to the surface more and more willingly. The only hope of salvation that she could see was in finally singing to every one of the men who had done this to her, and to be rid of her need for revenge. Once they all were dead, then she could stop.

But what if I can't stop?

Ana swam back and forth just above the edge of the cliff. She dug the shell into her hand again when the unwelcome thought came to her mind. She swam to the north, then turned and swam to the south. When she turned again, Mari floated right in the middle of the path she had been creating. A new necklace hung around Mari's throat.

Ana pulled up short and stared into Mari's eyes. Neither one spoke for the length of a thousand thoughts.

"How many has it been?" Mari asked at last.

Ana frowned. "Fifteen."

"How many are left?"

She knew the answer easily. She counted each knot on her tail; she counted every man that had tied her up, every day, every night, every hour. "Seven left."

"And when they're all dead?" Mari asked. "What then?"

Ana tried to put confidence in her voice. "Then I'll be done."

"And… what about when you realize that you're done… but you're not satisfied?"

Ana grabbed the rope hanging from where her knees had once been. The rope she had managed to untie while sinking had never fused to her legs. It dangled free, whipping around her when she swam at her fastest. Anger burned in her chest, anger at what the men had done, and it almost translated to Mari as well.

"I don't know," Ana spat. "I'll figure something out."

"You'll become a huntress," Mari said, "A temptress. A siren. You'll become the kind of mermaid sailors fear."

"What's wrong with that? It's what we mermaids were made for, isn't it?"

"Perhaps it is." Her eyes penetrated deep into Ana's soul. "But is it required? It doesn't make you happy."

"Happy?" Ana scoffed and shook her head. "I don't deserve to be happy."

"No." Mari grabbed Ana's hand and pried her fingers apart. "But you *want* to be happy." She took the red-stained shell from Ana and traced the jagged cuts and scars on Ana's palm.

Ana yanked her hand away. "What do you expect me to do? Become like you? I've *never* seen you go to the surface. Where are all the men who wronged you?"

"All the men who wronged me?" Mari shrugged. "I don't know. Probably dead. I have been here a long time. But I wasn't the one who killed them. At least…" She looked down. "Not most of them. After I saw what it was making me, and how it pained me, I refused to continue. I fought it every day for years. Sometimes I think I feel their sons or their grandsons passing by me overhead. Sometimes they tug at me. But I won't do that again."

"Do what?" Ana snapped.

"Become a victim."

Ana looked at her tail, stony at the bottom, ropes to her hips, remnants of a red dress. "But you were a victim."

"I was a victim of superstition, which is one thing. Becoming a victim to revenge is something else entirely."

Ana shook her head. "You're just afraid," she said. "You're afraid of the surface, the oxygen, the waves. You're afraid of the sun."

Mari smiled. "You're speaking to yourself, Ana. You can choose to heed my warning or not. Just think about what you will do when they're all gone. I have seen mermaids like you before. The drive, the pull. They are always the ones who are plagued with the most pain, even after it's all over."

Ana snatched her shell back from Mari and, with a strong kick, sailed away from her. She went down, down, down. Into the deep and penetrating darkness.

The waters went down for miles, never-ending. Eventually, all light from above went away, and Ana was left with nothing but darkness. Flickers and flashes of light flared up around her here and there as different creatures tried to lure her towards them. Small hints of demonic faces illuminated in their self-created light. Wide grins filled with sharp teeth. Big eyes tried to draw her in. She ignored them and kept going down.

The pressure on her chest got even harder, and before she could reach the bottom of this seemingly never-ending pit, she had to stop. She curled herself up into a fetal position and wrapped her arms around her tail, hugging the ropes tightly. That one strand she had pulled loose floated around her aimlessly. It was there in the blackness that she wept, mourning the life she had lost above, hating the weakness she had welcomed in.

Maybe it was better here in the darkness. Better amongst the demons of the deep. Better than turning herself into the same despicable creature that the men who threw her in had been.

Better than turning into her father; a monster controlled by desire, and not discipline.

Something brushed against her arm, and she shivered in the cold.

Demons. She was surrounded by demons.

Inside and out.

Ana lay in a state somewhere between awake and asleep.

The tug at first was gentle, soft. More like a tap than a pull.

Ana lifted her head from her ropes and looked up, but there was nothing to see. Not even the floating lights of demons of the deep.

She ignored it and tucked her head into her tail again.

This time it was two tugs. Distinct and strong. Like a man knocking twice on a door frame.

"No," Ana said out loud.

If Mari could somehow resist revenge, then Ana could, too. All she had to do was bury herself deep enough in the sea.

There was no sufficient depth to escape revenge, though. The anchor was set. The next yank pulled her body straight. She kicked her stone tail and moved upwards in the darkness.

"No!" she cried again, curling around her tail and trying to hold herself there. She squeezed her fist around that shell, cutting into her skin. It didn't help.

Pull, jerk, tug, yank. Inch by inch she was drawn upward in the water. Slowly, a dark blue haze shone above her. A little farther, and the haze turned to blue light.

She fought and kicked and tried to tear that anchor from her heart, but every thrash of her tail took her closer to the surface.

Mari had somehow overcome this addiction. But Mari didn't have Ana's father. She didn't have the blood of an addict in her veins.

It doesn't matter. There's nothing I can do to stop it.

No! Ana didn't want to be a victim. She gripped her shell so tight that it crushed to pieces in her hand.

And then her head broke the surface.

Intoxicating air filled her lungs. She grabbed a rope dangling from the hull.

It was like every other time. She was hopeless.

She knew the man who was on that boat. She told herself she wouldn't say his name, but as she opened her mouth to take another breath, the words tumbled from her lips.

"Trent."

His presence drew closer to her, and her desire for revenge grew stronger.

"Tre-ent," she called, more willingly the second time.

A face appeared over the edge of the boat. "Ana?"

He looked amazed, surprised, excited.

She didn't even have to reach for him. He threw off his jacket and dove over the side. "Ana! Ana!" He laughed as he swam for her.

She backed away. Frightened. Shocked.

"You're alive! How are you possibly alive? How…"

Trent's voice trailed off as his eyes drifted to the water and saw the stone and rope tail beneath her blue skirt. "Is this a dream?"

Ana didn't even know what to say to him.

She grabbed him and dove under the surface . . .

"What… what are you doing here?"

Ana pushed back between the barrels, as if she could hide again and not be found.

"Don't tell anyone," she whispered. "Please. I had no other choice."

Trent shook his head. "Stowaways are illegal. And womenfolk especially!"

"Please," Ana repeated. "Please."

Trent looked around for a moment and frowned. He stood up and opened the barrel above her, retrieving two soft apples from inside. "You look like you haven't eaten anything in days."

She shook her head. "I'm too afraid to come out. And I'm afraid someone will notice things missing if I steal."

"It's a three-month trip. You really think you're going to last that long?"

"What other choice do I have?"

Trent sighed and handed her one of the apples. "Maybe you need an ally."

Weeks went by, and Trent snuck her water and food. Sometimes at night when everyone else had gone to bed, he sat nearby, and they whispered to each other. Why had she stowed away? Why had he decided to become a sailor? What was it like in other parts of the world? What was it like to stay in one place for more than a week?

And then Devon discovered her and was not as forgiving as Trent had been.

The storm started shortly after she was dragged out from behind the barrels and told to stay in the hull until they arrived at port.

She'd tried to keep below deck like she'd been told, but the buffeting of the waves on the wood, the creaking of the boards, the screaming of the men as they tried to navigate through the gale was too much for her nerves. She made her way up, struggling through the torrents until she'd reached the bridge.

"Is there anything I can do to help?" she yelled above the gale.

Two sets of eyes stared back at her, one pair angry and murderous. One pair shocked and afraid. Trent shook his head at her, and she almost felt his terror in her own chest before Devon hissed, "You! You're responsible for this cyclone."

"Devon, no," said Trent. But in a move as sudden as lightning, Devon gripped Ana by the throat. She gasped and choked. Trent stepped forward and raised his hand as if to stop Devon. But he didn't come close enough to touch him.

"This is all *her* fault!" Devon yelled. "I knew we should never have allowed a woman on board. Bad luck. Bad luck this entire trip, and now we're about to get ripped in two..."

She kicked him, and she got enough purchase that he lost his grip on her throat. She stumbled backward and threw her hands up to stop him. "Stay away from me!"

Ana bumped into the railing of the bridge. She'd break a bone if she jumped, and that wouldn't help her.

Devon walked toward her slowly. Movement behind him caught her eye. Trent was no longer at the helm, and another sailor rushed up the stairs to keep them on course amidst the crashing waves.

Devon snatched her by the wrist. She screamed and tried twisting away, but his grip was crushingly tight.

"You know what we have to do, men!" Devon yelled above the roar of the storm. "We have to sacrifice her if we'll have any hope at all of surviving this cursed trip."

"No! No! Stay away!"

He was filled with devilish excitement as he said, "We'll have to drown her." He dragged her down the stairs, and all the men on deck gathered around. Asher brought ropes. Lucius brought the stone. Trent stood above her on the bridge, looking as buffeted by indecision as the ship was by the storm.

She screamed and thrashed about, trying to keep the men from carrying out their deed. But some men held her feet to the stone while others tied the first knots.

"Leave her alone!" Trent finally yelled. He pushed through the crowd and stood beside her.

"Get out of the way, Trent. Or you'll go over right beside her!"

"She's done nothing wrong!"

Another knot was cinched around her legs, and she tried in vain to push the sailor away.

"Of course she has!" Devon yelled as a wave doused him. "She's a woman! She distracts sailors from their duties, and that makes the sea gods angry!"

"There are no sea gods, only One God. And this storm has nothing to do with a woman or a god of any kind. It's a gale. We're out to sea. These things happen."

"Out of the way, Trent!" Devon exclaimed. "Or you'll go with her."

Devon backhanded Trent, sending him sprawling across the deck. Seawater poured over the starboard side and dragged Trent nearly over the edge. He screamed and caught a rigging, struggling to stay on board.

Devon laughed, then ripped Ana's shirt open.

"Now a naked woman." Devon grinned behind his wiry black beard. "That calms the sea." Devon turned to the man beside him. "Work faster. This storm is getting worse."

Every man on the boat lent their hand to tying the rope. The ones who had already performed their task held Trent back. But the fight he'd had before seemed to have diminished. His head was down, and his eyes narrowed to slits.

There was just one knot left to be made, just one piece of rope left to be tied. Devon stepped over to Trent who was still surrounded by three other sailors.

"You tie the last knot, Trent, or I'll find another rock."

He trudged forward slowly, angrily, and wrapped the last length of rope around her legs, ignoring her pleading looks as he halfheartedly tied the final knot.

How long had she been under the water? As the memory of her splashing into the sea woke her, she remembered Trent. They must have been leagues away from Trent's ship by now, and his face was pale and panicked.

Up!

Ana broke to the surface, and both she and Trent gasped a breath of fresh air. Trent coughed and hacked and gagged on the water but slowly came back to his breath.

They floated in isolation, not even a dot on the horizon in sight. Ana breathed hard as she considered what she had remembered. He had been kind to her. He had spoken up for her. But at the end of the day, he had tied the knot like the rest of them. Maybe he deserved death after all.

"Every day of my life since the day they threw you overboard I've been praying that somehow you survived," Trent sobbed. "I've been praying that somehow you got out of those ropes, away from that rock. That somehow someone saved you."

"No one saved me," Ana said in her hoarse voice. "I had to save myself."

He reached out, brushing her wet hair behind her ear. She felt no need to yell or chase him away. He had done the same thing to her many times before. When they spent hours talking in the dark of the night. Before she was a mermaid.

"I'm sorry." Two tears spilled from his eyes and dropped into the sea. "I'm sorry," he said again, shaking his head.

Ana's heart began beating faster. She dove under the surface for a moment and kicked hard with her tail to bring her up and out of the water, leaping into the air. She searched over the tops of the waves for his ship. It was nowhere to be seen.

She dove and jumped again, and again, until she heard him call her name over the waves.

She swam back to him. "I... I can't find your ship," she said in horror.

Trent flashed a little smile at her and shook his head. "It doesn't matter. This is precisely what I deserve."

"No." Ana stared into his face. "No. You don't deserve this."

"Ana." Trent treaded water with just his feet. He reached out and took Ana's hand in his, then hissed in pain. She looked down to see a shard of the shell she had shattered still stuck in her palm.

Trent pulled the piece out of her skin and slipped it into the pocket of his trousers. Then he brought her cut hand to his lips and kissed it gently. "I've been waiting uncountable years to say these two words to you, and I feel like you aren't hearing me." He looked straight into her eyes. "I'm sorry."

A tear trickled down her cheek and landed on her tongue. Salty and sweet, it was a taste she would never forget. And just like her shell had shattered earlier, that briny, iron anchor that had been lodged in her heart was crushed to bits.

"No, I'm sorry." She kicked her tail to lift herself out of the water one last time, desperate to find his boat. "I'm sorry! I never should have dragged you out here." More of her own tears cascaded down her cheeks and splashed into the water, filling her even more with that intoxicating taste.

The taste of forgiveness.

"I'm not afraid of this anymore," Trent said. "Right now, right here, in the water with you—this is where I belong."

That's what he said, but it couldn't be true. He would die. And she couldn't let that happen.

But what could she do? How was she going to find another boat to put him on? How was she going to fix what her need for revenge had done?

"Ana," he said, and put a hand on her cheek. "I have regretted that day ever since it happened. I was afraid then. When that wave almost took me off the boat, I knew what it meant, what Devon was threatening, and I was afraid. But I shouldn't have been a victim to my fear. I never should have tied that last knot. I should have let them throw me in with you."

She reached down and felt the rope at her knees, the last knot she had been able to loosen and get free. It was that knot that gave her one last shot of hope, that made her hold her breath those last few seconds instead of giving up. It was that knot that ensured she was alive when she reached the magic, instead of dead.

If he hadn't tied that last knot, she never would have become a mermaid. She would have drowned in the sea like the men intended for her to do. She knew what she had to do.

Ana took Trent by the hand and looked into his eyes, "Do you trust me, Trent?" she asked in her husky siren voice.

"Yes," said Trent.

She clasped his hand even tighter. "Take a breath. Hold it as long as you can. And don't give up. Don't ever give up."

He took a deep breath.

And then she dove, her stony tail propelling them deeper and deeper. Darker and darker.

Down into the all-consuming depths.

Beware the Sea

Rachel Kirkaldie

When I was seven years old, my father held my hand on the edge of a cliff and pointed down to the ocean. Far below us, the waves churned restlessly, crashing against rocks, black in the moonless night. "Stay away from the ocean, Emmy," he told me. "It will kill you if it can."

"Why?" I asked, both horrified and mesmerized by the ever-moving waves.

"Because you're a Carlin," he said simply, "and the Carlins are cursed."

That wasn't the first time in my life I had heard that word. People in town whispered it behind our backs when they thought we weren't listening. No matter that Father was one of the wealthiest men in town, descended from one of the original founders of Carlton Harbor, Maine. "Money can't save you from a curse," they whispered.

Father's black brows knit together, and he scowled the way he did when I talked back to Mother. "You must promise to never go near it."

I quickly nodded a promise, not knowing yet that promises never worked well for me. The ocean sounded like a mournful monster as it slammed itself against our cliff. Was it angry it couldn't have me? Or sad that it would never know me?

For years, I only knew bits and pieces about the curse; Mother covered my ears every time Father started ranting about it. It wasn't until I was eleven that I finally convinced my brother, Hiram, to tell me the details no one seemed to think I should hear. He ushered me out into the rocky garden that was also the Carlin family cemetery, shaded by a few shrubby alder trees and whipped by the winds that came in off the bay. Cracked and crumbling headstones marked ancient graves overgrown with sea grass.

Hiram sat down next to a stone cross that read "Captain Ephraim Carlin" and I sat cross-legged beside him. "They say the curse began with him." Hiram gestured to the cross, whispering as if fearful the ocean—or the ghosts of long-dead Carlins—would overhear him. "Our great-great-great-something-grandfather. His whaling ship was capsized by the biggest sperm whale you've ever seen. Somehow, Captain Ephraim survived, floating on a scrap of wood. He saw his best friend flailing in the water but was too afraid to swim out to help him. He let him drown. After that, so many Carlins died at sea, no one could shrug it off as coincidence."

"How?" I whispered, almost afraid to ask, but desperate to know. "How did they die?"

Hiram shrugged, leaning back against the cracked headstone. "Drowning, mostly. Falling off ships, getting caught in an undertow. Great Uncle Alistair slipped on the deck of a ship and cracked his head open. Great Grandfather's second wife threw herself off this very cliff. And then…well, you know about Father's twin brother. He drowned while they were playing on the beach."

The real reason behind Father's fear of the ocean. I shivered. Yet, as I looked out at the blue stretch of bay beyond the cliffs, the wind tossing my hair into my face, I was filled with longing. "Why do we still live here, by the ocean, if it hates us so much?"

Hiram smirked. "I don't think our ancestors could give up the ocean completely. You've heard Father say it—Carlins have more salt water in their veins than blood."

He said it often, explaining to people why he stayed in Carlton Harbor investing in whaling ships instead of moving to the city and becoming a businessman. I wondered if I could use it as an excuse for why I didn't fear the ocean the way I should.

"So," Hiram continued, "our forebears built Carlin Manor, where they could gaze upon the ocean, but never again venture out onto it."

I glanced up at our cliffside mansion, a red-brick monstrosity of weathered balconies, soaring turrets, and a high, peaked roof. It had seen several generations of Carlins suffer and endure. To me, Carlin Manor was more of a curse than the fear of death on the raging sea. It was there that I was trapped, being trussed and trained into a proper young lady with only one future—to someday make some man a suitable wife.

Hiram must have seen the sadness in my eyes and misinterpreted it. "I don't think the ocean hates us, Emmy," he told me. "It just wants our respect. I think...the Carlins have always tried to conquer it, instead of becoming one with it."

Hiram didn't fear the ocean the way Father did. I saw the same gleam in his eyes when he looked out over the harbor that I'm sure shined in mine. He was always pointing out its beauty to me:

"Look, Emmy, the ocean looks like silver."

"Look how the moon strikes a path across the water."

"The ocean moves like poetry, don't you think?"

Hiram and I never wanted to live our lives with our feet planted on the ground. We knew we were Carlins, and we didn't belong on the ocean, but nothing could stop us from dreaming about it.

"Will you take me to the docks with you, Hiram?" I blurted, surprising myself. Hiram was sixteen then, and already being groomed by Father to take over the family business someday. He had the freedom of spending time at Father's office and the harbor where the ships were docked. *He* wasn't trapped in the house with me and our sister, Lottie, learning piano and etiquette.

He took my question in quietly, pursing his lips. He should have said no without hesitation; Mother did not approve of her daughters spending time around sailors, and Father used the curse as the reason we couldn't go near the harbor. But Hiram's heart was as soft as warmed caramel. "Just once," he said at last, wagging his finger at me in mock sternness.

"Just once" turned into countless times over the next four years, until the docks—the tang of the sea air, the billowing of white sails, the screech of gulls overhead, and the *people*—became as familiar to me as the dim, carpeted halls of Carlin Manor.

At first, Mother and Father tried to forbid me from going, but Hiram came to my defense. Somehow, our parents never seemed capable of refusing Hiram, their only son, anything. Even when he came home one day with a big-eared, black and brown puppy, they sighed and relented. I convinced him to name her Brizo, and soon she came with us to the docks, too, trotting at our heels and chasing seagulls.

And so I learned the difference between a bark and a schooner, between square-rigging and fore-and-aft rigging. I learned what gurry was and mediocrely attempted to carve scrimshaw. I learned sailing terms like shivers, keep your eyes peeled, and mux. Some of the sailors taught me songs that Hiram made me swear to never repeat. Sometimes we went aboard the docked whalers, still reeking of blood and grease, and when I managed to hold in my vomit, the skipper told me I had the guts of a sailor.

Some evenings, when the sky was clear, Hiram and I would sit on the low sea wall and watch the color slowly leach from the sky as the sun set and the moon rose, lighting the ocean like a lamp. Constellations of stars spiraled through the heavens, a map with which to navigate the world. We talked, not usually about the unlikable present, but about what we dreamed for the future.

"Do you think you'll ever go sailing, Hiram?" I asked.

He shrugged. "I want to, someday. But right now, I think it would upset Father too much. Maybe…the time isn't right yet. I feel like we need to make a truce with the ocean. Give back, somehow, what we've taken."

I arched my eyebrows at him. "A truce?" I asked skeptically, "with the ocean? You hear yourself, don't you, Hiram?"

He laughed. "Yes, I know it sounds crazy. But so does the idea that an entire family could have as much bad luck as ours has. It has to end somehow, doesn't it?"

I was quiet for a while, watching a pair of moths flit toward our lantern. Finally, I said, "Just take me with you, all right? When you finally go out?"

He wanted to say no, I could tell. It was his natural brotherly protective instinct. But he nodded. "Of course I will, Emmy."

But Hiram didn't leave home on a sailing ship. America broke out into civil war, and, despite all of Father's objections, Hiram enlisted. I had never cried as many tears as I did the day he left, tall and handsome in his blue overcoat, his cap askew over his thick, dark hair.

"You have to be strong," he told me firmly, hands on my shoulders. "I know you're the youngest, Emmy, but you're the glue. You hold our family together. When Lottie frets and Father's temper flares, somehow you always smooth it all out. You have to be strong."

I didn't feel strong, but I told him I would be.

He smiled softly. "And take care of Brizo."

Mother made sure my days at the docks quickly came to an end, keeping me so busy with lessons and sewing for the war effort that I didn't even have time to eavesdrop on Father's conversations with his business associates and listen for stories of the sea. In a way, I didn't mind; the docks weren't the same without Hiram, and being there just reminded me how much I missed him. At least if I was busy, the days until he came home would go by faster.

Four years later, when the war finally ended, my heart breathed a sigh of relief. I was the very-marriageable age of nineteen, but the war had stalled all talk of such things. I allowed myself to dream of the days Hiram and I would spend at the harbor, maybe even a future day when we convinced Father that the ocean was ready for us to sail out on it again. Maybe I would see those brighter shores, after all.

But Hiram never made it home. He died in a riverboat explosion on the Mississippi. Drowned in the depths of an icy river.

"It's your curse!" Mother screamed at Father, the last passionate words to cross her lips before she, too, drowned—not in the ocean but in sorrow. She became confined to her bed, refusing to see anyone but her maid and the doctor.

I would never forget Father's face when Mother flung those words at him. He looked as if he had been slapped. I would argue that the Mississippi River was far from the ocean and couldn't have any connection to the curse. But Father seemed to take personal responsibility for Hiram's death. He spent more and more time alone in his study, waving off questions about his well-being with an, *"I'm fine,"* but I saw his bloodshot eyes, noticed his well-trimmed beard grow unkempt, saw a liquor bottle become a constant companion at his desk.

Visitors—some well-meaning, others not—came in a stream to Carlin Manor, but Mother and Father would see none of them. Lottie's music went silent as she tucked herself into a chair in the corner of her room and watched the ocean for hours on end.

Since there was no body to bury, the minister gave us a wooden cross to erect in the family cemetery in Hiram's memory. My family refused to come with me, so I went outside alone to pray over it, the blustery wind whipping at my black dress, my body shaking with sobs.

The curse had broken our family.

Wind and rain battered the windows as I carefully made my way up the creaky stairs, dinner tray balanced in my hands. I had dropped it more than a few times—Mother always called me clumsy—so I had learned to go slow. Generations of frowning Carlins stared down from the wall at me in judgment as I walked down the long, dim third-floor hallway. I tipped up my chin as I passed them, the way Hiram had taught me to do when sailors made a big deal over me being a girl.

Lottie hid like a ghost in the corner of her room, wearing her white nightdress, her long, dark hair spilling down her back. If I hadn't known she was there, I might have missed her. It was strange to me that she spent her time looking out over the ocean, when she, more than any of us, had always been so afraid of it.

I set the tray down on the side table. She was still eating, at least, though not a lot. "It's your favorite tonight," I said in my best forced-sing-song voice. "Meatloaf."

Lottie didn't smile back, but she said, "Thank you, Emmy."

"Are you ready to come downstairs yet? The piano is gathering dust."

Lottie shook her head. "Not yet. I'm…waiting."

I looked at her, hoping she'd say more. When she didn't, I pressed, "For what?"

"For a way to break the curse."

I—softly—blew out a frustrated breath. "What will that do? It won't…" My voice cracked. I fought a sudden onslaught of tears. "It's not going to bring Hiram back." Those words felt so final, like the dropping of an anchor I could never retrieve.

Lottie sat back in her chair, suddenly looking very small. "I know. But it will…fix things."

I knew better than to argue with her and distance her even further. I swiped away a stray tear on my cheek and put on a brave face for her, trying to liven her up with some small talk before retreating back into the hallway. Only then did my brave face crumple. I leaned against the wall as the tears slid down my cheeks.

I had promised Hiram I would be strong, but I was discovering I wasn't good at keeping promises. It was hard to be strong when I saw my family hurting. It was hard to be strong when I was hurting. When there seemed to be no way to make it better.

I slumped onto the couch beside the parlor window, watching the rain streak down the glass. It had been weeks since the sun had broken free of the clouds, as if nature itself was mourning Hiram. As was becoming typical lately, no one had bothered to light the lamps in this room, and I sat in near-darkness. The click of claws on wood announced the arrival of Brizo, who had become attached to me ever since the day we learned of Hiram's death. She sat down in front of me and pushed her soft brown head under my hands, eager for a pat.

I scratched behind her big black ears, lost in thought. Lottie's talk of breaking the curse reminded me of how Hiram used to talk about a truce with the ocean. It had seemed so right back then, but now, with a cloud of sorrow settled over our home, thicker than the morning fog over the bay, it seemed absurd. Nothing could fix this. Where would I even start? This was no fairy tale; curses didn't break with a whispered spell or a true love's kiss.

Brizo let out a low whine. I looked down and realized I had stopped petting her. I resumed scratching behind her ears and her tail thumped happily against the carpet.

For the rest of the evening, I was consumed with thoughts of curse-breaking and truces with the ocean, and even after I went to bed those thoughts tormented my dreams, sending me tossing and turning. I awoke with a start, pausing in the quiet, listening for the sound that had awakened me.

Brizo whined and scratched at my door.

I sat up and rubbed the sleep from my eyes. "What is it, girl?" I asked. As soon as I opened the door, she darted down the hallway. I sleepily began to close the door behind her, but then she started barking.

I hurried after her, shushing her and peering into the shadows of the stairs and the foyer, but saw nothing amiss. Everything was dark and silent. But Brizo was determined. She lumbered down the stairs and through the foyer, then began barking incessantly at the front door.

I sighed. She must really need to go out. Why did it have to be in the middle of the night? I threw a cloak over my nightgown and pulled on a pair of boots. "Make this quick," I told Brizo as I grabbed a lantern off a hook by the door.

She responded with another whine. Then, as soon as I opened the door, she bolted.

"Brizo!" It was as if she didn't hear me. "Brizo!" Through the misty rain, I saw her slip through the open gate and disappear.

I raced down the front walk, muttering curses I had learned while out on the docks. Confused as to why the gate had been left open, I pushed it wide enough for me to fit through and called Brizo again. Even when she found a squirrel to chase, she usually came back after only a few minutes. There was no sign of her.

With only a lantern to light the darkness, I had to carefully pick my way down the rocky path that led down the cliff to town. My pace was slow but my heart was racing. I couldn't let anything happen to

Brizo. She was all I had left of Hiram.

Near the bottom of the trail, over the crash of the ocean against the rocky beach, I heard Brizo's distant bark. I broke into a run then, lantern swinging, stumbling over the sandy trail. In a moment, my boots thudded on the weathered wooden docks, and I froze.

I had carefully avoided this place for four years. I gazed around at the shadowed ships, the glow of lanterns softly illuming the misty air. My heart started to ache. I had loved this place, once. I loved the salt in the air, the cry of gulls overhead, the interesting people that I imagined came from faraway lands. I loved Hiram's warm, reassuring presence beside me.

It was certainly different now, in the dark. The ships creaked eerily as they bobbed on the black, sinuous water. Moonlight peeked through the clouds, casting silvered shadows. A few ships were being loaded, rough voices called out to each other, and a drunken voice sang a bawdy, offkey tune. This was no place for a young lady, but somehow I wasn't afraid.

I should have been. The vengeful ocean was just beneath my feet, waiting to devour me just for being a Carlin. But instead, I was overcome with the feelings I had shoved away since Hiram left for war—love for the sea, a longing to meet the horizon, hope and possibility. They rose up inside of me with such strength that my sorrow lifted. It was as if Hiram was with me again, filling me with that distant dream of touching the sea.

"Hey, Brizo!"

I whirled, almost dropping my lantern. A dark-haired young man crouched there, rubbing Brizo's head while she licked his face and wagged her tail so hard her whole body shook. For one brief, heart-rending moment, I thought Hiram had come home, after all.

Then the young man looked up, meeting my gaze with eyes that were not Hiram's. Disappointment washed through me, mixed with relief at finding Brizo safe. I grabbed her collar and pulled her away. She licked my hand and showed no remorse for making me chase her to the docks. "I'm so sorry," I said. "She's not usually that friendly with strangers."

"I'm no stranger, am I, Brizo?" He grinned and reached out to pet Brizo again, almost making her wiggle out of my grasp. "We go way back."

I stared at him, uncomprehending. I didn't even think how absurd it sounded when I asked, "How do you know my dog?"

"She's Hiram's dog," the young man replied, rising to his full, lanky height. He squinted at me. "You're his sister, aren't you? Where's Hiram?"

I could only stare at him. Hiram had introduced me to many sailors over the years, and he always seemed to know everybody, so I couldn't immediately place this young man in my memories. But his question about Hiram, asked so casually, as if Hiram was just over at the market and would be back any second, sent my heart up into my throat, choking me so I couldn't speak.

He cocked his head slightly. "Are you all right?"

What was I doing here? It suddenly hit me that I had chased Brizo all the way to the docks in the middle of the night, that I was dressed in only my cloak and nightgown, and I was talking to a stranger who didn't know Hiram was dead. Gone. The hope and possibility I had felt moments before was quickly doused in dreadful truth.

"I have to go," I blurted.

He frowned. "All right. Maybe I'll see you tomorrow?"

I didn't answer, just pulled my cloak closer around me and hurried away before he could ask more questions about Hiram. Brizo lingered for one last pat, then trotted after me, apparently cured of whatever delusion had driven her out here in the first place. I resolutely started down the trail toward Carlin Manor, but my feet felt heavy, reluctant to leave the ocean behind.

When we got back to my room, Brizo curled up on my bed and fell into a peaceful slumber, while I lay awake, staring at the ceiling. The heartache in my chest stirred and throbbed as if I had just lost Hiram all over again. Tears stung my eyes, and I swore to myself that I would never go back to the docks; it just hurt too much.

And yet, I couldn't shake the feeling that Brizo's late-night escape to the docks had been purposeful. It was so unlike her, yet she had led me straight to someone who had known Hiram, straight to the ocean, straight to that feeling of Hiram being so close, as if we were still spending our days dreaming of sailing and the war had never come and torn it all away from us. Could I really stay away from that feeling forever, from the place I had always been happiest? If Lottie was right and the curse needed to be broken somehow, maybe this is where it could start.

Maybe I *could* do something. Maybe I could make a truce with the ocean.

Father would be furious if he found out I was going to the docks unchaperoned, but he wasn't around to stop me. As soon as the meager sunrise glowed through the overcast horizon, I was out of bed, getting dressed, then bringing Lottie breakfast and kissing the top of her head. Brizo hurried to my side when she heard me open the front door.

I wagged a finger at her. "No running away this time, got it?"

Brizo's fluffy tail wagged harder in consent, and she happily trotted at my heels as I hurried down the cracked stone path to our front gate. The morning fog soon swallowed us both, and aside from the occasional squirrel or sandpiper, we were the only two in the world.

As we neared the harbor, towering masts and jutting prows emerged from the gloom. It was too early for the docks to be terribly busy, but there were more people than the night before—weathered sailors tying lines and hauling cargo, fishermen bringing in their nets, a well-dressed merchant or two with servants in tow. Brizo watched it all with curious eyes but stayed right by my side.

I swallowed hard against the pain of resurfacing memories and let the salt breeze tug at my braided hair. Gulls squealed overhead. I wandered from ship to ship, remembering nautical terms and whispering them to myself like some kind of prayer. Once again, I felt that nearness to Hiram, felt the sorrow on my shoulders ease as if lifted by the ocean breeze. If only I could get on one of those ships and sail away. Maybe then I could keep these feelings with me forever.

But even I knew that sailing away on a ship would break my family even more, not fix it. I sighed, absentmindedly scratching Brizo's head, and glanced around, realizing I had been staring off into the fog like a fool. I called to Brizo to follow me, but she started barking excitedly, wagging her whole body at a figure moving through the fog.

"Oh, hey, it's you again!"

I recognized the voice of the boy from the night before as he crouched down and let Brizo bound to him, scratching behind her ears as she happily licked his hands. In the morning light, I saw that he had dark, curly hair, a smattering of freckles over his nose and cheeks, and vibrant green eyes sparkling with mischief. He seemed so genuinely friendly that I felt guilty for snubbing him the night before.

He ruffled Brizo's thick fur. "How's my little sea goddess?"

I smiled a little. Few people knew what Brizo's name actually meant. I took a deep breath. "I'm sorry for leaving in such a hurry last night."

He grinned, straightening and stuffing his hands in the pockets of his faded trousers. Brizo continued to sniff him and wag her tail. "No worries. I didn't expect you to remember me. I think you were this tall"—he held his hand up in the air around the height of his waist—"the last time I saw you." His grin widened, warm, contagious. "I'm Leander. I know it's a long, fancy name, but you can call me Lee for short, or Ann, or Der."

I laughed despite myself. "Der?"

He chuckled. "That's what Hiram always calls me, too."

My smile faltered.

Leander didn't seem to notice. "My mom named me. She was French, real sophisticated, and she thought giving me a sophisticated name might make my dad less…well, *un*sophisticated. Of course, it didn't work. No one can sophisticate a sailor, not even a pretty French girl. Or so my dad tells me. I never met my mom. She left right after I was born."

"Oh. I'm sorry," I said lamely.

He shrugged. "Hiram was always very protective of you. I don't think he ever told me your name."

"Emmeline." I cleared my throat. "But everyone calls me Emmy."

That face-splitting grin again. "Well look at that, you've got a fancy name like me. Does Hiram just let you come to the docks by yourself now, Emmy?"

It hurt so much I could barely breathe, but instead of answering, I forced myself to ask, "How do you know my brother?"

"I sail with my dad on the *Genevieve*. We come into this port a few times a year and usually stay for several weeks. We supply a lot of the whalers. I met Hiram years back. He had this adorable little puppy with him, with a little body and huge ears." He patted Brizo's head and her tail swiped back and forth on the dock.

I managed a tiny smile, remembering.

Leander tilted his head, regarding me like I was a perplexing knot. "What brings you to the harbor so early? You settin' sail somewhere?"

"I…" Telling him my reasons felt foolish. *I just want to stand on the deck of a ship like Hiram and I used to. I want to forget about the hurt in my heart. I want to make a truce with the ocean.* He was sure to think I was crazy. "I…just enjoy being here. Being near the ships. Getting out of the house."

He nodded like that was the most normal thing in the world for a nineteen year-old girl to be doing. "Come on, then, I'll show you the *Genevieve*. She's much lovelier than any of your whalers."

Startled by his offer, I hesitated a moment, then nearly tripped on my skirts as I turned to follow him down the row of ships, Brizo bounding along beside me. The *Genevieve* was a majestic schooner. She bobbed quietly on the water as Leander gestured me up the gangplank. It had only been four years since I had stood on a ship, but as my foot made contact with the freshly-scrubbed deck, I instinctively flinched, as if the entire ocean was going to open up and swallow me whole. It didn't. In fact, nothing happened—except Leander bumped into me from behind.

"What are you waiting for?" he asked.

I took another step, steadying myself against the ship's gentle rocking motion. Brizo immediately darted off, sniffing everything. The masts towered over me, half-shrouded in fog, creaking slightly. I could almost feel Hiram beside me, singing a sea shanty and laughing over the words he forgot.

Almost against my will, a grin spread over my face. "This is *your* ship?"

"Well, my dad's ship. We ship cargo up and down the coast, from Nova Scotia all the way to the Caribbean."

I felt a twinge of jealousy. I was a spoiled rich girl, and this rough sailor boy had the one thing I couldn't have: the life I wanted.

Leander showed me around the ship, unsurprised when I knew what everything was before he'd even told me. "Hiram taught you well, I see."

I smiled a little, though my heart hurt at the same time. "He did."

Leander's cheerful eyes sobered, his grin fading. "Where is he, Emmy?"

I swallowed hard. I couldn't say it. Tears pricked my eyes, and I hurried over to the rail, gripping it hard as if to steady myself. The fog was beginning to lift, and the silvery-blue harbor stretched into view. A view that Hiram would have loved.

Quietly, Leander came and stood beside me. I expected him to prod me for answers, but he just leaned his tanned forearms against the rail, looking out over the ocean. I took some deep breaths, composed myself and said, "Hiram was killed. In the war."

Leander sucked in a sharp breath. "No. Oh, Emmy, I'm so sorry. I didn't…We've been in the Caribbean for the last three years…"

I looked up at the mast, where a gull was perched, preening itself. "He loved the ocean. Being here makes me feel like he's not so far away."

"He's not. He belonged on the ocean. I think he loved it more than I do. I expected him to sail away before he ever enlisted in the army."

"He couldn't," I replied. "Because of the curse."

"Oh, yes," Leander scoffed. "The Carlin Curse."

"The curse is real," I snapped, indignant. "My family is doomed to die on the ocean. It started with one of my great grandfathers. Ever since, so many Carlins have died at sea that my father has forbidden us from going anywhere near it."

"This seems pretty near it," Leander said, glancing over the rail.

"Hiram and I used to get onto ships like this all the time. It seemed like the safest way to be on a ship without being *on* a ship. But we never sailed. That seemed too much like tempting fate. But we wanted to. More than anything."

"Then you should."

At my sharp glance, Leander straightened, holding his hands out to his sides. "You and Hiram spent your whole lives dreaming," he continued. "Where did that get you? Maybe your family is cursed, or maybe they're just unlucky. Either way, I don't think you should let it control your destiny. I think being kept from the ocean is more of a curse for you than any danger that waits upon it."

I had never thought of it that way before. "Did you ever tell Hiram that?"

Leander shrugged. "A time or two."

"Hiram thought we could make a truce with the ocean."

Leander nodded thoughtfully. "I think the ocean gives and takes, without malice. The ocean just is, and you have to learn to live on its terms."

That's what I wanted to believe.

But the sails on my heart dragged down as I thought of Hiram climbing aboard that steamship. What had been going through his mind? Had he been thrilled, hoping he was finally escaping the curse? Had he decided the risk was finally worth taking? "Do you think one family could just be so unlucky that there's no hope to fix it?"

Leander leaned against the rail next to me, a sadness in his eyes I hadn't seen before. "Most sailors believe in luck. They try to keep it with them by wearing a certain necklace or tying a knot a certain way. Some people have a lot of it. Some people don't. But I don't believe that. It seems so unfair to think that you're just born with what you get, and none of your choices matter."

That was a much more thoughtful answer than I had expected from him. I was familiar enough with my own heart-hurt that I could sense it in him, too. I let the silence hang between us for several heartbeats, then asked, "Do you and your dad not get along?"

He frowned at me. "How could you know that?"

"Just…a feeling."

Leander looked down at his hands resting on the rail, the worn, callused hands of a sailor, even a young one. "Dad could never get over Mother leaving us, and he blames me. I'm a constant, hateful reminder of her. He keeps me around to scrub the deck and bear the brunt of his anger. Then whenever we come to port, he abandons me, gets drunk, and gambles our money away."

My heart clenched. "Oh, Leander, I'm so sorry."

"I'll work my way out of it," he said fiercely. "I'm not a slave to luck. One of these days, I'll get my own ship and live on my own terms. I don't believe I'm cursed to an unlucky fate. And you can't think that about your family either, Emmy. What's broken can be fixed. I have to believe that. And you know Hiram would believe it, too."

It might have been the sea air in my lungs or the feel of the ship beneath me, but his words made me feel hopeful. "Thank you," I told him. "I feel…better than I have in a long time." I looked around for Brizo, who was sniffing around a coil of rope. She obediently came when I called her. "I should get going."

"Will you come back tomorrow?" Leander asked.

I looked at him in surprise. "Come back?"

His smile almost seemed shy. "I mean, it's hurricane season, so we're here for a while. The crew is on leave, and if I show my face around Dad when he's drunk, he'll do more than just yell at me. I could…use a hand around the ship."

I smiled so wide I could feel it stretching my face. I couldn't remember the last time I had smiled like that. "Yes, of course."

He grinned back. "And you, too, Brizo," he said, scratching her upturned head. "Come back whenever you like, sea goddess."

There was beauty in every curve of the road as I hurried home, my steps so light I almost floated. I twirled through the front gate of Carlin Manor and practically danced to the door. But inside, the house was so dark and quiet it nearly smothered my joy. I paused in the foyer, trying not to let the gloom overwhelm me.

I made my way to Lottie's room. No answer came when I knocked, so I let myself in. She hadn't moved from her chair by the window, her legs wrapped in a quilt. I frowned when I saw that the food I had left this morning was untouched.

"Lottie, aren't you hungry?"

She looked up at me, blinking in the dim light from the window. There were dark circles under her eyes. "No."

I crouched next to her chair. An opening in the clouds allowed a shaft of sunlight to shine through, painting the ocean golden and hazy. "The ocean is beautiful, isn't it?"

"It's angry," she whispered.

"Are you sure?" I asked, remembering the calm familiarity of being on Leander's ship. "I think Father's wrong about the ocean. It can be peaceful, joyful, even."

"Not for us."

I took her hands in mine. "Lottie, I went back to the harbor today."

"The harbor?" Lottie suddenly seemed to take an interest in our conversation. "Didn't Father forbid you from going there?"

"Not exactly. I walked the docks just like I used to do with Hiram."

"Only you weren't with Hiram."

"I *felt* like he was there, Lottie. The docks were where he was happiest. And I met one of his old friends, Leander. He showed me his ship, and he told me…"

"You went out on his ship?"

"It was docked." I fought to keep the strain of irritation out of my voice.

Lottie leaned forward in her chair, a flush rising to her cheeks. "I don't see how that matters. It's still the ocean. You shouldn't be going anywhere near the docks."

"I'm fine."

"Do you realize what could have happened?" she hissed. "You could have been killed. The ocean hates our family, Emmy. It's just waiting to take another of us."

Her words sent a chill up my spine, but I wouldn't let her deter me. "I think you're wrong. What happened to Grandfather, and our whole family's history, is tragic, but to let it keep us from the ocean forever…"

"Is so we'll be safe," Lottie cut in, her eyes wild. "How could you, Emmy? We just lost Hiram. I can't bear to lose you, too."

My excitement dwindled to guilt. "You won't lose me, Lottie."

She stared down at her hands, still clutched in mine. "I have to figure out a way," she whispered.

"What?"

"Promise me you won't do it again," she begged, turning to face me. Tears shone in her eyes.

I said the only thing I could. "I promise."

But I already knew I was no good at promises, and this was one I wouldn't keep. I was determined to meet up with Leander again, and nothing would stop me. Soon, joining him at the docks every day became a balm to my soul, much as going there with Hiram had been. The oppressive gloom of Carlin Manor lifted off my shoulders with the ocean breeze. Leander and I scrubbed decks, mended sails, sang off-key, and shared stories about Hiram. I felt hope stitching the wounds of losing him back together in new but beautiful ways.

The edges of my sorrow were being soothed away by something else, too, though I didn't notice it at first. I liked the mischief in Leander's green eyes, his warm smile, the easy way he had about him. He had been Hiram's friend and now he was mine, my connection to the sea. I didn't think there was anything more to it than that.

But when my heart started tumbling at the sight of him, I knew it was more than the harbor I loved seeing every day.

One unusually bright afternoon, Leander surprised me by meeting me and Brizo halfway down the beach trail. "I have something of a surprise for you," he said with that crooked grin. "Come on!"

Brizo bounded after him with delight, but I followed more slowly. When we reached the harbor, dark clouds building on the horizon, Leander proudly gestured to a small wooden boat tied and bobbing in the water. "Surprised?"

"Um, yes?" I replied uncertainly. "What is this?"

"The *Genevieve's* skiff, of course."

"I know that," I huffed. "But why?"

"I'm going for a row around the bay. And I'd like you to come with me."

My heart stammered. "Out on the bay? On a boat?" A tiny boat at that, not a big, comfortable ship.

"You can't let fear keep you on the shore forever."

"I'm not afraid," I snapped.

"Then why aren't you getting in?"

This was the moment I had been waiting for my whole life. Well, maybe not this exact moment; mine and Hiram's daydreams had always involved a sleek, majestic sailing ship. But maybe this was a better first step. I nodded, and Leander helped me into the boat. Brizo squeezed her way in next to me, not about to be left behind. Leander's knees brushed mine as he took his seat across from me.

Leander untied the boat, showed me how to grip the oars, and we started rowing away from the docks and onto the bay. The skiff rocked unsteadily over some rough waves, and I had a moment of panic. We were just two small, helpless people on a tiny wooden boat, floating in the middle of a vast, surging power. What was I doing? One strong wave could throw me overboard in a heartbeat.

Leander must have seen the fear on my face. "I won't let the ocean kill you, Emmy. Relax. Enjoy this." He grinned. "You're on the ocean."

I *was* on the ocean. I filled my mind with that miraculous thought and my grip on the oar eased. I focused on the waves gently rocking the boat, the oars dipping and splashing in a soothing rhythm. The docks fell away. Leander, in a low, even tone, told me stories of ocean adventures, tales of crotchety pirates with peg legs, of singing mermaids and ghost ships. All the while we rowed out farther into the harbor, the ocean all around us.

"Do you do this often?" I asked him.

"When I need to escape. I can't spend my days at the tavern like the rest of the crew. This is where my heart is. I'm free from everyone here, even my dad."

Freedom. Something I had never truly known, not even running barefoot through the gardens. There were always walls and gates surrounding me, and that warning to beware the sea. I was trapped. But the sea called to me, a promise of new horizons, the wind in my hair and fate held firmly in *my* hands, not dictated by some distant curse.

My heart was here too, I knew that with certainty. And perhaps the ocean could be appeased with taking my heart instead of my life.

After an interminable amount of time, Leander pointed up. "There's your house."

I followed his gaze to see Carlin Manor from a perspective I had never had before. It was tall and formidable atop the cliff, unyielding, unwilling to change despite the elements that constantly battered it.

I felt a stab of pain as I thought about the people in that house lost in sorrow, quietly grieving as if the pain would never go away. My grief over Hiram remained, but it was no longer a grief without hope. How could I bring that hope to my family?

I reached out over the side of the skiff and let my fingers graze the water. "Truce," I whispered.

The sun was low when we rowed the skiff back to the dock, the sky filled with dark, ominous clouds. Leander tied the boat while I pulled the oars in, then he jumped up onto the dock and held his hand out for me. I took it, but as he helped me out of the boat, I tripped over my skirts. He caught me by my arms as I fell forward into his chest.

"Sorry," I mumbled, my face warm, pushing against him as I tried to straighten.

Instead of letting go of me, he leaned forward and brushed his lips against mine. The warmth in my face spread, from the top of my head down to my toes. I kissed him back. Just a gentle kiss, a promise. One that I could keep.

He smiled softly at me. "You get to choose, Emmy. I hope you see that. Don't let fear keep you from living."

That night, dinner tray in hand, I opened the door to find Lottie's room empty. The window was cracked, letting in a drizzle of rain and salty wind. Worried but not yet panicked, I searched the other bedrooms, then the library, the music room, the parlor. No Lottie. Dread thudded in my heart.

Father snored over his books, so I did the only thing I could think of. I pushed aside Mother's protesting maid and burst into Mother's room. "Mother!" I exclaimed. "I can't find Lottie!"

She looked so frail against those white pillows, a shell of the formidable woman who would intimidate me into practicing French just by narrowing her eyes. It broke my heart that Hiram's death had done this to her, but right now I felt anger. How dare she allow her grief over her son's death to blind her to her living daughters—daughters who so desperately needed her.

Mother stared at me uncomprehending. "She hasn't been right," I pressed. "Lottie hasn't been well. Worse than you, I fear. And now she's gone. Gone! Mother, do you understand what that could mean?"

She slowly shook her head, which seemed to take a lot of effort. "There's nothing I can do..."

I moved in close to her, grabbing her cold hands in mine. "We all hate that Hiram is gone. But can you lose Lottie, too?"

She took a long time to respond. "No," she finally said in a cracked, tired voice.

"Please help me look for her."

"Your mother is in no position to help you," the maid interjected, hands on her hips. "She has been bedridden for weeks. The doctor said..."

Mother interrupted her by letting out a huff of breath. "Get my shoes and my coat."

When I emerged out into the hallway, Father was there, looming over me like a stranger. There was whiskey on his breath when he said, "You've been out on the ocean."

I stared at him, my worry over Lottie clouding over my ability to reason. "How could you possibly know that?"

"Lottie's in danger. You've been flirting with the ocean, ignoring the curse, and now your sister is going to pay the price."

"What are you talking about? Lottie won't go near the ocean; she's afraid of it."

"I saw her out on the cliff," he slurred.

Horror gripped me then, and I ran, flying out the front door, the rain instantly soaking through my nightgown. I ran through the gardens and the weary cemetery, screaming Lottie's name. Brizo rushed behind me, barking furiously.

There.

She stood out on the cliff, just as Father had said. Barefoot, with her hair and dress plastered to her skin, looking down from the edge as if planning to jump.

"Lottie!"

Somehow she heard me through the wind and rain. Her head snapped toward me. But she didn't move, didn't back away from the edge. She just smiled at me sadly and turned back toward the ocean.

I felt superhuman in those last moments, my strength and speed beyond what I would have thought possible. I leapt the last few feet toward Lottie, grabbed her arm, and yanked her back just as she was about to jump. She fell behind me, and I briefly saw Father there, holding her with shaking arms.

Yet my momentum threw me forward. I plummeted over the edge.

Lottie screamed. Brizo barked hysterically. I squeezed my eyes shut, bracing myself for the rocks that would end my life.

Instead, I hit the waves with a crash, the icy water driving me under. I flailed, reaching for the surface, but I was lost in the gloom and didn't know how to keep myself afloat.

Terror seized me. Leander had been wrong. I was cursed. After all my dreams of embracing the ocean, I was going to die in it, like so many Carlins before me.

The cold stole all feeling except for the burning in my lungs. I wondered, fleetingly, if this was how Hiram felt when he died. If this was how all those doomed Carlins felt—their last sight watery darkness, their last sound a scream, their last breath, water.

Faces flashed through my mind. Hiram. Mother. Father. Lottie. Leander. How would they deal with the heartbreak of losing another person they loved? How would they survive it? I couldn't bear the thought of another grave in that lonely cemetery.

I was not going to die like this.

I got to choose.

The curse was not my destiny.

Conviction shoved away my terror. I kicked my weary legs and my toes hit something hard. A rock. I pushed against it with all the strength I had left, which wasn't much, but enough to point me up toward a faint light wavering over the surface of the water. My head broke the surface with a gasp that filled my mouth with more seawater. I coughed and gagged and gripped the slippery edges of a rock with my numb fingers. Somehow, I managed to scramble atop the rock, drenched and shivering but alive.

The light I had seen underwater bobbed closer in the dark, a lantern on the prow of a small wooden boat. It illuminated Leander's worried, rain-soaked face, his swift, sure strokes bringing him closer to me. Maybe I was delirious, but all I could think as he pulled alongside my rock was that he was a gift from the ocean itself, saving my life instead of taking it.

He quickly helped me into the boat and threw his jacket around my shoulders, then frantically studied me for broken bones.

I gaped at him, water dripping into my eyes. "What are you doing out here?"

He cupped my face in his hands, heaving out a breath of relief I suspected he had been holding in for a while. "I just...had a feeling, Emmy."

I broke into sobs, and we sat there like that for several minutes before he started rowing us back to shore. When we neared the rocky beach, a figure was wading out toward us, fighting against the surf, stumbling then straightening and stumbling again. Father. He hadn't touched the sea in the forty years since his brother had drowned. And now here he was, coming for me.

I staggered out of the boat and waded toward him. He practically fell on me, hugging me so fiercely he almost knocked me back into the water. We stayed that way for a long time, drenched from the ocean and the rain, the surf beating against our legs.

The salt of our tears and the salt of the ocean mixed until there was no difference.

About the Authors

W. M. Ashley is a writing professor at BYU-I and BSU who loves to write short stories and poems. Currently, she's working on a novel and hopes to have it done soon! She enjoys reading and writing historical fiction with a hint of the gothic or supernatural. She has an MA in English Education, a BA in Creative Writing, and is currently pursuing a creative writing certificate. Some of her work has appeared in journals and anthologies like *diet milk*, *WhiteCat*, *Pirates of the Empyrean*, and *Women of the Woods*. Check out her website for more of her writing: wmashleyauthor.com.

Michelle Dennis Christensen connects Latter-day Saints with stories of heritage and faith that help them overcome darkness, embrace the light of God, and be a shining beacon in the latter days. Michelle is a kidney donor, award-winning author, speaker, avid family historian, and chocolate lover. She currently serves on the editorial staff of the Liahona Magazine. Her first book, *Mirrors of Jesus: Finding Parallels of Christ in Our Lives*, was published through Cedar Fort Publishing. You can connect with her at MichelleDennisChristensen.com.

Nurturer of plants and plots, **Kyro Dean** owns more greenery than shoes. She is the author of The Rogue Royals and co-author of The Fires of Qaf. When not writing by the seat of her pants, she is hiking in the Utah mountains and enjoying the delicious and creative humor of her children. Kyro speaks at conferences all over the U.S. and loves encouraging even the most nascent writers to tell their story. For updates, check her out @kyro_dean on Instagram and Twitter, or on her website at kyrodean.com.

D. Ogden Huff is a sun addict who moved to Arizona at the age of two. She's lived there ever since, except for a two-year stint in Utah where she discovered she even gets cold looking at pictures of snow. Thankfully, she lives in sunny Phoenix with the man of her dreams and a house often full of kids and grandkids. DeAnn is a multi-award-winning author who publishes as D. Ogden Huff. Her latest release, *Brooklyn Bridges, Heights, & Depths: A Novel and Two Novellas* is available on Amazon. Also look for *Michael 21* (a young adult science fiction romance), *Once Upon a Tour* (a contemporary romance), her *Too Sensitive* young adult urban fantasy series: *Master of Emotion, Supreme Chancellor of Stupidity, Dictator of Disaster,* and *Servant of NonSense,* and her stories and articles in five other ANWA anthologies.

Stephanie Kilpatrick worked as an RN before choosing to stay home with her boys and focus on writing and getting her English degree. She leads groups in ANWA and SCBWI and has a few awards and a short story, *Sister's Keeper,* published in 2023. She loves writing conferences, martial arts, reading, hanging out with her family, traveling, and sunshine. She also loves to laugh, and you can laugh along with her on YouTube, TikTok, and Instagram @Literary_Laughs.

Rachel Kirkaldie has been in love with writing since before she can remember, and has always been writing stories. After graduating from BYU-Idaho, writing took a backseat to "real" jobs and raising a family, but she persevered. Her first novel, *The Unicorn Hunter,* was published in 2017. She lives in a log cabin with her husband, four kids, two dogs, and a cat named Penguin.

Born and raised in the cloudy streets of the Seattle Area, **L.P. Masters** spent her fair share of time staring out rain-streaked windows and writing books in her free time. Masters has always had extremely vivid dreams, which often spark inspiration for her novels. These days she doesn't have as much free time, or as much time to dream, as she is currently raising a handful of rambunctious kids. But she still manages to write her dream-inspired science fiction books. You can find her published works on Amazon.

Erin Mindes writes fiction for children and teens putting her English degree to work. She is the author of THE LIFTING BALLOONS, an Award-Winning Finalist in the 2020 International Book Awards and BABE THE BALLERINA DOG (Lawley Publishing). While she grew up in the Arizona desert, she now lives in Northern Utah with her family and enjoys the beautiful mountains and baking bread.

Holly D. Morgan is a wife and mother of four. She has a Bachelor's Degree in Elementary Education and taught fourth graders that they were mathematicians, scientists, historians, and writers. It wasn't until after she left teaching that she realized she, too, was a writer (with some motivation from a friend leading her to accept the call). She can now be found in the fictional worlds of her stories from her home in Arizona.

Leah Moyes is a wife, a mother, a lifelong student with a background in Anthropology and History, and the author of a dozen novels featuring strong female protagonists, including her award-winning Berlin Butterfly Series and its Prequel, "The Polish Nurse". Between writing and archaeological digs, the world is her playground. She loves popcorn and seafood (though not together) and is slowly checking off her very long bucket list.

H. Linn Murphy (also known as Heidi L. Murphy and Heidi McKusick) divides her time between being her dog's butler, burning dinner for her husband, learning German and Gaelic on Duolingo, and huddling in her lair, writing a vast collection of fiction, including *Heart of the Enemy* (Whitney award finalist), *Summerhouse, Heart of Fire* and several in the process of being printed. She also writes a column for a national chimney sweep magazine (Random but fun).

L.M. Ontiveros has lived in the tiny town of Rainier, Oregon most of her life. She has had short stories featured in four previous ANWA Anthologies: From Ashes (*My Husband, My Hero*); Kismet, Tales from a Dating App (*App-ed to Fall in Love*); A Grimm Ever After (*A Grimm Prognosis*); and The Cold Cases of Saguaro Hills (*The Curious Case of Mrs. Carrington's Kidnapped Canine.*) She works as a substitute teacher, and she's an early-morning seminary teacher for the Church of Jesus Christ of Latter-day Saints. She and her husband Richard are parents of six children and have five grandchildren, with whom they love spending family time. They hope to serve a mission for the church next year after they retire. When she's not writing, she enjoys reading, flower and vegetable gardening, singing in her church choir, traveling, and taking care of their two cats, who let her snuggle with them when they're in the mood.

Jaclyn Rose Jaclyn Rose is a well-rounded creative writer of fiction, nonfiction, poetry, and is a master of the short story form in many genres. She graduated from the University of Washington with her Bachelor of Writing Studies in 2017 and has continued to pursue her passion ever since. Among Jaclyn's other published works are "Learning to Love Yourself" from the 2017 edition of Tahoma West Literary Journal, "The Art of Letting Go" from the 2020 ANWA

Anthology From Ashes, and "Arid Awakenings" from the 2023 ANWA Anthology The Cold Cases of Saguaro Hills. No matter what she is writing, she finds that each piece has its own unique story to tell and generally has inspirational undertones. Jaclyn lives in a small town in Washington state with her husband Brandon and their son, Patrick Jack. In her free time, Jaclyn enjoys cuddling up with her family on the couch, listening to true crime podcasts, baking, traveling, reading, and writing.

Skye Rosey doesn't normally write horror...but considering her favorite ride at Disneyland has always been The Haunted Mansion, she has a soft spot for ghosts. She was also published in ANWA's 2022 Anthology, A Grimm Ever After, with "Granny Lucy", a tongue-in-cheek account of the devil getting outwitted by his own sassy grandma. Skye has made a tenuous agreement with both Heavenly Father and her husband to live in reality rather than inside her own imagination, as long as she gets to take frequent trips to La La Land when the weather permits. She loves sparkles, lots of colors, and tropical rain, and lives in Arizona with her enchantingly sensible husband, four eclectic children, too many lizards, and a tiny diva of a dog. Find out more at www.skyerosey.com or on Instagram at @skye.rosey.stories.

C R Simper was raised seven miles north of a small town, with two sisters, thirteen dogs, and an open sky painted every night with billions of stars. This unharried childhood allowed time for much reading, which led into a desire to create stories of worlds beyond her own. She is a member of the American Night Writer's Association. She has two published short stories in the Steampunk genre. Besides writing, she has a passion for genealogy, volleyball, and bargain hunting.

Amy Trent is a longtime fan of happily-ever-afters, cookies, and staying up late to write happily-ever-afters and eat cookies. She writes novels and short stories that explore identity, whimsy, and love through the lens of fairy tales and folklore. A woman, a mother, a reader, and a devoted stan of her cat, Amy can think of nothing better than an afternoon of connecting with others over books and creature comforts. Her brand is cozy; her point of view is a slow-burning ember of hope. Please head to her website, amytrent.com, for a list of her publications, to sign up for her newsletter, or to say hi.

ABOUT ANWA

The American Night Writers Association (ANWA) is a unique professional organization for writers who are members of The Church of Jesus Christ of Latter-day Saints. ANWA supports writers of all levels and genres, published and unpublished, by matching them up with a critique group.

Our purpose is to encourage, assist, educate, and motivate members to write and, if they desire, to publish their works. ANWA members have varied writing goals: some are published, some seek publication, and some write for personal fulfillment.

Members are divided into chapters based on their geographical location. We also have online chapters for members who do not live in close proximity to a local chapter or whose schedule does not permit them to attend the local chapter meetings, as well as for members seeking genre-specific critique. Chapters meet monthly and consist of a writing-related lesson and inspirational thought, followed by a critique of each other's works-in-progress.

ANWA hosts a highly regarded annual Writing Conference that is open to the public. Each year we have nationally recognized faculty members including agents, editors and publishers, as well as noted authors, writers, and other instructors. We welcome all participants who are interested in writing, both members and non-ANWA members.

Find out more about ANWA at amerincanightwriters.org